AS IF BY MAGIC

Also by Dolores Gordon-Smith

A Fête Worse Than Death
Mad About the Boy?

AS IF BY MAGIC

A JACK HALDEAN MURDER MYSTERY

DOLORES GORDON-SMITH

Constable • London

Constable & Robinson Ltd
3 The Lanchesters
162 Fulham Palace Road
London W6 9ER
www.constablerobinson.com

First published in the UK by Constable,
an imprint of Constable & Robinson, 2009

First US edition published by SohoConstable,
an imprint of Soho Press, 2009

Soho Press, Inc.
853 Broadway
New York, NY 10003
www.sohopress.com

A copy of the British Library Cataloguing in Publication
Data is available from the British Library

UK ISBN: 978-1-84529-936-1

US ISBN: 978-1-56947-588-1
US Library of Congress number: 2009007865

Mixed Sources
Product group from well-managed
forests and other controlled sources
www.fsc.org Cert no. SA-COC-1565
© 1996 Forest Stewardship Council
FSC

Printed and bound in the EU by the MPG Books Group

1 3 5 7 9 10 8 6 4 2

For my sister, Barbara,
with love

Chapter One

London, October 1923

George Lassiter huddled against the entrance of Hyde Park Corner tube station, sheltering from the icy sting of the sleet-filled rain. Yesterday he had been well dressed in a top hat, evening clothes and thin patent leather shoes but now, although he still wore the same clothes, his hat was shapeless with rain, his shoes were like sodden cardboard and his white waistcoat and tail coat defenceless against the biting cold.

He looked to where taxis, cars and buses clogged Knightsbridge in a dark, noisy river. Their headlights caught the sleet-flecked crowds, secure in winter overcoats, gloves and hats. Umbrellas sprang up like black mushrooms, cocooning their owners in impenetrable, urgent circles. People: hundreds and hundreds of people. In such numbers they weren't really people any more. He wanted to reach out, to say, 'Stop!' He wanted someone in this barricaded, jostling mass of inhumanity to pause, to look, to speak, but no one spared him a glance.

His hands were numb and raw. He shielded them under his arms and leaned his head against the cold wet tiles of the tube station. He closed his eyes, hoping, like a gambler about to make a final, desperate throw, for a miracle. Perhaps when he opened his eyes there would be someone – anyone – who could help. The traffic ground on, the

1

newspaper seller shouted, the rain lanced down. He took a deep breath and opened his eyes. Nothing.

He turned up his collar and trudged away from the crowds pouring down the steps to the underground. They were heading for Acton and Ealing, Holland Park and home. They would have firesides and food, and perhaps a welcoming smile and the thump of a sleepy dog's tail. And as for him? Nothing. He loathed the rain and the bricks and the stones and the soot and the careless, unconscious cruelty of all who hurried through this man-made desert of London. His head ached and he had to lean against a shop window before he could walk on. His legs felt like rubber and the pavement swam dizzily in front of him. He stumbled across the road to the great dark emptiness of Hyde Park. Here at least were grass and trees and space, but the wind-whipped rain was even fiercer than it had been in the streets.

He walked on. George didn't know where he was and didn't care. He seemed to have been wandering for hours. He had spent last night in Euston station where, although uncomfortable, he'd been under cover. He'd been a fool to leave the entrance to the underground. He'd felt imprisoned by the crowds but at least the station had given some sort of shelter.

His head was really hurting now and he suspected an attack of malaria was in the offing. He left the park behind him and crossed a wide, traffic-choked road into a maze of quiet streets where flat-chested, elegant and forbidding houses ran in endless lines, caged in by iron railings. If they weren't caged in, thought George, all the houses might escape. He held on to the railings and laughed. The sound of his laugh shocked him. Dear God, if he really did go down with malaria now there would be no hope at all. He fought down the sick taste of panic. Sheer willpower made him take a deep breath, let go of the railings and straighten up. He needed to think of something else other than how he felt. He forced himself to look at his surroundings properly.

For some reason his spirits lifted. Although he was drenched to the skin and bitterly cold, the rain had subsided into ill-natured squalls and the empty streets glistening under the lamplight were oddly appealing. Sort of ... *cosy*, he thought. It was like a play-town on a nursery carpet. He looked at his hand and his hand seemed large enough to cover these toy-town houses and pick them up, one by one. He'd had a toy zoo and a gleaming ribbon of brass that encircled the nursery with an exciting noisy little train that chugged along with real steam. He could move the houses so they –

He stopped himself abruptly, alarmed. What the devil was happening to him? His mind was wandering and everything was too small, as if he had stepped into a shrunken world. His legs and neck were sore. Malaria, thought George again, with a touch of panic. He had to find somewhere to rest soon. Even a shop doorway or a park bench would have done but there were no shops and the park was far behind.

With clumsy, hesitant steps he walked on. His legs were stiff and it hurt to move. He half leaned, half fell against a set of railings and looked through them down to where light streamed from a window into the area of the house. He must be looking into someone's kitchen. There was a pair of hands – he could only see the hands – washing up, making the water dance in the bowl. The hands shook themselves and withdrew from sight. It was such a domestic scene that his eyes pricked with tears and he drew the back of his hand across them. These spear-railed houses were *homes* and people could be happy in them. He'd never thought of anyone actually having a home in London before. London was a dirty, complicated, alien sprawl, not a collection of homes. It must be strange to know one of these endlessly duplicated Portland stone boxes as home and yet, clinging to the railings and gazing down on to that wedge of light on the wet stone flags below, he thought he could find his way about inside one of these boxes. Everything had seemed too small and now

3

everything seemed too big. It would be like a fairy story or a folk tale. There would be giant rooms populated by giants ... His head swam and he tightened his grip on the railings.

The sound of voices and a basement door being shut in the yard of the next house made him look up. Three women, servants at a guess, came up the steps and on to the pavement. One, a plump, comfortable-looking sort, turned to her companion and made a face. 'I hope this is worth it, Elsie. I'd just as soon stay in my nice warm kitchen on a night like this.' Elsie laughed and replied, her words lost in a gust of wind. To his relief they went down the street, away from where he was holding on to the railings. He could hardly feel his hands any more. He waited until the echoes of their feet had died away before moving.

George walked slowly to the steps where the women had come from. A soft light flickered through the window. There would be a fire in there. Warmth. The rain slashed down again and he shivered. He wanted to be inside that house. A huge desire rose in him. It wasn't any house, it was this house which drew him. There was something about it which touched a shy, lost place deep inside. He was so very cold and the light looked so inviting ... but it was someone else's house and that, to George, was a mountainous barrier.

If the cook had banked up the fire properly or made sure the damper was close down, he would have walked on. As it was, he stood gazing at the light as if it were a glimpse of Paradise. There was something about the very bricks and mortar of this place which called to him. The street was totally deserted. Opening the iron gate, he went down the steps as quietly as he could, listening for any noise. From far away he could hear the measured tread of a policeman's feet and the sound made him panic. A policeman would stop him. He tried the handle but it was locked, of course. Minutes before, George would have been shocked at the thought of breaking into a stranger's house. Now it was unthinkable that he couldn't get in. As

4

the steps grew closer he even considered smashing the window, then suddenly smiled – his first smile for many hours – and felt under the mat. Seconds later he was turning the key in the door.

Inside the kitchen and with his back to the door he heard the steps pass by on the street above. Nerves on edge he approached the fire warily, then slumped to his knees on the hearthrug, wincing as the heat stung his frozen body. He sat in front of the black-leaded range, blissfully content. It must have been over five minutes later before he could think of anything but the fire, and with time came caution. He could almost imagine his ears had pricked like a dog's as he strained to hear any sound from the rest of the house. None came. Unconsciously he relaxed and, greatly daring, took the poker, stirred up the coals and raised the damper.

The fire blazed, sending light around the room. On the kitchen table was a plate of sandwiches, covered by a glass bowl. He hadn't eaten since yesterday . . . As he finished the last of the sandwiches, he guiltily realized he had probably stolen the servants' supper. He felt bad about that, remembering that plump, agreeable woman and her companions, but now the taste of food had reminded him how thirsty he was. A latched plank door stood to one side of the room. The larder? He opened the catch of the door and pulled it back as quietly as he could. On a marble slab, surrounded by the packets and boxes that lined the shelves, were two tin jugs full of milk. He couldn't see a cup so drank straight from the jug – another thing that until half an hour or so ago would have been unthinkable.

George slipped back into the kitchen. His clothes had started to steam in the heat, he could feel his hands and feet properly once more, and the savage desire for food and drink had been quelled. What he now wanted more than anything in the world was a cigarette. After the necessities, luxury, he thought, and realized, with a certain amount of irony, that the craving for the one was quite as great as the craving for the other. He walked round the kitchen with a boldness which would have horrified him

5

earlier and turned up a packet of Players, a box of matches and a tin ashtray beside the tea caddy. If anything he was now too warm, so he retreated into a corner chair behind the kitchen table and lit the cigarette, sucking in the smoke gratefully. He would have his cigarette and go. Of course he must go. The rain pattered against the window and he shuddered. He couldn't go yet. The servants were out. Surely he was safe for another hour at least? It had been many hours since he'd slept and he'd been walking all day and the kitchen was so blissfully warm. He'd just finish this cigarette . . .

He awoke with an alarmed start but was instantly still. There were other people in the room. The fire had died down and he shrank back against the dark wall. They'd switch on the lights, see him and it would all be over. He sat tensely in the darkness waiting to be discovered. What could he say? Why didn't they speak? Surprise tinged his fear: the people in the room were being very, very quiet. Why?

He narrowed his eyes, peering into firelit shadows. There were two men and a woman. What were they doing? Had they broken in too?

'Why here?' The whisper sounded clearly. He thought it was the woman who'd spoken.

'Are you sure we're safe?' It was one of the men.

'Stop worrying,' said the other man in a low voice. 'All the servants are out, he's having a bath and she's listening to the wireless. We'll be fine.'

The woman gave a dismissive laugh. 'In that case, let's get on with it, shall we?'

There was a pause. The shapes moved in front of the fire. One of the men stood back, then, without further ado, the other man took the woman in his arms and kissed her passionately. George watched in disbelief. Was he dreaming? The two shapes clung together, the woman's hair golden where the firelight caught it.

The shapes separated. 'Say you love me,' whispered the woman. 'Go on. You must say it. I want you to say it.'

6

The man held the woman at arm's length. 'I love you,' he said softly. With a little cry, she collapsed in his arms.

The man gave a stifled cry and then, still holding her, laid her down on the rug in front of the fire. He knelt down beside her and held her hand. He put his hand on her chest and breathed out in a long hissing gasp. He moved, black against the light, to look up at the man standing beside the hearth. 'I . . . I don't like this. She's not breathing. Really. She's not breathing.'

The other man laughed. 'Are you surprised? It's what you wanted. It's what both of you wanted. A perfect death. You've got it.'

The man on the rug stooped over the woman and touched her hair. 'I didn't know it'd be like this.'

'What did you expect? Stop worrying.'

A bell jangled from the next room, followed by the distant sound of three knocks. Both men froze, then the man kneeling by the hearth stood up. 'Damn! There's someone at the door. We'll have to go. We can't be found in here. What . . . what shall we do about *her*?'

'Leave her for the moment. It'll be all right.'

The two men walked to the door leading into the house and, going through it, shut it quietly behind them.

George swallowed and cautiously got up from his corner. It had to be a dream. He held on to the kitchen table and could feel the real, solid wood beneath his hand. But the girl was still there, stretched in front of the fire, and she couldn't be real. He must have dreamt it. Hardly liking to move, he forced himself to walk across the room to the fire. The girl's face was turned towards the softly flickering light. Half expecting to feel empty air, he reached out and started when his fingers touched her arm. She *was* real. George swallowed once more and delicately touched her chest where her heart should be. Nothing. No movement. She was real and she was dead.

He backed away, hand to his mouth, then stumbled to the kitchen door. He took a last look at the girl, flung open the door and fled in sheer panic, totally heedless of noise, wanting nothing but to get out of that room and away from the body on the rug. He crashed up the steps and raced through the open iron gate on to the street.

A few feet away were the steps up to the front door of the house. It stood open, sending light streaming into the road. George had a brief glimpse of a woman framed in the doorway, talking to the solid figure of a policeman in a glistening cape, then he ran for it. The policeman turned.

'Here! You! Stop!'

George heard the blast of a police whistle as he ran down the empty street, the sound deadened under the rasp of his breath and the thumping of his heart. Feet pounded after him, then another policeman loomed up, arms outstretched to stop him. George tried to dodge, wriggling helplessly in the man's grasp, but his arm was held fast. He tried to throw the man off but his strength deserted him. Another hand gripped his shoulder tightly. His legs gave way and he sank to the pavement.

A lantern was shone in his face and George twisted away from the blinding light.

'Now you come quietly, my lad,' said the policeman holding the lantern. 'No funny business.'

The second policeman looked down at him. 'What's he done?'

'I caught him legging out of number 19.' A hand descended on him. 'Breaking and entering, I'd say.' George felt his shoulder being shaken. 'Come on, you. Up you get.'

George tried to get up but his legs were like cotton wool. He reached out his hand for help and two puzzled faces looked down at him, swimming in and out of focus. He tried to speak but the words came out as a little gulp of a cry.

The two policemen stepped back in alarm. 'Strewth, I don't like the sound of that,' said one. He hauled George to his feet. George leaned heavily against him and vainly tried to speak once more.

The policeman shook him. 'Here, you! Stop that.'

George buried his face in his hands and waited, gasping for breath. 'You . . . you don't understand,' he managed to say. 'She's dead, I tell you, dead.'

The two policemen exchanged looks. 'I think he's off his rocker,' said one quietly. 'Who's dead?'

Panic welled up inside him once more. 'The girl,' he managed to say. 'The girl in the kitchen!'

There were footsteps behind him and a woman approached. She looked at him curiously. 'What's the problem, officer?' she asked. Her voice was clear but gentle and George felt instantly soothed. He could explain things to her. She'd understand. He could tell her what had happened.

Still holding George, the policeman answered. 'This is the man who broke in, miss.' He glanced at the other policeman. 'This is the lady from number 19. I was just telling her that her area gate was unlocked when this geezer shot out.'

'He doesn't look like a criminal,' said the girl doubtfully. 'I mean, look how he's dressed. Are you sure it's the right man?'

'Perfectly sure, miss. I caught him red-handed.'

'I'm sorry,' gasped George. 'I'm so sorry. I saw the fire and there's . . . there's a dead girl. She's been murdered. I'm sorry. I'm so sorry.'

The girl stepped back. 'A murder? Where?'

'In the kitchen,' George managed to say. Her face blurred in front of him and he held his hand to his eyes. 'I'm sorry.'

'In the *kitchen*?' said the girl sharply.

The policeman holding him coughed. 'Don't you believe a word of it, miss,' he said, adding in a quieter voice, 'I think he's a bit of a nutcase.'

She bit her lip. 'Perhaps . . . Look, would you mind coming into the kitchen with me? I don't know what this man's seen but there might be something.'

'Just as you like, miss,' said the policeman with the lantern. 'Come on, you,' he said to George. 'Come and show us what you saw.'

9

'No!' George struggled weakly in the policeman's grasp. 'I'm not going back. I'm not!' His voice was nearly a sob.

The policemen exchanged shrugs. 'You'd better have a look,' said the man holding George to the other policeman. George continued to struggle. 'Keep still, will you! You stay here with me.'

George subsided as the girl and the policeman went off, leaving him with his captor. They were back a few minutes later.

'There's nothing there,' said the policeman. 'Just as we thought.' He gave the girl beside him a long-suffering glance. 'And this lady says that as nothing was touched as far as she can see, she doesn't want to press charges. Let him go.'

The policeman holding him released him and George staggered to the railings.

'He's ill,' said the woman in sudden concern. 'Look at him.' She reached out and touched George on the forehead. 'Why, you're burning hot.'

George blinked. She'd got it wrong. He wasn't hot, he was cold, deathly cold. Hadn't she seen the girl in the kitchen? She must have seen her. 'Where is she?' he asked. 'Where's she gone?'

'There's no one there,' she said. 'You must have imagined it.'

Imagined it? Could he have done? He gazed at her and tried hard to speak but the words got twisted round. It was gibberish, he knew it was, but he couldn't help it.

'He's really ill,' said the woman.

Her voice came from very far away. George shut his eyes as the world split up into jerky, unrelated images. Then that intense cold seized him and dragged him off to a far-away Arctic of darkness.

Jack Haldean, two pints of bitter in hand, negotiated his way through the snug of the Heroes of Waterloo to the table where his friend, Inspector William Rackham, sat waiting for him. Jack liked the Heroes. It was a cheerfully unpretentious pub, minutes round the corner from his rooms in Chandos Row, with a welcoming fire, a resident cat, an agreeable landlady and oak panels which, dividing the snug into cosy little booths, were stained dark by years of London soot and placidly smoked pipes.

'Here we are,' he said, putting down the glasses. He took off his coat and hat, laid them on the oak settle and wedged himself in behind the table across from Rackham. Bill Rackham, a big, untidy man with vivid ginger hair, folded up his newspaper and picked up his beer. 'Cheers, Jack.' He took a long drink. 'My word, I needed that.'

'Is there anything wrong?' asked Jack, offering him his cigarette case.

'Not really. Should there be?'

Jack lit his cigarette. 'Not especially. You just don't look too happy with life.'

Rackham ran a hand through his hair. 'It's nothing. Just work. My sister's been down from Manchester,' he added after a pause.

'I know,' said Jack patiently. 'The three of us had dinner together, if you remember.'

'What? Oh yes, we did, didn't we. Sorry. I saw her on to the train before I called for you. I was supposed to be having a few days off but that went up in smoke.'

'Bad luck.'

It was a few moments before Rackham, who was staring moodily at the ashtray, apparently in a world of his own, replied. 'What? Oh, my sister, you mean. Yes, poor Sue. I had to more or less leave her to her own devices.' The conversation died down again, then Rackham made an effort. 'What have you been up to?'

'Nothing much. My cousin Isabelle's been up for a couple of days. We went to see *Hurry Along!* on Wednesday. You've seen it, haven't you?'

'Yes, I took Sue. Did you enjoy it?'

11

'Very much. Isabelle was a bit disappointed because Stephanie Granger's understudy was on, but I thought she was fine.'

The conversation lapsed once more.

'She lugged me round the shops yesterday,' added Jack when it became obvious Rackham wasn't tempted by a discussion of musical theatre. 'You know she's getting married in the spring?' Rackham nodded abstractedly. 'I think she must have bought half of Selfridges. I certainly seemed to be carrying half of Selfridges with most of Harrods thrown in by the end of the afternoon. Linen, you know, and so on.' Jack picked up his beer. 'She said she needed elephants so we bought three. I suggested a couple of walruses but she insisted on elephants.'

Rackham gazed past him blankly before saying, after an appreciable pause, 'Shopping, eh?'

Jack grinned. 'I knew it! I knew you weren't listening. Look, stop pretending there's nothing biting you and tell me what's wrong. You look whacked out and worried to death.'

Rackham half smiled and put his hands behind his neck, stretching his shoulders. 'All right. I'm sorry, I wasn't really listening. As I said, it's work.'

'Anything interesting?' asked Jack with a lift of his eyebrows. He tapped Rackham's folded newspaper on the table in front of him. 'I saw you had a naked man in the Thames. I read about it this morning. Is he your pigeon?'

'The naked man? Yes, he's mine, so to speak, but that's not the problem. You asked if there was anything interesting. It depends what you call interesting.' He picked up the paper and tossed it over to Jack. 'See for yourself. That's the evening edition. Another dead girl turned up in the Thames this morning. She'd been strangled.'

Jack unfolded the newspaper and read the headline out loud. *'Jack the Ripper! The X man strikes again!'* He looked at Rackham. 'Not another Ripper murder, Bill?'

Rackham winced. 'So the press says. Every time an

unfortunate, as the press delicately calls these women, gets murdered, the newspapers trot out Jack the Ripper.'

'Well, hang on,' said Jack. 'Someone must be killing the poor girls and the comparison with Jack the Ripper is inevitable. I mean, the bloke must be a lunatic.'

Rackham leaned back. 'You think so? Don't get me wrong. I want to nail him as much as anyone, but we're stuck. Over the past eighteen months or so there have been five unfortunates, to use that word, murdered, whose killer we can't trace. We know it's the work of one man because he has the nasty little habit of leaving all his victims marked with a cross, which is why he's also called the X man. All the women come from different areas of London and it's a devil of a job to guess where he'll strike next. We can't guess. There doesn't seem to be any pattern in it. One had her throat cut, two were beaten up and two were strangled, including this latest woman, Bridget Flynn. We haven't had a single sighting that's of any use to us. We're being hounded by the press but murder's far too easy, Jack, when the killer picks his victims at random.'

'And when the only motive is the desire to kill,' added Jack quietly. 'That's a nasty one. Don't the victims have anything in common?'

'Not a thing, apart from how they earned their money and the fact that they all end up in the river downstream of Blackfriars. Which,' added Rackham, reaching for another cigarette, 'leaves a fair old bit of London to cover. Between the two of us, I can't see how we're ever going to catch him. It's not for want of trying, I can tell you that.'

'Five women,' said Jack. He sat for a few moments in silence. 'Didn't the original Ripper murder five women?'

'Yes, he did,' agreed Rackham. 'But there, more or less, the comparison ends. We had a visit from Inspector Sagar.' Jack looked a question. 'Sagar's a bit of legend in the force. He played a leading part in the hunt for the original Ripper back in '88. It's a long time ago now, but he's well worth listening to. You see, Sagar's Ripper was obviously insane. If we don't know anything else about him, we do know

13

that. As a matter of fact, Sagar's convinced that his Ripper was a lunatic who lived in Aldgate. He was put into an asylum and the killings stopped, but from 31st August to 9th November he attacked and mutilated five women. That's a very short space of time. Now our man has been operating for eighteen months.' He took a long drink of beer. 'Eighteen months, Jack. It was only when a bright boy from the *Daily Despatch* put two and two together about the victims being marked with a cross and screamed *Ripper!* and the rest of the press took it up, that we realized we had a series of murders on our hands. That was after the third killing.'

'Eighteen months,' repeated Jack. 'It's a dickens of a time.'

'I know,' agreed Rackham. 'It bothered Sagar, too.'

'Could it be someone who's only in London every so often?' suggested Jack. 'You know, a sailor or someone like that?'

Rackham shook his head. 'We don't think so. According to the experts once this sort of homicidal mania gets hold of a man, it's like a drug. He can't stop and we'd expect a series of killings to follow him wherever he goes. There's nothing to suggest that. No. Sagar reckoned that our man – our very cautious man – isn't a lunatic at all.'

'He must be,' said Jack, startled.

Rackham shook his head. 'Not in the accepted sense, no. This man knows exactly what he's doing.'

Jack felt his throat tighten. 'You mean he kills for pleasure? Like a treat?' Rackham nodded. 'You've got to find him, Bill.'

'How?' demanded Rackham bitterly. 'I tell you, this bloke's sane. He doesn't leave clues. After all, we never found Jack the Ripper and he was barmy. There's damn all to go on. If you only *knew* . . .' He stopped and looked ruefully at his friend. 'I'm sorry. I didn't mean to bite your head off. It's just that everyone at the Yard wants this swine stopped and we haven't a clue how to go about it. That's the truth but it's hard to admit.' He blew out a mouthful of smoke with an irritated sigh. 'Forget it, Jack. It's not your sort of case.'

Jack's mouth twisted. 'No, thank God, it's not. If this bloke really is sane, then the only chance you've got is a lucky break and lots of police work.' He looked at his friend. 'No wonder you're looking so done in.'

Rackham stretched his shoulders. 'It's been tough. And, of course, I've got my naked man in the Thames.' He very nearly smiled. 'At least they can't blame Jack the Ripper for that one. Not that that's any help, particularly. So far we haven't been able to identify him. He had his face battered in very thoroughly. At first sight it looks like the work of a maniac, so what with a possibly insane killer and a probably sane Ripper, us poor beggars at Scotland Yard have got our work cut out. All we actually know is that his body was pulled out of the Thames at Southwark Bridge steps at just gone nine yesterday morning. The doctor thinks he had been dead for about nine or ten hours at that stage, which gets us back to eleven o'clock or midnight at the absolute outside. He didn't want to commit himself any more definitely than that because of the action of the water retarding the progress of rigor and so on.'

'Could his face have been bashed in to conceal his identity?'

'Well, I thought of that, of course, but his hands are still intact. Mind you, we haven't got his fingerprints on record, so that doesn't help much. The odd thing about him is that the surgeon states that the beating he got wasn't the cause of death. What's even odder is that the surgeon – it's Dr Harding, Jack, and you know he's good – can't say how he did die. Apparently he had some sort of heart problem so Harding's put it down as heart failure for the time being and that's as much as he can tell us.'

'Heart failure?' questioned Jack.

Rackham half smiled once more. 'Technically he's correct, of course. I can't say I've come across many dead men whose hearts are still up and running. It's simply medical terminology. Harding knows as well as I do that heart failure doesn't strip a man naked and cave in his face.'

'What about his teeth?' asked Jack. 'Or were they too damaged to help you identify him?'

'He didn't have any teeth. Presumably he had a dental plate but that's gone. All we can really say is that he's a middle-aged man, about five foot eleven and well-nourished, to use the usual formula. He'd eaten well before he died and was killed about eleven o'clock the night before last.' Rackham picked up his beer. 'Oh, forget about him, Jack. He's not your sort of case, either. I imagine what'll happen is that someone will eventually notice they haven't seen so-and-so for a time and tell us about it. We'll match up the description with our Mr X and that'll be it. It's a matter of simple police work.'

'And once that happens you can start to look for who-ever bumped him off. Which might not be so simple.' Jack leaned back against the oak of the settle. 'Haven't you had any other cases, Bill? Your bodies in the river aren't much fun.'

'Ghoul,' said Rackham with a grin. He stood up. 'Let me get some more beer and I'll think about it.'

When Rackham came back from the bar he looked more cheerful. 'I've thought of something,' he announced, sitting down. 'It happened about three weeks or a month ago now and it isn't really a case at all, more of an incident, but it made me think of you. It sounded like one of your stories. I only got to hear of it because one of my sergeants was grumbling that no charges had been pressed.'

'What happened?'

'A man broke into the kitchen of a house in Mayfair. He didn't steal anything, apart from a plate of ham and cheese sandwiches, which is why the lady of the house didn't press charges. He was ill, poor beggar, and we ended up carting him off to the Royal Free. The odd thing about him was that he was wearing full evening dress.'

'He sounds a very elegant tramp,' said Jack. 'So far, so good. That could be quite a nice point in a story. I suppose

16

the poor devil was actually an out-of-work waiter or musician or something. I don't suppose he was remotely elegant in real life.'

'As a matter of fact, he was – or had been, at least. According to Constable Newland, who nabbed him, the man's clothes were extremely good quality, if a bit the worse for wear. Newland worked in a gents' outfitters before he joined the force and knows what he's talking about. They were tailor-made in . . .' He frowned. 'Now where was it?'

'Savile Row?' suggested Jack.

'No. It wasn't in England at all. Cape Town, that was it. His name and the tailor's name were on the label of his tail coat. Anyway, he came up the kitchen steps like a bat out of hell, more or less straight into the arms of Constable Newland. He tried to get away, Newland chased after him, blew his whistle, Constable Thirsk showed up and between them they got him. Anyway, he started gibbering away about a murder he'd seen.' Rackham took a drink and laughed. 'He said there was a dead body in the kitchen.'

'And was there?' asked Jack, hopefully. 'This is getting really good.'

'Of course there wasn't. Sorry, Jack. He was making it up. The constables knew he was, but the lady of the house insisted that one of the policemen go and look, all the same. There was nothing there, as you'd expect. However, I thought that if there had been, it would make a cracking story.'

'It might,' said Jack. 'I like the bit about him being in evening dress, I must say. The lady who owned the house couldn't know anything about it, otherwise she wouldn't have insisted on the police inspecting the kitchen.' He ran his finger round the top of his glass. 'Kitchens. Who'd leave a body in a kitchen? It's a rotten place. The servants would trip over it.' He leaned back. 'In fact, it's odd that the servants weren't there. What sort of body was it? A man or a woman?'

17

'There wasn't a body,' said Rackham patiently. 'That's the point.'

'Yes, but he thought there was a body and by your account something must have scared him otherwise he wouldn't have done his bat out of hell impression. Hang on. Did you say he'd seen a murder? That'd scare him.'

'He didn't see anything, I tell you.'

'I wonder what he did see?'

'Crikey, Jack, I don't know,' said Rackham with a short laugh. 'Nothing but his own imagination, I should think. He wouldn't go back in the place to show them where his imaginary body was. He was frightened stiff.'

'It must have been some vision. Was he drunk?'

'Apparently not. He was ill, though, as I say. Look, old man, if you're that interested why don't you go and ask him? He's still in the Royal Free as far as I know.'

'I wonder if he'd appreciate a visitor?' Jack caught Rackham's expression and grinned. 'I know, you think I'm wasting my time chasing after some poor bloke and his vivid imagination but he does sound a bit out of the ordinary, you must admit. After all, that's why you told me about him in the first place. What's his name?'

'I've been trying to remember. Rossiter? George Rossiter? No, that's not quite right. Lassiter, that's it. George Lassiter.'

'George Lassiter?' Jack put down his beer and repeated the name sharply. 'George Lassiter? From South Africa? Are you sure?'

'Fairly sure, yes. Why? You don't know him, do you?'

'I certainly knew a George Lassiter and he was a South African. He was in my squadron. He was a first-rate pilot and a thoroughly good sort. He got shot down a few months before the end of the war and was taken prisoner. I don't know what happened to him after that. I haven't seen him for years. I wonder if it really is the same bloke? He was a big man with sandy hair.'

'I don't know what he looks like,' said Rackham, 'and to be honest I don't know if he's actually a South African, but his clothes were certainly made in Cape Town so it seems likely enough.'

Jack looked at his watch. 'I don't know what the visiting hours at the Royal Free are but I imagine I've missed them for today. Damn!'

'Don't worry about that,' said Rackham. 'Let me finish my beer and I'll come to the hospital with you. Even if they won't let you see the man himself, you can talk to the doctor or the matron or whatever about him. But remember, Jack, the man was apparently destitute. If you show too much interest you might end up being lumbered with him.'

Jack shrugged. 'I suppose I might but it wouldn't be for long. He was a very independent character. And after all, he's an old friend, or he could be. It sounds as if he needs one.' He stopped, frowning. 'What the devil made him do it? As I remember George, he was painfully honest. He must have been desperate. I'll tell you something else, too. He's the last person to suffer from an over-active imagination. He was a very prosaic sort of bloke. What the devil was he doing breaking into kitchens in Mayfair and seeing visionary corpses?'

Rackham drained his glass and stood up. 'Let's go and find out, shall we?'

Chapter Two

The man in the Royal Free was indeed George Lassiter, Jack's old friend, and, although Lassiter himself was fast asleep, the doctor in charge of the case greeted Haldean and Rackham with frank relief.

'You've solved a bit of a problem for us, Major Haldean,' said Dr Garrett, showing the two men into his office. 'Please, sit down, won't you? You see, although the patient will be well enough to leave us shortly, he has to have somewhere to regain his strength. I was attempting to place him in a suitable convalescent home but, as you can imagine, our funds are very limited. Your generous offer to take care of him couldn't have come at a better time.' He thought for a couple of moments. 'Let me see. Today's Friday. I imagine he'll be well enough to leave us on Monday. Tuesday at the outside.'

'What's actually been wrong with him?' asked Jack curiously. He had been shocked by the sight of the sleeping man. Poor old George, although perfectly recognizable, was thin and wasted.

'He's been suffering from influenza and malaria.' Jack whistled sympathetically. 'Yes,' continued Dr Garrett, 'it's a nasty combination. Frankly, I was surprised when he pulled through. I didn't expect him to. He must have a remarkable constitution.'

'He was always very fit and healthy when I knew him,' said Jack. 'He grew up on a farm on the veldt, as I remember, and was always a great bloke for the outdoors. He hated being cooped up inside for too long.'

The doctor nodded. 'That would explain his rapid progress. If you're able to provide good food and rest and he takes moderate exercise, I imagine a couple of weeks would see him completely recovered.'

'I'll do my best,' said Jack. 'He can either live with me for the time being or I'll see he gets into a convalescent home. It depends on my landlady to some extent, of course. I'll have to see what she says, but in any event, he'll be all right.'

'Well, Jack,' said Rackham, as they turned out of the hospital into the Gray's Inn Road. 'It looks as if you're going to have ample opportunity to ask George Lassiter what he did see in Mayfair.'

Jack clicked his tongue. 'I think I'll leave what happened that night alone for the time being. I know you said he was ill but I had no idea he was so washed up. To be honest, after having seen him, Bill, and hearing what the doctor had to say, I think you're probably right and he imagined the whole thing.'

George was discharged from hospital on Monday and, exhausted by the move to Chandos Row, spent most of the day dozing. On Tuesday morning, however, he was so much brighter that he was able to get up, have a bath, and eat a very substantial breakfast.

He sat in the brocaded armchair by the crackling fire, dressed in a spare pair of Jack's pyjamas, wrapped in an old and hairy dressing gown. As a final domestic touch, the kitchen cat, Boots, had wandered in to greet the new arrival. George, who liked cats, had given her some of his breakfast kipper on a saucer and Boots, with deep approval, was now curled up on his knee, purring loudly.

'You're honoured,' said Jack from over the top of the newspaper. 'Boots doesn't take to everyone.'

George smiled and idly scratched the top of the cat's head, resulting in a fusillade of purring. 'It's nice here, Jack,' he said.

21

He'd scarcely taken in his surroundings yesterday but he'd had a good look round the sitting room this morning. It was full of colour. There was a blue-and-red Turkish carpet in front of the fire, comfortable chairs and a sofa with cushions in green, blue and yellow. The table where they had just had breakfast was covered with a crisp white cloth and paintings hung on the cream-coloured walls. There were a couple of a large country house with a river and trees, with masses of gusty white clouds, one of Jack's favourite places of all. It was, Jack said, Hesperus, his aunt and uncle's house in Sussex, where he had spent much of his childhood. 'I go there for holidays,' he added with a smile. 'It's nice to pretend I'm one of the idle rich from time to time.'

The rest of the paintings were mainly, George guessed, of Mediterranean scenes, with big skies and a hot sun. He liked those; they reminded him of home. One, a striking study of a ruined white church set in dark pines against a brilliant sea, was signed with Jack's name. George had had no idea he was an artist. There was a gramophone with a mixed selection of classical and jazz records underneath. A collection of silver sports cups, mainly for boxing, stood on the sideboard, together with an agreeable array of bottles and a soda siphon. A Spanish guitar stood propped against the bookcase. The bookcase itself occupied the alcove next to the window and was filled from floor to ceiling. The stuff on the higher shelves looked fairly deep: poetry and philosophy. Further down were the sort of books George thought he might like to read, with bright spines and the words *Body*, *Murder* and *Death* in the titles. Underneath the blue-curtained window, through which came the faded noise of traffic on the Strand a few streets away, stood an office desk with a typewriter and, beside that, a very workmanlike filing cabinet, on top of which were reference books. There was a well-thumbed dictionary, an atlas, Whitaker's Almanack, something calling itself *Everybody's Pocket Companion* – you'd need damn big pockets – Burke's Peerage, Kelly's Street Directory and a book of quotations.

Jack, apparently, was an author, a choice of profession which caused George to raise his eyebrows. Even if old Jack wrote detective stories, which he said he did, it wasn't, in George's opinion, a proper job for a man, not the sort of man who'd been his flight commander, at any rate. It wasn't really work at all. He tactfully kept these views to himself, falling back on the comforting thought that it took all sorts to make a world.

Because Jack was all right. The first time he'd met him, Jack had been covered in oil and dressed in filthy overalls. George, secure in his immaculate uniform, had looked at his olive-skinned flight commander and inwardly sneered. A dago. Partly a dago, at any rate, who was too good-looking by half. And then, quite unaware that he had broken the twin South African taboos of dirt and mixed race, Jack had started to talk about flying. He knew his stuff, that was for sure, and George felt a grudging respect.

Jack, who was sitting in the opposite armchair, looked up from the *Daily Messenger*. He was also thinking about flying. It was George's voice that had done it in the first instance. That clipped South African accent brought back, more vividly than he'd have thought possible, half-forgotten details of the war. It seemed so long ago now, yet it wasn't, not really. Then, as if to reinforce his thoughts, the *Messenger* had had a long article about air travel and safety.

'Do you want the paper?' he asked. 'There's an article about this air crash in Paris the other day.'

'An air crash? What happened?' said George with interest.

'The undercarriage crumped as the plane came in. No one was hurt much to speak of, but a couple of sheds came off worse. Considering what could have happened, I think the pilot deserves a medal.'

'So do I.' He took the outstretched newspaper. Boots, outraged by the movement, stood up, glared, stropped her claws on the dressing gown and departed. George watched her go with a smile, then turned his attention to the paper.

23

He wouldn't have minded reading the article but the small print made his eyes ache.

'I'll look at it later, Jack. What I'd really like is a cup of coffee.'

'Right you are,' said Jack. He picked up the percolator which was making comfortable plopping noises on the hearth, poured two cups of coffee and gave one to George.

It was a simple action, yet George felt so ridiculously grateful he had to swallow hard to keep his voice from breaking. When Jack had turned up at the hospital on Saturday afternoon George could hardly believe it, and then, when Jack casually suggested he should come and stay, the relief had been so great George couldn't find any words to express what he felt. He simply reached out and clasped his friend's hand.

He'd hardly taken in what he'd said, all about his land-lady (Mrs Pettycure? Was that the name?) and how it was all okay and he could have the spare room and so on. All he really knew was that the ordinary things of life, things he'd scarcely thought of a few weeks before, such as warmth, food, shelter and companionship, had been snatched away and now they were back, given by some-one who didn't seem to have any idea of how much it meant.

George sipped his coffee. 'This,' he said with deep feel-ing, 'is absolutely wonderful. My word, I wish I'd known you lived in London. I've had the most ghastly time.'

Jack sat back in the armchair once more and stirred his coffee. 'Why did you come here?' he asked curiously. 'I know how you came to be in hospital, of course, but what brought you to London?'

'It was the legacy,' said George. He looked at Jack's enquiring face. 'It's a long story.'

'I love long stories,' said Jack cheerfully. 'Especially when they've got legacies in them. Go on.' George hesit-ated and Jack reached for a cigarette. 'Why don't you tell me what happened to you after the war?' he prompted. 'Did you go home? Back to South Africa?'

George hesitated once more and Jack could see him trying to think of the right words. 'I did go back,' he said eventually. 'I'd been longing to go back but I don't know . . .' He paused. 'I tried to get into the routine of the farm once more but after the war and flying and so on, it all seemed so dull. My mother had died while I'd been away and although my father was pleased to see me, I'd changed. He couldn't really understand what life had been like in France, Jack, or in the prisoner-of-war camp, and when I thought of what I'd been through, none of that ordinary stuff seemed worth bothering with any more. I couldn't settle.'

Jack nodded. 'You weren't alone in that feeling.'

George looked up. 'Wasn't I? I don't know. I didn't fit in any more. It was as simple as that. It might have been different if I'd had brothers and sisters but there was just me and my father. To be fair to him, I think he was ill. Anyway, he died a few months after I got back and then there really wasn't anything to keep me on the farm any longer. I sold up and headed north. I did a few things after that, including running a seaplane, a Short 184, along Lake Nyasa with a couple of pals. That was tremendously good fun while it lasted but the plane got damaged in a storm and we couldn't fix it. I lost a good bit of the money from the farm on that plane. Then I picked up a nasty dose of malaria and ended up back at the Cape. I tried all sorts of things – tourist guide, the railways, overseer at the diamond fields – and finally ended up taking parties to hunt big game. I got as far as Matabeleland. It was all going well when I came down with malaria again. I was looked after by the White Fathers on a mission station near Tulali.' He took another drink of coffee. 'And that, in a roundabout way, is what brought me to London. They had a stack of old newspapers. I was flicking through them one day when I saw my own name in a paper dated December 1921.'

Jack leaned forward. 'Your name?'

'Yes. It was an advertisement which said that if George Lassiter, late of my old address, and thought to be resident in South Africa, would apply to Marchbolt, Lawson and Marchbolt, solicitors of London – it gave the address – I would hear of something to my advantage. You could have knocked me over with the proverbial feather.'

'I can imagine. And this was your legacy, was it?'

'Yes, it was, but I'm afraid it didn't come off as I'd hoped.' George took a cigarette and lit it thoughtfully. 'I wrote to the solicitors and when their reply came, I was thunderstruck. It stated that the legacy – it was a legacy – had been paid in February 1922 to Mr George Lassiter and virtually accused me of attempted fraud.'

'Good grief,' said Jack, sitting up. 'What did you do?'

'I was furious. The solicitors had quoted the address of the farm in the advert and used my name and I thought someone had calmly stepped in and swindled me out of what was rightfully mine.'

'But that's appalling,' said Jack. 'Hang on a minute. Your father wasn't called George by any chance, was he?'

George shook his head. 'No, but I see what you mean. If I'd been called after him there would be two George Lassiters at the same address, but that idea doesn't hold water. Apart from anything else, the legacy was paid after he died. No, it wasn't my father.'

'And they gave the address of the farm?'

'Yes. It simply had to mean me, Jack.'

'It looks like it.' He paused. 'Who could have left you the money? Have you any idea?'

George shook his head. 'That's another thing I couldn't work out. I've had lots of friends and wondered if it might be an old pal, but from the tone of the letter I gathered there was quite a bit of money at stake. I couldn't think who the dickens it might be. I wrote to the solicitors again but they declared that they'd said all they were going to say and that, as far as they were concerned, was that. What would you have done?'

Jack considered the question for a moment. 'In your position? I think I'd have come to London. I'd want to know who had mentioned me in their will, I must say, let alone what had happened to the money.'

George nodded. 'That's exactly what I did. I packed up, got the train to Durban and when I found out the fare to London was twenty-two pounds, that seemed to settle it. I had just over twelve pounds left after I'd bought the ticket and got some kit together, and I thought the change would see me through for a few weeks. When I arrived in London I went straight to the solicitors. They were a bit frosty at first but I let them know I wasn't leaving until I had some answers. Eventually I was wheeled in to see the chief panjandrum, old Mr Marchbolt himself. He asked for my birth certificate but I've never had one. I'd wanted it when I joined the Royal Flying Corps but my father told me it had been lost years ago, together with a lot of other family papers. However, I had other papers with me, such as my RFC discharge certificate, and so on. Mr Marchbolt asked me some pretty piercing questions but my answers must have satisfied him, because he unbent as we went on and told me what had happened. The legacy was a pretty substantial one.'

Jack looked at him with interest. 'Go on. How much was it?'

'Forty-six thousand pounds.'

Jack stared at him. 'Forty-six *thousand*! That's a fortune.'

George nodded grimly. 'I thought so. Forty-six thousand pounds and it had been swiped. Nice, eh?'

'But who'd left it to you?' asked Jack. 'Did this Mr Marchbolt tell you?'

George leaned forward. 'Yes, he did, and again, I can't make any sense of it. A Mrs Rosemary Belmont had left the money to her son, George Alfred Lassiter, on her death in October 1921. Now I'm George Alfred Lassiter and the address given in the will was the farm, but Rosemary Belmont, whoever she was, certainly wasn't my mother. I couldn't figure it out. My mother was called Susan and her maiden name was Harrison. She certainly never had that sort of money and anything she did have went to my father. I've never known anyone called Belmont and who on earth she was is anybody's guess. Mr Marchbolt told me frankly he was giving me these details because I could go and look up Mrs Belmont's will for a shilling in Somerset House, wherever that is.'

'And who claimed it?'

George shrugged. 'Someone who said they were me. Apparently the solicitors had advertised in the *Cape Town Herald* and the other South African papers but I'd been up on Lake Nyasa. Anyway, they received a letter from a George Alfred Lassiter, enclosing a birth certificate, and, as everything seemed to be in order, they paid up.'

'Where had this other George Lassiter written from?'

'They wouldn't tell me, apart from the fact it was South Africa. I came out of the solicitors' office feeling skittled out. To be honest, I didn't know if I'd been rooked or not. As I say, the address was certainly mine but Mrs Belmont wasn't my mother.'

'Did you go to the police?'

George raised his hands and let them fall helplessly into his lap. 'No. No, I didn't. After all, the will clearly said "Rosemary Belmont to her son, George Alfred Lassiter," and that's not me, no matter what the address was. I should have gone to the police, I suppose, but my money was running out fast and I was desperately in need of a job.'

He put a hand to his mouth. It was some time before he spoke again. 'Jack, I had no idea how hard it would be. I'd heard about the unemployment, of course, but hand on heart, I thought it was because the men weren't trying hard enough. I'd always been able to pick up something back home but here there was nothing. I'd started off in a small hotel on the Tottenham Court Road but pretty soon real-ized I couldn't afford it and moved to a cheap boarding house in Bloomsbury. I'd wanted to make enough for a ticket back to the Cape but I was soon scratching round just to keep myself alive. I got a few odd jobs, portering and so on, at Covent Garden, but it was very little.'

'You poor devil,' said Jack quietly.

'I couldn't believe it,' broke out George. 'I was willing to work – work hard – but for every job there were dozens of men. I thought being an ex-officer would help but it cut no ice at all. For God's sake, Jack, all I wanted was some manual labour, anything to get enough money to return to Africa, but there seemed to be no chance at all. I looked at the poor beggars sleeping on the Embankment and knew I'd be joining them soon if something didn't turn up.'

Jack looked at his friend. George had gone pale, reliving that heartbreaking struggle. There was nothing he could say that wouldn't sound trite but he had to make some reply. He poured two more cups of coffee and handed one to George. 'It must have been pretty grim.'

George took the coffee and held it, warming his hands on the cup. It was a while before he spoke. 'Grim? Yes, it was grim. I've never felt so desperate in my life. Eventually I was down to my last few shillings. All I had left was one and ninepence, and I owed two weeks' rent. It may have been the worry which brought it on, because I couldn't think what to do, but I started to feel seedy. I came downstairs and met the landlord in the hall. He took one look at me and gave me my marching orders. He didn't want an invalid on his hands. I was feeling so wretched I let him take the money and swipe my clothes and things to pay for the room and turn me out without any argument. I was wearing my dress clothes, so he couldn't take them, and out I went. I spent that night in Euston station, pretending I was waiting for a train. The next day I wandered about, hoping for some sort of job, but I was feeling dreadful. It was raining and bitterly cold. I sat in the park for ages, hoping the fresh air would do me good, but as time went on I knew I was in for malaria.'

'Is this the night you were taken into hospital?'

George nodded. 'Yes.' He hesitated, looking at Jack. 'Your friend, the policeman – did he tell you what happened?'

'Yes, he did,' said Jack, lighting another cigarette. 'That's how I came to find you, of course. I'd like to hear your side of things, though, I must say.'

George didn't enjoy telling the story. As he spoke the desperation and the uncanny fear of that night returned. He remembered how the street and house seemed the wrong size; first too small, then too big. How the house, that creepily familiar house, seemed to draw him in, as if it was meant he should be there, to witness a murder in that quiet kitchen by the flickering firelight. Because he didn't enjoy telling the story, he knew his account was lame and unconvincing. He wouldn't have been able to piece things together at all if Jack hadn't helped him out with questions.

After George had finished, Jack sat for a long moment, staring sightlessly into the fire.

'Well?' prompted George anxiously. 'Do you think I was dreaming, Jack?'

Jack ran his thumb round his chin. 'To be honest, George, it sounds like it.'

George looked down at his intertwined fingers. He felt an unexpected stab of disappointment. He'd had a nightmare. Either that or he'd seen ghosts and he didn't want to believe in ghosts ... A bad dream was the only rational explanation and yet he felt oddly dissatisfied. It had all seemed so very *real*.

'What's wrong?' asked Jack softly.

George shrugged. 'After the men had left the room I wondered if I'd dreamt it. I felt the table. It was solid. I touched the girl. I could have sworn she was really there. Because I thought I might have dreamt it at the time, for some reason it makes it seem more real.' He looked up ruefully. 'Forget it,' he said with a dismissive gesture. 'It must have been a dream. Nothing else makes sense. Look, Jack,' he said, briskly changing the subject, 'it's damn good of you to take me in like this but I want you to know that I'll push off as soon as I can.' He gave a shy smile. 'I might

30

have to sponge the ticket money from you, but I'll repay you as soon as I can.'

'Ticket money?'

'To go back home.'

'Hold on.' Jack's voice was firm. 'You won't be fit to go anywhere for a few weeks. Don't worry, George. It's nice to have you here. Apart from that, you'll need somewhere to stay while we try and find out what's happened to this legacy of yours.'

George's eyes opened wide. 'But I told you. I don't know it's mine. Besides, it's been claimed.'

Jack snorted impatiently. 'Good God, man, I know it's been claimed. Who by? That's the point. We ought to be able to discover something between the two of us.' He stretched his long legs out in front of him, toasting the soles of his shoes by the fire. 'The question is, where do we start?'

Jack decided to start with the solicitors but his plans suffered a setback. That afternoon *On the Town* experienced a crisis which caused him to abandon his guest and completely overturn George's unvoiced opinion that writing wasn't really work. It wasn't until Friday afternoon, by which time he had hammered out a ten-thousand-word story (in which a golden-haired girl was mysteriously done to death not in a kitchen but a conservatory), three articles and a column, that he could call on Messrs Marchbolt, Lawson and Marchbolt. The results were unsatisfactory. Old Mr Marchbolt, although he received him courteously, could shed no light on the mystery and clearly thought the whole business was a misunderstanding. Major Haldean would surely appreciate, he added, steepling his fingers together, that any suggestion that the firm had acted other than in good faith was one they would treat with the utmost gravity. Indeed, if Major Haldean thought there was any chance whatsoever that a fraudulent claim had been made, it was Major Haldean's duty to go to the police.

Major Haldean, picking up his hat and stick, thought he'd do just that. He derived a certain amount of satisfaction from seeing the wind visibly taken out of Mr Marchbolt's sails.

The policeman Jack first thought of was, of course, Inspector William Rackham. But Rackham was not at the Yard. He'd been called out on urgent business and Jack, leaving a message for him, disconsolately went home.

The urgent business Rackham had been called away on concerned Mrs Margaret Culverton.

It had been that morning, the morning of Friday 9th November, a dark, fog-filled day, when she got the letters. Peggy, as Margaret Culverton was always known, held the letters lightly by the edges. They were both from Gilchrist Lloyd, Alexander's secretary. She could tell that from the writing on the envelopes. She had been waiting for this. The letters had been forwarded from the house in Richmond, the house she had shared with Alexander.

Alexander ... Her stomach seemed to turn to water. There had been a time – long ago, it seemed – when she had been happy. Then she had met Alexander. She had thought that happiness was her usual state. She was wrong. It was difficult to remember now why she had been so attracted to him. Alexander's dignified good looks (no one would ever shorten his name), his firm chin and Roman nose, suggested a thoughtful, temperate, far-seeing man. Even now, with that dignity coarsened into grossness, she knew he had a presence. Alexander would never be overlooked. He had charmed her. Oh yes, Alexander could charm. He was obviously going to be successful, too. He had vision and the knowledge to make his vision work. The hard core of ruthlessness, which she had always sensed, she had mistaken for tenacity. She had never met anyone like Alexander. She had been excited by his vision of the future, a future linked by the invisible highways of the air. Aeroplanes would replace ships and perhaps even railways. When you could breakfast in London and lunch in Paris, who would travel any other way? In a London tormented by war, she had listened, spellbound. She knew aeroplanes as things to be feared, with their bombs and their guns. Alexander showed her a glittering future of a prosperous peace, where the aeroplane would be the metaphorical sword to be beaten into a ploughshare. Alexander, like others before him, could quote the Bible for his own ends. He had invited her to share in that future. All he needed was money; her money.

She wasn't happy for long. Happiness had turned to dull content, and then, so subtly that she couldn't mark the change, to uneasy acceptance which merged into apprehension. Fear had followed close behind, then absolute revulsion seized her. She had left Alexander and had been dreading this moment ever since.

She took a deep breath and, picking up the paper-knife, slit open the first envelope. It was merely a note, written by Mr Lloyd and dated Thursday 1st November, to say that Alexander had gone to Paris. She smiled wryly. She hadn't told the servants she was leaving for good. She'd merely packed a bag and been driven to the station, as she had so many times before. They must have waited before forwarding the letter on, thinking she would be back soon. She opened the second letter and, as she read it, her eyes, which had been narrowed in unconscious defiance, opened in surprise. It had been written last Monday.

Culverton Air Navigation Limited,
23 Cooper Street,
London SW3.
Monday, 5th November 1923

Dear Mrs Culverton,
As you doubtless know, Mr Culverton should have flown to Paris on Thursday, 1st November. I do not wish to alarm you unduly but I have today received a telephone call from the

Paris office enquiring as to the whereabouts of Mr Culverton which I was unable to answer.

To the best of my knowledge Mr Culverton should have departed for Paris on Thursday morning but I now understand that, although he booked a seat on the 9.23 Culverton Air Navigation flight from Croydon, his seat was not, in fact, occupied. Following extensive enquiries I have ascertained that Mr Culverton has not flown to Paris on any of our subsequent flights.

I would be grateful if you would contact me at your earliest convenience.

Yours sincerely,
Gilchrist Lloyd
Secretary

Peggy Culverton put down the letter, staring blankly at the words on the page. With fingers that trembled slightly she lit a cigarette then, abruptly reaching a decision, she walked into the hall, picked up the telephone and rang Culverton Air Navigation.

William Rackham sat in the armchair in Margaret Culverton's sitting room. It was a pleasant room in a pleasant flat, if a bit on the small side. A pied-à-terre? He thought that was the right description. The flat was in a good area, furnished with classic good taste. The sideboard and table were of highly polished dark wood and the up-to-date chrome fittings of the fireplace caught the flicker of the agreeable wood fire. It was a lady's room, thought Rackham, taking in the shiny chintz of the sofa and the vibrant splash of colour from the chrysanthemums in their tall vase on the windowsill. Yes, a lady's room and Margaret Culverton was definitely a lady.

She was in her forties and still attractive, fashionably but quietly dressed in light brown. She didn't miss much, if he knew anything about it. That she was worried was

34

obvious, both from her expression and from the way she continually fingered the beading on the arm of the chair.

He cleared his throat and smiled, hoping to put her at her ease. 'It's very good of you to let me come and see you, Mrs Culverton.'

'Are you the person I spoke to on the phone?' Her voice was firm and clear.

'That's right, Mrs Culverton. I made a note of what you said, so we don't need to go over that again.' He coughed and came to the crunch. 'Your husband is missing?'

She nodded. 'Apparently he's been missing since 1st November.'

Apparently? That was an odd way to put it. Didn't she know? 'When did you last see him?' She hesitated. Rackham watched her curiously. 'Mrs Culverton?' he prompted.

'I saw him last on the morning of Monday, 29th October. We were at our house in Richmond. That's The Lampreys, River Grove Road.' She spoke in a nervous rush. 'Alexander was driven to the station to catch the 9.07. It was his custom to spend the week in town. He had rooms at his club, the Mulciber in St James's. I spoke to Mr Lloyd, Alexander's secretary, after I received his letter. He told me Alexander had arrived in the office on Monday morning.'

'And did you see him or speak to him – on the telephone, for instance – during the course of the week?'

'No. No, I didn't.' She sounded very uncertain and Rackham looked at her, waiting for the revelation he was sure was there. 'Mrs Culverton?' he prompted.

She took a deep breath. 'You might as well know,' she said in a rush. 'Having asked to see you it would be stupid to try and hide things.' She looked at him with troubled grey eyes. 'How much needs to be made public?'

'Nothing,' said Rackham quickly. 'You can put your mind at rest about that. What you tell me is entirely confidential unless, of course, it's a criminal matter.'

'In that case ...' She straightened her shoulders and plunged in. 'I had left my husband, Inspector.'

35

Rackham expected her to justify herself, to explain exactly why she had done what she did but, remarkably, in his experience, she simply left the statement as a record of bare fact. He schooled his face into blank and polite enquiry but Mrs Culverton hurried on. 'I don't particularly want to go into the reasons why I left him but I think any woman would have done the same.'

Again, she didn't seek to justify herself. Rackham sat back. 'When was this, Mrs Culverton? When did you leave, I mean?'

'Wednesday. Wednesday 31st October.'

'Did you let your husband know?' She shook her head. 'Did you leave a note or send him a letter?' Again, she shook her head. 'You see, Mrs Culverton,' he explained, 'I'm trying to find some reason why Mr Culverton should have disappeared and I thought that if he perhaps received a letter from you, saying you had left him, that could account for it.'

Her face cleared. 'I see what you mean. No, Inspector. I simply went. Not even the servants knew I intended to leave for good.'

And there again, frustratingly, she remained silent. The pause lengthened. Rackham waited for Mrs Culverton to explain further, to enlist, as most women would have done, his sympathy and support for their actions, but she simply remained silent. He put the reasons for Mrs Culverton's actions on the list of things he might have to investigate. It was probably another man but that didn't quite fit. *Any woman would have done the same.* What did that mean? Rackham mentally shrugged and moved on.

'Mrs Culverton, we know he should have gone to the Paris branch of the firm on Thursday. Presumably he was at the office on Wednesday?'

Mrs Culverton nodded. 'So Mr Lloyd says.'

'And when did he leave?'

'Nobody knows. Mr Lloyd was probably the last person to see him at the office. Alexander was still there when

Mr Lloyd left at half past five. Mr Lloyd tells me that Alexander had an engagement that evening. He had invited two business acquaintances to dinner at the Mulciber.'

'Did you know of this engagement in Paris?'

Mrs Culverton shook her head. 'No, but it wasn't unusual for him to have to go away at short notice.'

'Do you know who the business acquaintances were, Mrs Culverton? The men who had dinner with your husband on Wednesday evening, I mean?'

She shrugged. 'No, I'm sorry, I don't. Mr Lloyd might be able to tell you.'

'And that was on the 31st. Wednesday.' He had a picture in his mind, a picture of a naked, mutilated middle-aged man on a mortuary table, a man who had been found on Thursday morning. 'Could you describe your husband, Mrs Culverton? What did he look like?' He listened as she, hesitant as most people were when faced with such a question, answered him. Yes, that could be the body in the mortuary. 'Did he have any enemies? Is there anyone who might entertain violent feelings towards your husband?'

Her response intrigued him. Most people – most wives certainly – would hotly deny such a thing. Yes, she had left him, but that meant, as often as not, a catalogue of misunderstandings topped off by a quarrel. She, the injured wife, could see her husband's faults but that was a very different state of affairs from imagining an enemy, a real enemy.

Instead she dropped her eyes. 'There might be. I don't know of any,' she said at last.

'Mrs Culverton,' he said, his voice very gentle, 'have you considered the possibility that your husband may be dead?'

It was an appreciable moment before she raised her eyes to his and Rackham, who had been prepared to offer sympathy, was startled to catch a look of thinly veiled anticipation. It was almost triumphant, he thought, repelled. Damn it, the woman might have had a row with her husband but did she want him to be dead? Then, just as quickly, the look vanished to be replaced by conventional worry. She can hide her feelings, thought Rackham. Mrs Culverton was a woman he would have to treat with caution.

'I've . . . I wondered.' Once again she fingered the beading on the chair but this time Rackham wondered how much of her anxiety was caused by the thought that her husband might be dead and how much by the thought that he could be alive.

Rackham leaned forward. 'We have a body in the mortuary. The description matches that of your husband, superficially at least. Unfortunately his face is unrecognizable.'

Again, there was a gleam of anticipation followed by a puzzled frown. 'This body, Inspector. Is this the man I read about in the newspaper? The man who was found in the river?'

Rackham nodded. 'It's an unpleasant task to identify a body, Mrs Culverton, particularly in these very distressing circumstances. I would like to spare you if I could. Is there anyone who knew your husband well?'

Her mouth tightened. 'It has to be me, doesn't it? If what the newspaper said was right, he'd be unrecognizable to most people. I can't ask anyone else to do it.'

And that was true enough. She had courage, Rackham thought, even if he didn't really trust her. He rose to his feet. 'In that case, Mrs Culverton, perhaps you'd be good enough to come with me.'

Jack found a note from George on the table when he got home from Scotland Yard. *Gone for a walk. I borrowed some of your clothes. Hope that's okay. George.*

So he'd gone for a walk, had he? That was a first. There was no doubt George was getting better by the hour. He'd lost that awful wasted look and was far more himself again. Characteristically, he had been longing to get out.

38

What clothes had he taken? Jack looked in the wardrobe. His old blue suit, a sleeveless sweater and a Burberry. That should be all right. Some of his things made the poor beggar look like Charlie Chaplin.

He'd have to see about getting George kitted out. It was all very well saying expansively, 'Borrow my things' but George was a big man. They were about as tall as each other but George was a much sturdier bloke. Although his clothes did at a pinch, there was no denying George wasn't comfortable. He couldn't do up Jack's collars and the only shoes he had were his patent leather ones. Perhaps if George was up to going for walks, he'd agree to pay a visit to Butler and Furness? They could kit him up right away and clean and press his dress clothes into the bargain. Jack, thinking ruefully about the straining seams of his suits, rejected the idea of waiting for a proper tailor to do his thing. Besides that, Butler and Furness were all right and didn't cost a fortune.

Money. He stoked up the fire thoughtfully and put the kettle on to boil on the spirit lamp. He had to, as he had pointed out to George, work for a living and it was just as well he'd worked like a galley slave all week. That would be pretty handy, what with an increase in rent, the hefty donation to the Royal Free he'd felt honour-bound to make, a ticket to South Africa in the offing and now a visit to Butler and Furness. This Good Samaritan lark didn't come cheaply.

He made a cup of tea, relaxed into the armchair and lit a cigarette. George appreciated it all, though. George was a very straightforward character. He had something to be grateful for and was. Jack grinned. There was something deeply engaging about old George.

There was a noise in the hall and he looked up as George came in. 'Hello, old man,' he began, then stopped. He had been going to say something about it being a rotten day for a walk, but the excitement on George's face brought him up short. 'Whatever is it?'

'Jack,' said George, urgently. 'I've found the house!'

'What house?'

'The house,' repeated George, undoing his coat. 'The house where it all happened. You know, where I saw the girl. Well, where I thought I saw the girl, at any rate.' He tossed his coat and hat on to a chair. 'Jack, I don't know what it is about that place, but it's creepy. You know I said I felt drawn to it? Well, it's true. There's something about that house. When I was there before, I know I was coming down with malaria and so on but I'm not ill now. And yet, believe you me, I stood on that pavement and felt as peculiar as I had the other night. I don't know.' He stopped, hunting for the right expression. 'It's *meant*, Jack. It's as if I'm meant to be there.'

'Where is it?'

'The house? The address is 19 Eden Street. The place is called Mayfair, apparently. I asked a passer-by. I knew it was near a big park and I tramped around this afternoon until I found it. Look, I don't know the first thing about which bits of London are which, but is it a very grand area?'

Jack laughed. 'Mayfair? I should say so. It's seriously posh.'

George hunched down before the fire and warmed his hands by the flames. 'I thought so. I felt like the cat in the wrong warehouse, as the Boers would say, so what is it about the place, Jack? No one would call me grand and yet I kept on feeling I belonged there. I'm just a farmer. Not even that, now I've sold the farm. I've only been in London once before and that's when I was on leave in the war. I've certainly never been to Mayfair.' He stood up and braced his hands on the mantelpiece. 'I don't like it,' he said quietly. 'It's . . . Well, it's spooky.'

'Did you see who lived there?' asked Jack curiously.

George shuddered. 'Absolutely not. I'm . . . I'm *frightened* of the place. Besides, how could I possibly approach them after what I did? I broke into their house.'

'Didn't you say there was a woman? A woman with the policemen? You said she was nice.'

40

George's face softened. 'She was nice. She might understand if I could explain it to her but I can't face her again. She must have thought I was loco.'

Jack shook his head. 'Not from what you told me. She's the one who worked out you were ill.'

'That's true,' said George. 'She wouldn't let the policemen arrest me. If I'd seen her on Eden Street I might have said something.' He gave a short laugh. 'God knows what.' His eyes grew wistful. 'She was a corker. I wish I could talk to her again but I don't suppose I'll ever know her name.'

'Hang on.' Jack levered himself out of the armchair. 'Now you know the address, I can probably tell you who she is.' He walked to the bookcase, selected a book and opened it on the table.

'What's that?' asked George with interest.

'Kelly's Street Directory. It's a list of who lives where, indexed by street names. Where did you say it was? Eden Street?'

George joined him at the table. 'That's right. 19 Eden Street, Mayfair.'

Jack turned up the entry. He ran his finger down the page then stopped. He drew his breath in and stared incredulously at the book, his body rigid.

'Jack?' said George. 'Jack? What is it?'

For an answer Jack pointed at the name beside 19 Eden Street.

George read it and gasped. He turned so white that Jack put a hand on his arm to steady him. 'It's no wonder it's familiar, is it?' he whispered. 'Dear God, I live there. Me.'

Jack stared once more at the neatly printed entry. *Mr George Lassiter.* He took a deep breath. 'George,' he said, at length, 'that really is a stunner.'

Chapter Three

Jack and George looked at the entry in the street directory. 'It's got me stumped,' said George eventually. 'Jack, am I going crackers? I don't suppose it's a misprint or something, is it?'

'I wouldn't have thought so,' said Jack. 'After all, there you are.' He gave his friend a sideways look. 'So, there *are* two George Lassiters in the world, even if this one lives in London. I wonder if this one knows anything about your missing legacy?'

'By jingo, that's a thought,' said George slowly. 'He could be the man who claimed the money.'

Jack clicked his tongue. 'That's going a bit too fast. After all, you said your legacy was claimed from South Africa.'

'He might have come from South Africa. There's nothing here to say how long he's been living at that address.'

'No, that's true. He's not alone,' added Jack, putting his finger on the page. 'Mr David Lassiter, Mr Nigel Lassiter, and look, this presumably is the girl you met, Mrs Anne Lassiter. I wonder who she's married to? There's another raft of names, too. Michael Walsh, John Corby, Nora Nelson and so on. I bet those are the servants. George, don't the Lassiter names mean anything to you?'

George shook his head. 'Not a damn thing. It's got me beat. What do we do now?'

'We could go round and see them,' said Jack.

George drew his breath in sharply. 'I can't do that.'

'Why not?'

'Because of what I did. I broke in, remember? I stole their food, helped myself out of their larder and then, to top it off, caused a real scene. For heaven's sake, the police were involved, Jack. I was very nearly arrested. I can't walk through their front door and expect them to receive me with open arms. They'd throw me out on my ear and I couldn't blame them.'

Jack reluctantly agreed. 'Yes, you might be right. I can see you're bound to feel awkward about it.' He walked to the sofa and, sitting on the arm, ran his thumb round the side of his chin. 'You could write to them, I suppose,' he said eventually. 'Or I could go. I could explain what happened and say you've been ill and so on.' He looked at George. 'What d'you think? That might be the best thing to do.'

George sighed unhappily. 'Would it?' He hesitated. 'Look, don't you think you've done enough for me already? I appreciate it, Jack, really I do, but this is my affair.'

'All right.' Jack raised an interrogative eyebrow. 'So you want to go alone?'

George looked at him ruefully. 'I don't want to go at all.' He shook himself in irritation. 'I can't see the point of writing. I'd never be able to think of what to say. Damn! I'll have to see them. It's the only way.'

'Alone?'

George's mouth twisted. 'I can't ask you to come.'

'Why not?' asked Jack. 'After all, I know it's your business and not mine but I must admit I'm curious.' He didn't miss the relief in George's face. 'Come on. Let's go.'

'Now, you mean?' asked George, startled.

Jack shrugged. 'Why not? Now's as good a time as any.' He walked to the door, turning to smile encouragingly at his friend. 'Let's get a taxi.'

'What on earth do I say?' hissed George, as the bell jangled in the depths of 19 Eden Street.

'We'll tell them who we are and see what happens,' said Jack. The door was opened by a portly and glacially respectable butler. George gave a small, depressed sigh.

'Major Haldean and Mr Lassiter to see Mr George Lassiter,' said Jack with cheerful insouciance.

The glacier thawed and looked puzzled. 'Excuse me, sir, did you say Mr Lassiter?'

'That's right,' said George as firmly as he could manage.

The butler stood to one side to let them in. 'If you would care to wait, gentlemen, I will ascertain if Mr Lassiter is at home.' They were ushered into a large square hall furnished with, amongst other things, an oak table and a Jacobean settle.

As soon as the butler had gone George collapsed on to the seat. 'Jack, it's all wrong.' Jack put a hand on his shoulder and George glanced up, his face showing the strain he was under. 'The size is all wrong. The table's too small. Everything's too small.' Jack tightened his grip on George's shoulder. The table was a very substantial table in a very substantial house. There was nothing wrong with it. 'I feel like a clumsy giant in here,' muttered George. 'It's all *wrong*. Can't you see it?' He closed his eyes and took a deep breath.

'Come on,' said Jack awkwardly. 'The butler will be back soon.'

'He's wrong too,' said George savagely. 'Everything's wrong.' He looked round the hall. 'I wish I hadn't come.' He sat in silence until the butler returned.

'Mr Lassiter will see you now. Allow me to take your coats, gentlemen, then if you will come with me, please.'

They followed the butler's stately progress down the hall. He paused outside a door, coughed, then showed them into a big room made cosy by curtains and lamps. A fire burned in the grate at the further end of the room, surrounded by modern and inviting easy chairs. Above the fireplace hung an oil painting of an aeroplane in flight, which, from its graceful outline, Jack immediately recognized as an LE4c.

A white-haired old man, who, at a guess, was well into his seventies but still bright-eyed and vigorous, stood on the rug in front of the fire. There was something vaguely familiar about him and Jack wondered where he'd seen him before. A woman in her late twenties, with dark hair and intelligent eyes, attractively dressed in blue and green, stood beside him. Mrs Anne Lassiter? Probably, thought Jack. So this was the woman who had refused to let the police arrest George after the incident in the kitchen. He looked at her with concealed interest. She seemed a thoroughly dependable sort, who could take charge when necessary. Exactly, in fact, as she had done that evening when George needed her help so badly. He wasn't surprised she had made such a strong impression on George. As they were shown into the room her face was alive with interest.

'Major Haldean and Mr Lassiter,' said the butler.

As the door shut behind the butler, the old man moved forward a pace. 'I wondered if Corby had heard your names correctly,' he began, when George stepped into the lamplight. The man gasped and swayed. The woman beside him caught his arm. He stared at George, his mouth open and his eyes wide. 'Charles?' he mumbled. 'Charles? Charles, it can't be you!' He made a fluttering movement with his hand and groped his way into a chair. Quickly but without fuss, Mrs Lassiter took a bottle of brandy from the cabinet behind her, poured some into a glass and added soda water. She put it into his outstretched hand, standing by with a calm, reassuring stillness.

He gulped it down, then handed the glass back to her, colour returning to his cheeks. 'Thank you, Anne.' So it was Mrs Lassiter. The old man looked at George in bewilderment. 'Who the devil are you?'

George took a deep breath. 'Lassiter. My name's George Lassiter,' he said. 'I –'

'Wait.' The old man held up his hand. 'Please, before you say anything more, wait. Anne, there's a photograph

45

on the cabinet. A photograph of Charles. Can you bring it to me, please?'

A collection of silver-framed photographs stood on the cabinet. After a short search she found the one he wanted and gave it to him. He motioned with his hand to Jack and George. 'Come and look at this.'

It was a studio portrait of a young man dressed in the fashion of thirty-odd years ago. Jack looked at the stiffly posed figure, then at his friend. 'But it's you, George,' he said in astonishment. 'Hang on, it's not quite . . . Well, it's nearly you,' he finished.

George shook his head. 'No, it's not. It's my father. We had that photo at home.' He looked from the old man to the photograph, his forehead creased in a frown. 'I don't understand, sir. Who are you? Why have you got my father's picture?'

'Charles is your father?' The old man looked George up and down and tentatively reached out to him with an expression of such tenderness it made Jack catch his breath. 'And you're George. You were called after me. You don't know this, but I've thought about you a lot.' George took his outstretched hand. 'You're my grandson.'

The next ten minutes or so were spent in a tumble of explanations, most of which were so fragmentary that, with the best will in the world, Jack didn't see how anyone could follow them. He watched George's earnest face as he leaned forward, listening to his grandfather. He should have seen the likeness immediately. It was no wonder old Mr Lassiter reminded him of someone. It was George, of course – those similarities in the shape of the nose and the line of the jaw. There were mannerisms too; how they sat, how both men would give a sharp tilt of the head before speaking and little unconscious gestures of the hands.

George had embarked on an account of his bewilderment at how oddly familiar the house and surrounding streets seemed, when his grandfather interrupted.

'But of course it all seems familiar, George. You were

born here, here in this house. You lived here until you were nearly three.'

George looked at him with a puzzled frown. 'I was born in South Africa.'

His grandfather smiled. 'No, you weren't. Not a bit of it. This is where you were born and this was your home when you were very young.'

George turned to Jack. 'That must be it, Jack! I must have remembered without knowing I did.'

'I bet that's why everything seemed the wrong size,' said Jack. 'When you go back to somewhere you knew as a kid it all seems too small. I've had that experience.'

'It explains the other night as well,' said George eagerly. 'It explains why I felt so drawn to this particular house. That and the fire.' He gave a shy smile, braced himself and looked at Anne. 'You don't seem to have recognized me, but I was the man in the kitchen. You know, with the police and so on.'

'*You?*' Anne sat up and stared at him sharply. 'Of course you are! I thought I recognized you. Ever since you came in I've been trying to think where I've seen you before.' She turned to Mr Lassiter. 'You remember I told you about it? A man broke into the kitchen. The police took him to hospital.'

Mr Lassiter drew back, shocked. 'You broke in, George?'

'He was desperate,' put in Jack, seeing his friend's face. Poor old George was brick-red with embarrassment and the atmosphere in the sitting room had suffered a sudden chill. 'He was completely on his uppers – destitute, I mean – and had nowhere to go. He was coming down with malaria and flu and, from what I can make out, half-dead with cold.'

Old Mr Lassiter relaxed but still looked at George warily.

'I told you I was attracted to the house,' said George. 'I seemed to remember what it would be like inside. I . . . I so wanted to be inside.' He stood up. 'Look, I'm sorry.' He hesitated. 'It's as Jack said. I was desperate, but I still

47

shouldn't have done it. I know that. All I can say is, I'm sorry.' He glanced at Jack. 'I think we'd better go.'

His grandfather rose to his feet. 'Go? For heaven's sake, boy, you've only just arrived.' He reached his hand out once more. 'Please, George, sit down. You were ill, you say?'

George looked at Jack for support.

'George was completely broke and very ill indeed,' said Jack, seeing his friend needed helping out. 'I don't think it's any exaggeration to say that he would have died that night if it hadn't been for your help, Mrs Lassiter. As it was, he got taken to the Royal Free and very nearly didn't make it, even then. George and I are old friends,' he continued, seeing that further explanation was necessary. 'I found out from a pal of mine in the police what had happened, recognized the name and, to cut a long story short, George is staying with me until he recovers completely.'

'But, George, how did you come to be in such dire straits?' asked Mr Lassiter wonderingly. 'Sit down.' He turned the command into a request. 'Please?'

George hesitantly sat down again. 'I think I'd better tell you the story of the legacy,' he said. He did so, as briefly as he could. 'But who this Rosemary Belmont is, I don't know,' he finished.

His grandfather looked at him thoughtfully. 'Rosemary?' he said quietly. 'Rosemary. I knew she'd married again but I'd forgotten her husband's name. She must be the woman I knew as Rosemary Vernon. She . . .' He broke off, looking at George. 'I'm sorry, my boy. I don't know quite how to break this to you. You see . . .' He hesitated once more then, gathering himself, spoke in a rush. 'Rosemary was your mother.'

There was dead silence. George sat bolt upright, his hands clenched. 'No,' he said at last. 'No, she wasn't. My mother wasn't called Rosemary. She was Susan. Susan Harrison. You're wrong, sir. You must be wrong.'

'I'm not,' said Mr Lassiter quietly. 'I'm sorry if this is a shock to you, George, but Rosemary Vernon was your mother.'

George looked at him in bewilderment. 'But how can she be, sir?' he protested. 'I know who my mother was.'

Mr Lassiter put down his glass. 'I'm sorry, George. Your father should have told you.' He shrugged. 'It's obvious that he didn't. All I can say in mitigation is that he was hurt. Badly hurt.' He sighed. 'Rosemary Vernon was your mother and the reason why you lived here.' His eyes became distant. 'Your father was a stubborn boy. Mary – your grandmother – always said that he took after me.' He blinked rapidly. 'Maybe he did. Poor Charles. I wish I could have seen him again. It's too late now.'

George gazed at him in complete disbelief. 'Can you explain, sir?' he said at last.

There was a long pause, then Mr Lassiter shook himself. 'Charles married Rosemary Vernon against my wishes. I don't wish to speak ill of your mother, George, particularly as she is dead, but I considered her to be flighty and spoiled and the very last person who Charles should have married.' He looked at George apologetically. 'I have to tell you the truth as I see it, otherwise you'll never understand.'

George sat back in his chair. 'I think you'd better.' He glanced at Jack. 'I didn't know what to expect, but certainly nothing like this.'

Mr Lassiter turned to Anne. 'Would you get drinks for us, my dear? I think we could all do with something.'

Both George and Jack accepted a whisky and soda gratefully. 'As I say,' continued old Mr Lassiter, 'I never thought Rosemary was the right wife for Charles.' He picked up his glass and grimaced. 'It gave me no pleasure at all to be proved right. She was an actress and Charles was dazzled by her. They very quickly grew apart. Rosemary wasn't interested in making a home for Charles and it was in an attempt to bring them together that Mary and I suggested they live here until you were born, at least. The idea was to take the cares of running a household off her shoulders so she could concentrate on you, but Rosemary was never cut out to be a mother. She was fond of you, don't think she wasn't, but she couldn't cope with responsibility. She left Charles when you were a few months old and went abroad.' He looked away. 'She went to Paris with Belmont. He was far more her type. He was an artist, a successful one, I believe.' He cleared his throat awkwardly. 'She wasn't a conventional woman, George. Much to Charles's distress, she lived an openly scandalous life with Belmont until the divorce was granted. She married him after that.' He looked at his grandson with worried eyes. 'I'm sorry I had to be the one to break such unpalatable news.'

'It's not your fault, sir,' said George. 'It's just – well, it's a bit of a shock, you know?' He paused, then shrugged helplessly. 'I don't suppose there's much I can say.'

'She obviously never forgot you, George,' said Anne, gently. 'I don't suppose it's much consolation, but she left you all her money.'

He looked at her bleakly. 'I don't think that's very important. Not now.' He heaved a sigh. 'I wish I'd known. My father should have told me.'

'He probably wanted to put it behind him,' said Anne. 'We've never talked about it but I know David – David's my father-in-law – still finds it difficult. We were in the Tate a few months ago and some of Jerome Belmont's paintings were there. I knew something was wrong and asked what the matter was. David looked at the paintings and said, "I don't know much about art but I know about the devil who painted these. He's the swine who ran off with my brother's wife." He wouldn't tell me much more. I gathered it was a painful subject still.' She glanced at Jack. 'You've heard of Jerome Belmont, haven't you?'

'Jerome Belmont? Yes, of course I've heard of him, but the name didn't ring a bell when George told me about his legacy, I'm afraid.'

'I imagine the money came from Belmont's paintings,' said Mr Lassiter. 'Rosemary certainly never had any of her own.'

'I wonder what happened to it?' asked Anne. 'You say it was claimed from South Africa, George? There must be

50

some mistake. I'm sure the solicitors will be able to sort it out.'

'They weren't very helpful when I saw them before.'

'Yes, but things are different now. I mean, you know who Rosemary Belmont was now, and where you fit in and so on. There must be a mistake.'

Mr Lassiter looked grave. 'If there has been a mistake it might be more difficult to put right than you imagine, Anne. In my experience lawyers are very reluctant to admit an error.'

'Excuse me for asking, sir,' said Jack, 'but one way George can put the matter right is to prove who he is. I don't suppose you've got George's birth certificate, have you?'

'His birth certificate?' Mr Lassiter looked surprised. 'I imagine it's in the desk in the library with all the other family papers. If you think it will help, George, I can look it out for you but even then, I'm afraid it may be some time before you see the money.' He looked at his grandson. 'Rosemary did have feelings for you. You mustn't think otherwise. She did write once, many years ago, I remember, wanting to know where you were. I forwarded the letter on to Charles but I don't know what happened afterwards.'

'He must have answered her, Grandfather,' said Anne. 'That must have been where she got George's old address from.'

'That's true enough,' agreed Mr Lassiter. He took a deep breath. 'My word, I haven't thought of either her or Belmont for years. I'd forgotten his name until you mentioned it just now.' He sipped his drink thoughtfully. 'I had no idea David still resented what happened but he was very close to Charles. It all seems so long ago, now. You must remember how different things were before the war,' he added reflectively. 'We hushed things up a great deal more but that wouldn't do for Charles. He was determined to get a divorce. I was horrified. I don't approve of divorce now but then it was unthinkable. Charles and I quarrelled

51

and I said a great many things which I now regret. After the divorce was granted, Charles went to South Africa. You were here anyway, so he left you with us. When your grandmother died I wrote to him but all I got in reply was a brief note.' He looked at his grandson with an oddly hungry expression. 'Did he tell you much about us?'

George met his eyes, then looked away. 'He never mentioned you. I honestly believed I had no relations at all.' He spoke as gently as he could but his grandfather sagged and looked suddenly much older.

'He was always stubborn,' he said quietly. 'So terribly stubborn.'

George moved uneasily. 'Where did my mother – I suppose I should call her my stepmother, really – come into it?'

'Charles met her in the Cape. I got a short letter from him to say that he'd married again. Now that he had a home to offer you he wanted you back, so we sent you out to him in the care of your nurse. I believe she stayed with you in South Africa.'

'I certainly had an English nurse,' agreed George. 'I liked her a lot.'

'Your grandmother picked her. She was heartbroken when you left. She missed you terribly.'

George sat back in his chair and let his breath out in a long sigh. 'I'm stunned,' he said eventually. 'Everything I believed about myself has been turned upside down. My mother wasn't my mother and I've got a family I never knew about.' He shook himself. 'I can't tell you how strongly I felt drawn to this house. I wish I'd known why.' He looked apologetically at Jack. 'It would have saved you a lot of trouble, old man.' He glanced at Anne. 'After I'd found the house again we looked you up in a street directory. I saw there was a David and a Nigel Lassiter. You said David was my father's brother. Are you married to Nigel?'

Anne looked surprised. 'No, Nigel's a lot older than I am. He's my uncle-in-law, I suppose, if I can call him that.'

George looked puzzled. 'Well . . . Excuse my asking, but who's in the family?'

'I had three sons,' said Mr Lassiter. 'The eldest was Charles, your father. He never took any interest in the family firm.' He gave a rueful smile. 'We argued about that, too.' Anne laid a hand on his shoulder and he looked at her gratefully. 'My other two sons,' he continued in a stronger voice, 'are still very much with us. There's David. You'll like David. He's your uncle, of course.' He said the name with infectious warmth. 'He looked up to your father. They used to argue all the time, but it never stopped them being friends. David could never understand why your father wanted to strike out on his own. He's as committed to the firm as I am. I should have retired years ago but I could never bring myself to take the plunge.' He smiled. 'It's lucky I'm here. I'm usually at the works but I'm recovering from a nasty cold. David's taking over the reins. I rely on him tremendously.'

'And your other son, sir?' asked George. 'Is that Nigel? He'll be my uncle, too, I suppose.'

Mr Lassiter raised an eyebrow. 'So he will. It's hard to think of him in that role. Nigel.' Jack heard the chill in the old man's voice as he said the name. 'Don't expect any great show of affection from Nigel, George. It's not that there's anything wrong, mind, but he can seem a bit cold at times.'

'The thing about Nigel,' put in Anne, 'is that he's either a genius or the next best thing to it. He's completely absorbed in his work.' She smiled at George's expression. 'I'm sorry. You look a bit worried and I'm not surprised. I'm just saying that he probably won't throw his hat in the air at the sight of you.'

'Well, why should he?' said George. He looked at Anne. 'What about the rest of the family? You said David was your father-in-law. That means I've got a cousin, doesn't it? Your husband, I mean.'

Jack felt genuine sympathy for his friend. It was an innocent enough question but the silence which followed was nearly tangible. George flushed. 'I'm sorry. Have I said something I shouldn't? I didn't mean to put my foot in it.'

'You haven't,' said Anne quickly. 'Really, you haven't. It's just having to spell everything out is a bit stark. My husband died, you see.'

George shifted uneasily. 'I'm sorry to hear that.'

'Yes. There was an accident. It's two years ago now. David was heartbroken.' As you were, thought Jack, watching her consciously bright eyes. She sat very straight in the chair. 'David's wife died years ago and his other two boys had been killed in the war, you see, so Tom was all he had. It was tragic. Awkward, too,' she added, to Jack's surprise. He felt very sorry for Anne, and David, too, come to that. He had an idea he'd heard of David Lassiter before. Where? He dismissed the notion, more interested in Anne's choice of words. Tragic? It was certainly tragic, but why was it awkward? He might have asked why, but Anne continued speaking, obviously concerned to put George at his ease. 'After Tom died, Grandfather asked me to come and live here.'

'It was very kind of you to accept, my dear,' said old Mr Lassiter.

She smiled briefly at him. 'I'd rather be here than on my own.' She looked at Jack and George. 'David feels much the same. Nigel lives here, too.'

Mr Lassiter leaned forward. 'George,' he said, 'tell me about yourself.' He was another one who had suffered, thought Jack. Poor devil. Old Mr Lassiter seemed so outwardly prosperous that most men of his age would envy him, yet behind the façade lay a pretty rocky past. He knew how oddly sensitive George could be and it looked as if he'd inherited that trait from his grandfather. 'You said you sold the farm. What did you do after that?'

'All sorts of things,' said George, clearly relieved by the change of subject from Anne's husband. 'I worked on the railways and led parties big-game hunting and did a stint at the diamond fields. What I enjoyed most, though, was my seaplane.'

'Your *seaplane*?' echoed his grandfather.

George blinked at his grandfather's surprise. 'Yes, I had

a seaplane, a Short 184, on Lake Nyasa with a couple of pals. We set up an air service around the lake.'

'Bless my soul. What did you do in the war?'

'I was in the RFC with Major Haldean here.'

Mr Lassiter laughed. 'The Flying Corps? It must be in the blood.' His smile broadened at George's expression. 'That's the firm, the family firm. The Lassiter Aircraft Company.'

'What?' George leaned forward excitedly. Perhaps, thought Jack, he was relieved to find a topic that didn't seem to lacerate anyone's feelings. 'You mean you made the LE4c?' He glanced up to the oil painting above the fireplace. 'I wondered why you had a painting of one. It was a lovely machine.'

'It was a shame about the LE4c,' said Mr Lassiter, shaking his head. 'We were all ready to start full production when the war ended and the contracts were cancelled. It was a bad time for us. We weathered it, but it was touch and go at one time. Fortunately Nigel managed to win a seaplane contract with the Sprite but it was a close-run thing.'

'You're developing another flying-boat aren't you, sir?' asked Jack, his memory stirred by the mention of the Sprite. 'I saw a picture of it in *Modern Flight*. It said it was going to be one of the largest aircraft in the world.'

'The Pegasus,' said Mr Lassiter with a wry note in his voice. 'It's supposed to be the biggest aircraft ever made. It's Nigel's design. I sometimes wonder if he's bitten off more than he can chew.'

'He lives and breathes for his flying-boat,' put in Anne.

Mr Lassiter leaned back in his chair. 'I can't get over you being a pilot, George. We'll have to get you involved in the firm. Obviously you're going to see the solicitors again but it'll take some time to get the matter cleared up. I think the best thing would be to find you a temporary position until we see where your talents lie. Perhaps the best introduction to the firm would be some sort of secretarial role.'

Anne looked startled. 'You wouldn't replace Michael Walsh, would you, Grandfather?'

'Good Lord, no.' Mr Lassiter looked at George. 'Michael Walsh is my secretary,' he said in explanation. 'He's a very competent man.' He sucked his cheeks in. 'Nigel's the one who really needs help. He works far too hard and the only assistance he's got is that precious clerk of his, Miss Aldryn.'

'She suits Nigel, though,' said Anne. 'What about David? I'm sure he could find work for George without any trouble.' She looked reassuringly at George. 'Being a pilot gives you a huge advantage. You'll be able to pick up everything else you need to know easily enough.'

Mr Lassiter looked at George. 'Are you interested?'

'Well, of course I am,' began George awkwardly. 'The only thing is, I've never done an office job before. I don't know what David – my Uncle David, I suppose I should call him – will think about it.'

'Naturally we'll have to ask him, but he'll be glad of your help. You'll see.'

George thought for a moment. 'I'll do it,' he said. He smiled rather shyly. 'Besides, I want to get to know the family. When can I start?'

'At once, if you like. The works are on the river near Tilbury.'

'I don't think that's a good idea, George,' said Jack quickly. 'You're still convalescing. After all, it's not so long ago the doctor was convinced you were on the way out. It'll be a while before you're fit to do any sort of work.'

George looked disappointed. 'I suppose you're right. It's a shame, though. I was looking forward to meeting the family.'

'That can easily be arranged,' said his grandfather. 'I'm sorry, George. I should have remembered how ill you'd been. I shouldn't have mentioned work at this stage. You get better, my boy. We'll talk about work afterwards. However, when you're feeling up to it you must come down to the factory, and both you and Major Haldean must stay for dinner this evening.'

'That's very kind of you, sir,' said Jack, answering for both of them. 'Are you feeling up to it, George? You're looking a bit washed out.'

'I'll be fine,' said George stubbornly.

'Perhaps you can have a rest beforehand,' suggested his grandfather. He looked at the clock. 'Let me see. It's nearly five o'clock now. David will be in about six, I imagine. Heaven knows when Nigel will arrive.' He stopped as Corby, the butler, entered the room. 'Yes?'

'Mrs Culverton is here, sir, with an Inspector Rackham from Scotland Yard.'

Jack started. Bill? What on earth was Bill doing here?

Anne Lassiter looked at Corby in surprise. 'A police inspector?' she repeated. She shook her head. 'You'd better show them in.' She turned to Mr Lassiter. 'That's all right, isn't it?'

'Of course, my dear.' He stood up. 'This sounds serious.'

Anne turned to George and Jack as Corby left. 'I don't know what this is about. Peggy Culverton is one of my closest friends. She's highly respectable. I can't think why she'd have a policeman in tow.'

Rackham, accompanied by a well-dressed woman in brown – Peggy Culverton, Jack presumed – entered the room a few minutes later. Rackham's eyebrows rose at the sight of him but he said nothing.

'Peggy? What is it?' asked Anne, stepping forward. She reached out her hands to the older woman. 'Peggy! You're upset. What's happened?'

Mrs Culverton tried to speak but couldn't. Anne looked a question at Rackham, who coughed.

'I'm afraid to say that Mrs Culverton has had a distressing experience. She has just come from the mortuary.'

Peggy Culverton managed to speak. 'Anne,' she said, her voice breaking. 'Alexander's dead.'

Mr Lassiter started forward. '*What?* Alexander Culverton?' He put a hand to his mouth. 'Dear God.'

Anne put an arm round her friend. 'Come and sit down near the fire. You're cold. Peggy, this is awful.'

'I shouldn't be so upset,' said Peggy, holding on to Anne's arm. 'You know what it's been like, Anne, but seeing him there . . .' She swallowed. 'He was murdered,' she said starkly with a break in her voice. 'I had to come here. It was the only place I could think of.' She looked up at Mr Lassiter. 'You don't mind, do you?'

'No. No, not all,' he said in a dazed voice. 'Culverton dead!' He seemed to pull himself together. 'You know you have my sympathy, Peggy. My greatest sympathy. Did you say *murdered*?' Mrs Culverton nodded dumbly. Mr Lassiter stepped back and breathed deeply. 'Anne,' he said quietly, 'I'll telephone Nigel. He needs to know about this right away.'

As Mr Lassiter left the room, Rackham drew Jack to one side. 'What the dickens are you doing here, Jack?' he asked in a low voice. 'And is that George Lassiter? The man in the Royal Free? Is he part of the family?'

'He is,' said Jack, 'but he didn't know anything about it. It's a long story. I'll tell you later. Look, I don't want to sound like a parrot, but what are you doing here?'

'Mrs Culverton and Mrs Lassiter are old friends. After seeing her husband in the mortuary she wanted to come here and she was far too upset for me to let her come alone. You know who the dead man is?' he added. 'It's Culverton of Culverton Air Navigation.'

Jack gave a low whistle. 'My God, is it? This'll hit the headlines and no mistake.' He looked sharply at Rackham. 'I say, he's not your naked man in the Thames, is he?' Rackham nodded. Jack's eyes widened. He looked at Mrs Culverton. 'The poor woman. That must have been really nasty for her.'

'Yes,' said Rackham, in an odd voice. 'I think it probably was. Look, Jack, I need to go to Culverton's office. Lloyd, his secretary, has promised to wait for me there. Do you want to come?'

'Absolutely,' said Jack. 'Of course I do. The only thing is, I'm here with George.' He motioned to George to join them. 'George, this is Inspector Rackham. You've heard me speak of him. Rackham and I could do with sloping off for a while. Will you be all right without me? I'll be back later. I don't know what time dinner will be.'

'It looks as if dinner might go by the board,' said George quietly.

Jack shook his head. 'No, it won't. You'll see. I know this sort of house. If I'm not back in time, go ahead without me. I'll skip dinner if necessary. Look, when your grandfather comes back, get him to show you where you can have a rest. There must be a sofa in the library or something. You need it.'

George nodded. 'I don't particularly want to stay, not with them all at sixes and sevens, but I know my grandfather would be hurt if I left right away. You go, Jack. I'll see you later.'

'Good man. Make my excuses for me, will you?'

'I'd better have a word with Mrs Culverton before I go,' said Rackham. 'I won't be a minute, Jack.'

On Anne's instructions, Corby showed them to the door. As soon as they were on the street and could speak freely, Jack turned to Rackham. 'Alexander Culverton? I can hardly believe it.'

'Neither could I when I realized who he was. It's incredible that the man disappeared for days before anyone noticed he was gone.'

'Didn't his wife know?' asked Jack.

'I can't help thinking his wife knows a lot more than she's telling me,' said Rackham in dissatisfaction. 'She didn't like seeing him on the mortuary slab, Jack, that was real enough, but, God help me, she's glad he's dead.'

His meaning was so unmistakable that Jack stopped short. 'Bill, what are you saying?' Rackham didn't answer. 'Are you telling me that you think she murdered her husband? She can't have done. The murder was brutal.'

'So what if it was? I don't like to think a woman's tied up with it, but she really was glad he was dead. She's obviously a very determined sort of person. Just because the crime was brutal doesn't mean we can rule her out. After all, when a married man's killed, the first person we usually look at is his wife – and vice versa.'

'Yes, I know,' said Jack impatiently, falling into step beside Rackham once more. 'But for heaven's sake, Bill, his face was battered in. She wouldn't do that, surely?'

Rackham shrugged. 'Why not? I mean, look at your reaction. You've automatically excluded her *because* it was a brutal crime. I think she's clever, Jack. Clever enough to work that out. After all, it only needs a few blows with something heavy and the job's done. She was a nurse in the war. If she saw a fraction of what we did – and she must have done – she must be fairly proof against most horrors. She's not some fragile little thing. Physically, she'd be perfectly capable of it.'

'But . . .' Jack was silent for a few moments, putting his thoughts in order. 'How did you find her? Did she tell you her husband was missing?'

'That's right. She'd left him, so she says. She's got a flat in Kensington and she telephoned me from there. She'd had a letter from his secretary, a Mr Gilchrist Lloyd, to say that he'd vanished. I went round to see her, hoping that it might be my naked man in the Thames and, as you know, was proved right. She identified him.'

'But that doesn't make sense, surely? If she killed him and walloped him afterwards, presumably that was to conceal his identity.'

'I tell you, she was glad he was dead. It could be sheer hatred, Jack.'

'Well, even it was, I still don't see why, after having bumped him off, she runs and tells you that he's gone. If she hadn't come forward you'd still have an unidentified body on your hands. All she has to do is sit tight and no one's any the wiser.'

'Yes, that's true enough,' admitted Rackham. 'However, his secretary knew he'd disappeared and if Mrs Culverton hadn't reported the fact, he would have done. There's the other point that it takes years before death can be presumed and she might not want to get tied up in legal wrangles. Look, Jack, I'm no happier about the idea than you are, but I can't exclude Mrs Culverton from suspicion on the grounds she's a woman. Having said that, we have to know a great deal more about Culverton before we can suspect anyone. That's why I'm going to his office. It's as good a place as any to start.'

Chapter Four

If Culverton's taste was reflected in his offices, then he must have been a rum sort of beggar, decided Jack. His first impression of Culverton Air Navigation was of grandeur hovering on pretentiousness. The building stood on the prosaically named Cooper Street, SW3, but the street name was the only prosaic thing about it. The office was a cross between one of the more pompous banks and a Hollywood film set.

The entrance hall was a riot of green marble which splashed across the floor, pillared up in columns and finally wound in an architectural frenzy round the central skylight. Two discreetly, if precariously, draped and vaguely female winged forms – symbolic, Jack was willing to bet, of Flight – stood wingtip to wingtip, guarding the lift at the far end of the hall. The lift doors appeared to have been constructed for Tutankhamun's tomb, as did the reception desk over which a pair of stiffly carved goddesses of the Nile extended winged arms. Jack fought hard to subdue a smile. Culverton Air Navigation might be a temple to aviation, but anything as utilitarian as the internal combustion engine was ignored. It seemed as if the human race had got aloft with the aid of feathers.

The commissionaire looked at Rackham's warrant card. 'Mr Lloyd is waiting for you gentlemen in his office,' he said. He escorted them across the empty, echoing hall to the lift, up to the third floor and along an imposing pillared corridor to the secretary's room.

Gilchrist Lloyd, a thin, spare man with a worried expression, was waiting for them inside. 'Inspector Rackham?'

'Yes, sir. And this is Major Haldean.'

Lloyd nodded briefly to both of them. 'This is a perfectly awful business,' he said. 'I only hope the firm can survive. It's been a dreadful few days, first with the Paris crash –'

'Was that one of your aeroplanes?' asked Jack.

Lloyd looked at him in weary surprise. 'Didn't you know? Yes, it was one of ours. The only good thing was that no one was injured but that, to be honest, was more a matter of luck than anything else. Then Mr Culverton, whom I believed to be in Paris, disappeared, and I couldn't get in touch with Mrs Culverton. My very worst fears were confirmed when you telephoned, Inspector. I haven't made any announcement to the staff yet. I need to speak to Mrs Culverton before it's decided what will happen to the company.'

'Was Mrs Culverton involved in the running of the business?' asked Rackham.

'Not the actual running of it, no. Mr Culverton had very firm ideas how the business should be conducted and arranged matters accordingly. I suppose if anyone was Mr Culverton's second-in-command, I was. We're a private limited company, Inspector, and the shares were held by Mr and Mrs Culverton. He took all the decisions but the company itself belongs to Mrs Culverton. She's the majority shareholder.' Rackham's raised eyebrows invited a further explanation. 'It was a purely business decision, Inspector. It enabled Mr Culverton to safeguard some assets that might have otherwise have been endangered.'

Rackham pondered this for a moment. 'In fact,' he said slowly, 'to use the common phrase, he put it in the wife's name?'

Gilchrist Lloyd winced but had to agree. 'As you say, Inspector.'

'As I understand things,' said Rackham, 'it was Mrs Culverton's money which provided the foundation for the entire business.'

Lloyd nodded. 'That also is true. However, it was Mr Culverton's vision and ability which made it grow. Some of the risks he took were breathtaking, but he always got away with it.' Jack could see that the significance of the phrase 'got away with it' had not been lost on Rackham. 'However,' continued Lloyd, 'you came to see Mr Culverton's office.' He led the way to a pair of oak doors. 'It's through here.'

Alexander Culverton's taste in interior decoration had, it seemed, been faithfully reflected in the hall below. His office ran to rather fewer statues, but the theme of green marble was continued. The massive oak desk was held up by eight Egyptian goddesses, two to each corner. The chairs, judging from the carving on the legs and backs, had been made not for an office but for a pyramid. The desk and chairs aside, the man might as well have set up in an Italian church, thought Jack. It was all very well to dream of dwelling in marble halls, but it was a bit overpowering at close quarters. A large framed map of the world, with lines marked in red showing, presumably, the routes flown by Culverton Air Navigation, looked out of place against such luxuriant surroundings. Beside the map was hung an enlarged photograph of three men in front of the propellers of an aeroplane.

Jack pointed to the photograph. 'Is Mr Culverton part of that group? I never met him.'

'Yes, that's him,' agreed Lloyd. 'He's standing with Carlton Lascelles, the actor, and Samuel Hoare, the Minister for Air. Mr Hoare flew with us to Paris last year.' He indicated a substantial oil painting on the wall over the desk. 'That's Mr Culverton, too.'

Jack looked at the pictures of Culverton. It was remarkable what a picture could say that a description couldn't. Culverton was a well-built, fleshy man in his middle fifties, exuding confidence and self-satisfaction. Jack was reminded of something or someone completely out of context. It was the eyes which struck a chord. He'd seen eyes like those before . . . something to do with the Tudors . . . With a shock of recognition he realized it was the Holbein portrait of Henry the Eighth. Culverton's thin lips and watchful, cold, calculating eyes were akin to those Holbein had captured in that devastating and surely truthful portrayal.

'Did you like Mr Culverton?' Jack asked curiously.

Lloyd, prowling apprehensively by the window, looked surprised by the question. 'Like him? What do you mean?'

Jack smiled disarmingly. 'Just that. Was he a pleasant man? Did you like him?'

'I respected him,' said Lloyd reprovingly. 'My personal likes and dislikes hardly enter into the matter, Major. He was an excellent businessman who saw a future for commercial aviation very early on.'

'Did you like him, though?' asked Rackham.

Lloyd wriggled uncomfortably. 'Do I really have to answer that question, Inspector?'

Rackham raised his eyebrows. 'I think you probably have,' he said quietly. He opened his notebook. 'Tell me about the company. When did it start?'

Lloyd brightened, clearly relieved to drop the topic of Culverton's personality. 'Mr Culverton set up the firm after the war. He had two Handley Pages which he converted into passenger aircraft flying the London to Paris route, and that's still the nub of the business. Unlike many of our competitors, the aeroplanes were ready to fly when restrictions on civilian flying were removed in May 1919, and by July of that year we were well established. Since then the business has expanded greatly, of course. We fly from London to all the major British cities and two circular routes. One, our most popular, flies from London to Paris then on to Brussels, Antwerp, Rotterdam, Harwich and back to London. The other route goes from Paris through Orleans, Tours and Bordeaux to Toulouse and Marseilles, up to Lyons then to Berne and Dijon and back to Paris. However, there has been a certain amount of opposition from the French authorities and that route is hotly contested by both our British and foreign rivals. Mr Culverton was actively looking for other routes, preferably within the Empire.'

'Where there's no foreign opposition?' asked Jack.

Lloyd nodded. 'Exactly, Major. Cairo to the Cape is a possible and potentially lucrative route. Van Ryneveld flew it in 1920 and since then a good few others have gone the same way. However, it's one thing to fly it as a special expedition and quite another to set up a commercial air route. Mr Culverton would have done it, though.' He drew a deep sigh. 'I don't know what we're going to do without him. He had such vision! He had a route planned to India.'

'*India?*' repeated Jack incredulously. 'You can't fly a commercial aircraft to India.'

Lloyd smiled at Jack's reaction. 'Mr Culverton had every intention of doing so. It would, gentlemen, be the proverbial goldmine.' He indicated the route on the map. 'Look. Down through the Red Sea to Aden, on to Kamar Bay and then either to Karachi or Bombay.'

'But that last leg's a journey of around a thousand miles,' said Jack. 'There's no commercial aircraft that can tackle that distance.' He paused. 'I suppose an airship could do it. Is that what Mr Culverton had in mind?'

Mr Lloyd smiled once more. 'No, he wasn't thinking of an airship. Mr Culverton was working in close association with the Lassiter Aircraft Company. Mr Nigel Lassiter, with funding from Mr Culverton, is developing a flying-boat which will be quite unlike any seen before. Mr Lassiter is probably the best designer in Britain today. In my opinion he's nothing short of a genius.' Lloyd took a cigarette from the box on the desk and lit it thoughtfully. 'The trouble is, it's all a race against time and now Mr Culverton's dead I don't know if it'll ever happen. There are two other investors, Dr Roger Maguire of Harley Street and Martin Ridgeway of Croft and Ridgeway, the merchant bankers, but compared with Mr Culverton their stake was very small beer. Mr Lassiter's flying-boat is near completion but time is running very short.'

'What's the hurry?' asked Rackham. 'Is anyone else in the running?'

Lloyd shook his head. 'No, it's not that. Nobody else, as far as I know, has even considered a route to India. It's the government that's the problem. There are too many British airlines and the foreign companies, who receive assistance from their governments, are gradually chipping away at British concerns. So there's a plan afoot – it should come off next year – to amalgamate all the major British airlines into one government-backed company. Now if Mr Culverton could have got the India route established, the chances are it would have been taken over as a going concern and he would have been appointed as a director of the new company.' He shrugged. 'A great deal depends on Mrs Culverton. Without the funds from this company I doubt if Mr Lassiter will be able to complete the project. Not for some time, anyway.'

'Is she likely to withdraw funding?' asked Jack. 'I mean, if the flying-boat is nearly ready, why should she? You said the route was a goldmine.'

Lloyd paused before answering. 'I am not, you understand, making any sort of criticism of Mr Culverton. However, if I was called upon to advise Mrs Culverton, I would suggest that a formal contract be drawn up between us and Lassiter's before she continued. We have plunged huge amounts of money into the aircraft and I am unclear as to the exact nature of the return. I have tried to ascertain the details of the arrangement before now but without success.'

'What if she simply pulls the plug?' asked Jack.

'You mean if she stops the funding altogether?' Lloyd paused again. 'I don't know,' he said eventually. 'In that case it would be unlikely that Mrs Culverton would get the directorship of the new government-backed airline but, as you can imagine, that's rather unlikely anyway. Even today, people would be unwilling to accept a woman in such a role. As a matter of fact, we might be better off. As I say, we are putting a great deal of money into this aircraft of Lassiter's and I can't deny the company is suffering as a result. Work that should be done as a matter of course is not being carried out . . .'

'Such as checking the undercarriage of an aeroplane landing in Paris?' asked Jack softly.

Mr Lloyd blenched. 'You did not hear me suggest any such thing, Major Haldean.' He pulled nervously on his cigarette. 'However . . .' He left the sentence hanging in the air. 'Mr Culverton in many ways played things close to his chest. I will be in a better position to advise Mrs Culverton once I have checked the documents I have not hitherto been able to see. My feeling is that the business is essentially sound. We might find that in these changed circumstances we are well advised not to pioneer a new route but to stick to the routes we have already established. However, that decision is not mine to make.'

Rackham drew himself forward in his chair. 'I'd like to ask you about the last time you saw Mr Culverton, sir. That was Wednesday, 31st October.'

'That's correct. I left the building at five thirty. Mr Culverton was still here.'

'How was his manner that day, sir? Was Mr Culverton his usual self?'

Lloyd frowned. 'I thought you'd ask me that, Inspector, and I've been trying to think how best to answer. At first sight his manner was perfectly ordinary but a couple of times during the day he seemed abstracted.'

'Was he annoyed or irritable?'

'No, not especially.' Lloyd's frown deepened. 'He seemed pleased about something. It's difficult to describe exactly. It was as if he had a scheme in mind, something he was looking forward to.' He shook his head impatiently. 'I can't tell you any more. Mr Culverton was not given to confidences and it was just an impression.'

'It's worth bearing in mind though, sir,' said Rackham. 'Was it customary for Mr Culverton to work late?'

'Fairly customary. He lived in Richmond, as you know,

Inspector, but he had rooms at his club, the Mulciber in St James's, and usually stayed there during the week.'

Rackham nodded. 'Mrs Culverton said as much when I spoke to her earlier on.'

'He often changed here, as a matter of fact.' Lloyd walked across the room and opened a door in the far wall. 'This is all fitted out as a dressing room. There's a bath, a wash-basin, a dressing table, wardrobes and everything he needed.'

'Did he change here on Wednesday night?' asked Rackham.

Lloyd thought for a moment. 'Yes, he would have done. He told me to see the charwoman on my way out and tell her to do this room last. That meant he was going to be using it.'

'Did you know he was supposed to be flying to Paris on Thursday?'

'No, Inspector. The first I knew of it was a note I received the next morning. I still have the note, in case you want to see it, but the gist is that he was leaving for Paris on Thursday morning. He asked me to cancel his appointments for the next couple of days and inform Mrs Culverton he had been called away. He said he would advise me later as to his return. He didn't actually say that he was going to Paris as a result of the accident but that must have been the reason. If you recall, the accident happened at four o'clock and I imagine the Paris office contacted Mr Culverton in the course of the evening.'

'That's something we can probably check,' said Rackham. 'Have you any idea what he did when he left the office?'

'I thought of that, too,' said Lloyd. He walked to the desk and took a book from the drawer. 'This is his appointments diary.' Lloyd opened the book and turned it round so Jack and Rackham could see.

'*Wednesday 31st October*,' read Rackham. 'There's a couple of meetings and so on during the day but the entry for the evening reads, *Dinner – Mulciber – N.L. and R.M. – 7.30. Paris.'*

'Who are N.L. and R.M.?' asked Jack.

'I imagine that's Mr Nigel Lassiter and Dr Roger Maguire.'

Rackham looked pleased. 'Well, if they did have dinner with him that's another part of the evening accounted for.' He closed his notebook. 'I think that's about all we can find out here.' He glanced at Jack. 'Is there anything you'd like to know?'

'I wouldn't mind looking round for a few more minutes, if that's all right with you, Mr Lloyd.'

'Be my guest. If you can dispense with my services for the time being, I'll be in my office. I have quite a lot of work to catch up with, as you can imagine.'

'Just before you go,' said Jack, 'can you tell us the names of any of Mr Culverton's friends?'

Lloyd looked blank. 'I really can't say, Major. As far as I know, Mr Culverton had no close personal friends. He was devoted to the business and any social engagements were usually connected with the firm in some way.'

'So no interests or hobbies at all?'

Lloyd very nearly smiled. 'No, Major. If you had known Mr Culverton you would realize how improbable a suggestion that is.' He walked to the door. 'I shall be in the next room if you require anything further.'

Lloyd left the two men together. 'Mr Culverton sounds a barrel of laughs,' said Rackham. 'What did you want to look for in here, Jack? Anything in particular?'

Jack hitched himself on to the massive desk. 'Some sort of clue as to who he was, I suppose. He doesn't sound a very well-loved sort, does he?' He nodded towards the painting behind him. 'I might be reading too much into it but I don't think our Mr Culverton was a very pleasant bloke.'

'Someone obviously agreed with you,' said Rackham drily. 'I'll say this for him though, he clearly had personality. I know his wife left him but she married him in the

70

first place and she was the one with the money, don't forget. He must have had something going for him.'

'Yes,' agreed Jack. The image of the Holbein portrait was very strong in his mind. 'I think he was a bully.'

Rackham laughed. 'He might have been. I don't see how you can possibly be so sure though.'

'It's the pictures of him. That and Mr Lloyd's reactions.' Jack got off the desk and wandered round it, opening the drawers at random. 'What can this desk tell us? There's clean blotting paper in the blotter, so no clue there.' He opened a drawer. 'Pens, paper-clips, a hole-punch and so on,' he said, rummaging through the contents. 'Headed notepaper, a box of cigars and two lighters. There's something else right at the back. It's a box of some sort.' He pulled it out. It was about the same size as a cashbox but made of highly ornamented polished rosewood.

'That's a striking thing,' said Rackham. 'I wonder why he buried it at the back of his desk?' He picked it up. 'How does it open? It seems to be a solid block of wood. There's no keyhole.'

'Try pressing the sides in,' said Jack. 'That might do it.'

They both tried but the box stayed obstinately shut. 'I think I'll leave a receipt with Mr Lloyd and take this with me,' said Rackham. 'You never know, it looks as if it might be important. Someone at Scotland Yard ought to be able to open it.' He looked round the room. 'What next?'

'His dressing room?' suggested Jack.

He led the way to the dressing room Gilchrist Lloyd had shown them and into the bathroom. It was fitted out as luxuriously as the office, but with pink rather than green marble, gold taps, a full-length gold-framed mirror and soft white towels. A huge white bath stood against the wall. Jack opened a door off the bathroom. 'The lavatory. Good God!'

'What is it?' asked Rackham eagerly.

'He's got pink curtains to match the wall. Now that really is a bit much.'

'Honestly, Jack,' complained Rackham. 'I thought you'd found something.'

'Well, it is a bit much. Don't you think?'

'I think he certainly liked his home comforts,' said Rackham. He looked at the shelf by the wash-basin which held gold-and-tortoiseshell-backed brushes and combs with the initials A.C. inscribed on them, a collection of little bottles, a soap-dish, shaving brush and razor. 'I'll take a couple of those bottles with me. They should have his fingerprints on them.'

Jack looked at the shelf. 'I bet even my cousin Isabelle hasn't got as much stuff as this.' He opened a bottle and sniffed it. 'Cologne. Rather a nice one if you like that sort of thing. Soap in a very fetching little dish and various unguents, all from Floris. Well, he certainly went for the best.' Jack picked up the shaving brush and held it idly. 'A hugely expensive shaving brush and a razor. He went in for the safety variety, I see. It's easier to shave yourself with one of those.'

'I'm surprised he didn't get his valet to shave him,' commented Rackham.

Jack put the brush back on the shelf. 'It's a bit far to pop down to Richmond for a wash and brush-up.'

Rackham shook his head. 'His valet stayed at the Mulciber Club during the week. Mrs Culverton told me. He's on my list of people to interview.'

Jack turned to look at his friend. 'His valet stayed at the Mulciber Club? But . . .' He frowned at Rackham. 'That doesn't make sense.'

'What d'you mean?'

Jack indicated the bathroom shelf. 'Look at all this stuff, Bill. The bloke must have been as vain as a peacock. At the very least he was unduly careful of his personal appearance, wouldn't you say?'

'Undoubtedly so.'

'Then why does a man who goes to such lengths about his looks change here when there's a valet waiting for him

72

at the club where he's going to spend the evening? If you have a valet, the evening is when you need him most. He could have been going to see someone else first, I suppose, and had to change for that, but if he was meeting Nigel Lassiter and this Dr Maguire at half past seven it doesn't give him much leeway.'

Rackham started to speak, then stopped. 'That is odd,' he said eventually. 'That really is odd. I wonder if he was meeting anyone else first? I have to talk to both Nigel Lassiter and Roger Maguire anyway, so I'll ask them. They might know. Is there anything else you want to have a look at?'

'We've not searched the dressing room yet,' said Jack, leading the way out of the bathroom.

The dressing room contained a chest-of-drawers, a large wardrobe and another full-length mirror. Jack opened the top shallow drawers of the chest. They contained winged collars, ties and cuffs, all for evening wear. Jack idly noted that Culverton had taken a size seventeen in collars and moved on to the next drawer. Here there was a collection of small boxes from Asprey's. He opened them in turn. 'Diamond studs, pearl studs, ruby studs.' He moved on. 'Three sets of cuff-links, also sporting, variously, diamonds, pearls and rubies. A small Wedgwood tray containing a signet ring with A.C. in entwined initials. Empty box which did contain studs. Ditto cuff-links. Presumably those were what he was wearing when he bought it.' He put down the empty stud-box. 'Let's have a look at his clothes.'

Jack swung open the wardrobe door. Two evening coats, three suits of dress clothes and various shirts hung inside with a suit of morning dress, consisting of a black coat, waistcoat and pin-striped trousers. A shoe rack containing three pairs of patent leather shoes and a pair of black brogues stood underneath. A square wicker basket sat neatly at one end of the wardrobe. 'What's in here?' asked Jack, lifting the lid. 'Dirty linen. Not for washing in public, I presume. Silk underwear, silk socks, and a shirt. I like that shirt.' He picked it up and looked at the label. 'Rothbury and Co., Jermyn Street. These are the things he changed out of, of course.' He closed the lid of the basket and picked up the shoes, looking at them in turn. 'Size ten and a half at a guess.' He turned one of the dress shoes over in his hands. 'Bill, these shoes have been cleaned by a valet. There's polish caught on the instep between the sole and the heel. That's where a valet or a bootblack from a decent hotel always leaves his mark.'

'You're right,' said Rackham, looking at the shoe. 'And, Sherlock, your inference is?'

Jack grinned. 'I haven't got one yet. Let's have a shufti at his clothes.' He took a dress suit out of the wardrobe and looked at it intently. 'I'd say this has been valeted too, wouldn't you? It looks very fresh.'

'I don't suppose it's new, is it?' asked Rackham. 'Look at the label, Jack. That usually gives the date it was made.' Jack turned back the breast of the coat. 'Where is it?' asked Rackham. He pointed to where the label had been stitched into the seam. 'That's odd. It looks as if it's been sliced off with a razor blade.'

'The suit's made by Lockyer and Co.,' said Jack, examining the trouser buttons. 'I wonder why he took the tab off? Hold on.' He put the suit back in the wardrobe and looked at the rest of the suits in turn, before rifling through the dress shirts. 'There's no tailor's tab on any of the evening clothes but there is on the morning suit.' They looked at the tab together.

Lockyer and Co.
A. Culverton Esq.
June 1921
17 Savile Row, London

Rackham looked frankly puzzled. 'I don't understand this, Jack. Why should he take the labels off his clothes? It doesn't seem to make any sense.'

'Off his evening clothes,' corrected Jack, absently.

'Well, off his evening clothes then. It still doesn't make any sense.'

'No . . .' Jack drifted away to the dressing table once more. There was a silver cigar case and a book of matches lying next to an ashtray. Jack opened the cigar case, looking at the elaborately engraved *Alexander Culverton* inside. The matchbook, with three matches gone, was a shiny black cardboard packet with *C* embossed on the cover. Jack raised his eyebrows slightly. Did he have his own matchbooks printed? Three cigars about the size of young torpedoes were left in the case. He picked out one and sniffed it, raising his eyebrows in unconscious approval. He wouldn't have left a cigar like that behind. He stopped as the significance of his unspoken phrase struck him. *Left behind!* Culverton had left all this stuff behind.

He whirled round. 'Bill! I think I've got it!'

Rackham looked startled. 'Got what?'

Jack indicated the room with an impatient hand. 'Look at these things. Just look at them. There's the cigar case with his name inside, a signet ring with his initials and his name's been removed from every single piece of evening wear. If the clothes he was wearing had been treated like the clothes in his wardrobe then they'd have their tabs removed too. Now why this modest self-effacement, Bill? He doesn't seem to have been a shrinking flower in any other walk of life. He was concealing his identity.'

Rackham stared at him. 'Good grief, Jack, I wonder if you're right. What about his valet?' he asked. 'Where does he fit in?'

'He doesn't,' Jack said positively. 'Look, this is Culverton's private room. This is where he keeps his private clothes, his unidentifiable private clothes.'

'What about the morning suit?'

'That doesn't count. That's for the daytime.'

'But the valet's seen these clothes, even the ones with no labels.'

Jack gave a sudden grin. 'I think you're going to find the valet's a bit dumb. I think you're going to find he's the sort of man who doesn't ask questions. He's probably a perfect treasure. Naturally Culverton wouldn't mind his valet – especially if he is dumb – seeing his stuff because the valet knows exactly who Culverton is. But there's someone else, someone who *doesn't* know who Culverton is, and our Alexander isn't giving them any clues.'

Rackham stood for a moment, thinking. 'Who?' he said eventually. 'It can't be Nigel Lassiter or this Dr Maguire. They know who he is, too.'

'So?' prompted Jack softly.

'So it must be someone he's going to see afterwards.'

'Exactly,' said Jack. 'What's more, if you include the clothes he was wearing, he had no fewer than four sets of evening dress, all doctored, so it must be a fairly frequent occurrence.'

'But you don't normally examine the label on a man's coat to see who he is,' objected Rackham.

Jack grinned once more. 'You might, if the man had taken his clothes off.'

Rackham whistled. '*That'd* do it. By crikey, Jack, I wonder if you're on to something. If he wasn't behaving himself he'd be frightened of blackmail.' He jabbed his finger at the photograph again. 'You can't hang around with government ministers and suchlike and be involved in that sort of scandal. I'll tell you something else, too. If he was involved in a scandal then he could kiss goodbye to his hopes of being a director in this new government airline Lloyd was talking about. It'd really scupper his chances.' He rubbed his hands together. 'Could he have been leading a double life?'

'A mistress, you mean? That's possible,' said Jack. 'That's certainly possible. Judging by the tabs on his clothes, though, he only ever saw her at night. That means no weekends away and no little nest in the country or St John's Wood or wherever.'

'And I can't see a mistress dumping him in the Thames with a mutilated face. Someone attacked him, viciously attacked him. He was in the river, damn it, Jack. How did he come to be there?'

Jack walked away and leaned against the desk. *'What was he doing, the great god Pan, down in the reeds by the river?'* he quoted softly to himself. 'Look, Bill, whatever he was doing, he was doing it fairly frequently, as I said. As to where he was doing it, it was upstream of Southwark Bridge steps.'

'Which leaves a lot of London.'

'Which leaves a lot of London,' agreed Jack. 'Could he have been going to a club? A dodgy club, I mean? It can't be too vile if he was wearing evening dress and jewelled studs. He'd have to be wearing decent clothes because he met Nigel Lassiter and Dr Maguire for dinner.'

'He could have been doing a few things,' said Rackham. 'But none of it tells us how he came to be murdered.' He shook his head impatiently. 'I've got some leads to follow up, though.' He gestured to the secretary's door. 'I think I'll ask Mr Lloyd a few more questions before I go. I think he's perfectly above board but he might know something or have guessed something about Culverton's private life. I need to see the valet and I also need to talk to Nigel Lassiter and Dr Maguire.'

'What about Mrs Culverton?'

'I'll have to talk to her again,' agreed Rackham. 'D'you know, looking back, I think she might have been trying to tell me what Culverton was like. I didn't see it at the time but now, now we know something, certain remarks of hers don't half chime in.'

'So you think I'm right about our Alexander?'

Rackham nodded slowly. 'It explains things, doesn't it? It's not proof but it explains things. I think you're on to something. Are you going to stay and talk to Lloyd?'

Jack glanced at his watch. 'As a matter of fact, I think I'd better get back to Eden Street. George isn't up to staying out too late yet. Nigel Lassiter should be there, if that's any help. Old Mr Lassiter was telephoning him as we left.'

'In that case,' said Rackham, 'that's one more place to visit. Look, what are you doing for the rest of the evening? If you're not busy I wouldn't mind calling round.'

'Be my guest,' said Jack. 'If you don't mind cold grub, you can eat with me if you like.'

'Thanks, Jack. I can't imagine I'll have time for dinner anywhere else. I'll see you later on.'

Chapter Five

It was gone ten o'clock by the time Rackham made it to Chandos Row. 'I haven't eaten a thing since lunchtime,' he said, drawing his chair up to the table and loading his plate with the cheese, bread, cold sausage and pickles Jack had left out for him. 'I'm starving. I've been knuckling down to it tonight and no mistake,' he added, between mouthfuls. 'I talked to Gilchrist Lloyd again, then I went to the Mulciber. I saw Culverton's valet, then the porter who was on duty in the lobby the night Culverton went west, before I went on to Eden Street.' He looked round the room. 'Where's your pal, Lassiter, by the way?'

Jack jerked his thumb at the door of the spare room. 'He's gone to bed. This was his first day up and about and the poor beggar was all in. He was wiped out by the time I got back to Eden Street, so we made our apologies and came back here.'

'How's he getting on with his new-found family?'

'Pretty well. He and his grandfather obviously hit it off. When his grandfather understood he was well and truly broke, he gave him a fair old chunk of money to see him through.'

'Lucky George,' commented Rackham.

'Well, he really didn't have a bean and it's not a straight-forward gift. As George is being drafted into the firm, he insisted on treating the money as an advance on his wages. That pleased his granddad, I could tell. He's taken a real shine to Anne Lassiter, as well. I liked her, too. Neither of us saw much of David Lassiter but he seems all right. The

79

only one we didn't meet was Nigel Lassiter, the chap who had dinner with Culverton.'

'Nigel Lassiter, eh?' said Rackham, meaningfully. 'Well, I don't want to do down your friend's family, but I wouldn't pay you in washers for Nigel Lassiter.'

Jack looked at him, his head to one side. 'Why not?'

Rackham speared a piece of sausage. 'He's one of the awkward squad and no mistake. He told me he couldn't see it was any of my business what Culverton had for dinner. He's been knocked sideways by Culverton's death but he couldn't give a damn who killed him. You'll probably come across him at some stage. Let me know what you think, but I'd be surprised if your opinion was very different from mine.'

'I'm going to come across him tomorrow, I imagine. George and I have been invited for lunch and, as it's Saturday, I suppose all the family will be there. I'm not sorry to have the chance to meet them. You know I told you about George's missing legacy? Well, he's got his birth certificate.'

'Has he, by Jove?' said Rackham, adding a pickled egg to his plate.

'Yes. It was in the desk in the library at Eden Street, together with a lot of other family papers. Anne Lassiter looked it out for him. Now, George was told that the legacy was claimed from South Africa on the strength of that certificate.'

Rackham ate thoughtfully for a few moments. 'What are you saying? That someone used George's birth certificate to snaffle the loot?'

'Either that or the certificate the solicitors saw was forged.'

'Can a birth certificate be forged?'

Jack shrugged. 'I don't see why not. The details would have to be correct, of course, but they're all on record at Somerset House. All a certificate is, when you come down to it, is an extract from the register. Anyone who pays a

80

shilling can take a dekko, which isn't a bad investment when there's forty-six thousand pounds in the offing.'

'How would anyone know there's that amount of money up for grabs?'

'They might not know,' said Jack. 'However, the advert was in the South African press, and it's fairly obvious there must be something to gain. It might be sheer speculation or someone at the solicitors may be on the make or it might have been someone who knew George's mother and realized she had a fair old bit to leave.'

Rackham finished the rest of his supper and pushed his plate away. 'Thanks for that, Jack. It was just what I needed.' He stood up and took his pipe from his pocket. 'Look, you'd better get Lassiter to call in at Scotland Yard to make a formal complaint. I'll leave a note that it's to be referred to me.' He covered a yawn with his hand. 'I've got my work cut out with the Culverton case but I'll make time to go and see the solicitors on Monday.'

'Thanks, Bill. I couldn't get a damn thing out of Mr Marchbolt. He was very frosty.'

'I'll use the strong arm of the Law,' said Rackham with a grin. 'An official warrant card works wonders.'

Jack poured out two glasses of whisky, gave one to Rackham and put the tobacco jar on the table between them. 'So what did you find out about Culverton?' he asked, sitting down in an armchair. 'Could his valet suggest where he might have gone in his carefully de-labelled clothes?'

Rackham sighed in irritation. 'That valet could give two short planks a run for their money. You know you said he might be a bit dim? Absolutely, he was. I asked him why Culverton had taken the tabs off his evening clothes and he told me he'd never thought to enquire. He knew about them, right enough. He'd call at the office, collect the used linen and valet the suits, but he never wondered why the tabs had been removed. He showed me Culverton's dressing room at the Mulciber. It was as lavishly furnished as

81

the one at the office but the evening wear in the wardrobe had all its tabs intact.'

Jack nodded. 'That bears out my theory in a way. He changed at the Mulciber when he was going to a respectable function. Could Gilchrist Lloyd shed any light on the mystery?'

'No. He knew Culverton frequently changed at the office but he didn't know anything about his evening clothes. I'll tell you something, though. He wasn't remotely surprised that Culverton could have had a private life, as I delicately put it.'

'I wonder if that's an angle you could try? If Culverton was a bit of a philanderer then he might have caused some trouble with the female servants or office staff.'

'Mr Lloyd didn't say anything,' said Rackham doubt-fully. 'I think you might be right about a dodgy club. Culverton was a well-known man and his picture got into the papers often enough to worry him if he was trying to keep his identity a secret.' He frowned. 'Mrs Culverton knows something, I'm sure of it. She was very much on her guard.'

'Do you really think she might be guilty? I know you floated the possibility earlier.'

'And you didn't like it one bit.' Rackham smiled. 'Well, relax, Jack. She didn't do it. On Wednesday the 31st, the day she left Culverton, she went to see Anne Lassiter. Both old Mr Lassiter and Mrs Lassiter bear that out. Mrs Culverton stayed at Eden Street for a while, then she and Mrs Lassiter went to her flat in Kensington. Anne Lassiter stayed with her until after midnight.'

'So she's got an alibi, has she?' asked Jack, reaching for the tobacco jar.

'Yes. What's more, old Mr Lassiter spoke to Anne after she got back. Apparently he's a bit of a night owl and, although he phrased this quite carefully, he was obviously agog to find out exactly what was going on between Mrs Culverton and her husband.' Jack stuck a match and lit

82

his pipe, frowning over the smoke. 'What's the matter? I thought you'd be pleased that Mrs Culverton's out of it.'

'Well, I am,' agreed Jack. 'It's just that I thought your reasoning was pretty good. You know, about it being a brutal crime an' all so therefore we wouldn't suspect a woman. By the way, how come Mrs Culverton and Anne Lassiter are such friends? I mean, there's no reason why they shouldn't be, but Mrs Culverton's a good deal older than Anne Lassiter.'

'I wondered that, too,' said Rackham. 'Apparently they nursed together in the war and always kept in touch. Mrs Culverton was very good to Anne after Thomas, her husband, died. Mrs Lassiter told me that she always thought of her as an older sister. Be that as it may, I'm sure Mrs Culverton knows something. What I find frustrating is that she won't even hint at why she left Culverton. She just states she did and that's that.'

'Perhaps I'm right about his philandering tendencies. Wouldn't that be enough reason?'

Rackham frowned. 'It *might*. I'm not sure that's the top and bottom of it, though. However,' he added with a shrug, 'her alibi's borne out by Mrs Lassiter and I can't believe Mrs Lassiter would be involved in murder. She didn't strike me as the type.'

'No,' said Jack with certainty. 'Me neither.'

'Nigel Lassiter, on the other hand, struck me as the sort who'd murder his own grandmother if she got in the way.'

'You really didn't like him, did you?' said Jack with a grin.

'He rubbed me up the wrong way, the arrogant devil. I don't think he'd have condescended to speak to me at all if it wasn't for Dr Maguire.'

'Is that the same bloke who had dinner with Culverton the night he was killed? What was he doing there?'

'He's a friend of Nigel's and informally engaged to Anne Lassiter.'

'Is he, by Jove?'

'That's right. I'm not sure about Maguire. He's a bit smooth. Having said that, he's a Harley Street psychiatrist, so I suppose he has to be fairly smooth. He was ready enough to answer my questions, though. Interestingly, he'd been Culverton's doctor when he was in general practice. He couldn't tell me a lot about Culverton but he kept Nigel on this side of politeness – just.'

'I don't suppose Nigel is a possibility, is he?' Jack asked hopefully. 'For bumping off Culverton, I mean.'

Rackham laughed. 'Unfortunately, no. That's a big no. I don't suppose he gives tuppence about Culverton, as such, but it's given him a real headache as regards his aeroplane. Apart from that, he's got an alibi. He came home after the dinner at the Mulciber and talked to his father about something called stringers, whatever they are.'

'They're part of the innards of a wing,' said Jack.

'Well, he's got problems with them. Apparently that's what the dinner in the Mulciber was about. Culverton agreed to fund the extra work Nigel needed to put in on them. And that, even more than his alibi, is why he's such a big no. Nigel Lassiter's obsessed with his seaplane and was depending on Culverton's support to finance it. Maguire's one of Nigel's investors too, but very small beer compared to Culverton. He only has five thousand or so invested in it.'

'*Only* five thousand?' Jack's eyebrows shot up. 'Good God, Bill, when did you join the plutocracy? Five thousand isn't chicken feed, you know.'

Rackham grinned. 'You haven't heard the rest of it yet. I confirmed how much Dr Maguire had at stake with old Mr Lassiter. He's a nice old boy, isn't he? I asked him about the costs of the seaplane as I wanted to know just how heavily Culverton was involved. Apparently he brassed up about eighty thousand.'

'*Eighty thousand?* No wonder Mr Lloyd wanted to talk to Mrs Culverton about the future of the firm. Culverton put in eighty thousand? That's unbelievable. I always thought air travel was too expensive.'

84

'Mr Lassiter thought Culverton had used his wife's money. She was a very rich woman before she married. I don't know if she's very rich now. Apparently her father was one of the original investors in Wisemann and Levy's, the New York store. He never touched the income and it built up for years at compound interest. He was worth well over two hundred thousand.'

'What?' Jack shook his head disbelievingly. 'But she was a nurse. By golly, I wish she'd nursed me.'

'She's too old for you,' said Rackham with a laugh.

'I could age very convincingly,' muttered Jack.

'Anyway,' continued Rackham, 'Mr Lassiter told me all this to fill in the background. There's no two ways about it, Culverton's death has left Lassiter's in a real hole. You said you met David Lassiter?'

'Yes. I liked him. I got the impression he's the one who really controls the firm.'

'So did I. He bore out everything his father said. He thinks Culverton's death has more or less kicked the seaplane into touch. They're finding things difficult anyway and he can't see why Peggy Culverton should invest in the seaplane as no one's going to offer her a directorship in any state airline, whatever she does. He's a very worried man.'

'Poor beggar.' Jack put down his pipe. 'To get back to our own concerns for the moment, I don't suppose either Nigel Lassiter or Dr Maguire can suggest where Culverton went after they left him at the Mulciber?'

'They haven't a clue, or so they say. The only thing which did strike me as not quite right was Dr Maguire's expression when I asked him what he did for the rest of the evening. He said he went on to the Continental. That's a restaurant off Northumberland Avenue with a well-frequented bar and dancing and so on. Now, there's nothing wrong with the Continental, as far as I know, but he looked me straight in the eye as he said it. It made me wonder if he really did go there. He didn't like the question, I could tell. It's something and nothing but you never know. If he's not telling the truth, it might just lead us to this club of Culverton's.'

'That'd be a handy short-cut. I bet you're right about his expression, Bill. That sort of impression is difficult to put into words but fairly unmistakable. What time did they leave?'

'About nine. I checked that at the Mulciber and it's right. The porter remembered it as he had a cable for Mr Culverton.'

'A cable?' asked Jack with sharpened interest.

'Yes. Culverton came into the lobby with Maguire and Nigel Lassiter just as the porter was about to send one of the staff to look for him. Culverton said goodbye to the two men, and the porter, who hadn't wanted to interrupt, gave him the cable after they'd gone. I'll get a copy of it, but I think it must have been from Paris. Culverton read it and obviously wasn't very pleased. He wrote a note to Lloyd, as we know. Lloyd showed me the note. Culverton ordered the porter to post it in the Late Fee box so it would arrive next morning. Then he went back into the club and had a drink at the bar. He left the Mulciber about quarter to ten or thereabouts. He didn't have a taxi so the porter couldn't tell me where he was going.'

Jack frowned. 'You say the cable arrived at the Mulciber? But ...' He broke off and drank his whisky perplexedly. 'That doesn't make sense. Culverton wrote *Paris* in his appointment diary, didn't he? But he wrote it in the space for Wednesday, not Thursday, when he should have flown out.'

'Maybe he got the wrong day,' said Rackham, puzzled by his friend's intensity. 'It's an easy enough mistake.'

'So when did he write it? We assumed he knew he was going to Paris before he left the office but he didn't.'

Rackham stared. 'That's a thought,' he said slowly. 'Maybe he had to go back to the office to pick up some papers.'

Jack got up and stood beside the mantelpiece. 'So why post the letter to Lloyd?'

'He could have only worked out he needed the papers or whatever after he'd sent the letter.'

'That's true,' agreed Jack. 'Damn! That might be it. Could you ask Lloyd if there's any way of telling if Culverton came back to the office that night? Any papers which should be there that aren't?'

'I'll ask him, certainly,' agreed Rackham, 'but what's the point? If he added *Paris* to his diary he must have gone back to the office.' He stared sightlessly into the fireplace. 'This is a beggar of a case, Jack. Culverton left the Mulciber about quarter to ten and was killed before midnight. If he went back to the office there's not much time for him to have gone anywhere else. It's odd, isn't it?'

'It's damned odd,' agreed Jack. 'I wonder where the dickens he got to?'

The next morning Jack and George went to Scotland Yard where, armed with his birth certificate, George made an official complaint about his missing legacy. That was followed by a visit to Butler and Furness, the gentlemen's outfitters. Next on the agenda was lunch at Eden Street. It made a pleasant change, thought Jack, as he rang the bell at number 19, to see his friend in clothes that actually fitted. He was about to say as much when he noticed how apprehensive George seemed. 'What's the matter?' he asked.

George adjusted the lapels of his new jacket. 'Nothing, really,' he said with a sigh. 'It's just that coming here still feels odd, and it's even odder to think this is my family's house. I'm looking forward to meeting my Uncle Nigel, though. Everyone seemed a bit iffy about him yesterday but if he's anything like my grandfather and Uncle David, he should be all right.'

Jack, too, was looking forward to meeting Uncle Nigel, but, with Bill Rackham's comments firmly in mind, he lacked George's optimism.

Corby, the butler, opened the door and, ushering them into the hall, took their hats and coats.

'I'm afraid we're a bit early,' said George, glancing at the clock.

'It doesn't matter, sir. Mr Lassiter gave instructions you were to be shown into the library. He's going over some papers with Mr Nigel and Mr David.'

As Corby led the way along the hall they heard the muffled sound of raised voices which grew louder as they approached the library. Jack swapped glances with Lassiter. There was obviously a heated argument going on. Corby hesitated with his hand on the handle, then opened the door, stepped into the room and coughed. 'Mr Lassiter and Major Haldean, sir.'

Everyone was abruptly silent but the room was crackling with tension. Jack recognized David Lassiter from the previous evening, a tall, grey-haired man with kindly, worried eyes. He looked up as they entered and nodded a greeting. He was standing with his arms braced on a table strewn with papers. Across the table from him stood George's grandfather and another man, who was, presumably, Nigel Lassiter. Nigel Lassiter's body was rigid, his arms were folded and his face flushed.

Jack saw old Mr Lassiter's rather harried expression lighten in relief. 'George! And Major Haldean. It's a pleasure to see you both. As you're going to be part of the firm, George, I said you might as well be shown in here but I think we're about finished.' He turned to David and Nigel. 'That's right, isn't it?' There was a definite command in the question.

Nigel, a man in his forties with shadowed eyes and dark, untidy hair, unfolded his arms. He was radiating anger. He hardly glanced at Jack and Lassiter but spoke to his father. '*You* might have finished but *I* certainly haven't. I need some answers. What am I going to do?'

David Lassiter looked apologetically across the room. 'I'm sorry, George, Major Haldean. We really have finished.'

'Stop saying we're finished!' snarled Nigel in frustration. 'For God's sake, David, we haven't begun. Listen to me! You don't seem to realize what Culverton's death means. You can't seem to grasp how truly awful it is. What's going to happen to the funding of the seaplane now? I need another few thousand at least. Culverton would have paid up. What does Mrs Culverton say?'

'Mrs Culverton,' said David with weary patience, 'told you she wasn't making any decisions until her secretary, Gilchrist Lloyd, has gone through the paperwork.'

Nigel tossed his head impatiently. 'That's not good enough. I haven't got the time to wait. Doesn't she know how urgent it is?'

'You can't expect her to make a snap decision. For heaven's sake, she's just lost her husband.'

'Don't give me that,' said Nigel with a dismissive snort. 'She couldn't care less about Culverton. She left him, for heaven's sake. This is a matter of business.'

'Well, she's not going to be hurried, no matter how important you think it is,' said David acidly. 'So what if we do have to suspend production on the seaplane?'

'Suspend production?' Nigel Lassiter stared at him. 'For God's sake, don't start that again. We're only ten days away from the press presentation. I've got ten days to get the Pegasus in a fit condition to show to the public. *Ten days!* We can't stop now. It'd be disastrous. If Mrs Culverton won't pay up then the company will have to fund it.'

His father made as if to speak but David beat him to it. 'What d'you think we've been doing? Your blasted flying-boat has cost us thousands and for what? The entire company's been turned upside down because of it. We can't afford to pump any more money into the Pegasus, Nigel. You know that.'

'You'll have to.'

'We haven't got it!' David Lassiter swallowed and forced himself to speak calmly. 'Look, as I said before, if we could only suspend production we could concentrate on making some sort of profit. Then, when things are more settled, we can go back to the Pegasus.'

The door opened once more and a thin, nervy-looking man with a file of papers under his arm came in. He looked at Jack and George, smiled briefly, and spoke to Mr Lassiter. 'I've got the papers you wanted, sir.'

'Thank you, Walsh,' said Mr Lassiter. 'Nigel, perhaps you can look at these figures later on.'

Walsh gave the file to Nigel who glanced at it contemptuously.

'Balance sheets,' he said with deep sarcasm.

Walsh straightened up. Jack remembered Mr Lassiter referring to his secretary, Walsh, yesterday. He was a taller man than Nigel but much slighter. There were deep-set lines etched round his eyes and mouth. He was, thought Jack, not a well man. He had very little colour in his face but his eyes were glittering with suppressed anger. 'Balance sheets, Mr Lassiter,' he said, picking his way through the words. 'I was only able to give you a very brief idea of the figures involved when we talked about this earlier, but if you would care to look over the balance sheets –'

'Damn the bloody balance sheets,' ground out Nigel. 'And damn you, too.'

'Nigel!' exclaimed his father, shocked. 'Withdraw that remark immediately.'

Nigel clenched his fists and took a deep breath. He glanced at Walsh. 'Sorry.' The word was like the flick of a whip.

Walsh met his eyes unflinchingly, reining in his temper with a visible effort. A spot of angry colour flamed on his pale cheeks. 'You might not like what the balance sheets show, Mr Lassiter, but you cannot ignore them.'

Nigel brought his fist down on the table. 'For God's sake, stop talking about balance sheets! I'm days away from the press presentation. The Pegasus is *important*.'

'The Pegasus is damned expensive,' snapped David. 'It's one thing after another. Last month's flight trials were a disaster. The aeroplane isn't safe, Nigel. Not yet.'

'Safety! Don't you ever think about anything other than safety?'

The cold gleam in David Lassiter's eyes startled Jack. He'd been angry before but now he was suddenly murderous. 'It's not surprising, is it? Let me tell you –'

'David,' said Mr Lassiter sharply. 'I'd rather you and Nigel had this conversation in private.'

David Lassiter froze. He stood very still, then, with a long-drawn-out breath, and his shoulders rigid, stretched his hands out on the table. After a few moments he looked ruefully at Jack and George. 'I'm sorry. For the moment I forgot you were here. I apologize.'

The door opened once more and Corby came into the room. 'Dr Maguire has arrived, sir. Shall I show him in?'

'Don't bother,' said Nigel in disgust. He looked at his brother contemptuously. 'Apparently, we've finished.'

Walsh coughed. The flush of colour on his cheeks hadn't faded. 'You really should look at the balance sheets, Mr Lassiter,' he said evenly. 'They tell their own story.'

'Bloody *hell*!' shouted Nigel, goaded beyond endurance.

A well-dressed man came into the room behind Corby. 'Excuse me finding my way in here but I heard voices,' he said calmly. He looked at Nigel. 'Is there a problem?'

'A problem?' repeated Nigel. 'Of course there's a problem, Roger.' Jack looked at the newcomer with interest. So this was the smooth Dr Maguire. Nigel ran his hands through his hair. 'I've been trying to explain the situation with the Pegasus and all anyone can talk to me about is balance sheets.'

'They will repay study, Mr Lassiter,' said Walsh.

Nigel glared at him speechlessly then, taking the papers from the file, ripped them across and flung them down on the table. 'That's what I think of you and your balance sheets. Why don't you drop dead, you little runt?'

'Nigel!' exclaimed his father, David and Maguire together but Nigel was past hearing.

'Because if you don't drop dead, then God help me, I'll kill you. In fact –'

'Nigel!' said Maguire in a voice as sharp as the crack of a bullet. 'Shut up!' His eyes blazed. Nigel, startled, looked at him, then dropped his head. 'That's better,' said Maguire curtly. 'I think an apology's in order.'

Nigel met his gaze, then glanced away. 'All right. I'm sorry.' He wearily stuck his hands in his pockets and looked round the room, seemingly noticing Jack and George for the first time. 'I'm sorry.' He picked up the torn papers and put them back in the file. 'I'll study these,' he said to Walsh with an effort. 'Sorry about that.'

Walsh let his breath out slowly. 'Don't mention it.'

The gong sounded in the hall. 'Lunch,' said old Mr Lassiter.

'What d'you think of your Uncle Nigel?' asked Jack softly as they walked across the hall.

'Happy families,' said George with a grimace. 'What have I got myself involved in?'

Leaving George at Eden Street for the afternoon, Jack walked to his club, the Young Services. He was pretty sure that he would bump into Joe Hawley of *Aviation Monthly* there and he could rely on Joe, a former pilot and a journalist with a real nose for a story, to be both knowledgeable and gossipy about Culverton and the Lassiter Aircraft Company.

Hawley was unsure about the Pegasus. In his opinion, Nigel Lassiter was a wayward genius. 'The trouble is,' he said, 'you're never quite sure how his designs are going to work out in practice. Things are tough for everyone in the aviation world at the moment, particularly the small fry. Because of all the old surplus from the war, there's not many new craft being sold. Lassiter's might have bitten off more than they can chew with the Pegasus. They're not a big company, although they did some good work in the war. Mind you, David Lassiter, although he's nowhere near as brilliant as his brother, isn't a bad designer, either. Surely

92

you remember all the to-do about his plane, the Urbis, last year? There was enough in the papers.'

Of course! Jack had thought David Lassiter's name was vaguely familiar. The Urbis was a small aircraft which sold for three hundred and fifty pounds and had been the subject of a well-publicized competition. Ten lucky winners received an aeroplane and their first flying-lesson from David Lassiter himself. The aeroplanes were presented to the winners in the course of a much-talked-about flight round Britain. The aerial photographs of the trip, featuring such far-flung places as Cape Wrath and homely scenes of holiday-makers at Margate, had been a regular feature in the newspapers, together with quotes from David Lassiter emphasizing the simplicity and pleasure of flying the Urbis and the benefits of owning an aeroplane to any frequent traveller. It was the Urbis, according to Joe Hawley, which was keeping the company going. As he said, David Lassiter was a sound businessman.

Jack went thoughtfully into the smoking room, turning over what he'd heard. Here, as an unlooked-for bonus, he ran into an old acquaintance, Dr Anthony Brooke.

Dr Brooke, late of the RAMC and now of London University, didn't answer Jack's question right away. 'Maguire? Yes, I know Maguire,' he said eventually, halfway down the cigarette Jack had offered him. 'Not very well, mind, but I do know him. To be honest, Haldean, I don't care for him. He's too sleek for my taste, but he's fashionable. He used to be a real doctor but now rich women go and talk to him about sex. Rich men, as well, I suppose. All our problems are meant to be tied up with sex nowadays. Freud's got a lot to answer for. Maguire charges them a fortune for it. I believe he's got a wonderful manner. Still, why not?' He grinned. 'It beats working for a living.'

Jack had been home for some time when George arrived, time enough for him to have a bath and change into evening dress.

'Hello,' said George morosely. 'What are the glad-rags for?'

'I thought,' said Jack, checking his tie in the mirror, 'I'd take in a few clubs this evening.' He was hoping to get some idea of where Culverton might have been, but he didn't want to spell that out to George.

'By yourself?' asked George with a frown. 'It doesn't sound much fun.'

'I usually run into someone I know. We can go somewhere for a bite to eat if you like first, though.'

'I don't know if I'm very hungry,' said George unenthusiastically. 'I had afternoon tea so I'll just have a sandwich or something later on. I don't really fancy going out. I think I'll have an early night. Thanks, anyway.'

'Is something wrong?' asked Jack, watching his friend pace round the room. 'You were a fair old time at Eden Street.'

'Yes,' said George absently. He hesitated before the fireplace, fiddled with the ornaments on the mantelpiece, rearranged the clock and distractedly straightened up the spills in their wooden jar.

'George?' repeated Jack. 'What's wrong?'

George sighed and ran a hand through his hair before perching on the arm of a chair. 'Do you want to come to the factory on Monday?' he asked. 'My grandfather wondered if it would be convenient for you. He said we could all go down together in his car.'

'I've got to go into the office on Monday. I don't suppose you can make it Tuesday, by any chance?' asked Jack. 'I'd like to come.'

'I'll ask,' said George. 'I'd rather you were there.' He got off the chair, walked over to the sideboard and started to rearrange the silver cups.

'What on earth is it?' demanded Jack.

George didn't answer.

'Family?' asked Jack with a lift of his eyebrows.

George sighed once more. 'Yes, damn it, it is,' he agreed reluctantly. He put down a cup and turned to face him.

'Look, Jack, I don't like saying this. Yesterday was wonderful, what with meeting my grandfather, to say nothing of Anne.' His voice softened. 'She's really something, isn't she? She's younger than me, you know, yet my grandfather relies on her completely. She really understands people. Neither she nor my grandfather have said a word to the rest of the family about how I broke into the kitchen, by the way. Anne said that she thought I'd find it difficult to explain, and he agreed.'

'That's very tactful of them.'

'Yes, isn't it?' He paused for a few moments then shook himself. 'It was like a dream. After everything I'd been through, to find myself not only with a family, but with the offer of a job as well, was like a miracle.' His face lengthened. 'And then today . . .'

'What happened?' said Jack, offering George a cigarette.

'Nigel was just about unbearable,' said George in a rush. 'One of these days he'll go too far. It didn't get any better after you left, you know. Nigel started sniping about a dinner he's having tonight.'

'What dinner?'

'It's a formal thing at the Savoy to try and drum up money for the Pegasus. There's a whole bunch of worthies invited, an MP, a bloke called Ridgeway or something, and a few others. Culverton should have been there. My grandfather isn't going, and neither are David or Anne, and Nigel was hugely sarcastic about their lack of support. Anne told him straight out that she can't stand Ridgeway and my grandfather pointed out he hadn't wanted them there in the first place. That simmered down, but Walsh was there, still seething about his balance sheets. Walsh spoke out of turn and Nigel was really foul to him. It was rotten. Walsh is a sick man, poor devil. He was badly gassed in the war and it left him with his heart and lungs on the blink and it didn't do him any good to have Nigel turn on him. I tell you, Jack, I was worried Walsh was going to keel over there and then after Nigel had finished with him. What he said was completely not on.'

'What on earth did Nigel say?' asked Jack, curiously.

George snorted in disapproval. 'It was about a girl, of all the cheap shots to take. Poor old Walsh obviously isn't in any sort of condition to go running round after girls, but he's got a real thing about Nigel's clerk. From what I can make out, he worships her from afar, which is all he's really capable of. He's dippy about her, apparently, poor beggar. Anyway, Nigel caught Walsh on the raw, saying it was pathetic to see him follow her about endlessly, looking sorry for himself, and no girl would ever look twice at a washed-up crock like him.'

Jack frowned in distaste. 'That's a bit off. What on earth did your grandfather say? Surely he didn't let Nigel get away with that sort of remark?'

'Maguire and I were the only others in the room. Nigel chose his time very carefully. Maguire didn't like it and told Nigel to pipe down but he was spoiling for a fight. When David came in, Nigel started another row with him. You probably gathered there's not much love lost between David and Nigel but there's more to it than you realize.' His mouth became a thin line. 'David holds Nigel responsible for Thomas's death.'

Jack drew back. 'Thomas? His son, you mean? Why?'

'His son and Anne's husband,' said George grimly. He was silent for a few moments. 'Thomas crashed in one of Nigel's planes,' he said eventually. 'It went up in a fireball.'

Jack looked at him sharply. 'The poor devil,' he said softly. 'Was it really Nigel's fault?'

George nodded. 'To be honest, it sounds like it. Thomas was the test pilot for the company. He sounded like a terrific bloke. I really wish I'd known him. Anne thought the world of him. Anyway, the plane was a fighter and Nigel had built in instability. Now, I know you need that in a fighter, but David thought it was dangerously unstable. Nigel agreed to amend the specifications before Thomas took her up but he didn't. He was convinced his design would work.'

96

Jack looked at his friend in shocked silence. He understood now the reason for that sudden, murderous gleam in David Lassiter's eyes during the argument before lunch. 'That's appalling,' he said at last.

'Isn't it though?' agreed George. 'Apparently David had to be dragged off Nigel when he found out the truth. He very nearly killed him.'

Jack gave a soundless whistle. No wonder Anne Lassiter had used the word 'awkward' to describe Thomas's death. Downright impossible would be another way of putting it. 'How on earth can they live in the same house?'

George shrugged. 'Stubbornness. Nigel's never lived anywhere else and he certainly wasn't going to shift when David moved back in.' He smiled faintly. 'My father was a stubborn beggar. It seems to be a Lassiter characteristic.' He would have said more but a ring sounded at the door.

Jack glanced up, surprised. 'I wasn't expecting anyone. Were you?' George shook his head and Jack went to answer it.

David Lassiter was outside. His rather weary face lit up in a smile as Jack opened the door. 'You'll excuse me calling unannounced,' he said, taking off his hat and stepping into the hall. 'I was hoping to have a word with George.' He hesitated, looking at Jack's clothes. 'Were you going out? I don't want to hold you up.'

'There's no rush,' said Jack, leading the way into his rooms. 'I hadn't any definite plans. George, you've got a visitor,' he called. 'Come in and sit down, Mr Lassiter. Can I offer you a drink?'

'Whisky, if you've got it,' said David. 'Thanks.' He looked at his nephew thoughtfully. 'It's about this idea of the guv'nor's that you join the firm as my secretary. I wanted to talk to you.' He gave a wry smile. 'Today should have been ideal but it was difficult, wasn't it? I had the impression you found it heavy going.'

'I've just been saying as much to Jack,' admitted George.

David nodded. 'I thought so.' He sipped his whisky. 'I'm glad to say it's not always like that. Nigel's a bit hard to

97

take at the moment but, to be fair to him, he's worried sick. Culverton's death really has put the cat amongst the pigeons. Anyway, I thought I'd call in and see you here, where we could have some peace and quiet. Have you ever done any secretarial work before?'

'No,' said George. He spoke quickly. 'Look, Uncle David, I feel as if I've been wished on you and that's not what I want at all. If you're not happy, say so.'

David held up his hand. 'Easy does it. Believe me, George, if you can't do the job, I'll tell you. But . . .' He hesitated and smiled. 'I thought the world of my brother, you know, and you remind me of him no end. Silly beggar,' he added wistfully. 'Burying himself in South Africa. I used to think of going to see him, but I got involved with the firm and then there was my family to think of.' He bit his lip. 'It's too late now. I should have made the effort.'

'Did any of the family ever get out there?' asked Jack.

David shook his head. 'No, never. The guv'nor's too old and it's not the sort of thing that would occur to Nigel. He was a lot younger than Charles and they didn't really know one another. Dad was too upset to talk about it much, so I'm afraid it all just got forgotten, more or less. I doubt Nigel really remembered he had another brother until you showed up, George. I should have tried, though.'

'It was my father's decision,' said George awkwardly.

'He was a stubborn devil,' said David affectionately. 'It's a family failing. And he'd been hurt, you know. I'm not surprised he thought it was up to us to make the first move. Anyway, George, you'll want to know what sort of thing I expect you to do. The first thing is to get acquainted with how the firm works . . .'

George and David went into details while Jack, legs stretched out in front of him, lit a cigarette. If none of the Lassiters had been to South Africa that surely ruled out the possibility of any of them claiming the legacy – and yet who else could know there was a legacy to claim? The solicitors were the obvious answer. He'd just have to wait and see what Bill could dig out of them on Monday.

George, he was pleased to see, seemed to be getting on well with his uncle. That should cheer him up after his uncomfortable afternoon. David Lassiter, he thought, was a very likeable man. He was clearly in reality, if not in name, the head of the firm and Jack admired the tact he showed in dealing with his father who was so reluctant to let go of the reins. In fact, what with old Mr Lassiter on the one hand and Nigel on the other, diplomacy seemed to be the virtue David chiefly required.

The telephone jangled in the hall and, a few minutes later, he heard Mrs Pettycure's tread up the stairs. He opened the door and looked over the banister.

'Is it for me, Mrs Pettycure?' he called.

'No, Major. It's a lady. She wants to know if a Mr David Lassiter is here,' she said.

'David Lassiter? Yes, he's here.'

David, with a puzzled frown, went down to the hall.

He returned a few minutes later, looking grim. 'That was Anne,' he said without preamble. 'Thank goodness I mentioned I was calling here. Something's happened at the factory. Michael Walsh has been found dead.'

Chapter Six

George started to his feet. 'Dead?'

'Yes, poor devil.' David Lassiter's face was grave. 'It sounds as if his heart's packed in. It was always on the cards but . . .' He broke off. 'I'll have to leave. Fielding, the nightwatchman, found him and rang Eden Street. I've told Anne to get the doctor immediately and ask him to meet me at the factory. I'll go down there as soon as I can.' His brow furrowed. 'I'd better get a cab. It'll take far too long to fetch my car. I just hope I can find a taxi driver willing to make the trip.'

'I'll drive,' offered Jack. 'My car's garaged in Wilson Street mews. It's only round the corner. It'll be much quicker than trying to find a cab.'

David looked at him in relief. 'Thanks. That solves one problem at least.'

It was about twenty-six miles to Tilbury. That would, Jack thought as he drove out of the mews, take forty minutes or so at this time of night. David sat beside George in the back of the car.

'I really appreciate this, Haldean,' said David, leaning forward.

'What on earth was Walsh doing at the factory?' called back Jack over the noise of the engine.

'I suppose I'll have to say he was catching up on some work,' said David wearily.

'Wasn't he?' asked George.

David didn't answer for a few moments. Then he gave a heavy sigh. 'Look, George, you might as well know what was behind it. You're going to be working for us and you're part of the family, after all.' He leaned forward once more. 'Can I ask you to keep it under your hat, though, Haldean? You've been so decent to George I feel I can trust you, but if Nigel found out what the real reason was, then the fat would be in the fire and no mistake.' He shifted in his seat in irritation. 'It's so damn stupid. The worst of it is, it's my fault, in a way. It all comes back to Culverton.'

'Culverton?' repeated Jack.

'That's right.' David Lassiter's voice was thin with frustration. 'I was dead against the idea of the Pegasus. I thought it was ridiculously ambitious, far too big a task for us to undertake. Nigel argued that we had to produce a plane that was radically different and my father agreed. Now, Nigel's got real creative talent and he's a first-rate engineer but he hasn't a clue about business. If only the firm was organized properly, then we wouldn't have half the problems we do, but the guv'nor simply won't let go. He thinks we can muddle along as we did years ago. Anyway, I said that if Nigel could arrange the funding, we'd match it. I thought that would scotch the idea, but it didn't. Nigel teamed up with Culverton. There's a couple of others, such as Ridgeway and Maguire, but what made the Pegasus possible was Nigel's agreement with Culverton.' He paused. 'I don't know how much you know about Culverton.'

'Not much,' said Jack cautiously, unwilling to betray too much knowledge.

'He was a hard man. A very tough customer indeed. To be honest, I couldn't stick him at any price but I'll say this, he was a perfect investor. Too perfect, I thought. I couldn't work it out. There didn't seem to be any limit to what he would do and he became more generous as time went on. I didn't like it. I discussed it with my father and we called Nigel in and asked him outright. The key to it all was the India route. Culverton was desperate to have that route established before this government-assisted airline comes into being next year. If Culverton could get on the board, he'd be in clover. This is where I blame myself.'

Jack heard the bitterness in his voice. 'Why?'

'It had been a very heated discussion, as I'm sure you can imagine. When Nigel left, I remarked to my father that the India route was all very well, I just hoped there wasn't more to it, something that would blow up and land us all in the cart.'

'What sort of thing?' asked George, puzzled.

'Oh, damned if I know. Some secret agreement, some deal Nigel had worked out. It was the sort of comment Nigel invites, you know? You've got to dig information out of him. He acts as if he's got something up his sleeve and there's nothing to it, apart from the fact that he can't be bothered explaining himself properly. Anyway, Walsh was in on the meeting, sitting there with his ears flapping. Walsh can't stand Nigel and vice versa. Mind you, although Nigel could be absolutely foul to Walsh, I can see why Walsh annoyed him. He was a real old woman in some ways. He was clever enough and if it wasn't for his wretched health he could have amounted to something, but as it was, he had far too much spare time. He always wanted to know what went on behind the scenes and this idea about Nigel got to him. No matter how much I said I hadn't really meant it, Walsh was convinced I was on to something and managed to persuade my father that there was more to Culverton's support than met the eye. Anyway, to cut a long story short, Walsh searched Nigel's office.'

'What?' said George incredulously. 'He can't do that.'

'He shouldn't have done,' agreed David. 'That was a few weeks ago. The first I knew of it was Nigel sounding off about Walsh snooping round his office. He caught him in the act. It's virtually impossible to find a time when you can guarantee Nigel won't be there. Even if he leaves, he's liable to come back. He even sleeps there, sometimes. Walsh made some excuse but Nigel was furious. So was I.

I knew exactly what Walsh was up to and had a fair old row with him and my father as a consequence. Apart from the ethics of the thing, it was crazy. If Nigel had a secret contract, he'd have it locked away in a safe somewhere, not lying around in an office drawer. The trouble is, once my father had the idea in his head, he was certain it was right and Walsh conspiring away like Machiavelli made it worse. I thought Walsh might try again, despite all I'd said. If Nigel guesses what Walsh was doing, there'll be hell to pay. He was in my father's room, but that's next door to Nigel's.'

'Are you sure Walsh was intending to search your brother's office?' asked Jack.

'Absolutely I am,' agreed David. 'There simply isn't any other reason why he should be there at this time on a Saturday night. The stupid thing is, it's completely unnecessary. I don't believe there is a deal and, if there is, Peggy Culverton will let us know.'

'I suppose your father could have wanted to know before she did,' said Jack thoughtfully. 'It'd make life very awkward for your brother if he was caught out in something secretive. It'd be better if you all knew about it.'

'Not as awkward as it'll be if Nigel guesses what Walsh was up to,' said David grimly. 'I can do without all this cloak-and-dagger stuff. Oh, damn Walsh! As I say, he was a clever man. Too clever to waste his time on the bits and pieces my father could find for him. He needed something to occupy his mind. I'm sorry he's dead. I really am sorry, but he was living on borrowed time, you know. He caught a packet in the war and it's nearly done for him a few times. Poor beggar,' he added, more to himself than to George or Jack. 'He had a pretty thin time of it. Anyway, that's what's behind it. Anne knows as much as I do, but I'd appreciate you keeping it quiet. The doctor's meeting us there. It's Moorhouse, who sees to any problems at the works. He's a good man. He's attended Walsh before now. It's just as well, I suppose, that Walsh was one of his patients. It'll probably make things easier and, just at the moment, I can do with all the help I can get.'

Jack saw the great dark bulk of the factory stretching down towards the river as he drove through the lodge gates. David Lassiter directed him to the front and he pulled up outside a pillared entrance. The door was standing open, the light spilling down the flight of steps.

Dr Moorhouse, who was obviously meant by nature to be a cheerful soul, was looking out for them. He was waiting for them in the lobby with Fielding, the night-watchman. 'This is a very sad turn of events,' he said with professional sobriety.

'Terrible, sir,' put in Fielding sombrely. He looked really shaken, thought Jack. 'When I found poor Mr Walsh, I hoped he might have just had a nasty turn, like, but he'd gone, poor young beggar.'

'Have you moved him?' David asked Dr Moorhouse, leading the way up the stairs.

'Well, I had to move him to examine him, of course, but he's still in the room where Fielding found him. I wanted your instructions before I took any further action.'

They turned on to the upper corridor, a passageway lined with office doors. It was a rum thing, thought Jack, but places that should be full of people always seemed a bit creepy when they were empty, as if there were unseen ghosts and unheard echoes just beyond his senses. At least the lights were on. That was something.

'When did you find him?' asked David, turning to the nightwatchman.

'It was eight o'clock or so, sir,' said Fielding. 'I got here at seven thirty, as I always do on Saturdays, and started my rounds. I looked round downstairs first, then I came up here. I saw there was a light on in Mr Lassiter Senior's room. I thought it was Mr Nigel's room at first, and didn't think much of it, because he's often here, sir, as you know. Anyway, when I realized it was Mr Lassiter's room, I had a look in, and there was poor Mr Walsh, stretched out on the floor. I tried to wake him up, hoping I could help, but he was past saving. I tell you, sir, I had to sit down and pull myself together before I could telephone, then I spoke to Mrs Lassiter. She was very good.'

'I came as soon as I got the message,' said Moorhouse. 'I've examined Mr Walsh before, of course, and, to be truthful, this has come as no great surprise. He had a marked disordered action of the heart. His own doctor prescribed bromide of sodium for him, which would have been beneficial, but there was very little anyone could have done. He had to be careful not to overdo it and to beware of sudden exertion and shock, but I'm afraid time caught up with him in the end.'

They came to the office. The light was on, left by Dr Moorhouse after his previous examination. Walsh's body lay in the middle of the room.

Jack drew his breath in, aware that his reactions were mirrored by both the Lassiters. Walsh was lying with his face turned towards them, his hands by his side and his face showing the waxy pallor of death.

'He was very much like that when I saw him first,' said the doctor. 'I moved his arms, of course. There's not much doubt what he died of, poor devil. The symptoms are pretty clear. It's his heart, all right. Among other things, he suffered from auricular fibrillation, if that means anything to you.'

'Not an awful lot, no,' confessed Jack. He dropped down on one knee beside Walsh. His eyes were closed and his jaw had fallen open. 'Poor devil,' he said softly. 'When did he die, doctor?'

'About seven o'clock or thereabouts.'

David nodded. 'He can't have been here long. He left Eden Street about five, as I recall, and he would have got the train down. Why did it happen now, doctor? Any particular reason?'

The doctor shrugged. 'Not really. If he was nervous or apprehensive it wouldn't have helped. Any sudden shock,

105

such as a door banging or so on, might have done it. He was in a bad way, you know. It was mustard gas that caused his condition, I understand. I intend to say as much on my certificate.'

Jack stood up and looked at David. 'Is your brother's office next door?' he asked. David nodded. 'I'll just see if it's undisturbed.' He was back in a couple of minutes. 'All clear,' he said quietly. 'I don't think he went in there.'

David heaved a sigh of relief. 'I suppose that's something.'

Jack stood back, looking round the room, his hands in his pockets. 'These offices would have been cleaned last night, I suppose?'

'Yes, that's right. The charwomen come in the evening.'

Jack looked at the ashtray on the desk. There were two cigarette stubs in it. They both looked as if they'd been smoked using a holder. 'Do they empty the ashtrays?' he asked.

David looked at the ashtray in surprise. 'Yes, of course they do.' He shrugged. 'Walsh must have smoked those. Except . . .'

'Yes?'

'He hardly ever smoked. Only on social occasions and not often then. He didn't carry a cigarette case, I know.'

'Did he use a cigarette holder?'

David shrugged. 'He might have done. Yes, I think he did.'

Jack flipped open a silver box on the desk. 'There are cigarettes in here.'

'That's probably where he got them from,' said the doctor. 'You're quite right about him being a very occasional smoker though, Mr Lassiter. I remember asking him about it when I treated him last.'

Jack frowned. 'Mr Lassiter, are you thinking of calling the police?'

'The police?' David looked at him in astonishment.

'There's no need for the police, Major Haldean,' said Dr Moorhouse. 'No need whatsoever. What on earth makes you suggest such a thing?'

'Those cigarette ends.' Jack was still frowning. 'I don't like them.'

'But . . .' Dr Moorhouse stared at him. 'Major Haldean, we can't possibly call the police because of two cigarette stubs. I can assure you there's no possibility of foul play. It's my duty to report to the coroner any cases of violent, unexplained or unnatural death, but nothing of the sort has occurred. Mr Walsh died as a result of a pre-existing heart condition. There's no question of anything but purely natural causes and I can testify to that. If we did call in the police, Major, I would be reprimanded by the coroner for wasting police time.'

'That's true enough, isn't it, Haldean?' said David Lassiter. 'I mean, there's nothing for them to investigate, is there?'

Jack looked round the room in a dissatisfied way. 'I don't suppose there is.'

'What's happened to Walsh's body?' asked Rackham the next morning, pouring out a cup of coffee and handing it to Jack. They were in Rackham's rooms off Russell Square, the Sunday sound of church bells and the occasional car coming faintly through the window. 'Milk? Sugar?'

'Just milk, thanks,' said Jack, stretching his long legs out towards the fire. 'The doctor took charge and I imagine the body's filed away in the mortuary until it's released to the undertakers for the funeral. That will be next week, I imagine. I dunno, Bill. The doctor didn't find anything fishy, but I don't like those cigarette ends. There was one short stub and one longer one. They suggested someone had been in the room with him.'

'They might do,' said Rackham, unconvinced. 'I'm not so sure. The trouble is, Jack,' he added, stirring his coffee, 'the doctor was quite right. If this bloke Walsh had a ropy heart and keeled over, that's natural causes, not suicide or murder, no matter how many fag-ends were in the ashtray. If Dr Moorhouse had reported it to the Essex police he'd have got a very formal flea in his ear.' He sat down in the chair across from Jack. 'He had a heart attack, something that was very much on the cards. You said yourself he looked a real crock. If, as you say, he was sneaking round like something out of a spy thriller, I bet he was jumping with nerves. He probably smoked a couple of cigarettes on the strength of it.' He grinned. 'It sounds as if that could have seen him off from what you've told me.'

'But he only smoked on social occasions,' countered Jack.

'So David Lassiter says. I don't imagine Walsh consulted him every time he lit a cigarette. The doctor said he died of natural causes,' repeated Rackham patiently.

'Look, Doubting Thomas, the doctor said Culverton died of natural causes,' pointed out Jack.

'Yes, damn it, so he did, but natural causes didn't take his clothes off, cave his face in and dump him in the river, did they? That's very unnatural indeed. Incidentally, we got the result of the fingerprints I took from the bottle in the washroom. The body in the Thames was Culverton, all right.'

'Did you doubt it?' asked Jack.

'Not really,' said Rackham, 'but it's always as well to be sure. The point is, we know there's been some funny business with Culverton. Apart from these cigarette ends there's nothing to show there's anything amiss about Walsh.' He looked at Jack's face and sighed. 'Okay. Let your imagination rip. What d'you think happened?'

'That's just it,' said Jack in irritation. 'I can't see what can have happened. On the one hand, there are those two cigarette ends and an odd discrepancy in times.' Rackham looked up, enquiringly. 'Walsh left Eden Street about five o'clock and died about seven. The train journey takes approximately forty-five minutes. Now, even leaving him a generous allowance for walking to and from the station at either end, he's got at least half an hour unaccounted for. What was he doing in that time? He wasn't searching Nigel Lassiter's office. I don't think he'd been in there. What was he up to?'

'Smoking cigarettes by the sound of it,' muttered Rackham. 'Perhaps the train was late.'

Jack shook his head. 'No, the trains were running fine last night. I checked.'

'Well, maybe he stopped off for a drink somewhere to steady his nerves.'

'Maybe,' said Jack. 'Yes, I suppose he could have done that.'

Rackham frowned. 'The trouble is, there could be any number of reasons. I bet Dr Moorhouse didn't give seven o'clock as an absolute, did he? All these times of death are always very approximate. You want to argue, I take it, given that he publicly hoped Walsh would drop dead, that Nigel Lassiter bumped him off, yes? The motive, presumably, being that Walsh was on the right lines in thinking Nigel Lassiter had a shady deal with Culverton.'

'I don't know as I want to do anything of the sort,' said Jack, plaintively. 'Nigel Lassiter was vile to Walsh but he can't be the bumper-offer. He was hosting a highly publicized and well-attended dinner at the Savoy last night – it's mentioned in the newspaper this morning – in the presence of Dr Maguire, a sprinkling of investment bankers and a couple of luminaries such as Sholto Bierce, the MP. It was the fact that Nigel was so safely engaged elsewhere that drew Walsh to the factory in the first place. Nigel and all his guests really were at the Savoy,' he added. 'I checked that, too. I called in on my way here.'

'That was very keen of you,' said Rackham. 'So what are you saying?'

'I'm saying it's odd, damn it!' Jack sighed in exasperation, then relaxed, picking up his coffee once more. He grinned ruefully. 'Sorry. I'm probably barking up the wrong tree but it feels *wrong*.'

Rackham raised his eyes to heaven. 'There's enough to think about without you having feelings. What are you doing tomorrow?'

'Working. Why?'

'Because I hope that, come tomorrow, I'll find out what was in that rosewood box we found in Culverton's office. Following your suggestion, I intend to see if Culverton had been caught making trouble with any of his female staff, too. I thought, as you were in on it, I'd bring you up to date.'

'Cheers, Bill,' said Jack. 'We could go for a quick one in the Heroes in the evening if you like. Look, I know you're busy, but if you could find time to call on Marchbolt's, George would be really grateful.'

'I'll do it first thing,' promised Rackham.

The next morning Rackham, as promised, went to see Mr Marchbolt, the senior partner of Marchbolt, Lawson and Marchbolt. Mr Marchbolt, keen to dissociate his firm from any suggestion of fraud, was eager to help.

The firm's first action on being called upon to execute Rosemary Belmont's will had been to write to the address in South Africa, but the letter had been returned marked *Gone Away*. They had written to a Mr George Lassiter of Mayfair, London, whose address they had found in the telephone directory, to see if he was, by any chance, the man they were looking for but Mr Lassiter had not replied.

'We can only request information,' said Mr Marchbolt, steepling his fingers, 'not compel it.' If Inspector Rackham would care to see, the correspondence was still contained in the file.

Their next move was to advertise in the South African press and that did bring a result. The legacy had been claimed by a George Alfred Lassiter in February 1921 who enclosed his birth certificate for identification. Mr Marchbolt examined George's birth certificate but was unable to say if it was the same document which the firm had seen earlier. Marchbolt, Lawson and Marchbolt, he informed Rackham, were not in the habit of marking personal documents. He was able to produce the letter they had received but Rackham could glean nothing from it. It was a neat,

110

typewritten document from the Faulkner Hotel, Cape Town, signed in the name of George Lassiter. The signature didn't look like Lassiter's, but Rackham hadn't expected it to.

What was interesting about it was that whoever had written the letter obviously had some knowledge of Rosemary Belmont. Rosemary Belmont, so the letter said, had been married to the writer's father, Charles Lassiter, and, after her divorce, had married Jerome Belmont in Deauville in 1902.

Mr Marchbolt, although he had never met Mrs Belmont, she being one of the clients inherited from his father when he took over the practice in 1911, was able to confirm that the details were correct and added to them from the information they had in Mrs Belmont's papers. Mrs Belmont's will, said Mr Marchbolt, had been drawn up shortly after her marriage. After Belmont's death in 1915, caused by a too-free indulgence in absinthe, Mrs Belmont had taken to drink, isolated in France by the outbreak of war.

Old long before her time, she had spent the last three years of her life being cared for by the nuns of the convent of St Germain-des-Prés, Mantes, who specialized in such cases. The first that Mr Marchbolt knew of Rosemary Belmont's death was a letter from the Mother Superior of the convent, detailing what the Reverend Mother knew of their patient's life and the fact that Mrs Belmont had been incapable of any form of rational communication for the last year she spent in their care. The Reverend Mother believed, she added, that Mrs Belmont had no living family. Certainly she had had no visitors. Her only possessions had been a cardboard box full of letters, old theatre programmes and invitations. A letter from Marchbolt's, dated 1902, confirming the drawing up of the new will, was the reason why the Mother Superior had written.

'Blimey,' said Jack, when Rackham told him the results of the interview on the telephone later on. 'You're sure that letter – the one from the Mother Superior, I mean – was genuine?'

'It certainly was,' said Rackham, recalling the spidery French of the Mother Superior's communication. 'I can't see Marchbolt's being on the fiddle either, Jack. I mean, if they were, Mr Marchbolt wouldn't have given me all that information.'

Jack let his breath out slowly. 'At this rate I'm going to convince myself that George claimed the money then forgot all about it. That's a joke, by the way. But where do we go now, Bill? If the information didn't come from Rosemary Belmont and Marchbolt's are squeaky-clean, how the dickens did anyone know that there was any loot in the offing? Did the nuns know she was rich?'

'The Mother Superior was aware that she'd been married to an artist but all she knew about him was that he'd killed himself with absinthe. She certainly didn't know Mrs Belmont had a small fortune tucked away. That was obvious.'

'Then it has to be the solicitors,' said Jack. 'There's nowhere else the information could have come from.'

Rackham's voice was doubtful. 'What can I do? I've seen Mr Marchbolt and he's convinced the firm acted properly. On the evidence he has, they're in the clear. I suppose I could write to the South African police.'

Jack sounded unimpressed. 'That'll tell us what, exactly? That a George Lassiter stayed at the Faulkner Hotel, Cape Town, about two years ago? I suppose it's worth doing but I can't see it's going to get us much further.'

'Neither can I,' admitted Rackham, 'but you never know.'

Rackham, without much hope of success, wrote to the South African police and there, for the time being, the matter rested.

Chapter Seven

At eight o'clock that evening, Jack was standing by the bar in the Heroes of Waterloo. He looked up with a smile as Bill Rackham came into the snug. 'Ah, Bill. I've only just arrived. I've nabbed a table by the fire. Can I get you a drink?'

'Thanks,' said Rackham, tersely, taking off his hat and unbuttoning his coat. He didn't smile back but rubbed a weary hand over his freckled face. His eyes had shadows underneath them and he looked, thought Jack, whacked out. 'I'll have a pint of Young's, thanks.' He looked round the oak and brass interior of the pub, saw the table Jack indicated, walked across the room and sank gratefully on to the wooden settle. Jack picked up the two pewter mugs and carried them across to his friend. There was obviously something wrong. When he'd spoken to Bill earlier that day, he'd been fine. Now he looked washed out and, more than that, angry. Jack put the drinks on the table and sat down.

Apart from a group of young men who looked like bank clerks and were cheerfully and loudly analysing Arsenal's performance on Saturday, they had the snug to themselves. There was no danger of them being overheard. 'What is it, Bill?' he asked quietly.

Rackham heaved a deep sigh and took a long drink. 'You were right,' he said simply.

Jack frowned. 'What about?'

'You were right about him,' said Rackham. 'Culverton,' he added bitterly. 'The big boss, the big cheese, the friend of cabinet ministers and just about the worst eighteen carat gold-plated swine it's ever been my fortune to run up against.' He shook his head. 'I said you were good at guessing. What did you say? That Culverton was unpleasant? You took one look at those pictures in his office on Friday and you had him nailed.'

'What did he do?' asked Jack. He knew he hadn't been mistaken about that face in the pictures in Culverton's office. He put his cigarettes on the table and waited for Rackham to speak. He had never seen Bill look so grim.

Rackham gave a shudder, ran his hand through his ginger hair and took a cigarette from the case, tapping it on the table. He was obviously finding it hard to put his thoughts in order. A burst of laughter came from the group of football supporters and Jack suddenly wished that he, too, had nothing more to think about than the everyday pleasures of life. Whatever Rackham had to tell him, it had clearly shaken his friend.

'Culverton,' said Rackham eventually. 'Let's take the public man first. He seems to have had genuine ability. Gilchrist Lloyd admired him. He's been with him from the beginning. During the war Culverton set up a transport company, buying and repairing old commercial vehicles and selling them to the government at a very healthy profit. And, of course, with any vehicle, however clapped out, being shipped to France, he finished the war a great deal better off than when he started. He sold out just before the Armistice and got a huge price on the deal. As soon as the Armistice was declared he started nosing around after old aeroplanes and dropped lucky. He bought two aircraft for next to nothing and spent some money in fitting them up. Then, as soon as civilian flying was permitted again, he was there. He made a real killing. He got married at the end of 1919 and, with Mrs Culverton's money behind him, went from strength to strength.'

Rackham rolled his cigarette between his fingers. 'He was a big personality, Jack. I've got to give him that. I've had a long talk with Mrs Culverton today and she found him overwhelming. He could charm, too. It was his energy, she thinks, that really attracted her.'

'So what went wrong?' asked Jack.

'He did. You know that rosewood box you found in his desk? Well, after I'd been to Marchbolt's this morning and spoken to you, I was able to examine the contents. You know you thought he might have caused trouble with the female staff? That box proved it. It contained a couple of packets of grubby photographs – the sort you get offered in Paris – a few newspaper cuttings and three letters from a girl called Katherine Forrest. After I'd read the letters I went round to see Gilchrist Lloyd, as it was obvious that Katherine Forrest had worked for Culverton at one time. Gilchrist Lloyd remembered her. She was a pretty, amiable girl who'd been Culverton's stenographer about three years ago. She wasn't, thought Lloyd, outstandingly bright, but she was pleasant enough. She resigned and Lloyd had no idea what had happened to her.'

'I presume Culverton had an affair with her,' said Jack. 'Did she land up in trouble?'

'Yes, she did.' Rackham took a deep breath. 'And if that was all, it would be bad enough but that's the way of things, Jack. No, it was everything else that turned my stomach. You see, Culverton didn't merely get the poor girl pregnant.' He leaned forward, his voice low. 'He also gave her syphilis.'

Jack stared at him. 'The bastard.'

'Absolutely.' Rackham looked at him with hooded eyes. 'The last letter was a plea for help. It would have melted a heart of stone. It was written from Charing Cross Hospital. I went to Charing Cross and got the whole sorry story. The baby was stillborn and Katherine Forrest died shortly after-wards. By that stage, you see, the disease was far too advanced to be cured.' Jack made a noise in his throat. 'The hospital,' continued Rackham, 'said that she seemed to have no friends or relations. He left her to die, Jack. How anyone after reading those letters could leave the girl to die without offering a single shred of comfort, I don't know.'

115

Jack covered his eyes with his hand. It was a long time before he spoke. At the other end of the snug the bank clerks were talking, drinking, smoking and laughing, swapping stories, being happy in ordinary, everyday ways. Why the hell – why the bloody *hell* – couldn't Culverton have been happy like them? There must have been some reason Culverton kept those letters. He had made no move to help the girl and, given that the letters were with a packet of obscene photographs, they hadn't been kept as a goad to his conscience. No; they were a record of one of his conquests. 'What then?' he asked quietly.

'I went back to the offices on Cooper Street. Lloyd had told me that Mrs Culverton would be there this afternoon and I wanted to see her.'

'You didn't tell her about Katherine Forrest, did you?' said Jack, startled.

'I did, Jack. I was angry, you see, blisteringly angry. I don't think I've ever felt like that before. Mrs Culverton had never heard of Katherine Forrest. She was appalled.'

'Well, she would be,' said Jack. 'How d'you expect the poor woman to react? What on earth did she say?'

'It helped that she'd been a nurse.' Rackham took a long pull at his cigarette. 'That meant I could state things clearly without beating around the bush. She was shocked – disgusted might be a better description – but she wasn't surprised.'

Jack looked up sharply. 'No?'

'No. She knew what her husband was like. However, she didn't realize he'd had syphilis. Not that she doubted it, mind you. "I should have known," she said. "I should have guessed." She remembered him going to Maguire for treatment. Culverton told her he was suffering from overwork but the symptoms fitted those of syphilis. We checked the dates with his old appointment diaries. Culverton had been seeing Maguire for some time when Katherine Forrest joined the firm. I saw Maguire to confirm the dates and the diagnosis. He said he'd warned Culverton about the importance of not passing the disease on.'

Jack nodded. 'Of course he would.'

'Maguire treated him with a course of intramuscular injections of mercurial cream and, apart from an enlargement of his aortic valve, a common side-effect of syphilis, Culverton made a good recovery. One fact that Mrs Culverton found significant with hindsight was that it was about then Culverton complained of heart trouble. She also said that his personality began to alter and that, too, can be a symptom.'

'How did his personality alter?' asked Jack. 'He doesn't sound any great shakes to begin with.'

'He doesn't, does he? However, he had some good qualities, if you count all that shrewdness, energy and charm as good points. She says that she went from being charmed to being wary but then – and the dates fit his treatment from Maguire – she started to be afraid. I know we've only got her word for it but I was convinced she was telling the truth. Things came to a head the morning of Wednesday, 31st October. What she found in his room terrified the life out of her.'

Jack looked a question.

'Culverton was up in London, of course,' said Rackham, stubbing out his cigarette and lighting another. 'Mrs Culverton went into his dressing room. It was a room which, according to her, she rarely entered. Culverton's valet looked after his things and she never had occasion to go in, but the Richmond Red Cross were having a jumble sale and she'd been asked to look out some old clothes. While going through Culverton's wardrobe, she saw there was a loose panel at the base. The wardrobe had a false bottom and tucked into it was a folder containing yet more obscene photographs and a bundle of newspaper cuttings.'

Rackham stopped and looked at Jack. 'There were newspaper cuttings in the rosewood box in his office. These were on the same subject.' He paused. 'You seemed to have a good idea what he was like, Jack. You seemed to have him pegged right away. I don't suppose you can guess what these cuttings were about, can you?'

117

Jack leaned back. Images and sensations jumbled together in his mind. A cold-eyed predatory face, the sensuous luxury of Culverton's office, a dying girl, a terrified woman, the obscene photographs, a string of unsolved murders, the intrusive memory of a Holbein portrait, and an imaginary but oddly convincing picture of a bundle of newspaper cuttings gloated over in private. It was huge leap but he was going to make it. He took a deep breath. 'He's the X man. He's your Jack the Ripper,' he said quietly.

Rackham brought his fist down on the table.'You've got it. *That's* what the cuttings were about. They were all accounts of the murders and when Mrs Culverton saw them hidden away under the bottom of the wardrobe she said she felt sick. All of a sudden, all sorts of details, all sorts of comments and, most of all, her growing feeling of terror seemed to make sense. She's utterly convinced of it.'

'Was she going to tell you?' asked Jack.

Rackham splayed his hands out in a questioning gesture. 'How do I know? After she found the cuttings she had no thought beyond getting out of the house and to the safety of her own flat. She says she felt paralysed. She had no proof, only conviction, and was terrified that if she did approach the police Culverton would find out what she'd done. To be honest, I think she was nerving herself to come to us when she got the letter from Lloyd to say he was missing. After that . . .' He shrugged. 'What was the point? Culverton was dead and she couldn't help his victims.'

'Is there any proof?' asked Jack, suddenly cautious. He would have preferred Rackham to argue the toss with him, to point out all the reasons why he could be wrong, to test his sudden insight against hard fact. 'I mean, it's all very well us swapping nightmares with each other but is there any evidence?'

Rackham raised his hands and let them fall. 'No. No, there isn't and if we can't find any, this will never be made public. What sort of evidence could there be? I'm going to look, believe me I'm going to look, but I wouldn't be surprised if the X man murders are never officially solved.

The Assistant Commissioner is going to interview Mrs Culverton but he told me there's no real doubt in his mind that we've got the truth.'

'What about his papers? Did he keep a diary?'

'Only that appointment diary.' Rackham leaned forward. 'That threw up a bit of a question. In the last eighteen months there have been five murders we've attributed to the Ripper. On all the relevant dates Culverton had written *Paris* in his diary and that's a lie. I think he might have been arranging an alibi for himself. Lloyd was able to check from other paperwork where Culverton was. It took a bit of doing but he hadn't been in France, he'd been in London, all right.'

'He'd written *Paris* in his diary the other night,' Jack said. 'The night the last girl was killed.'

'Yes. On that occasion, of course, he actually was going to Paris, even if he didn't get there.' He gave a humourless smile. 'There's only one way of really being certain, and that's if the murders stop. In the meantime, I still have to try and find who killed him.'

'If Culverton really is your Ripper, whoever saw him off deserves a medal.'

'I couldn't agree more,' said Rackham, stretching his shoulders.

Jack picked up his beer and raised an eyebrow at his friend. 'So can't you just let sleeping dogs lie, so to speak?'

'No.' Rackham leaned back on the settle. 'For one thing, we don't work like that. Police procedure is police procedure and I can't get round it. Besides that, think of the consequences if we don't crack it. Thanks to you, we believe Culverton was frequenting a dodgy club, a club where, granted he's our man, he's been able to pick up and go on to murder no less than five women. I want that club found, Jack, and our key to finding it has to be to work out who killed Culverton. We haven't got anything else to go on but it's a damn sight more than we had before. The AC's agreed to detail some men who can go into clubs – men who won't stand out like a sore thumb by wearing uniform boots with evening dress and so on – and see if they can pick up any traces.'

'I was going to have a look round myself tonight,' said Jack. 'I don't know if I'm really in the mood any more. I always run into someone I know and I've got to be jolly. I don't feel the least jolly after what you've told me.' He smoked his cigarette down to the butt and crushed it out in the ashtray. 'What about the other angle? Where was the last Ripper victim seen?'

'We found out as much as we could about the latest victim, Bridget Flynn, at the time. She was last seen a bit the worse for wear with drink at Wednesday lunchtime in Carrowgate Road, Chelsea. Then, like Culverton himself, she seemed to vanish into thin air until she was found on Friday morning. She'd been in the water longer than Culverton so it was difficult to state exactly when she died but the police surgeon, Dr Harding, puts it sometime on Wednesday night or the early hours of Thursday morning, which ties in with Culverton right enough.'

'I don't suppose you've got photographs of these girls, have you?'

'We have,' said Rackham doubtfully, 'but you wouldn't want to see them. They're all taken after we found them.'

'In that case, is there a photo of Culverton I can have? If I'm going to join the hunt, it'll help.'

'You can have a picture of him and welcome,' agreed Rackham, 'but for heaven's sake if you do find anything, let me know right away. Don't try anything off your own bat. I don't want to haul your body out of the Thames.'

Jack spread his hands wide. 'Pax, *amigo*. I'll be good.' He picked up his glass. 'C'mon, Bill. I know this has got to you, but he's dead, remember. He can't do any more harm.'

'There's still the club,' said Rackham. 'We have to find the club.'

The next day brought the promised trip to the factory. In a way, Jack was surprised it was going ahead but old Mr

Lassiter, according to George, wanted to keep as much to his plans and usual routine as possible. Michael Walsh's funeral was planned for Thursday and George intended to be there, principally to support his grandfather. Old Mr Lassiter had been upset by Michael Walsh's death – very upset – but Dr Moorhouse's reassurance that it could have happened at any time had helped. 'My grandfather knew that,' said George. 'It was because poor old Walsh was such a basket case that he took him on in the first place. He felt very strongly about the men who were injured in the war and employing Walsh was one of his ways of showing it. It was decent of him, wasn't it?'

Jack agreed. It was probably, he reflected, because of the easy life Mr Lassiter had been able to give him that Walsh had survived as long as he did.

The roomy Armstrong-Siddeley, which drew up in Chandos Row after lunch, contained not only Mr Lassiter but Anne Lassiter and Dr Maguire as well.

'I have to thank you, Major,' said Mr Lassiter, after they'd settled themselves in the car, 'for taking David down to Tilbury on Saturday night. It was a grievous loss. A very grievous loss. I miss poor Walsh enormously.'

'Why was Mr Walsh at the factory in the first place?' asked Maguire curiously.

Mr Lassiter hesitated. 'He had undertaken a commission I had entrusted him with,' he said eventually. 'A matter of looking out some papers, doctor.'

Jack admired his way of putting it. It was the truth, when all was said and done, and wouldn't raise any suspicions in Maguire's mind. However, Mr Lassiter was clearly uncomfortable and, to divert Maguire's attention, Jack chipped in with a question about the dinner at the Savoy on Saturday night.

'It was a great success,' said Maguire, 'or seemed so, at least. That's why I'm here today. Nigel's arranged another meeting for those who seemed particularly interested and I've been roped in to enthuse about the flying-boat.' He smiled. 'That being so, I thought I'd better come and see it

for myself. After all,' he added, 'it's as much for my benefit as for Nigel's, especially now there's a question mark
over what Culverton's are going to provide.'

George, who had clearly heard enough about
Culverton's and their problematical finances to last him a
long time, spent most of the journey looking out of the
window in discontented silence. 'Why on earth,' he said,
looking at the drab streets, 'would anyone live here?'

Jack had to admit that George had a point. Parts of the
journey would have been enough to curb the highest of
spirits. The city appeared as mile after mile of dingy
blackened-brick boxes where even the occasional grass
verge seemed grubby, and autumn showed only as a dis-
mal foretaste of winter.

Weary of the view, he turned to the occupants of the car.
Mr Lassiter was wrapped in reflective silence. It must be
hard for him, thought Jack, with a stab of sympathy. He'd
obviously thought a lot of Walsh.

Anne Lassiter sat next to Roger Maguire. Anne was still
in her twenties and Maguire was a well-preserved forty-
odd. That by itself wouldn't matter but he couldn't see
why the sophisticated, worldly Maguire was attracted to
Anne. She was a good-looking girl, in a fresh, outdoor way.
She was wearing a red coat and hat which set off her dark
hair and bright eyes, and she looked really something. No,
it wasn't a question of looks, it was a matter of personality. That was the puzzle. Material possessions, thought
Jack, didn't make much appeal to Anne. He could imagine
her making the cheerful best of hardship, as the mother of
a large and happy family with constant visitors, where
the dinner would always be made to go round rather than
turn anyone away. She seemed the sort of woman who
instinctively understood large dogs and small boys and
must have been a cracking nurse.

Maguire, on the other hand, would recoil from any sort
of hardship as a cat recoiled from water. Sleek was about
the best word to describe him. Psychiatry, in some of its
forms at least, was probably a good choice of profession.

Armed with Anthony Brooke's insights in the club on Saturday, Jack could easily believe that Maguire would be indulgent to a whole range of conditions which Anne had never heard of and which would bewilder her if she did. Sensuality and the problems thrown up by its gratification would be second nature to the knowledgeable Dr Maguire. Jack doubted Anne could even begin to understand the man. So what did she see in him? He was handsome, with an easy, if well-practised, courtesy of manner, and the poor girl must have been lonely after her husband died. Her kindness would excuse his faults. No; Anne's attraction to Maguire was no mystery but Maguire's attraction to Anne was baffling.

After a wearisomely long journey they left the buildings behind and turned down the broad road which ran down the long spit of land to the factory. On this sullen November day, the gloomy clouds seemed to hang at hand-height over the endless iron band of the Thames, in a landscape whose colours varied from grey to black.

They went through the lodge gates and got out of the car beside the long, high brick bulk of the factory. The clank and rumble of a train sounded clearly somewhere out of sight.

Mr Lassiter looked at George. 'I know you've been here before, my boy, but I can't imagine you took much in, granted the very distressing circumstances.' He pointed down the length of the factory. 'This is the main building, where the aeroplanes are actually made and, as you know, the offices are at the back. This is only part of the site, of course. We've got about fifteen acres altogether. On the other side there's the testing field and our harbour.'

He led them up an imposing flight of steps, through a pillared doorway and into the hall. A clerk, who had been seated at a desk, stood up respectfully as they came in. Mr Lassiter spoke to him briefly then turned to his guests. 'I'll show you the factory first.'

With a slight touch of showmanship, Mr Lassiter opened the door from the hall into the factory, ushered them in and stood back with an attitude of modest pride.

Blinking in the bright lights, Jack took in the factory. The doorway they had come through led them into the side of the building. At first sight it was impressive. The factory itself was a sort of indoor street, open at both ends. Half-formed aeroplanes stood at intervals, each surrounded by khaki-coated workers. The noise was tremendous. It was the smell of the place that hit him, a smell consisting of hot oil, warm metal, new wood, leather, varnish and the heady scent of aircraft dope. For a couple of seconds he was whisked into the skin of his sixteen-year-old self, nearly sick with excitement, climbing into a plane for the first time. Then he realized how empty it all seemed. You could have fitted four or five times as many planes and far more men into the space. He had been told, he reflected, that things were tough for Lassiter's.

Eighty feet above their heads a glass roof covered the entire building. Arc lamps blazed down, making hard black shadows. In the apex of the roof a wooden board-walk ran the entire length of the street, under which ran a thick double chain supporting a huge lump of machinery that hung suspended at one end. Jack narrowed his eyes, then smiled in recognition. 'Why, sir, it's an overhead crane,' he said loudly to Mr Lassiter, pitching his voice to carry over the thump of machinery.

'That's right.' Mr Lassiter pointed with his stick again. 'If you look through the open doors at the end there you can see the railway yard. The crane extends over the trucks and we can pick up and unload all the bulky heavy materials right to the door of the various shops. There's timber, of course, which is mainly ash and spruce, which we get in the baulk, metal and linen.' His face lit up as he looked at a group of men standing to the side, about halfway down the factory. 'There's David with Benson, the foreman.'

David Lassiter looked up as they approached. 'The lodge-keeper sent word to say you'd arrived,' he said, signing the clipboard Benson had given him. 'Take a look at that last lot of spruce,' he said to the foreman. 'The spar shops will need it by this afternoon.'

124

'What are you making here?' asked George.

'This is the Urbis,' said David. He smiled. 'It's an excellent machine, even though I say it myself. Yes, all things considered, we're not doing badly with the Urbis but I wish you could have seen the factory in the war when we had the LE series in full production. We employed nearly a thousand hands then and turned out over fifty aeroplanes a month. If you look outside –' he turned and pointed – 'you can see the land stretching down to the river and the old sheds. You can just see the corner of Nigel's new hangar down by the river. That's where the Pegasus is.'

Jack felt his interest quicken. So far he'd only heard of the Pegasus as a problem, but he was looking forward to seeing the aircraft itself. After all, it was going to be the biggest craft ever constructed and the idea of an aeroplane that could make commercial flights to India was staggering.

'In here,' continued David, indicating the shops to his left, 'we've got the workshops. There's metal-working, fabric-cutting, spars, dope and varnish.' He grinned. 'If you want a plot for a story, Haldean, this would be a good place to start. We have to treat the aeroplane fabric with dope and the fumes are lethal. We ventilate the room properly, of course, but dope's dangerous stuff. Then there are the ovens where we dry out the timber. That's 125 degrees of dry heat. Get stuck in there and you wouldn't last long.'

'I imagine you could have any number of interesting accidents,' said Maguire. 'Fatal, for sure.'

'Our safety record is excellent,' said old Mr Lassiter stiffly. 'And really, David, considering what happened on Saturday night, I think that remark is in very poor taste.'

David Lassiter looked stricken. 'I'm sorry. I wasn't thinking of poor old Walsh or anything or the sort. I was only trying to make things more interesting for Haldean.' He glanced at George. 'I'll give you a proper idea of my side of things when you've got more time. I know you're only here for a brief visit and Maguire wants to see the Pegasus.'

125

'We'll go up to Nigel's office,' said his father. 'He's the best person to show us the new plane.'

They retreated out of the factory back into the corridor, the sound of machinery muffled behind them.

'How did the firm get started, sir?' asked George as they walked up the stairs.

'We were boat builders,' said his grandfather, after a pause to catch his breath. 'However, Nigel was fascinated by the experiments in flight and I caught his enthusiasm. You won't have heard of it, but there was an Air Week in Reims in 1909 where the American and the various European aviators got together. I attended it with Nigel and David. I came away convinced that heavier-than-air flight was the way of the future and started experimenting with building our own craft.' He smiled reminiscently. 'I was in my sixties then and had been thinking of retirement, but the idea of starting a fresh enterprise gave me a new lease of life. The first of the LEs, the Lassiter Experimental Number One, was flying by 1910. It was the war that really set us on our feet, of course. That's when we dropped the boat part of the business. We still use the boat yard, but nowadays it's to build floats for seaplanes. Nigel's keeping them all busy at the moment.'

They heard a shrill whistle from the factory and the noise of machinery was abruptly cut off. A swell of purely human sound filled its place. Mr Lassiter, who had evidently been finding the stairs difficult, stopped, took out his pocket watch and nodded. 'Three o'clock. Tea break.'

'Are you all right, sir?' asked George.

The old man smiled deprecatingly. 'I had a bad cold a few weeks ago and it's left me a bit chesty. It's at times like this I realize that I'm not as young as I was. I just need to wait here for a couple of minutes. I'd like a cup of tea, I must say.' He held on to the balustrade with one hand and leaned on his stick with the other. The window on the stairs looked out across the yards and the new steel-built hangar. Mr Lassiter shook his head. 'There it is. It's a vast thing for a vast aircraft. I sometimes wonder if Nigel's taken on more than he can cope with.' He sighed, gathered his strength, then straightened his shoulders. 'Let's get on.'

They climbed the remainder of the stairs and came to a door marked *Mr Nigel Lassiter*. Maguire knocked and, in response to a shout from Nigel, opened the door.

'There you are,' said Nigel Lassiter. He smiled, the smile lighting up his rather sulky face. He seemed happy and relaxed and a very different character from the furious man Jack had encountered on Saturday. He crushed out a cigarette, got to his feet and came out from behind the desk. 'I've been expecting you. Let's go to the hangar. Wait till you see the Pegasus, Roger. You'll appreciate the progress I've made.'

'I wouldn't mind sitting down for a while,' said his father. 'Could we have some tea, Nigel?'

'Tea?' Nigel looked blank. 'I suppose so. Yes, of course, if you must. I never bother as a rule.'

'I was impressed by the Urbis,' said Dr Maguire.

Nigel grinned. 'The Pegasus makes the Urbis look like a paper aeroplane. If only Mrs Culverton will see sense, it'll revolutionize flying.'

It was the mention of Mrs Culverton which had brought it to mind, but Jack couldn't help comparing the grandeur Culverton had surrounded himself with to the very workman-like setting Nigel Lassiter preferred. A desk with neatly stacked papers stood in the middle of the room and pinned to the wall were draughtsman's drawings of various sections of an aircraft. Another door led out of the room, presumably to the clerk's office. A drawing board, with a detail of the inside of a wing fastened to it, stood where it received the natural light from the window. The window itself looked out on to a wide reach of the Thames. The only concession to comfort were the yellow-and-black cushions which softened the angular chairs.

Mr Lassiter sank gratefully on to a seat. 'Can you arrange for some tea, Nigel?'

'Just as you like,' said Nigel. 'I'll tell my clerk.' He rang the bell on his desk.

The door from the next room opened and Jack glanced up, raising his eyebrows in involuntary appreciation at the girl who stood in the entrance. For some reason he had expected her to be very ordinary. It was probably the word 'clerk' that had done it, but he had imagined a dowdily dressed female with scraped-back hair and spectacles on a chain. This girl wasn't dowdy and she certainly wasn't in the least ordinary. She was fair-haired and blue-eyed with a timid, hesitant charm, the sort of charm that would make most men want to open doors, help her on with her coat, carry her shopping and generally – he could almost hear his cousin Isabelle saying it – behave like absolute idiots in her presence.

She walked to Nigel's desk. 'You rang, Mr Lassiter?'

As she spoke, Jack saw her face alter, and she stared in bewilderment at George. For George gave a choking gasp, stepped forward and, before anyone could save him, crumpled to the floor.

Chapter Eight

Jack reached George first. Kneeling down, he put a hand on his friend's shoulder and turned him over. To his relief, George's eyes flickered open.

'Let me see him,' said a calm voice beside him. Anne Lassiter, kneeling on the floor, undid George's tie and collar and, taking his hand, felt for his pulse. 'Be still,' she warned, as George tried to move. 'Roger,' she added, without turning her head, 'get a glass of water, will you, please?'

'I'm sorry,' began George in a weak voice but Anne stopped him.

'Just lie there for a few moments. You've fainted and need time to recover.'

'What the devil's wrong?' asked Nigel. 'What on earth came over him?'

'I don't know,' said Maguire, stooping down. 'He's been ill, though, hasn't he?'

George tried to speak but Anne stopped him once more. 'Keep quiet.' She looked at Maguire. 'Roger, we need that water.'

'A tot of brandy might be better,' said Maguire. 'Nigel, have you got any?'

'Brandy?' repeated Nigel. 'Of course I haven't got any brandy.'

Anne sighed impatiently. 'Roger, can you help?'

'Nigel,' demanded Maguire, 'is there any brandy in the factory?'

Nigel shrugged. 'How the devil do I know?'

Maguire sighed, controlling his irritation. 'Look, old man, don't you have anything to drink? Perhaps in one of the other rooms?' He took Nigel by the elbow. 'Can we at least go and see? The poor devil needs something to bring him round.'

'There might be something in the meeting room,' said the clerk. She glanced at Nigel. 'I don't know if I'll be able to take it without permission. Perhaps . . .' She hesitated before making the suggestion. 'Perhaps it would be better if you came with me, Mr Lassiter.' She cast wide appealing eyes at her employer.

'Come on, Nigel,' said Maguire. 'Let's go and find it.'

They left the room. After a couple of minutes George took a ragged breath. 'Can I sit up now?'

'Carefully does it,' warned Anne. With Anne's help, Jack got George to his feet and sat him down in a chair.

'Are you all right, my boy?' asked old Mr Lassiter anxiously. 'You look washed out. I'm sorry if the trip's been too much for you. I should have postponed it.'

'It isn't that,' said George. 'I'll be fine, sir. I will, really.' He put a shaky hand to his forehead and breathed deeply. 'I'm awfully sorry,' he said after a while. 'I couldn't help it.' He looked at Anne. 'Who is she? That girl, I mean? The one who was here just now.'

Anne looked puzzled. 'Nigel's clerk? That's Miss Aldryn. Stella Aldryn.'

George shuddered, looking at Jack helplessly. 'I don't know if you're going to believe this. She's the girl I saw in the kitchen.'

'*What?*' Jack stared at him in disbelief. 'She can't be, George. You said the girl in the kitchen was dead.'

'I thought she was. She was dead, God help me. I know she was dead. She was dead in the kitchen.'

Anne exchanged worried looks with old Mr Lassiter and Jack. 'Perhaps we'd better ask Roger about it,' she suggested tentatively. 'He is a doctor, after all.'

George gave a humourless laugh. 'A loony-doctor. You

130

think I'm crazy, don't you?' He buried his head in his hands. 'Maybe I am.'

It was nearly ten minutes later before Nigel Lassiter returned, together with Dr Maguire and Miss Aldryn. David Lassiter, holding a bottle of brandy and a soda siphon, brought up the rear. He had come across the others on the way to the meeting room and wanted to see how George was.

Jack, for one, was glad when they arrived. It had been an awkward few minutes. Mr Lassiter was anxious about George and tried to fuss, which didn't improve George's temper. Anne, although clearly worried about George, had irritated him by repeating her suggestion he consult Maguire, and Jack, although he didn't fuss and thought Anne's idea was remarkably tactless, was, in addition to being concerned, badly puzzled. George was making such a good recovery that his relapse seemed inexplicable.

'What happened?' asked David, pouring brandy into a glass and filling it up with soda water. 'I know you've been ill. Did you have a bad turn?' He put the glass into George's hand. 'Drink this, old man, and get some colour in your cheeks. You look done in.'

George took a gulp of brandy. 'No, it isn't that.' He took a deep breath, looked past David to Stella Aldryn, shuddered, and tried to speak. 'It's no use.' His voice trailed off miserably. 'I feel such a fool.'

'Can I tell them, George?' said Anne. George nodded. She put her shoulders back and spoke in a no-nonsense voice. 'George was the man in the kitchen.'

'What d'you mean, the man in the kitchen?' asked David. 'What kitchen?'

'The kitchen at home.' Anne's hand tightened comfortingly on George's arm. 'You remember a man got into the kitchen and the police took him to hospital? Well, poor George is the man.'

David Lassiter gazed at her. 'What? *George* was the man who broke in? Why didn't you tell us?'

131

Mr Lassiter coughed. 'We thought it as well not to mention it.'

'They were being tactful,' put in George with a whey-faced smile.

Maguire looked at George with a puzzled frown. 'I don't quite understand. Anne told me about the man in the kitchen, of course, but why did you faint?'

Seeing that George couldn't bring himself to answer, Jack took up the story. 'George was very ill that night. He was coming down with malaria and flu. He got into the kitchen at Eden Street and saw what he thought was a girl, a dead girl. That's why he made a run for it.'

Stella Aldryn still looked puzzled. 'Excuse me, but I don't see –'

'You're the girl,' said George, desperately. 'You're the dead girl I saw.'

Stella Aldryn drew back, her eyes wide. '*Me*? But it can't have been. I'm not dead.'

'No,' agreed George. 'Of course you're not. I'm sorry. I've mixed you up with some sort of nightmare and I can only say I'm sorry. I've made a complete fool of myself and put you all to no end of trouble.' He made as if to stand up but Anne restrained him. 'I feel an absolute idiot,' he added.

Maguire sat down and looked at him thoughtfully. His voice took on the professional sympathy of the psychiatrist. 'I'd like to know what you did see, Mr Lassiter. You say you were suffering from malaria and flu? Perhaps you wouldn't mind just going through the story.' He held up a hand as Nigel tried to interrupt. 'Let me hear this, Nigel. This is my province. I might be able to help.'

'It was all so *real*,' said George helplessly. 'I was completely desperate. I got into the kitchen because it seemed warm and I found something to eat and drink and I fell asleep. Then, when I woke up –' He broke off. 'It's no use. I dreamt it. I must have dreamt it but I thought I saw you, Miss Aldryn. The only thing is, you were dead.'

She gazed at him, frozen into speechlessness. Then she

132

shook herself and gave a puzzled laugh. 'But I'm not dead. You can't have seen me.'

George looked at her miserably. 'I know that.'

Maguire cleared his throat. 'What were you doing before you went into the kitchen at Eden Street, Mr Lassiter?'

George shrugged. 'Nothing much. I hung around various railway stations and so on, then I went into the park for a time.'

Maguire nodded. 'I think you must have seen Miss Aldryn earlier in the day.' He glanced at Stella Aldryn. 'I don't know if you recognize Mr Lassiter at all?'

She shook her head. 'I've never seen Mr Lassiter in my life.'

Maguire clicked his tongue. 'I think he probably saw you.' He turned back to George. 'When your illness started to take hold, you mixed up the reality of what you'd seen earlier with your dream.'

'I must be going crazy,' George stated flatly.

Maguire looked shocked. 'Of course you're not. If you were suffering from malaria and flu, then it's only natural that you should be confused. That's a very different state of affairs from being crazy, as you put it.'

George sat silently for a few moments. 'Thanks,' he said quietly.

'However,' continued Maguire, 'it might be as well if you consulted me professionally. There could be some underlying tendency –'

'I'm fine,' said George sharply. 'Thanks, but I don't need any help.'

Jack put his hand on his friend's shoulder. 'Shall we go home?'

George nodded. 'Yes, I'd like that.' He broke off, turning to his grandfather. 'I'm sorry, sir. I'll wait for you, of course. You wanted to see the aeroplane.'

Mr Lassiter got to his feet. 'I can see the Pegasus any time. I'm rather more concerned about you.'

Maguire reached out for Anne's hand and held it reassuringly. 'Why don't you go back with the others?' He glanced at George. 'It might be as well if you were there. I'd like to stay and see the plane but I think it's probably just as well if you're with them.'

David Lassiter showed them down the stairs to the car. He clapped a friendly hand on George's shoulder. 'You get better. I don't want any more shocks like that.'

'Neither do I,' agreed George fervently. He got into the car, leaned back against the seat and heaved a sigh as Marsh, the chauffeur, started the engine. 'Look, can I apologize?' he said as the car pulled out of the factory gates. 'I was really looking forward to this afternoon. I know you were as well, Jack, and now I've spoilt it.'

'Forget it,' said Jack. 'You didn't want to keel over.'

'No,' said George. 'No, I certainly didn't. It knocked the stuffing out of me.' He gave a small smile. 'Poor Miss Aldryn. She must think I'm nuts.' His expression softened. 'I hope I didn't scare her, talking nonsense about her being dead, poor girl.'

'She'll get over it,' said Anne robustly. Just for once, Anne's sturdy common sense seemed to make little appeal to George.

Mr Lassiter, on the other hand, approved. 'Exactly, Anne.'

He was about to say more but George spoke first. 'Has she worked for the company long?'

Anne gave him a quick look. 'She's been there for about a year and a half or so. Why?'

'I just wondered,' said George, colouring. 'No reason, really. I thought she seemed rather nice, that's all. Pleasant, you know?'

Mr Lassiter sniffed in disapproval. 'She may be pleasant but it's a pity she's not a better clerk. Her time-keeping is appalling.'

'Well, if Miss Aldryn's been there for over a year she can't be that bad, surely?' said George. 'If Nigel's happy, that's all that matters. Unless . . .'

He stopped, his face lengthening. Jack knew what was on his mind as clearly as if he'd bellowed it at the top of

134

his voice. There were other reasons for middle-aged men to be indulgent over the foibles of their attractive young female clerks, quite apart from their ability with typing and filing, and George had obviously just thought of them.

Anne shrugged. 'Nigel wouldn't notice if she was there or not half the time.' George, observed Jack, looked remarkably pleased by this piece of information. 'What he really wants is to be left alone. He's happier when she's not there.'

'Then Nigel should be a very happy man,' said Mr Lassiter drily. 'Anne, leaving aside Miss Aldryn for the moment, do you think we should consider changing the lock on the kitchen door? I said as much at the time but the matter slipped my mind. I know you didn't mean any harm, George, but I wouldn't like to think anyone could stroll in and out of the house as they pleased.'

'They can't, Grandfather,' said Anne. 'You needn't worry. That evening was very much the exception. On any other evening at least one of the servants would have been in the kitchen.'

Jack looked at her with interest. 'So it wasn't usual for them all to go out together?'

'Of course not,' said Anne. 'That would be very inconvenient, as you can imagine. No, it was all because of Mrs Nelson's nephew. She's our cook,' she added, smiling at Jack's expression. 'She has a nephew on the stage. He was appearing in London for the first time and she was terribly excited about it. She asked me ages before if she, Elsie and Pat could have the evening off to go and see him. Mrs Nelson was talking about it for weeks beforehand. She still is.'

'But they aren't your only servants, are they?' asked Jack.

'No. There's Marsh,' she said with a nod in the direction of the chauffeur. 'He sleeps over the garage, though. There's a gardener and his boy, too, but they don't live in. And there's Corby, of course.'

'Did Corby go to the theatre as well?'

135

Anne grinned. 'I don't think it would suit Corby's dignity to go out with the cook. No, he was in bed with a bad cold. It was a real snorter. He was laid up for a few days.'

'He gave it to me,' said Mr Lassiter with feeling. 'My chest hasn't been the same since. I remember that evening. I'd been feeling off-colour anyway and the worry about what I thought was an attempt at burglary made it worse.'

'I am sorry,' said George. 'When I think about that evening I feel rotten. I hate having caused such a scene.'

'Well, in the end it all worked out for the best,' said his grandfather. 'I had to have the doctor and he said your adventure probably saved me from a serious illness. We should have gone to Norfolk for the weekend, shooting with some old friends of mine, the Leightons. The doctor said that if I'd done any such thing, with my chest the way it was, I'd have been courting pneumonia.' He looked at Anne. 'We must arrange another weekend with the Leightons, my dear. They wanted to meet Maguire and, as Nigel agreed to come with us once, maybe he will again. He could do with a rest. He works far too hard.'

'I don't think Nigel will leave London until the Pegasus is well and truly launched, Grandfather,' said Anne. 'Even then, there's a great deal to do.'

'No,' agreed Mr Lassiter reluctantly. He sighed uneasily. 'If only Culverton was alive it would all be so very much easier. It's a pity he wasn't spared to us. A very great pity. Sometimes I don't know if we can go on without him.'

The following evening, Jack, resplendent in full evening dress, knocked at the door of Bill Rackham's rooms.

Rackham opened the door. 'Hello,' he said in surprise. 'I wasn't expecting you. Come on in. Can I get you a drink?'

Jack followed Rackham into the sitting room. 'Thanks. I'll have a gin and lime, if you've got it. I was on my way to see a bit of night-life,' he added, taking off his coat. He sat on the arm of a chair. 'I wondered if you fancied ankling along with me. It isn't mere pleasure-seeking. I was hoping to pick up some trace of Culverton's dodgy club.'

Rackham, bottle in hand, turned. 'Not really. I'm fairly tired and was looking forward to an evening in. Besides that, we've got some men trying to track it down.' He stopped, staring at his friend. 'Jack, stand up.' Jack did so. 'Come into the light for a moment.' Jack obligingly stepped forward. 'What,' asked Rackham in awe-struck tones, 'are you wearing, for heaven's sake?'

Jack, grinning broadly, tweaked his tie, picked up his top hat from the table, gave the nap a brush with the sleeve of his coat and twirled the hat on his stick. 'You've noticed?'

'*Noticed?*' Rackham looked Jack up and down, taking in the gleaming, slicked-down hair, the sparkling diamond shirt-studs and the white tie edged in silver.

'Well?' demanded Jack. 'How do I look? The studs are paste, by the way.'

'You look like a damn dago,' said Rackham bluntly. 'The sort that gives dagos a bad name.'

Jack laughed. 'Exactly. I am Señor 'Aldeanez, ze 'unter of ze clobs.' His dark face grew harsh. 'I am an Argentine. I am on the prowl, *si usted entiende?*'

'Just say that again slowly, Jack. You can't expect a Northern boy like me to understand foreign lingo.'

'I'm an Argentine on the prowl, if you understand.'

'Oh, I understand, all right.' He came closer and peered into Jack's face. 'Good God, you're wearing *make-up!*'

'Theatrical make-up. Just a touch round my eyes.' Rackham breathed in heavy disapproval. 'Nobody will be able to tell it's false in a nightclub. The lights aren't strong enough. I needed to look a trifle more dissipated than nature intended. D'you know, if I'd been a major in the Romanian army it'd be expected of me to wear make-up? They had to forbid the use of it to junior officers.'

'Foreigners,' grunted Rackham. 'What do you expect? If it cheers you up, I think you look perfectly awful and I imagine most men would want to kick you. God knows what most women would want to do.'

'Well, that's the point, isn't it, old scream,' said Jack, sitting back down in the chair. 'I went out last night as my usual suave self and the answer was a lemon. I thought if I was hunting for a den of secret vice I'd better look as if I was in the market for some. Vice, I mean.'

'Our chaps haven't turned anything up yet either,' said Rackham, putting Jack's drink on the table. He sat down, took another look at Jack and shuddered. 'What did your pal Lassiter have to say about the fancy dress?'

'He went out before I appeared in all my glory.' Jack drank his gin reflectively. 'It's probably just as well. I didn't want to explain what I was up to. No,' he added, swirling the liquid round in the glass. 'George has got a date.'

'Has he, by jingo.'

'Yes. He got a letter by this morning's post from the lady in question, a letter written, I may say, on lilac-coloured scented notepaper, enquiring after his health and well-being and asking if he could telephone as she was worried about him. He was on the telephone quicker than lightning and that resulted in supper and a show. He's been like a dog with two tails all day, bombarding me with questions as to what he should do and where they should go. He's settled on *Hurry Along!* followed by that little restaurant off Montague Place.'

'I've seen *Hurry Along!*,' said Rackham with interest. 'I enjoyed it. Er . . . who's the girl and why's she so worried about him?'

'A Miss Aldryn. Stella Aldryn. She's Nigel Lassiter's clerk. George met her yesterday, when we visited the factory. She worried about him because she gave him the dickens of a shock.' He related George's encounter with Stella Aldryn.

Rackham stared at him. 'He can't be serious, Jack. He dreamt it. There wasn't a girl in the kitchen. We know that.'

'Well, yes, we do,' agreed Jack. 'Funnily enough, George thinks so too.'

'So what does the girl say about it?'

138

'She's completely baffled. When Dr Maguire explained things she was no end relieved and, really, it's the only explanation I can think of which holds water.'

'It more or less has to be, doesn't it? That's if your pal isn't simply making it all up.'

'He gave himself a pretty nasty scare if he is.'

Rackham frowned. 'I don't like it, Jack. It all sounds very odd to me. What's the girl like?'

'A stunner,' said Jack positively. 'Really something. George was pleased as punch when he got the letter. She's a shy sort of girl, a bit of a shrinking violet. It's obvious he thinks she's the bee's knees and he'd convinced himself that he'd frightened her rigid, talking about this nightmare or whatever it was he had.'

Rackham shook his head. 'Well, it sounds a little out of the ordinary, I must say. Is he all right? After his relapse, I mean?'

'Physically he's fine,' said Jack. 'He was a bit shaken up yesterday, as you'd expect, but he had an early night and was okay this morning. He's as puzzled as we are about what happened, though, and there's a definite atmosphere between him and Mrs Lassiter as a result.'

'Anne Lassiter?' asked Rackham. 'Why's she upset?'

'She rang him last night. She wants George to see the boyfriend, Maguire, to have his bumps properly felt. George dug his heels in and said there was nothing to see Maguire about, that Maguire had given him his opinion at the time and, as far as he was concerned, that was that. What's more, he couldn't afford the fancy fees that a Harley Street loony-doctor would stick him for. Anne said he was just being stubborn and that Maguire had offered to see him free of charge, and so George got het up about the idea of accepting charity and all in all it was a bit of a relief when Miss Aldryn's letter arrived. It stopped him brooding, even if I have had to listen to him on the subject of Stella Aldryn for most of the day. Mind you, she's quite something. She's the kind of girl that makes you want to leap up and open doors for her. Sort of asks to be looked after, you know? She's got lovely smudgy blue eyes with a kind of My Hero expression in them.'

'That's the second time you've raved about her,' said Rackham with a grin. 'I thought it was Lassiter she made the impression on. It sounds as if he might have some competition.'

Jack laughed and shook his head. 'No takers. I could see why she got to George, but she's a bit round-eyed and wondering for me.'

'What in Manchester we'd call a bit gormless?'

'Not gormless, exactly,' said Jack, 'but I'd think you'd run out of conversation pretty quickly. She might have hidden depths. I don't know. Anyway,' he added, 'despite Dr Maguire's explanation, the whole business puzzles me. To be honest, that's my real reason for calling in. I wanted to talk it over with you.'

'Why? Dr Maguire's explanation seems likely, wouldn't you say?'

Jack scratched his chin. 'Yes,' he admitted. 'When George asked me if I believed it, I said it sounded plausible and it does, Bill, there's no doubt about it. But talking about that night in the kitchen to Anne and old Mr Lassiter threw up some odd details. For a start, on that evening and that evening alone, the servants were out and the kitchen was empty. The cook had taken everyone to see her nephew on the stage and Corby, the butler, was confined to bed with a bad cold. Just assume for the moment George saw what he said he did.'

Rackham shifted uneasily in his chair. 'He can't have done.'

'I don't think he could have done either,' said Jack. 'But don't you see? If Maguire's explanation is correct, then George's girl could be anyone, a passing stranger in a railway station or on the street. However, not only does the girl turn out to be real, she's connected with Lassiter's. And that, when you think about it, is weird.'

Rackham sipped his whisky. 'Yes,' he said reflectively.

'It *is* weird.' He looked at Jack. 'Couldn't it be a fantastic coincidence?'

'Of course it could,' agreed Jack, 'but I don't like it, Bill. Look, George said the house seemed creepily familiar. That was partly why he was attracted to it in the first place. He was getting himself all worked up about ghosts and so on, but his creepy feeling had a perfectly natural explanation. I was just wondering if this girl, Stella Aldryn's, appearance in George's nightmare had a rational explanation too.'

'Like what?' asked Rackham, offering Jack his cigarette case.

Jack took a cigarette, frowning. 'I'm damned if I can think of one. The point of George's story was that the girl died – and she hasn't done.'

Rackham shook his head. 'I'd think a lot more of Lassiter's story if Constable Thirsk and Mrs Lassiter had found Stella Aldryn either alive or, as he insisted, dead. We know he was ill, really ill, and the hospital told us he was half-starved.' He lit his cigarette. 'He must have imagined it, Jack. What are those things blokes see in the desert?'

'Camels?' asked Jack, his eyes crinkling.

Rackham laughed. 'Not camels, idiot. Mirages, that's it. Well, they're not real but people see them, don't they?'

'Actually,' said Jack, entranced by this new departure, 'mirages are real. It's to do with the atmospheric conditions. The image is projected from the actual place by a trick of the light so you see it where it isn't, if you see what I mean.'

Rackham laughed once more. 'Call it a projected image if it makes you feel any happier. I still think he imagined it. Incidentally, you know I appealed for any taxi driver who'd driven Culverton on the 31st? A Mr Albert Kyle came into the Yard. He picked up Culverton in Cooper Street just after six thirty and got to the Mulciber about quarter to seven. There's a rank not far from Culverton Air Navigation and he'd driven Culverton before. No other driver's come forward but I'm still hoping.'

141

'I don't suppose you checked up on Dr Maguire's alibi, did you?' asked Jack. 'I haven't got any earthly reason to suspect him but I'm thinking of the look of limpid sincerity he gave you when he said he'd been in the Continental.'

'Unfortunately, he was telling the exact truth. Irritating, isn't it? I thought there was something not quite right about that part of his story as well, but the cloakroom attendant knows Dr Maguire and remembers him coming in that evening.'

'How can he be so sure?' asked Jack. 'After all, it's some time ago now.'

'The cloakroom bloke took Maguire's wet coat and umbrella – it was raining – and made some reference to the fact that it was the last day of October and it had been a chilly autumn. Anyway, he referred me to a crowd of Maguire's particular cronies and he'd been there, sure enough.'

'I suppose he could have sneaked out,' said Jack. 'He very well might have done, in fact, and gone on somewhere he doesn't want us to know about.' He frowned. 'Even if he did, so what? I can't see he's got the slightest motive to bump off Culverton. He's fairly close to Nigel Lassiter and he must know the situation the company's in.'

'And what situation's that?'

Jack leaned forward. 'They're up against it, Bill. They really needed Culverton. I spoke to Joe Hawley on Saturday. He works for *Aviation Monthly* and he said that Lassiter's are very nearly next door to Queer Street. If Nigel's plane isn't ready soon, they've had it. It should have been ready weeks ago but the flying trials are supposed to have gone badly and the press presentation, which they're pinning a lot of hope on, might have to be called off. The maiden flight should have been at the presentation but it's had to be put off until Friday the 30th, if it comes off at all. They're planning a dinner on board the aircraft to mark the occasion. Joe thinks it could be all right, but with Culverton dead, there's been an unholy spanner thrown in the works. Lassiter's might do it but it'll be a close-run thing. It's an open secret how close to the edge they've been sailing and they'll find it difficult to raise the money. Apparently all the usual investment bankers are very leery of them. Joe thinks that David Lassiter should consider cutting loose, ditching the seaplane and concentrating on the Urbis and the LE series.'

Rackham looked at his friend thoughtfully. 'Are you sure that's not just journalists' chit-chat?'

'Joe's pretty reliable. Besides that, although he didn't spell it out quite so starkly, it's what old Mr Lassiter thinks too. He's very worried indeed now Culverton's gone. He said as much.'

Rackham's brow wrinkled. 'That seems like an odd conversation to have. After all, he's only met you a couple of times. I'm not surprised the company's in trouble if Mr Lassiter's spilling the beans to everyone about how hard pressed they are.'

'He wasn't really talking to me. I just happened to be there.' Jack drained his glass and stood up. 'Anyway, I didn't get dressed up like this for nothing. I'd better get a move on if I'm to seek out the raptures and roses of vice, as I've heard it expressed.'

'Just as long as you don't seek out a knife in the ribs,' said Rackham. 'The Lassiters might have needed Culverton but he worried someone, Jack. Don't you do the same.'

Jack leaned over the Embankment, watching the Thames lap against the green-slimed stone of the walls. It was now Saturday morning and, he thought moodily, he was still no further forward than he had been at the beginning of the week. There was one thing: Bill needn't have worried about his safety. Despite spending the past three evenings as a true child of the Jazz Age, Jack had uncovered nothing of the slightest interest to Scotland Yard. He was feeling distinctly chewed up, a fairly predictable result, he told himself, with a rueful smile, of a series of late nights, smoky clubs, loud music and bad champagne. However, there hadn't been even the slightest hint of the raptures or, worse luck, the merest whiff of the roses of vice.

There were, if he cared to pursue them, opportunities – his smile broadened at the thought of one particular opportunity who assured him she *loved* Argentines and *adored* the way he spoke – but they were all very private enterprises and he was looking for something a great deal more organized.

This chasing round in and out of nightclubs was crazy. Rather than trying to match the club to Culverton, it was surely far better to match Culverton to the club. But what clubs had the blasted man been in? He didn't, according to Mrs Culverton, particularly care for clubs as such, preferring dining rather than dancing. Gilchrist Lloyd had provided the police with a list of Culverton's favourite restaurants, but they all seemed to be wearisomely respectable.

He was going to another respectable restaurant for lunch, the Continental, on Tilford Lane off Northumberland Avenue. George had been there on Thursday evening with Stella Aldryn and run into Roger Maguire. As Maguire said, it was one of his favourite haunts. The encounter had resulted in Maguire inviting not only George and Stella but Jack as well, to lunch on Saturday. George, once reassured that Maguire didn't intend to bring up the idea of offering his professional services once more, had warmed to him. For one thing, Maguire was very pleasant to Stella and sympathetic about the trials she endured in working for Nigel Lassiter and, for another, Maguire said that Anne would like it.

George was feeling guilty about Anne and the brusque way in which he'd spoken to her on the telephone. He had made amends, so he believed, at Michael Walsh's funeral, but hoped lunch would smooth down any remaining ruffled feathers. They were meeting at one o'clock. Jack looked at his watch with a start. Crikey, he'd better get a move on. Plunging into the traffic, he threaded his way across the road, up Savoy Place and fetched up at Chandos Row at twenty-five to the hour.

'I know, I know,' he said to the waiting George as he walked into the sitting room. 'I'll be ready in two ticks.' George's face showed just how impatient he was. Not only that, but Boots, the kitchen cat, was wrapping herself in and out of George's legs – Boots adored George – and was being completely ignored.

'Come on,' said George, glancing at the clock. 'I don't want to be late.'

'Relax,' said Jack, taking off his coat. 'I'll be with you in a jiffy. I'll just have a quick wash and brush-up.'

He glanced at the table on the way to his bedroom. There was a tray with two coffee cups, a milk jug and a sugar bowl. 'You'd better move either the cat or the milk,' he called over his shoulder. 'We can't leave them in the same room.'

'There's an easy answer to that,' said George, pouring out the last of milk into a saucer for the expectant Boots.

'Who was your visitor?' asked Jack, coming out of his room after a hasty wash, towel in hand.

George looked at him blankly. 'I didn't have a visitor.'

Jack frowned at him. 'You must have done.' He walked to the table and picked a cup up from the tray. There were the remains of sugar visible at the bottom and a trace of what looked like lipstick on the rim of the cup. George never had sugar in either tea or coffee and he certainly didn't wear lipstick. Jack wiped his finger over the stain and rubbed his finger and thumb together. It was a dark-ish rich red, rather like a morello cherry in colour. A very faint perfume seemed to cling to the cup. 'It's all right, you know,' he said, puzzled. 'I don't mind you having people round, George.'

George looked equally puzzled. 'But no one's been here.'

Jack held out the cup. 'There's sugar in the bottom of this cup and lipstick on the rim.'

'Lipstick?' repeated George in surprise. He took the cup

and looked at it by the light from the window. 'What are you talking about? I can't see any lipstick.'

'I wiped it off. It's on my fingers,' said Jack with growing impatience.

George shrugged and handed the cup back. 'It must be something else. There certainly haven't been any girls up here, if that's what you mean.' He gazed at Jack, drawing himself up in reaction to his puzzled hostility. 'I'm telling you the truth. No one's been here all morning. I don't know about lipstick but you know I never have sugar. You must have had it. I certainly didn't.' Jack didn't reply. 'Look,' added George. 'We had breakfast, then you went out. You must have had a coffee before you left. All I've done this morning is walk to the newsagent's for the paper. No one's called, Jack. I'd tell you if they had.' He glanced at the clock again. 'Come on, we've got to go.'

Jack let his breath out in a long whistle, shrugged and put down the cup. He wasn't mistaken about the lipstick. Yes, he'd had coffee at breakfast but not only had that cup been collected with the rest of the breakfast things by Mrs Pettycure, but, like George, he never had sugar in either tea or coffee. Someone – presumably a woman – had called and that someone had stayed long enough to drink a cup of coffee. Why on earth should George deny it?

Anne Lassiter, Roger Maguire and Stella Aldryn were waiting for them in the entrance hall of the Continental. 'I'm sorry we're late,' said Jack, handing his coat to the cloakroom attendant.

'Not at all,' replied Anne politely, immediately undermining her words by glancing at her watch. 'Shall we go in? Roger's booked the table.'

A waiter showed them to their table and handed out the menus. Jack looked round with interest. The place was larger than he had thought, with a separate bar and a dance floor beside which a five-piece band was playing 'I Love My Chili Bom Bom' with a good deal of zip. The outside was ordinary enough, the ground floor of a four-storey brick building, but the inside was colourful with brightly painted and very well-executed murals.

'They specialize in European food,' said Maguire, looking at the menu. 'That's one of the reasons I like it here. It's virtually all good, but there's a Spanish dish with rice and prawns I particularly like.'

Jack looked at him in surprise. 'Paella? I've never come across that outside Spain.'

'I like that Italian one,' said Anne Lassiter. 'Escalope something or other.'

George studied the menu dubiously. 'I hope there's not too much garlic. I can't stand the stuff.'

'You can hardly avoid it in a place like this,' retorted Jack shortly. That coffee cup still rankled and puzzled him in equal measure. He leaned back in his chair, looking at his surroundings.

The club was split up into separate areas and each area had a European scene painted directly on to the white plaster walls. The Continental. They were sitting under the leaning tower of Pisa. Spain was represented by a bullfight and a fairy-tale castle stood high above the Rhine.

'What shall we have to drink?' asked Maguire. 'There's Chianti, if you want to try an Italian wine – that's red – or there's hock, of course, and there's always champagne.'

The Colosseum stood for Rome and Mont Blanc for Switzerland. Gondoliers plied the waterways of Venice and the Brandenburg Gate indicated Berlin. Berlin, eh? Ah well, the war had been over for ages . . .

'So we'll have a bottle of hock and a bottle of Chianti,' said Maguire. 'Is that all right with you, Major?'

The little mermaid of Copenhagen, an Alpine pasture in springtime, a Dutch windmill and polder and the Parthenon. 'Yes, that's fine,' agreed Jack, his mind roaming across Europe. Why did a bullfight stand for the whole of Spain? You could have the Alhambra, Madrid, Barcelona, Toledo . . . He looked at the menu and concentrated on food. 'I'll have the paella.'

Stella Aldryn pursed her lips. 'I think I'll be adventurous and try it too.' She inserted a cigarette into a holder that seemed to be about a foot long and leaned across the table for him to light it. 'Mr Haldean, I must tell you how much I enjoy your stories. When George told me who his friend was I was really excited.'

'That's very kind of you,' said Jack with a grin. 'I hope you don't feel let down now you've met me in the flesh, so to speak.'

Her eyes widened. 'Oh *no*, Mr Haldean. You're famous. George told me. He said you'd been in the newspapers.' She heaved a sigh. 'I've always wanted to write but I've never had the time to sit down and do it.'

'D'you think it would be better than working?' asked Jack wickedly. He had come across this curious idea before, that all anyone needed to write successful fiction was a chair and time.

'Well, it must be more fun than working,' she began then stopped awkwardly. 'That is . . . I suppose for you it *is* work, in a sort of way.'

'To be honest, it is more fun than working,' replied Jack, throwing her a lifeline. 'I know, because I work as well. I've got a job on a magazine.'

'Oh, have you?' she said with less enthusiasm and rather more respect. 'That must be *so* interesting.' She plunged into a series of questions.

Jack answered her readily enough – *Do you really make up all those stories? How long does it take you to write one? Where do you get all those clever ideas from?* – but he was actually thinking about Stella Aldryn. She really was a corker, with that classic English rose peaches-and-cream complexion and a heart-shaped face. The only thing which made him wary was the occasional hard glint in those lovely eyes as she glanced at George. There was a calculation there that sat oddly with her open innocence. A gold-digger? In that case he'd have expected her to make a play for Nigel Lassiter.

He glanced at George. George wasn't rich exactly, but the

boss's grandson wasn't a bad bet and was probably a damn sight easier material to work on than the boss's son. There was his legacy, too. Jack was willing to bet George had told her about that and, however remote it now seemed, it wouldn't diminish his charms.

His discussion of the literary life came to a welcome end and he sat back, watching her as she chatted animatedly to George. He looked round the room once more. There was a little niggle of dissatisfaction at the back of his mind. Something wasn't quite right and he couldn't work out what it was. He dismissed his train of thought and paid attention to Anne, who was, he had to admit, rather more interesting.

She was talking about the Pegasus. Nigel had confounded Joe Hawley and the rest of the aviation press by announcing that he was going ahead not only with the press presentation on Tuesday, the day he'd originally announced, but with the airborne dinner in the Pegasus, too. That was to take place on Friday the following week and would mark the official maiden flight of the aeroplane.

Nigel, according to Anne, wanted to give the impression that everything was proceeding as planned. So it was, on the surface, but production on the Urbis and LE series had stopped while all the workforce was drafted in for a supreme effort. Nigel himself hadn't been home for the last few nights. Stella Aldryn pitched in with a couple of anecdotes illustrating Nigel's dedication and Maguire topped it off with a wry recital of his own experience of Nigel's complete absorption in his work and indifference to everyday affairs.

It was all very friendly and the food was excellent, but Jack was unsettled. George was simply being George, as open, good-humoured and seemingly honest as ever, and he couldn't understand why he'd denied having a visitor.

'Would you care to dance?' Maguire said politely to Stella once the meal was over. George escorted Anne on to the floor and Jack was left momentarily to his own devices. The dance hostess, who was employed for just such occasions, saw he was alone and stopped by the table. She might have been an attractive girl, if her face hadn't been hidden under a fashionable mask of dead-white make-up.

George, seeing him put a pound note on the table for the hostess, glowered disapprovingly from the dance floor as Jack stood up. The look annoyed him. What right had George to approve or disapprove? Mainly because he was irritated with George, Jack danced twice with the hostess, who called him *Dharling!* and whose name, she confided in a low, supposedly thrilling, husky whisper, was Isadora. He didn't want to be unfair to the girl but, in addition to leaving white make-up on the shoulder of his jacket, she did nothing to improve his temper.

'Dharling, what's wrong?' she murmured as they shimmied round the floor to the tune of 'Don't Keep Me Guessing, Baby'. 'Is it something I have done?'

Jack made an effort to kick his bad temper into touch. After all, it wasn't the girl's fault that George had been caught out in a silly lie. 'Look,' he said with a rather forced smile, 'd'you mind if we sit the rest of this dance out?' She nodded willingly and allowed herself to be steered to a table.

'I'm sorry,' he said, drawing out a chair for her. 'What with one thing and another I'm not really in the mood for dancing.' He leaned forward and lit the cigarette she was holding out to him. 'I've got a few things on my mind.' She attempted to look interested and he suddenly grinned. Professional dancers, like barbers, shop assistants and the priest in the confessional, had to at least pretend to be interested in their clientele; they didn't have any choice. The poor girl must be used to having blokes maunder on about Life and what was wrong with it.

'Such as?' she asked huskily.

Struck by a sudden thought he took out the photograph of Culverton he carried in his inside pocket. 'For one thing, this chap. I don't suppose you recognize him, do you?'

She took the little cardboard picture, turning it round to the light. He saw the way her fingers suddenly gripped down on her cigarette holder and heard the quick intake of breath. 'No. No, I don't,' she said quickly. The husky accent vanished leaving a sharp London twang behind.

Jack looked at her curiously. 'Are you sure?'

'Yeah, perfectly sure.' She put the photograph face down on the table and pushed it back to him. 'Look, I might have seen him, but I don't think I've ever seen him here. I can't remember everyone who's been, mind, but I don't think I've seen him.' She took her cigarette from its holder and crushed it out. 'Sorry. I can see somebody waiting. I'll have to go.'

With almost indecent haste she got up and hurried across the room towards the door marked *Staff* by the bar. Thoughtfully he got up and strolled back to his table, where the others were sitting. They had ordered coffee in his absence. If that girl didn't know something, he was a Dutchman.

'Are you okay?' asked George, as he sat down.

'Fine,' he said absently, his mind still on Isadora, forgetting for the moment that George had been the cause of his bad temper.

'Would you like some coffee?' asked Anne Lassiter, picking up the pot. 'I told the waiter to leave the tray. Do say yes. Roger never drinks coffee and always makes a fuss about ordering it, but I told him the rest of us wanted some, including you.'

'Too much coffee is the cause of a lot of over-excitement and nerve trouble,' said Maguire. 'I've explained that before, Anne.'

'Yes, but I still like it. Major Haldean?'

'I'd love some, thanks, if Dr Maguire thinks my nerves can stand it,' he said with a smile. 'Black, please, with no sugar.'

'Are you sweet enough?' put in Stella Aldryn with an arch little giggle.

Jack privately winced. Even if she was a corker, he didn't see how George could put up with this sort of thing. *'Ruddier than the cherry, sweeter than the berry,'* he quoted. 'I presume that's a coffee berry.' Stella Aldryn giggled again and put her cup down in the saucer. Jack idly watched her actions, then froze. Almost immediately he relaxed, anxious not to arouse anyone's attention. *Ruddier than the cherry* . . . A morello cherry. Surely that was a trace of dark red lipstick on the rim of her cup? 'Would you care to dance, Miss Aldryn?' he asked. He saw her glance at the cup in his hand and smiled. 'I wouldn't mind letting this cool down before I drink it.'

He escorted her on to the floor. As they started to dance, Jack felt a surge of triumph. Her perfume was unmistakable. *That* was the scent that had clung to the cup. 'I like these paintings,' he said, indicating the scenes on the walls. He nodded towards the fairy-tale Rhine castle. 'I've got one very similar to that in my rooms.'

'Have you? I . . .' she began to say, then stopped abruptly.

'You didn't see it?' he finished with a lift of his eyebrows.

She bit her lip in vexation. 'I don't know what you mean.' She drew away from him. 'I think I'd better sit down.'

Jack gently pulled her back. 'No, wait. Please wait. Look, I knew George had a visitor and I thought it might be you. For some reason he didn't want to tell me about it. I don't know why.'

She flushed. 'I've got to be careful.' He looked at her enquiringly. 'I don't suppose it would matter if I was a lady like Mrs Lassiter or someone,' she said with a trace of bitterness. 'It's different if a girl's got to earn her living. Everyone's very quick to find fault and if it was known I'd been alone with a gentleman in his rooms, it's only too easy to put the wrong construction on it. I met him this morning on the Strand and he suggested I might like to call in for a few minutes.' She looked at him with wide appealing eyes. 'I wasn't there for long and there wasn't anything wrong, Major Haldean, there really wasn't.'

'I don't suppose for a minute there was,' he reassured her. 'It's just that George annoyed me by insisting no one had called.'

She smiled. 'That was very sweet of him.' She looked at him sharply. 'How did you guess?'

'The coffee cup. It had lipstick on it.'

'The coffee cup?' Her face cleared. 'I see I shall have to be careful. I know you write detective stories, but I don't know if I really like you detecting me.'

'From now on I'll only do it with your permission,' he said gravely and was relieved to see her smile once more.

'Were you detecting earlier? I saw you talking to that dancer.'

'I was trying to,' he said lightly. 'I was remarkably unsuccessful.'

'Bad luck. Major Haldean, would you mind if we sat down? And please don't be too cross with George. I asked him not to mention it and he promised he wouldn't. Please don't say anything.'

'Trust me,' he promised, mentally crossing his fingers.

They went back to the table. Jack picked up his coffee and drank it, looking thoughtfully at George and pushing down a sense of unease. He'd had no idea that George could be such a damn good liar. Yes, he probably was concerned about Stella Aldryn's reputation and, although it was a mere convention, she could be criticized for being alone with an unmarried man in his rooms. George knew that. It was likely that the conservative and South African George was rather more alive to the conventions than most men of their age, but even so, it seemed an exaggerated reaction.

He had his opportunity to bring the subject up when the band started to play 'Whoops, Daisy, That Was Me'. Anne Lassiter turned to Maguire with a broad smile. 'We've just got to dance to this, Roger. It's from *Hurry Along!* I loved the show.'

153

Once they had gone, Stella Aldryn stubbed out her cigarette, fiddled for a few moments with the clasp of her bag and then announced she was off to powder her nose.

'Why the dickens,' said Jack, watching her depart, 'didn't you tell me that it was Miss Aldryn who had called?'

George frowned at him. 'Called? Telephoned, you mean?'

'No, of course I don't mean telephoned. I mean called. She called this morning when I was out.'

George stared at him. 'She did no such thing. Jack you're getting an absolute bee in your bonnet about this. Miss Aldryn didn't call and neither did anyone else.'

Jack started to feel annoyed. 'For heaven's sake, George, stop pretending, will you? I couldn't care less if she calls or not but I do mind you denying it.'

George shook his head. 'But it's the truth.' A note of indignation crept into his voice. 'It's the absolute truth. We went through this earlier. Drop it, Jack. I didn't have a visitor. I don't know why you won't believe me.'

His face was so earnest and his voice so compelling that, even though he knew he was right, Jack felt his belief momentarily shift. This was frankly incredible. Until this morning he would have sworn – sworn in any court of law and on any number of bibles – that George was utterly and completely honest. Damn it, he *knew* George. He'd trusted him, both as a fellow officer and as a friend. He'd relied on his courage, his skill and, underpinning all that, his integrity. A sliver of uncertainty icicled into his mind. Was George subject to delusions? After all, he knew George still believed in his heart of hearts that he'd seen a murdered girl in the kitchen that night. Yes, he'd been ill, but he still believed it. Jack felt suddenly chilled. 'All right,' he said. 'All right.' He put his hands palms outwards and tried to smile. 'Just as you say.'

George sat back, mollified. 'Thank God for that.' He looked round for a distraction and saw the waiter. 'Will you have another drink?'

Jack stood up. 'Look, d'you mind if I don't?' What he really wanted was to get away, to think things over, and he had to tell Bill Rackham about Isadora. He was sure she knew something. 'I'll see you back at Chandos Row, George.'

He made his goodbyes, collected his hat, stick and coat and walked out on to Tilford Lane. The short November afternoon was rapidly turning to dusk but there was about an hour of daylight left. He turned down Saffron Place, past the huddle of alleyways at the back of Tilford Lane and on to the Embankment. The seagulls swooped over the barges on the Thames and the wash of the boats left broad wakes of dull pewter. He was glad to be out of the stuffy, overheated restaurant. He felt stale and ill at ease. Even if George was honest, in the sense of not telling deliberate lies, it was scarcely more comforting to think that he was subject to delusions on such a scale. He shook himself. He needed a walk and set off on a circuitous route home.

Absorbed in his thoughts, he turned into Leicester Square. The usual street entertainers were performing for the passing crowds of Saturday afternoon shoppers. There was a man with a dog that could jump through a hoop and die for the King, a man who looked like an ex-prize-fighter being unexpectedly gentle with a flock of trained canaries, and a man who was offering to sell real, genuine gold watches as worn by the crowned heads of Europe. He wasn't doing much trade. There was a magician who put a dove into a box where it was mysteriously transformed into handfuls of red, white and blue handkerchiefs. The handkerchiefs joined together in strings before patriotically knitting themselves into a Union Jack and were, in turn, stuffed back into the box which, when opened, proved to be empty. The box was ceremoniously closed and, when it was opened, revealed the long-suffering dove once more.

With a flourish the magician doffed his hat and held it out to the crowd. Moved by a sudden impulse, Jack took out half a crown and dropped it in. The man's eyes gleamed. 'Why, thanks. You're a gent.'

'That act of yours. It's an illusion, isn't it? I mean, you're deluding us, aren't you?'

155

The magician winked broadly. 'What do you think?' He raised his voice. 'Thank you very much, ladies and gennel'men, thank you *very* much.' He looked up and groaned as rain spattered heavily about them. 'I wish this blinking weather was an illusion.'

Jack opened his umbrella, drew his collar up and started for home, head down against the driving rain. It was an illusion, nothing more. It was the second time that afternoon he'd thought of swearing to the truth on oath. He'd just seen an illusion; he knew that but, if he'd been asked to testify in a court of law, he would have sworn he had seen a dove come from an empty box . . .

Chapter Nine

It was after four o'clock when he arrived home. Rather to his relief, George was still out. Mrs Pettycure had long since cleared away the coffee cups and the tray. She couldn't rightly swear to it but she thought that Mr Lassiter had had a visitor that morning. She'd heard Mr Lassiter come in and then heard voices in the hall. She knew it was Mr Lassiter by the way Boots behaved, scratching and meowing to get out. The way Boots watched out for Mr Lassiter was more like a dog than a cat. She'd heard Mr Lassiter say something like, 'This old lady's taken me to heart,' and it was remarkable how attached Boots had become, wasn't it?

Jack, who wasn't feeling nearly as attached to Mr Lassiter as Boots evidently was, was glad to be alone in his room. He picked up his guitar, feeling the pleasure of the smooth wood in his hands and the strings beneath his fingers. The guitar was a beauty, brought from Spain. *George was dishonest . . .?* He fretted a succession of chords, strumming the strings idly, his hands occupied and his eyes abstracted. Somewhere, somewhere so close that he could nearly reach out and touch it, there was an explanation; a rational, coherent explanation. *George was deluded . . .?* The music became a discord and he put down the guitar and sighed. *George was a problem . . .* He had to give himself time.

It was only because of an earlier promise that Jack joined George for Sunday lunch at Eden Street. He felt an odd reluctance to concern himself any further with the Lassiter family's affairs. The feeling was so indefinable he couldn't express it – certainly not to George – but he shied away from the thought of witnessing yet another argument between Nigel and David. That was something he could say and did.

'We're safe enough, by all accounts,' said George cheerfully, who was looking forward to lunch. 'I don't think Nigel will be there. According to Stella, he's virtually moved into the factory. It's perhaps as well because Anne said Mrs Culverton was coming and he'd only start bally-ragging her about his wretched aeroplane again. By the way, Jack,' he added, 'is there anything wrong? You don't seem yourself somehow.'

No, I bloody well don't, thought Jack sourly and you should know why. And yet, seeing George's friendly, puzzled and seemingly rational face made the whole affair of that damn coffee cup even odder. So what if Stella Aldryn had called? All he wanted was for the man to admit it. George, on the other hand, seemed to have forgotten it altogether.

Even without Nigel, the main topic at lunch was, predictably, the Pegasus.

'I grant that the Pegasus will *look* all right,' said David Lassiter, reaching for the horseradish sauce to go with his roast beef. 'Looks aren't the problem. Tuesday should be fine. The press will love it, I'm sure, but I think he's taking a big risk by announcing this airborne dinner. The Pegasus has to be totally airworthy by a week on Friday and I'm not at all sure it can be.'

'He's been testing the plane all week,' said his father. 'He's pleased with the latest results. You can't judge anything by last month's flying trials. That was a blow, I admit, and there are still some faults, but he's addressing those.'

'At least he's flying the plane himself instead of relying on a test pilot,' said Anne.

'There's that about it,' conceded David. 'Mind you, I really would have put my foot down if he'd tried to persuade anyone else to take her up at this stage, particularly after what happened last month.'

'What did happen?' asked George curiously, cutting his Yorkshire pudding into neat squares. 'Last month, I mean.'

'The starboard side strut buckled. If he'd only use bracing wires like everyone else instead of trying to rely on fixed struts alone then he wouldn't have had the problem in the first place.' He sighed in exasperation. 'I know it's a new design but there are too many innovations.'

'We have to try new designs,' objected Mr Lassiter. 'If we never tried anything new we'd still be bumbling round in glorified gliders.'

Jack, visualizing the artist's impression of the giant biplane that had appeared in *Modern Flight*, frowned. 'I can understand why he's trying to do without bracing wires because they can be an absolute pest to rig, but I'd have thought it'd cause more problems than it solved.'

'Exactly, Haldean,' said David in satisfaction. 'Because the Pegasus is so large, the wing is very flexible and, to make matters worse, the flexing point is on the centre-line of the top wing. The strut runs between the lower wing panel outboard of the engine attachment and the upper wing overhang. The wing twisted and buckled when he engaged the aileron because he'd exceeded the compression strength of the long diagonal strut.'

George blinked. 'The wings tried to come apart, you mean?'

'That's about the size of it,' agreed David. 'Fortunately he was over the river and able to get down in one piece.'

'Nigel sorted it out,' said Mr Lassiter. 'He's worked endlessly on this, David. You have to give him credit for how hard he's working.' He looked at Mrs Culverton. 'He's slept at the factory for the last few nights.'

'It's his choice,' said David. 'He's convinced that once the Pegasus is airworthy you'll buy it.'

Peggy Culverton put down her knife and fork. 'I can't promise anything of the kind.' She saw Mr Lassiter's unhappy expression and looked away. 'I'm sorry but I simply can't. I know that Nigel wouldn't have started the project in the first place if Alexander hadn't been so keen on the India route.' She sighed. 'I know that, but I have to say it's looking increasingly doubtful the more Gilchrist Lloyd and I discover about the real state of the firm.'

Mr Lassiter looked crestfallen. 'I wondered if that would prove to be the case.'

'I'm meeting Mr Lloyd tomorrow,' said Mrs Culverton. 'He's been working hard too, trying to establish exactly what the situation is. Alexander liked to play his cards very close to his chest and it's taken Mr Lloyd ages to work out where we stand.'

Mr Lassiter looked at her in resignation. 'You must do what you think best, of course.'

'I can only do what's possible. Alexander's much-vaunted talents as a businessman seem to have deserted him in the last few months.' She picked up her glass but paused before drinking. 'I'm not looking forward to the meeting tomorrow. I think I might have to make some very hard decisions.'

Mr Lassiter took a deep breath and straightened his shoulders. 'You can only do what is right for your own concerns, Peggy, my dear. There's one thing: Tuesday should be a real gala occasion and we've got the dinner to look forward to as well. The press will be out in force and the publicity should help to stimulate some interest amongst other air passenger companies.' He looked at Jack. 'Would you like to join us for the presentation, Major? I wish I could invite you to the dinner as well but space is extremely limited.'

'Thank you very much, sir,' said Jack. 'I'll look forward to it.'

'You've arranged all the social side of things, haven't you, Anne?' said George. 'Miss Aldryn was telling me about it.'

'I've booked Howgrave and Cheriton to do the catering,' said Anne. 'They do a wonderful job.'

David Lassiter looked puzzled. 'Miss Aldryn? Stella Aldryn, you mean? I didn't know you knew her. Not socially, I mean.'

Jack caught the disapproving look Mr Lassiter gave his grandson.

'We've been out a couple of times,' said George, colouring slightly. He had seen the look too. 'You know, dinner and the theatre, that sort of thing.'

'You saw *Hurry Along!*, didn't you?' put in Jack, trying to steer the conversation away from the thorny topic of Stella Aldryn. 'It's an excellent show.'

'I've seen *Hurry Along!*,' said Anne, helping him. 'I really enjoyed it. The music's terrific. I only wish Stephanie Granger had been on the night I went. Her understudy was all right, but Stephanie Granger's meant to be really something.' She turned to Peggy Culverton. 'You've not seen it, have you? We must go.'

'I'd love to,' said Peggy Culverton. 'It's ages since I've been to the theatre,' she added, and George, on safer ground, relaxed.

After lunch George went for a game of billiards with David. In the drawing room Mr Lassiter slumbered under the newspaper and Peggy Culverton, supported by Anne Lassiter, sought out Jack.

He was sitting on the sofa. He had a cup of coffee but he'd drunk it scarcely noticing the taste. There was something he had missed, a little niggling something, and he couldn't figure out what it was. He looked up as Peggy Culverton and Anne Lassiter sat down by his side, grateful for the distraction.

'Forgive me, Major,' said Mrs Culverton quietly, 'but I was hoping to have a word with you.' She hesitated.

'Fire away,' said Jack, putting his empty cup on the table in front of him.

She hesitated once more. 'I'm not quite sure how to put this, but you know about Alexander's death, don't you? More than the rest of us, I mean.'

'I only wish I did,' said Jack, with feeling.

'You do, though, don't you?' said Anne. 'George has mentioned how friendly you are with Inspector Rackham and Roger says you're a real Sherlock Holmes.'

Jack could have made a joke but he didn't. Instead he looked expectantly at Mrs Culverton. 'What is it you want to know?'

Her hands were clasped very tightly together. 'Have the police any idea who killed Alexander?'

Jack shook his head. 'I'm afraid they haven't, Mrs Culverton.'

'In that case . . .' She hesitated and plunged on. 'Do they know what was behind it? Have they discovered any motive, I mean?'

Jack looked at her harried eyes. She was strapping down her emotions but she seemed brittle with worry. 'Not yet.'

'Why?' she demanded bitterly. 'Major Haldean, if you really are close to Inspector Rackham, you must know what sort of man my husband was. Surely, *surely* there must be a motive linked to his way of life.'

'Can't you make a guess?' asked Anne. 'An intelligent guess, I mean.'

Jack put his hands wide. 'That's exactly what we can't do,' he said. 'We haven't anything to go on. The lack of motive is a real sticking point. If Rackham could find someone with any sort of a motive, even one which might seem trivial at first sight, then he would have a real chance of finding the killer.'

Peggy Culverton's eyes widened, dark against her pale face. 'That's what he's looking for? But . . .' She swallowed and sat for a few moments without speaking, her brow furrowed in concentration. 'Does he think I've got a motive?'

'Peggy!' cried Anne, shocked.

Peggy Culverton turned to her swiftly. 'It's true. You must know it's true, Anne. I told Inspector Rackham everything. Perhaps that was stupid.'

'You needn't worry, Mrs Culverton,' said Jack reassuringly. She was right, though. She did have a motive, as Rackham had seen very early on. She had been pleased

162

that Culverton was dead but that was understandable. Besides that, motive alone wasn't enough; she needed the opportunity. 'I can assure you that Inspector Rackham doesn't suspect you. After all,' he added, 'as well as motive, Rackham's looking for someone with the opportunity and you were with Mrs Lassiter all evening, weren't you?'

Anne put her hand on her friend's arm. 'It's all right, Peggy. It's going to be all right.'

Peggy breathed deeply. 'I hope so.' She tried to smile. 'I wish it could all be forgotten. That would probably be the best for everyone. I'd like to forget about it.'

She tried to smile once more but her eyes were still dark-shadowed; and Jack felt, as he had felt earlier, that there was something he had missed.

Tuesday, the day of the press presentation, brought a change in the weather. Jack's spirits lightened. The depression which had been sitting over London for over a week, bringing a succession of dreary, damp days, had lifted and blown away in the night and the morning was crisp, clear and invitingly sharp. Far too inviting, thought Jack, as he turned into the Strand, to sit indoors. He seemed to have done nothing for days but scurry from room to room. He was looking forward to his trip to Tilbury. Apart from anything else, the Essex marshes should blow his cobwebs away.

He walked past the bulk of Charing Cross hospital. A surge of anger gripped him as he thought of Katherine Forrest and her lonely death. Poor kid, she would have been helpless against a predatory swine like Culverton. Unconsciously he quickened his step and came, almost before he realized where he was, to the King Edward's theatre, where *Hurry Along!* was playing, as the poster outside said, to *ecstatic audiences*. Stephanie Granger, it added, was *simply wonderful*. Trying to put Katherine Forrest out of his mind he concentrated on the poster. How did the song go? *Whoops, Daisy, that was me,* he hummed under his breath, then the tune died on his lips. He stared unbeliev-ingly at the poster. He knew it! He knew what he had missed on Sunday and yet it couldn't be true. If it was, it turned everything upside down.

Bill Rackham gaped at him. 'Are you sure, Jack?'

'Of course I'm damn well sure,' said Jack unhappily. 'When I was at the Lassiters' for lunch on Sunday I knew I'd missed something but I couldn't place what it was. I still haven't got to the bottom of it. There's something else I've missed but what, I don't know.' He sighed. 'Anyway, I've checked with the theatre. You'd better do the same, of course. The only time Stephanie Granger hasn't appeared in *Hurry Along!*, the only time her understudy has been on in the entire London run of the show, was the night of 31st October, the performance Isabelle and I saw, the per-formance Anne Lassiter saw, and the night Culverton was murdered.'

'And the night Anne Lassiter stated she was with Mrs Culverton in her flat in Kensington.' Rackham shook his head in disbelief. 'Hold on a minute.' He crossed the room to a filing cabinet, rummaged in the drawer and produced a manila folder. 'I've got both Mrs Lassiter's and Mrs Culverton's statements here.' He flipped open the folder and found what he was looking for. 'This is Mrs Culver-ton's. *Called on Anne Lassiter at Eden Street . . . went to my flat together . . . had dinner. . . Anne stayed with me until about half past twelve.* Let's see what Anne Lassiter has to say for herself. *Dined in the flat with Peggy . . . stayed with her all evening . . . took a taxi home after midnight.*' He looked up, his lips a thin line. 'Can you credit it? I believed them. I believed the pair of them and all the time they were string-ing me along. It's a service flat; there are no servants to say if they were there or not.' He pushed his chair away from the desk and walked angrily round the room. 'All we had was their word and I took it. Damn it, Jack, I told you Mrs Culverton looked pleased that her husband had died.'

'I can hardly blame her for that,' said Jack.

Rackham's face twisted. 'Neither can I, knowing what we do about him.' He leaned his elbow on the filing cabinet, drumming his fingers on the metal. 'Those injuries were savage, Jack, and she hated him, right enough. She's made no secret of the fact.' He rubbed his hand though his hair. 'There's a lot we don't understand about this, though, an awful lot.' He sighed. 'I'll get on to the theatre and then I'd better go and see her. This isn't going to be pleasant.'

Jack glanced at his watch. 'She'll be on her way to the Lassiter factory by now for the press presentation.'

Rackham clicked his tongue in annoyance.'I don't want to interrupt that. It's going to be difficult enough without having most of Fleet Street watching my every move. I'll see her and Mrs Lassiter this evening.'

Jack got up. 'I'll have to go, Bill. I've been invited to the factory too. I'm taking George in the Spyker.' He winced. 'I'm not looking forward to meeting either Mrs Culverton or Anne Lassiter there, knowing what I do. Damn it, I *like* Anne Lassiter, and Mrs Culverton must have gone through hell. I think she's a remarkable woman.' He looked thoroughly unhappy. 'If it wasn't for knowing you, I might have kept quiet about Anne's broken alibi.'

'I can understand that,' said Rackham seriously. 'But look, Jack, you mustn't reproach yourself. You haven't broken any confidences or let anyone down. Anne Lassiter told an outright lie. I want to know why.' He gave his friend an appraising look. 'You won't drop any hints, will you? I know you feel torn, but it's not your fault she didn't tell the truth. She might look as if butter wouldn't melt in her mouth but that's obviously not so. As for Mrs Culverton, I always knew she was capable of hiding her feelings. I don't know what either of them would do if they realized we'd tumbled to it, but there's a chance that Mrs Culverton might do a runner. She's got enough money to be able to disappear anywhere the fancy takes her.'

'Do you really think she'd do that?'

'She might, if it's a choice between that or being arrested. I've got a healthy respect for her resourcefulness.'

'I'll be careful,' promised Jack.

'Good man. By the way,' added Rackham, walking with Jack to the door, 'you know you said that dancer at the Continental recognized the photo of Culverton you showed her? Well, we've questioned her and she said she did recognize him, but on reflection she thinks it must have been because his picture was in the paper. She's right as far as that goes. The photo you've got is the same one we issued to the press.'

'D'you think she knew him apart from that? She seemed pretty startled when I produced the photo. She didn't like it.'

'No, she said she didn't. She wondered what your game was, if you were a reporter or someone trying to stir up trouble.' Rackham shrugged. 'I can't prove she's wrong. And the Continental seems all right, Jack. We've checked it.'

'Yes,' agreed Jack thoughtfully, putting on his coat. 'Which is frustrating, isn't it, Bill? Where the devil is this club?'

'I only wish I knew. We haven't had a sniff of it.'

'That's odd, isn't it? I mean, they must get their clients from somewhere. How does anyone know it exists?'

'Invitation only? It must be a very select group indeed.'

Jack shuddered. 'Don't. That makes it more creepy than ever.' He picked up his hat. 'I'll let you know if anything interesting happens this afternoon.'

With George beside him, Jack nosed the Spyker through the lodge gates of the factory and the lodge-keeper directed them to the main building where a workman, dressed in what were obviously his best clothes, escorted them into the building.

'I've heard how hard everyone's been working to get the Pegasus ready,' said Jack.

'I've never known anything like it, sir,' said the workman earnestly. 'It's been worth it, though. Wait till you see the plane, sir. She's a rare beauty.'

Although George had said, casually enough, that Anne Lassiter 'had arranged all the social side of things', neither of them had any idea of the scale of the preparations.

Production had been stopped for the day and the inside street that ran the length of the factory was virtually unrecognizable. Where workmen usually trundled cargoes of aeroplane parts, tables, white with shining cloths and glinting with silver dishes and ice-buckets with green gold-topped bottles, stood waiting. The factory wasn't full, but the crowd was very select indeed, thought Jack. Samuel Hoare, the air minister, was among a group of black-coated men standing round old Mr Lassiter, and there were other faces he knew from the newspapers.

Most of the hands had been given a very welcome day off, whilst a carefully picked selection of the workforce stood by their machines, ready to answer any questions that might occur to the guests. Howgrave and Cheriton, the leading London caterers, had transformed the street with flowers and decorations. Waiters weaved their way respectfully through the crowd of fur-coated, cloche-hatted women and morning-suited men, ensuring that no glass was unfilled and no plate empty. Lassiter's were really pushing the boat – or should that be flying-boat? thought Jack – out in style. The swell of noise rose, and under the high glass roof, glistening with the autumn sun, the factory resembled a Soviet poster of Ideal Labour mixed up with a society ball in a conservatory.

Anne Lassiter was standing halfway down the factory, flanked by Roger Maguire and Stella Aldryn, chatting animatedly to a group of pressmen. Jack recognized Joe Hawley of *Aviation Monthly*, Freddie Talbot of *Modern Flight* and Eric Laing of *Twentieth Century Transport* amongst them.

'Anne's terrific,' said George quietly to Jack as they walked through the crowd towards her. 'It was her idea to make this more like a party, rather than just a press event.

She must have worked like a galley slave to bring it all off and yet you'd never guess to hear her talk. I'm not surprised my grandfather thinks the world of her, you know. So does David.' Jack privately winced. 'She's tried to get Grandfather to see sense about Stella. He listens to Anne, you know, but it's an uphill struggle.'

'Has he said anything to you?' asked Jack. He didn't know and, even as he asked the question, he was surprised he didn't know. That showed, more than anything, the barrier that had sprung up between them in the last few days.

George nodded. 'Didn't I mention it? My grandfather made a couple of pointed remarks when he joined David and me in the billiard room on Sunday. He wasn't happy.' He looked at Anne and sighed. 'Anne's made an effort to get to know Stella.' A waiter stopped beside them and they took a glass of champagne each. 'I don't see why my grandfather shouldn't come round. She's a corker, you know, Jack.'

'Who? Miss Aldryn?'

'No, Anne, I mean. Roger Maguire's a lucky devil. I wonder if he knows how lucky he is?'

Anne Lassiter caught sight of them. 'Come and join us,' she said cheerfully and Jack, who was feeling like an absolute heel, managed a smile. Looking at Anne, with her expression of sincere friendliness, it was hard to believe she'd made a deliberately false statement. Damn it, what was wrong with everyone? The most trustworthy people seemed to be able to lie like troopers without turning a hair and she wasn't suffering from delusions, that was for sure. He knew that if he tried to speak to her at that moment he would give something away so, with an abruptness that made George look at him very oddly, he turned and made a point of talking to Freddie Talbot. 'What sort of press are you giving Lassiter's?' he asked.

Talbot, glass of champagne in hand, shrugged. 'So far, so good, if I was writing about food and drink, but I'm here to see the aeroplane. I'll say this, all the right people have been invited. Did you see Hoare? It's quite a coup getting him here, and there's Gilbert Sanderson of London and Colonial, as well as Sir Samuel Instone. Instone Air Lines might go for it. This India idea isn't so bad if the Pegasus lives up to the publicity. I want to see the plane put through its paces, though. I gathered from the grapevine that should have happened today but it's had to be put off until next week. It'd help if Nigel Lassiter could make an appearance. He hasn't shown up yet.' There was a buzz in the crowd and Talbot glanced round. 'Hello, where's Joe Hawley off to? Blow me, if that isn't Lassiter himself.' He slugged down the rest of his champagne. 'S'cuse me, Jack,' and taking out his notebook, he joined the rest of the pressmen who had formed an eager circle round Nigel at the door.

Anne, suddenly deprived of conversation, glanced round. Stella Aldryn, having claimed George, was talking exclusively to him, so that left only Maguire and Jack in the immediate vicinity. 'Perhaps we'd better mingle with the other guests, Roger,' she said, looking round the room. The only guest who was alone was a stout, middle-aged man by the table, ladling down food together with generous amounts of champagne. 'I suppose I should go and have a word with Mr Ridgeway,' said Anne unenthusiastically.

'I didn't think you liked him,' said Maguire.

'I don't much but I'd better be polite.' She looked at George. 'He's Nigel's chief investor after Culverton's and, consequently, a very important person. He's a senior partner in Croft and Ridgeway, the merchant bankers.'

George detached his arm from Stella's. 'I'll come with you, Anne.'

'Me too,' said Jack, trying to make up for his earlier curtness.

Anne gave them a glance of gratitude and led them over to the table. Mr Ridgeway looked up expectantly.

'Hello, Mr Ridgeway,' said Anne politely. 'You know Dr Maguire, of course, but I'd like to introduce you to Miss Stella Aldryn, Nigel's confidential clerk. This is Mr George Lassiter and his friend, Major Haldean.'

169

Ridgeway dabbed his bulldog jowls with his napkin. 'Pleased to meet you. I must say, Mrs Lassiter, this is excellent champagne. Excellent.' He looked at the men. 'Nigel Lassiter tells me this project will transform aviation. It sounds a magnificent achievement. Quite outstanding.' His enthusiasm, Jack noticed, didn't animate his face. Martin Ridgeway leaned forward confidentially to George. 'You're a Lassiter, eh? As a member of the family, sir, you are in a privileged position to know what sort of return can be expected on the project.' Now that did animate him, Jack noticed, seeing how the small, shrewd eyes lit up. 'I would like to know what interest has been expressed by the commercial air companies.'

George looked blank and Anne stepped into the breach. 'The best person to ask about future sales is Nigel himself, Mr Ridgeway. Unless Miss Aldryn knows anything?'

Martin Ridgeway glanced at Stella Aldryn, then, his eyes widening, gave her the benefit of his full attention. He looked her up and down slowly, with an expression amounting to a leer. The colour sprang up in Anne's face, Maguire frowned in disapproval and George, two white spots on his cheeks, curled his hands into fists.

Jack felt as if someone had drenched him with cold water. He knew that expression and he knew those eyes, those lascivious, cold, appraising, Holbein eyes. The face was different but this man was essentially the same sort as Alexander Culverton.

The leer broadened. 'I can't believe that such a pretty young thing likes to bother her head about such dull matters as sales, eh, my dear?'

Of all the people present, Stella Aldryn seemed to be the only one not to realize what was so evidently passing through Ridgeway's mind. She was either completely innocent or completely dumb, thought Jack. Whatever the reason, he mentally applauded her tact.

'I'm afraid you're right, Mr Ridgeway,' she said affably. 'Mr Nigel Lassiter's the person that you have to speak to.'

170

She glanced across the factory. 'He's engaged at the moment but he'll be happy to see you once he's free.'

'I'm sure Mr Ridgeway can speak to Nigel in his own time,' said George stiffly, drawing her away. He nodded his head abruptly. 'Pleased to meet you,' he said, curtly and quite untruthfully.

'George?' asked Stella once they were out of earshot. 'What's wrong?'

George's face was like thunder. 'Didn't you see how he looked at you? The man's an absolute creep. I felt like hitting him.'

Stella Aldryn giggled delightedly and caught hold of his arm. 'Are you jealous? That's so sweet of you.'

George's frown melted into a sheepish look and Stella giggled again. Jack, feeling that three was definitely a crowd, faded into the background. He might as well listen to Nigel Lassiter, he decided, and edged his way into the group of pressmen. Nigel, his face alive with enthusiasm, was going at full throttle.

'. . . we have encountered various problems connected with the sheer size of the machine that have had to be overcome. The top wing span is a hundred and fifty feet and we had to go back to fundamentals when it came to the interior construction of the wings. If you would care to visit the spar shop, the foreman will show you the radical solution we employed. As far as the passengers are concerned, the most striking innovation concerns the seating. Instead of building a car into the fuselage, the pontoons, or floats, which are sixty feet in length, are designed to serve as commodious saloons. We hear a great deal about the luxurious conditions aboard airships. I can safely say, gentlemen, that the passenger accommodation will easily rival, if not surpass, any airship either in existence or currently under construction, without, of course, the appalling hazard of fire justly associated with lighter-than-air flight.'

Freddie Talbot of *Modern Flight* ventured a question.

Nigel Lassiter nodded gravely. 'Safety has been our major preoccupation, as it is with all our machines.' It was just as well the pressmen didn't know about the wings try-ing to twist apart, thought Jack. 'I am pleased to say that most parts of the seaplane have a safety factor of five and certain parts, which endure the biggest stress, have a safety factor of six.' The men from the aviation papers looked impressed. The men from Fleet Street looked baffled. 'Which means, of course,' said Nigel, so smoothly that no one would suspect him of talking down to his audience, 'that the machine is capable of sustaining at least five or six times the strain which it will ever be called upon to bear.' The crowd made approving noises and Jack slipped away.

Old Mr Lassiter had briefly escaped his guests and was having a breather with David by the entrance to the dope and varnish room. David caught sight of him and beckoned an invitation to join them.

'Those were very impressive statistics Mr Lassiter was quoting,' said Jack, hoping for a reaction. He got one.

'Lies, damned lies and statistics,' said David ironically. 'It's all right,' he said in response to his father's anxious frown. 'I'm not going to say anything out of turn. It's just that with all the emphasis on the Pegasus, any other ideas have been kicked into touch. Perhaps now the aeroplane's finished I'll be able to go ahead with my plans.'

'Do you have a new aircraft in mind?' asked Jack.

David Lassiter shook his head. 'Not so much a new air-craft but a new way of owning an aircraft.' Jack looked a question and David Lassiter warmed to his theme. 'You're a pilot, Haldean, and knowledgeable about aviation. You might not know this, but as far as most people are con-cerned, buying a private plane is still a rather daring thing to do.'

It was a shatteringly expensive thing to do, thought Jack as he looked at David Lassiter, schooling his face into blank and polite enquiry.

'What I want to do is to take the average man and show him how easy it is to own an aeroplane. We'd build him a hangar – the Urbis has fold-back wings, so the hangar need be no bigger than a garage – lay out an airstrip in his garden or fields, sell him a flying kit, provide flying lessons if he wants to fly it himself or hire out pilots to act as chauffeurs if he doesn't. I wanted to set up lorries which would act as mobile garages staffed by our mechanics to repair and service the planes regularly at the customers' own homes. I did manage to get a decent insurance deal arranged through a City firm. It's honest and more economical than anything an individual could arrange for himself. We make a small but worthwhile profit on that but it's nothing compared to what we could make if only I could get things under way.'

Jack, whilst boggling slightly at David Lassiter's conception of the average man, was intrigued.

'You see,' continued Lassiter enthusiastically, 'I want to make owning a plane as easy as owning a car. It could be done. And when I say "man" don't think I just mean "men". There's a huge unplumbed women's market out there, and women make excellent pilots. They have a light touch which men often can't master, but it's the mechanical side of things that puts them off. I'd take care of all of that.' He finished his drink. 'Anyway, I suppose I'd better go and do my bit.'

'You won't say anything out of turn, will you?' asked his father. 'After all, the whole company, you included, needs the Pegasus to be successful.'

David Lassiter suddenly grinned. 'Don't worry, Dad. I want the plane to succeed as much as anyone else. We've put far too much in to see it thrown away.'

'Why don't you talk to Mrs Culverton?' suggested his father. 'I know she had to warn us on Sunday that she might pull out but the India route is still a good commercial proposition. There's a lot of money to be made there, David.' He put down his glass. 'There are some people I could do with seeing, as well.' He looked across the room. 'Instone's taken up with Samuel Hoare but there's Burton of City and Commercial and John Frazier of Capital Air. I know Frazier had hopes of a directorship in any state

173

airline, so if you'll excuse us, Major Haldean, we'd better be off.'

Jack, temporarily alone, looked round the crowded room. Nigel Lassiter had finished addressing the crowd and was talking earnestly to Martin Ridgeway.

Anne Lassiter and Roger Maguire joined him. 'Wasn't Mr Ridgeway horrible?' she said in a low voice. 'Did you see how he looked at Stella Aldryn? I thought George was going to hit him.'

'It's as well he didn't,' murmured Maguire. 'That would really spoil the party. You're making too much of it, Anne.'

'You must be blind,' said Anne with a toss of her head. 'The kindest explanation I can think of is that he's drunk too much. What's your opinion, Major Haldean?'

'I think if Ridgeway sinks any more of that champagne he'd buy a brick balloon,' said Jack. Maguire grinned. 'He's been shovelling it down. I didn't like the way he goggled at Miss Aldryn, either.'

'*In vino veritas*?' suggested Maguire. He took Anne's arm. 'She's a pretty girl and he noticed. So what? Don't get so upset. Hello, what's Nigel doing now?'

Nigel Lassiter had finished talking to Ridgeway and, in a consciously dynamic pose, mounted the first few steps of the ladder up to the crane. 'Ladies and gentlemen,' he began in a carrying voice. 'Thank you for your attention.'

The hum of conversation in the room petered out and the crowd looked at Nigel obediently and expectantly. 'On behalf of the Lassiter Aircraft Company and all the Lassiter family, I am happy to welcome you this afternoon. I am not going to make a speech.'

I bet you are, thought Jack.

'Very shortly you will be invited to see the Pegasus. I would be lacking in my duties as a host if I failed to point out what a huge step forward the aircraft represents. It is a completely new departure in civil aviation, one that will surely both pioneer and set the standard for trans-oceanic flight for years to come.' Nigel Lassiter's voice took on a sorrowful note. 'You will all have heard of the tragic and premature death of Mr Alexander Culverton. I may say that it is in some degree because of his vision that this unique aircraft, the Pegasus, exists at all.'

And that, commented Jack to himself, was true enough.

'His generous and unstinting support was valued more highly than he could ever have known. Mrs Culverton, who has, I am sure, the sympathy of everyone here, has graciously consented to come here today to see what can only be regarded in very large part as a memorial to her husband.' He stooped down, picked up a glass from the table beside him and raised it high. 'Ladies and gentlemen, I give you Alexander Culverton.'

Jack drank the toast, wondering how many others in the building felt as hypocritical as he did.

'My most grateful and sincere thanks are also due to our other two principal supporters, Mr Martin Ridgeway and Dr Roger Maguire. Mr Culverton is beyond the reach of such petty considerations as a just and generous return on his investment. Mr Ridgeway and Dr Maguire are, I am glad to say, on the verge of seeing a very tangible reward for their faith and vision in bringing into existence the Pegasus, the aeroplane of the future. Ladies and gentlemen, the future is here.'

On which exit line and to a burst of applause, he climbed down from the ladder and led the chattering group out of the factory towards the new hangar. It had been nicely done, Jack reflected, as he walked round the testing field in the company of the others. Just the right amount of very respectful pressure on Peggy Culverton and a heroic interpretation of the role of money-lender.

They followed Nigel round the bulk of the building towards the inlet of the Thames. And then he saw it. In that moment nothing but the aeroplane existed. Riding at anchor was a huge, graceful biplane. The sun, which had been fitfully hidden behind scudding clouds, shone down as if it, too, had been orchestrated by Nigel, turning the dull Thames into a shimmering lake supporting the shining craft. The wood of the pontoons glowed a deep rich

175

chestnut in the fleeting sun and the varnished fabric of the wings over the water caught the light and lanced it out in glittering, dancing darts.

Jack swallowed. The workman at the gate had said the Pegasus was a beauty and she was. Behind that beauty lay obsession, unfairness and greed, and yet it was still beautiful. Nigel Lassiter made little appeal to him, but there was no doubting what he'd achieved. Perhaps his very aloofness was essential to keep his dream intact. Jack had heard often enough that the Pegasus was a breakthrough in civil aviation but, confronted with the actual craft, the phrase was hopelessly inept. This aircraft could leap oceans and it was as if a new world had dawned.

Then, as always when confronted with a new aircraft, came the questions. How did she handle? Had Nigel Lassiter solved the problems with the wing? Did she – although this seemed an unnecessary question when he looked at the four meaty Rolls-Royce Condor engines – have enough power to support the enormous weight?

A gang-plank was laid from the shore to the pontoons and various guests were ushered aboard. Jack found a baulk of timber and sat on it, back to the hangar wall. Safety; he was glad David Lassiter, at least, was concerned about safety. He'd trust David Lassiter. He knew how dangerous aircraft could be. He grinned to himself and unconsciously patted his lame leg, souvenir of a long-ago flight when safety had been the last thing on his mind. By God, he'd been lucky. The sky had been full of Germans, his propeller was smashed and his petrol tank had been hit. One stray spark from an incendiary bullet or the magneto and he'd have been toast, not sitting here grumbling about his dodgy leg. He lit a cigarette and sat back, soaking in the impressions. People were coming and going from the craft, but he just wanted to sit and look.

Peggy Culverton, with Nigel and David Lassiter in tow, came down on to the shore and walked up the path towards him. 'I'll let you know soon, Mr Lassiter,' Mrs Culverton said to Nigel. 'I'm very impressed. The Pegasus is a wonderful machine but there are other considerations to take into account.'

Nigel's eyes narrowed, then he swallowed, nodding his head stiffly. 'In that case, I await your decision, Mrs Culverton.' He turned and walked along the path, stopping as he noticed Jack for the first time. 'Major Haldean? What do you think of the plane?'

'I think she's superb,' said Jack, rising to his feet. 'I must congratulate you, Mr Lassiter. It's an extraordinary achievement.'

'Would you like to be part of it? I understand you're a successful author. We're looking for new investors, you know.'

Jack laughed. 'I only wish I had the money. If I had . . .' The sentence finished abruptly as Nigel Lassiter walked away. Jack stared after him, taken aback by this monumental display of bad manners. Although the sun still shone, some of the gloss seemed to wear off the plane.

He walked back along the gleaming railway track to the factory. Before he turned the corner he looked once more at the Pegasus. It was still beautiful but the beauty was marred by the crass behaviour of its creator. Damn Nigel Lassiter, thought Jack. He wanted another drink.

Back inside the factory George was standing by one of the tables, champagne in hand. He looked ill at ease. 'What's the matter?' asked Jack, picking up a glass from the tray.

'I don't know if I should mention it,' said George awkwardly. He paused, obviously hunting round for something to say. 'What did you think of the plane, Jack?'

'Terrific. I don't think much of Nigel Lassiter, though. He's just snubbed me for not being rich enough to invest in it.' Jack took a drink. 'What shouldn't you mention?'

George wriggled uncomfortably and looked round. The nearest people they knew were Anne Lassiter, Roger Maguire and Stella Aldryn. They were standing by the ladder of the crane a few yards away. Anne was pointing upwards, indicating the board-walk. No one was paying either Jack or George any attention. George drew closer and lowered his voice. 'Look,' he said. 'You know Culverton was murdered?' Jack raised his eyebrows in puzzled enquiry. 'Well, you haven't told me much but I gather that you and Inspector Rackham are trying to find someone with a motive for bumping him off. Is that right?'

Jack looked sharply at his friend. 'That's absolutely right. Why?'

'It's all a bit awkward. You see, Jack, I'm sure there's nothing in it but if it got out I can see how things could be misinterpreted.'

'What on earth's happened, George?'

George sighed. 'The only reason I'm telling you is so you won't hear it from someone else. It must be all right and quite honestly, if I was the only one involved I probably wouldn't have said anything.' He hesitated, then plunged on. 'The four of us, myself, Stella, Anne and Dr Maguire, walked round the side of the hangar and . . .' He paused once more and his voice sank to a whisper. 'Well, we saw Mrs Culverton and my Uncle David. They didn't see us right away. He had his arm round her and they were completely absorbed in each other. Then she looked up and they sort of sprang apart. Mrs Culverton looked horrified. Anne said "Sorry" and we all pushed off.'

Jack mentally kicked himself. He should have guessed. After lunch on Sunday he knew there was something he had missed and this was it. When Peggy Culverton heard the police were searching for anyone with a motive she'd looked stricken. She'd accused herself but that was a deliberate blind. She'd put herself forward, dragging a broken wing across the trail to protect David. She knew exactly what the police would think if they knew she and David Lassiter were having an affair.

'I could see that beggar, Maguire, putting two and two together, working it out,' added George unhappily. 'This could mean trouble for Uncle David somehow or other, but it can't be true, Jack. He can't have bumped off Culverton. I like him, really like him, but I know what it looks like.'

'It looks as if he had a motive,' said Jack quietly.

'This is my uncle we're talking about,' George hissed fiercely. 'I don't care if he did have a motive. He wouldn't hurt a fly.'

Jack looked at George. 'Didn't you tell me he once tried to throttle Nigel?'

George's face twisted. 'Good God, Jack, he thought Nigel was responsible for his son's death. Can you imagine how he must have felt? He'd been provoked beyond endurance. This is different.'

Jack was silent. Peggy Culverton hadn't simply disliked her husband, she'd been terrified of him. That alone could be enough provocation for David Lassiter. And Peggy Culverton had lied about how she spent the night Culverton died. He'd never really believed in Peggy Culverton acting alone, even when her alibi was shown to be false, but if she was working with David Lassiter? That was different.

Anne glanced round and saw the two men. 'Come and join us,' she called, with a wave of her hand. She brushed her brown hair away from her face. 'We're talking about cats.'

'Cats?' asked George with assumed cheerfulness. 'What about cats?'

Stella Aldryn's smile faded as George and Jack walked towards them. George wasn't particularly good at concealing his feelings and his supposed jollity wouldn't have fooled anyone. 'Never mind about cats, George,' she said accusingly. 'You haven't told Mr Haldean, have you?' George didn't answer and she looked at Jack. 'Do you know what happened? With Mrs Culverton, I mean?' Jack nodded. 'That's rotten of you, George,' she said indignantly. 'It's none of our business.'

George looked acutely uncomfortable. 'I'm sorry, Stella.' Stella tossed her head. 'I don't think it's fair.'

'What's this about cats?' asked Jack, trying to smooth things over. Cats were a safer topic than David Lassiter and Mrs Culverton.

179

Maguire pointed up to the board-walk, eighty feet above their heads. 'We're wondering if there's a cat on the roof.'

'I can't see it,' said Anne. 'I really should wear glasses but I don't need them all the time.'

Jack looked upwards. The low autumn sun glinted through the glass roof making it difficult to see. He narrowed his eyes in a squint. 'I can't see it, either.'

George gave him a puzzled look. 'Can't you? The poor creature must be terrified.' He swung himself on to the iron-runged ladder. 'Don't worry, I'll get it down.'

Stella looked up anxiously as George swarmed up the ladder. 'I hope he's all right.'

'He'll be okay,' said Jack reassuringly. After all, if George wanted to impress the girlfriend by saving cats, that was his affair. He just hoped he actually found an animal to save, otherwise he'd look pretty silly.

George reached the top and gave them a cheery wave from the platform at the top of the ladder. The board-walk, guarded by a handrail, ran above the chains of the crane-hook to the operator's cab at the other end. Stella Aldryn drew her breath in anxiously. 'I hope he's all right.'

'Relax,' said Jack easily. He knew George had a good head for heights and chasing cats was probably as good a diversion from David Lassiter and Peggy Culverton as any other. 'It's perfectly safe up – *My God!*'

For as he watched George slipped, stumbled, and, with a despairing scream, fell.

Chapter Ten

George's scream ripped out, echoed by a gasp from the people below. Arms flailing, he clutched air and found the chains of the crane. Hanging by one hand, he swung above their heads.

For a fraction of a second Jack stood frozen with shock, then, with an explosion of movement, raced up the ladder, ran along the board-walk and flung himself out at full length on the walk above George, looking into his friend's white face. He stretched out, trying vainly to touch him, but the distance was too great. George was a full three fingers out of reach. 'Get your other hand on to the chain,' Jack commanded.

'I can't.' George's voice was a thin whisper of despair. Jack looked at the clutching hand so frustratingly close. George's hand only just encircled the link of the chain. To get his other hand up would mean shifting his weight and if he did that he would certainly fall. George's fingers tightened convulsively on the link. 'I'm going, Jack.'

'No, you're not.' Jack wrapped his legs round one of the metal struts of the guard-rail and flung his body out from the board-walk, his fingers clawing forward. He grabbed George's wrist with both hands. George's body swung forward. Vaguely Jack heard the shouts from below and then with a rattle the chain started to move. George clutched at his arm with his other hand. With a feeling of sick horror Jack felt himself being pulled over the edge. His leg screamed a protest as he tried to force the tortured muscles to obey him. His arm was cracking, but it was his leg, his damned useless damaged leg, that was giving under the strain. Underneath him flash-bulbs flicked like lightning as the press caught the agonizing moment. He shut his eyes, trying to hold on by sheer willpower, when a voice, calm and controlled, sounded beside him and the intolerable weight was gone.

He hung limply for a moment then with a shudder clutched on to the guard-rail, heaved himself back on to the board-walk and, eyes shut, lay without moving. Gradually the noise of his harsh breathing was replaced by other sounds and he flickered his eyes open. In a sharp focus that filled all his world he saw the dust and the grain on the wood of the planks, and beyond them, a pair of boots. A hand awkwardly encircled his shoulders, helping him to sit up. It was Benson, the foreman, a large, kindly man. Jack slumped against his rough jacket, deriving enormous comfort from the man's solid bulk. 'What happened?' he managed to say at last.

'It was Mr David who did it, sir. He got up the other ladder to the cab of the crane and was coming with a rope, when we saw that you'd got Mr George's hand off the links. So Mr David stood on the hook of the crane and I sent him along underneath Mr George and he was able to catch his legs and take the weight off you. I think we were just in time as well, sir. Begging your pardon, sir, but do you think you can climb down the ladder? I'll help you, of course.'

Jack nodded, and with a hand from the foreman, stood up, clutching the guard-rail. The man looked critically at Jack's dragging leg. 'Done some damage to that, haven't you, sir?' Jack tried to take a step forward and his knee buckled. The foreman caught hold of him. 'Hold up, lad! Let me help you.' He put his arm under Jack's shoulders and helped him limp to the ladder.

With Benson below him he made a slow and jarring descent, wincing every time his foot touched metal. As he reached the ground, he turned and faced the circle of people crowding round the foot of the ladder, screwing up his eyes to avoid the jabs of light from the flash-guns.

Mr Lassiter, his face white, shook his hand. 'Major Haldean, thank God you're in one piece. That was one of the bravest bits of work I've ever seen. If you hadn't held on to George I dread to think what would have happened.' He stopped and swallowed. 'Thank God you were able to get to him in time.'

Jack took a deep breath. 'It was just as well David came along when he did, sir. He deserves a good deal of the credit.'

'He's getting it, don't you worry. He showed marvellously quick thinking.' Mr Lassiter turned to the foreman and held out his hand. 'And you too, Benson. I saw what you did. Thank you.'

The foreman smiled shyly and shook the outstretched hand. 'It wasn't anything really, sir. Not put against what this gentleman did.'

'It won't be forgotten, Benson, I can promise you that. Can I get you anything, Major Haldean?'

'I'd like my stick, sir,' said Jack tightly. 'I don't usually need it, but just now I could do with it.'

Mr Lassiter picked up the stick Jack had flung at the foot of the ladder in his dash upwards. 'Here you are.' He turned to the crowd pressing round them. 'Make a bit of room there, please. George is over here, Major. If you come this way, you can sit down.' The crowd parted and, leading the way, Mr Lassiter took him over to where George, nursing his arm, was sitting with David Lassiter. Mr Lassiter beckoned to a waiter, took a drink and pressed it into Jack's hand.

Jack held the glass and raised it in salute to George and David. He took a sip but the reaction had set in and the alcohol made him feel slightly sick. Flash-bulbs flared again as the pressmen caught the moment. He held up his hand to ward off the barrage of questions from the reporters. 'I'll talk to you properly later. We all will.' He saw Joe Hawley and motioned to him. 'Joe, call off the pack, will you? I promise I'll give you all a lovely quote for tomorrow's paper but just give us some time, will you?'

'Gentlemen?' said Mr Lassiter.

The pressmen grinned. 'Very well, sir.'

Jack put the glass down as the crowd thinned out and looked up to see Stella Aldryn and Peggy Culverton. Habit made him try and stand.

'Don't get up, Major Haldean,' said Mrs Culverton quickly, 'When I think what could have happened . . .' She broke off, sat down beside David and shot him an anxious glance. David smiled reassuringly at her.

Stella Aldryn put her hand on George's arm. Her eyes were frightened.

'I'm all right,' he said awkwardly, constrained by his grandfather and the crowd around them. 'Honestly, I'm all right.' He tried to cover her hand with his and gave a sharp intake of breath.

'What is it?' asked Stella anxiously.

'Nothing much. I've crocked my arm, that's all.' He gave a covert glance at Mr Lassiter. 'I'll see you later.'

Stella swallowed, followed his glance and nodded in understanding. With a deep breath she let go of his arm and pushed her way back into the crowd.

'What happened, George?' asked David. 'Why were you up there in the first place?'

George raised his hands in a helpless gesture. 'It sounds stupid, I know, but there was a cat stuck on the board-walk. It never occurred to me there was any danger. After all, the workmen are up there all the time. Even now I don't know what went wrong.'

'You slipped,' said Jack.

George put his hand to his mouth. 'My feet just seemed to go from under me. There might have been some oil spilled up there or something.'

'Oil?' David Lassiter's eyebrows rose. 'Someone's going to hear about it if there was. Are you sure, George?'

'No, I'm not. I wish I was sure but it was over so quickly it's hard to pin down exactly what did happen. I know I was treading on solid ground and then it all seemed to open up in front of me. I just managed to grab that chain in time.' He smiled ruefully at Jack. 'And then you came along. Thanks, old man.'

Jack offered him a cigarette with a grin. 'I feel as if my arm should be as long as an orang-utan's after having you dangling off it.' George laughed and Jack looked at David. 'Thanks for the way you weighed in there. I couldn't have held him much longer.'

David Lassiter shook his head. 'It was the obvious thing to do.' He stood up and offered his arm to Mrs Culverton. 'Nigel was about to make a speech. I think we'd better go and listen to him.'

Followed by Mr Lassiter, David and Peggy Culverton walked away, the crowd drifting after them.

Across the room a hammer banged on the table for silence and Nigel Lassiter started to speak. George leaned forward and, nodding towards Nigel, lowered his voice. 'He's a bit of a contrast to his brother, isn't he? The plane's fantastic, Jack, but I can't say I like Nigel much.'

'Me too,' agreed Jack. It seemed to be a long time since Nigel had snubbed him yet it could only be half an hour or so.

'I think he's a bully,' said George unexpectedly.

Jack raised his eyebrows. 'Why?'

'It was what he said to Stella. When I got down from the crane everyone was fussing over me and David. Nigel was speaking to Stella. She'd come forward to see how I was. Nigel looked at her and said something – I couldn't catch what – and then he added, "Bloody fool." He was furious, Jack. You should have heard him.'

'Bloody fool? That's a bit rich. If it makes you feel any better, I imagine he was talking about you. There's no doubt which story's going to be headline news and he probably resents his press coverage being taken over.'

George frowned. 'I didn't think he was speaking about me,' he said doubtfully. 'He didn't look in my direction at all. I'm sure it was Stella he was angry with. Now I'll grant you he might think I'm an absolute idiot, fooling around on top of the board-walk, but what's Stella done? I can't stand the idea of him talking to her like that. He shouldn't swear at any girl, especially not one who works for him. She can't tell him to go to the devil,' he added. 'It's not fair.' There was a long pause. 'Jack,' he continued hesitantly, 'are you going to tell Inspector Rackham about David and . . . and well, you know what I mean.'

Jack took a deep breath. 'I've got to.'

George's eyes narrowed. 'Even after what he's done?'

'Yes.' He flinched at George's expression. 'What else can I do?' he demanded. George didn't answer. 'I've got to, George,' he repeated. 'I've got to play fair with Bill.' Again George said nothing but his silence was more telling than any words could be. 'I'm going to tell him the whole story though, not just part of it. David saved both of us. I know that.'

And he had. That's what made it so very hard.

William Rackham rang the doorbell of Mrs Culverton's flat. He glanced at his watch. Eight o'clock in the evening.

He had already seen Anne Lassiter and, although she was the one caught out, it was Rackham who felt like the guilty party, as if he had done something utterly crass, such as using bad language in church or taking pennies from a beggar's hat. She was – Rackham felt the full force of this – a lady. She greeted him with guarded politeness and, in the quiet of the library at Eden Street, listened while he stated his case. Reduced to its brutal essentials it was that she was a liar. Anne listened in silence, then raised her head.

'You're right, Inspector. When Roger realized what I had done he advised me to tell you what actually occurred. I chose not to take his advice.'

She was, astonishingly, going to leave it there.

'When did Dr Maguire realize that you had given Mrs Culverton a false alibi?'

'This afternoon, Inspector. I foolishly said more than I intended and Roger guessed what had happened. You mustn't think that Dr Maguire was involved in my deception.'

He demanded more details and Anne, reluctantly, provided them. She had left Eden Street with Peggy Culverton as she had stated and gone to Peggy's flat. That was true. Then – she couldn't exactly recall but it must have been after six o'clock – she had left Peggy. She was hungry and had called into her club, the Three Arts in Piccadilly, for something to eat. There she had met some friends – Rackham had their names and addresses – and they had decided to go to *Hurry Along!* and for supper afterwards. And that was that. She refused to offer any defence or any explanation and Rackham had unhappily taken his leave.

And now he was standing outside Mrs Culverton's front door waiting to tell another woman she was a liar. David Lassiter, whom he proposed to tackle later, would make a nice change, he thought ironically.

Jack hadn't envied him the interview. He had sounded tired and dispirited on the phone, as if the colour had been drained out of him. David Lassiter, Jack had been at pains to point out, had saved his and George's lives that afternoon. The man was a hero. Jack had left him in no doubt. The story would be in tomorrow's press, and he had to be cautious with heroes. However, Jack's very depression pointed to the fact that he believed that at long last there seemed to be a credible motive attached to a credible suspect in the Culverton case.

There were footsteps behind the door. Rackham straightened himself up as the door was opened not by Mrs Culverton but by David Lassiter. The startled apprehension in the man's eyes told him that Lassiter knew why he was there. Lassiter hesitated, then held the door open. 'You'd better come in.' He turned and called down the corridor of the flat. 'Peggy, Inspector's Rackham's here.'

Following David Lassiter, Rackham went into the sitting room. Mrs Culverton stood by the bay window. She wore

187

a red, square-necked dress and, as she stood, framed against the tapestry curtains, she fleetingly reminded Rackham of a picture he'd seen of Mary, Queen of Scots. Mary, Queen of Scots, Rackham thought, had been well loved if controversial, with great dignity and unquestionable presence. She'd also been accused of murdering her husband, her adulterous, deeply unsatisfactory husband. The parallel caught him off guard. 'I'm sorry to disturb you, Mrs Culverton,' he said. That wasn't what he'd intended to say but her still presence demanded courtesy. She didn't answer but stood, waiting with a questioning, wary smile and guarded eyes. 'The fact is,' he continued, hoping he didn't sound as awkward as he felt, 'I've got good reason to believe that your account of how you spent the evening of 31st October is inaccurate.'

She gave a little sigh.

'Are you calling Mrs Culverton a liar?' demanded David Lassiter.

She held up her hand. 'David, please.' Her shoulders dropped and her smile faded, leaving only tiredness. 'What exactly do you know, Inspector?' she asked quietly.

'I know,' said Rackham, 'that you did not spend the evening with Anne Lassiter.' Looking at her defeated face he felt like a clumsy brute. And that's ridiculous, he told himself savagely. This woman had lied to him and if it wasn't for Jack she would have continued to lie. He looked at David Lassiter, glad to turn away from that pale, weary face. 'I'm sorry to talk about your private affairs, sir, but I also have good reason to believe that you and Mrs Culverton are more than friends.' He glanced apologetically at her. 'I'm sorry, Mrs Culverton, but the lack of motive for your husband's death has plagued the investigation. You must see that your failure to tell the truth about that evening makes you – both of you – open to suspicion.'

'For God's sake!' David Lassiter stepped towards him. 'What are you saying, man? That I killed Culverton?'

Mrs Culverton held out her hand to him. 'David, be fair.

188

After all, it's what we were afraid of. It's what I've been afraid of all along.' She looked at Rackham. 'You're wrong, Inspector. You're very wrong.' She indicated the armchairs either side of the fireplace. 'Please, sit down. David, we have to tell the truth.'

She sat on the edge of the chair and wrapped her hands around her knee. 'We were frightened, Inspector. Both of us knew perfectly well the construction that could be put on our actions but it was all so much simpler than you believe.'

She glanced reassuringly at David Lassiter, still standing beside her. 'You know what my husband was like, Inspector. Everything I said about him was true. There's a new law which makes it possible for a woman to divorce her husband. I had been thinking about leaving him for some time but it's a huge step to take.' She shrugged. 'I was nervous and unsure. Alexander wasn't the sort of man to make things easy for me. I . . .' She hesitated. 'I was worried about what people would say.'

She smiled, fleetingly. 'That matters to me, Inspector. It's silly to pretend it doesn't.' She took a deep breath. 'It all changed when I found the newspaper cuttings and those postcards. I told you what happened. I fled. I honestly can't think of another way of putting it. I went to Anne and it was she who pointed out I had a ready-made refuge in this flat. I could have stayed at Eden Street, I know that, but it would have meant explaining exactly what I was so afraid of. I couldn't bring myself to do it. After all –' she smiled briefly once more – 'I knew it sounded ridiculously melodramatic. If Mr Lassiter had any hint of what I believed he would have first tried to reason me out of it and then, if I did convince him, insisted on my going to the police. I didn't want to do either of those things. All I wanted to do was hide.'

'Did you tell Mrs Lassiter about the newspaper cuttings?' asked Rackham.

Peggy Culverton nodded. 'Oh yes. I don't know if she agreed with my interpretation of them but she saw how scared I was.' She smiled once more, a genuine smile this time. 'Anne knew exactly what to do.' She reached up and took David Lassiter's hand. 'She called David.'

Rackham coughed. 'Did Mrs Lassiter know you were . . .' He stopped, warned by the sudden, dangerous light in David Lassiter's eyes, and tried again. 'Did Mrs Lassiter know about your relationship?'

'But we didn't have a relationship,' said Peggy Culverton. 'Not then. I liked David, liked him a great deal, but it had never occurred to me to do anything about it.' She squeezed Lassiter's hand. 'As I said, Inspector, it matters to me what people think and – well, I suppose I'm rather a conventional person.'

Lassiter's hand tightened on hers. 'You believe in marriage, Peggy,' he said quietly. 'Don't apologize for that. So do I.' He looked at Rackham. 'I hadn't realized that Anne knew anything about my feelings for Peggy. They were real enough, even though there was nothing between us. When I got the phone call from Anne saying Peggy was desperately upset, I came straight here from the works at Tilbury. Anne, very tactfully, faded away.'

'I didn't know she'd gone,' said Peggy Culverton thoughtfully.

'What happened next?' asked Rackham.

'For God's sake!' said Lassiter desperately. 'What d'you think happened?'

Rackham held up his hand. 'Don't misunderstand me, sir. As I say, I have no desire to poke around in your private affairs. What I meant was, granted what you've told me, it would be natural for you to try and find Mr Culverton. I know that in the same circumstances, I'd be tempted to get hold of him, if for no other reason than to warn him to stay away from Mrs Culverton.'

'You did think that, David,' said Peggy Culverton. 'You asked me where you could find him. You said you wanted a word.'

Lassiter suddenly grinned. 'As a matter of fact, I think I put it rather more strongly.' He let out a deep breath.

'All right, Inspector. When Peggy told me how scared she'd been and what she believed Culverton to be, I wanted to find him. I had visions of giving him a damn good hiding – I would have beaten the truth out of him – then hauling him off to the police. Peggy said he had rooms at the Mulciber Club. My idea was to go there and either see him right away or wait for him to turn up. However . . .' He shrugged. 'Peggy didn't want me to leave her.'

'I couldn't bear the thought of being alone,' she said quickly. 'Not then.'

'So you stayed here?' asked Rackham.

Lassiter nodded. 'So I stayed here. It was the early hours of the morning before I finally left. The next day I went round to Culverton's office, hoping to see him, but his secretary, Lloyd, told me he had gone to Paris. I left a message for Culverton to get in touch when he got back and that was about that.' He shrugged and, walking to the sideboard, poured himself a whisky and soda. Leaning against the sideboard he held the glass thoughtfully. 'Anne covered up for us. Peggy didn't want anyone to know how things were between us.'

Peggy Culverton drew her breath in. 'No. No, I didn't.' She looked at him. 'I didn't want you to see Alexander, David. I simply wanted to get a divorce as quickly and as painlessly as possible and if he had any idea we cared for each other he would have used that against us. I wanted you to stay away from him. I said so. You thought you could get the truth out of him but you didn't seem to realize – nobody ever did seem to realize – just how dangerous he was. Even if you had taken him to the police he'd have got out of it somehow. He'd have destroyed you, David.'

Lassiter took a long drink. 'I wasn't frightened of him.'

Mrs Culverton turned away for a moment. 'Perhaps you should have been.'

Rackham looked from Peggy Culverton to David Lassiter. 'So when you got the news Culverton was dead, why didn't you tell the truth?'

David Lassiter gave a short laugh. 'Because neither of us is stupid, Inspector. As it happened, Anne had given Peggy an alibi. When we heard the news of Culverton's death she wanted to tell the truth but I asked her to keep stumm. I expected you to find the killer pretty quickly and then, after a decent interval, I was going to ask Peggy to marry me. But, as time went on, it became obvious that you couldn't find the killer and would be very interested in anyone who'd had a motive. What happened? Did Anne's conscience get the better of her?'

'David!' said Mrs Culverton, shocked. 'Anne wouldn't let us down.'

'She didn't,' said Rackham. 'The truth came out by accident, as it often does.'

Lassiter grimaced. 'I don't suppose this afternoon helped. I know Maguire put two and two together. I could see him doing it.' Rackham didn't contradict him. Lassiter put down his glass with a sharp click. 'How could we have told you the truth? I didn't kill Culverton but there's no denying I might have done if I'd got hold of him that night.'

'Is there anyone who can support your story, Mr Lassiter?' asked Rackham. 'Is there anyone who saw you leave this flat, say?'

David Lassiter shook his head. 'I wish there was, Inspector, but no.' He smiled ruefully. 'I was trying not to be seen, you understand. I simply slipped away as quietly as I could.' He cleared his throat. 'I'm innocent but I know how it looks. What will you do?'

Rackham got to his feet. 'At the moment, nothing, sir. However, I must ask both you and Mrs Culverton to stay in London for the time being.'

Peggy Culverton rose to her feet. 'Thank you, Inspector.' She sounded genuinely grateful. 'The last few days have been awful. Watching, wondering . . . Just being afraid.' She gave a little shudder. 'I'm glad in a way the truth's come out. Now it has, it's not nearly as bad as I thought it might be.' She glanced at David. 'Thank God I stopped you

192

going to find Alexander that night. He was dangerous, David. You were so sure you'd have it your way but he would have struck back, you know.'

'So you tell me,' said Lassiter. 'You've been frightened of him for too long, Peggy. It's over now.'

She breathed a deep sigh of relief. 'Yes, it's over now.' She half-smiled. 'I'm glad. It's hard to believe. I feel as if I'm coming back to life again.' She looked at Rackham. 'I'm sure, as sure as I can be of anything, that he was the man you were looking for. I don't know if this makes sense, but he was empty, empty in a frightening way. He could only destroy, not create.' She shook her head with a little choking noise. 'I never knew that about him until afterwards. Even the things he had cared about he destroyed. When I first met him he really did care about his business and he had plans, great plans in a way. That was real but even that was destroyed.'

'Wasn't he successful?' said Rackham, startled.

'Like everything else, Inspector, it was all show. Empty show. The company couldn't have lasted, the way he ran it. It would have gone under.' David Lassiter moved towards her protectively. 'David knows the truth. Alexander was no longer a rich man and I am certainly no longer a rich woman.'

'That doesn't matter,' said Lassiter quickly.

She turned and smiled at him and, for the first time since he had met her, Rackham could sense she was happy. 'No, it doesn't, does it, David? I'm glad I stopped you from going to find him that night.'

Which was, Rackham thought as he walked down the stairs from the flat, very moving and very convincing. He wanted to believe it was true. The trouble was, as he remarked to Jack the next day, even though it chimed in with Anne Lassiter's story and Gilchrist Lloyd confirmed that David Lassiter had enquired after Culverton on 1st November, he wasn't completely sure it was.

* * *

193

Nigel Lassiter strode into his father's office, slamming the door behind him.

David, who was standing by his father's desk, jerked his head up. 'What the hell's got into you?'

Nigel ignored him and threw down a letter in front of Mr Lassiter. 'Read that. Just read that. That *bloody* woman!'

Mr Lassiter gazed at his furious son, then picked up his reading glasses and glanced at the superscription. 'From Mrs Culverton. *Thank you . . . efforts involved . . . of great interest . . . long association . . . cannot see my way to . . . however . . .*' He put down the letter and drummed his fingers on the desk. 'It could be worse,' he said at last. 'It could be a great deal worse.'

'How?' demanded Nigel, flinging himself into a chair. 'We don't get another penny from her until the maiden flight to India. India, for God's sake! I don't care about India, it's a week on Friday I'm bothered about. If I can't get some more money we'll have to call off the dinner and we'll look like complete idiots.'

David picked up the letter and read through it. 'She says she expects the final cost of the aircraft to reflect the money already paid towards the project by Culverton Air Navigation.'

'She says she'll fund part of the production – *part*, mind you – if we agree to virtually give her a blasted plane. How the blazes are we supposed to make any money out of that?'

David's voice was deliberately calm. 'I can't help thinking that's fair enough, Nigel.'

'You would. You've never believed in the Pegasus. Why didn't you tell the bloody reporters it was going to crash on take-off? It's what you expect, isn't it?'

'I'm not expecting anything of the sort,' said David patiently. 'For God's sake, Nigel, you know it needs more work.'

Nigel Lassiter buried his head in his hands. 'Work! That's all I ever do. I've worked so hard and this – this *bloody* letter – is all the thanks I get for it. We need sales. I need money.'

'The press presentation caused a lot of interest,' said Mr Lassiter. 'Some of the comments make wonderful reading.'

Nigel looked up. 'So what? They were bound to like it. They couldn't but like it. I was relying on Culverton's. What the devil does she mean, she expects a substantial reduction? Does she want me to be grateful? Why the hell should I be?'

David folded his arms and sat on the corner of the desk. 'What now? The company's stretched as it's never been before. If we had the funds we could carry the seaplane until orders came in but we haven't. I'll freely admit it, Nigel, the plane's a beauty. Once you've had a successful maiden voyage to India, the aircraft will virtually sell itself. But and it's a big but – you've got to get her to that stage. Is there anyone else you can approach?'

Nigel's shoulders sank. 'I don't know.' He bit his nails broodingly. 'The firm will have to pay up. You'll just have to give me the money.'

'We haven't got it!' said David angrily. 'I always said this was too big a project for us.'

'Yes, I know. You wanted to stick with your business-men's bus. You've got it in for me, David. You want me to fail. Ever since Thomas's crash you've been trying to undermine me. Don't deny it. You know it's true but it was his fault, not mine. He couldn't control the plane.'

David Lassiter got to his feet and, hands opening and closing, towered over his brother. 'You think I've got it in for you, do you?' he said in a deceptively quiet voice. 'You think Thomas was to blame?' His hand shot out, grasping Nigel's shirt and hauling him to his feet. 'Well, let me tell you –'

Nigel, his dark eyes alight with fear, wriggled as help-lessly as a worm on a hook.

Mr Lassiter brought his fist crashing down on the table. 'David! Calm down.' David Lassiter didn't respond. 'David!'

David slowly turned his head to look at his father, then, like a man coming up from underwater, looked at his hands, shook himself and released his grip.

Nigel dropped back into the chair, staring at his brother. 'You damned lunatic,' he said softly. David was staring at his hands. Nigel straightened out his shirt. 'It's not safe to be in the same room as you.'

Mr Lassiter smacked his fist down on the table again. 'Nigel! That was completely uncalled for. David, you mustn't let your temper get the better of you, no matter what the provocation.'

David, still staring at his upturned hands, blinked and looked at his father. It was as if he was coming back from somewhere very far away. 'I'm sorry, sir,' he said hesitantly. 'I forgot myself for the moment.'

Nigel, still straightening his tie, continued to stare at David. 'What about me? Don't I deserve an apology?'

David, white-lipped, swallowed and flexed his hands. Nigel instinctively started back in his seat.

Mr Lassiter leaned forward warningly. 'David!' he said urgently.

David Lassiter took a deep breath and relaxed his shoulders. 'Sorry,' he said evenly.

A thin smile curled Nigel's mouth. 'That'll do, I suppose. Now, if we can return to business, I'd like to point out that Mrs Culverton has given us all a problem. This firm needs the Pegasus and I'd like to remind you both that you promised you'd see the Pegasus through, not abandon it at the last minute. I need *money*!'

'The press presentation –' began Mr Lassiter.

Nigel cut him off. 'The press presentation! Don't talk to me about that. Yes, we got mentioned in the aviation papers but the Pegasus should have been headline news. What happened? All the coverage was about that South African idiot and his pal, to say nothing of Daring David here, cavorting around the roof. I wish the bloody idiot had fallen off. It would have served him right.'

Mr Lassiter took off his glasses and stared very hard at his son. Then he placed his hands flat on the desk in front of him and concentrated on keeping them steady. Nigel, suddenly aware that he had gone drastically too far, swallowed and waited. When Mr Lassiter eventually spoke, it was in a quiet, even voice that Nigel had only heard a very few times before. 'That South African idiot, as you call him, is my grandson. I do not feel I have to add to that statement. If *you* –' here he gave Nigel such a withering glance that he flinched – 'had an ounce of his concern for others then I would be a far happier man. I could describe your character; I prefer to leave such things unsaid. As for the Pegasus, unless fresh money is forthcoming soon, then I am afraid that the seaplane will have to be postponed until we have recouped at least some of our losses.'

Nigel glanced at him then fumbled for a cigarette. 'Postponed?' He rubbed his forehead and gave his father an agonized look. 'You don't mean it, do you? You can't.' He mouth twisted. 'Look, it'll be all right. I'm sorry I said that about George. I didn't mean it. You must know I didn't mean it. You can't hold it against me, not now. All I need is a bit more money to bridge the gap. It's going to be a success. You must help. We've got to fly next week. It's all arranged. It was Anne who suggested I host a dinner, a dinner in the air over London. If it wasn't for Anne I could have postponed the first flight but I've got to fly next week. She said it would be a success. She's put a lot of thought into it. You can't let Anne down. You wouldn't let Anne down, would you, David?'

'That's a bit transparent,' commented David.

'She really has put a lot of effort into it,' said his father. 'I can see she'd be disappointed if it didn't come off. There's been quite a bit of excitement in the press about it. And Nigel's quite right. It would cause some very adverse comment if the dinner were to be cancelled.'

197

Nigel stubbed out his cigarette and lit another. 'I can't let that happen. I'm so close,' he said, more to himself than to the other two men in the room. 'I'm so very close . . .'

It was Sunday afternoon. Jack, alone in his rooms, lay in drowsy comfort full-length on the sofa, the *Messenger* discarded in a heap beside him. Outside, the rain-filled wind rattled against the windows. He felt a warm sense of pleasure at the contrast. A coal fell on the glowing fire, sending a shower of sparks up the chimney. From the hallway below a distant telephone bell jangled. It was probably the telephone which had woken him up. He snuggled back into the cushions, gazing abstractedly at the ceiling. George was at Eden Street and it was pleasant to have only his own thoughts for company.

George had suffered as a result of his experiences at the factory. He'd wrenched the muscles in his arm and had to wear a sling all week. Still, compared with what could have happened . . . He thought once more of George's white face and the agonized clutch of his hand and shuddered. That moment when he felt himself being pulled inexorably over the edge of the board-walk was easily one of the worst in his life. My God, but he was grateful to David.

David: his mouth tightened as he thought of David. It seemed incredible that, granted the sort of man Culverton had been, the only person who seemed to have any motive to kill him was David. Bill had put in no end of work, chasing up Culverton's associates, but there was nothing. Peggy Culverton had a motive, of course, and, like David, a trumped-up alibi, but that was all. Bill had had a long discussion with the Assistant Commissioner about them. As the AC had pointed out, there wasn't a shred of any real evidence, only a circumstantial case. In the AC's opinion, once Anne Lassiter, David Lassiter and, most of all, Peggy Culverton had explained those circumstances, no jury in England would bring in a guilty verdict. And Bill's opinion? Agnostic would probably sum it up. However, he agreed with the AC about the reactions of any jury, especially if Mrs Culverton even hinted what she believed about her husband.

There was a knock at the door. 'Major Haldean?' It was Mrs Pettycure. 'There's a telephone call for you, sir.'

Damn. 'Thank you,' Jack called back as he levered himself off the sofa.

Bill Rackham was on the phone. 'Jack?'

His voice was urgent and Jack was instantly alert. 'What is it?'

Rackham's voice was sharp and thin with worry. 'We were wrong about Culverton. Another girl's been found in the river.'

'Dead?'

'Very dead.' Jack could hear the emotion in Rackham's voice. 'She was marked with a cross. I thought this was over. I thought it had stopped but we were wrong, Jack, wrong. We're back to square one.'

Chapter Eleven

At half past nine on Tuesday morning Jack walked briskly down the Strand to Fleet Street, crossed at the Cheshire Cheese, weaved his way through the traffic and stopped by the newspaper seller standing in the shelter of the doorway of the steps leading up to the third-floor offices of *On the Town*.

'Paper, Major?' asked the newspaper seller, holding out a copy of the *Chronicle*.

'Thanks, Stan,' said Jack, feeling in his pocket for change.

'I see they're no further forward catching this Ripper,' said Stan. 'I don't know what the police are playing at. Useless, they are.'

'Umm,' said Jack diplomatically, glancing at the headlines. Politics had moved the Ripper into second place but the story was essentially the same as in Monday's paper. Yesterday the victim had no name. Now she was identified as Martha Palmer of Sheffield Court, Marylebone, thought to be twenty-six, originally from Brighton, who had, until last April, been employed as a waitress at the Golden Road Café in Soho and had twice been cautioned for soliciting. No one had seen her since Saturday morning.

Jack had an idea of the work behind that simple statement. He felt an unexpected wave of anger. Her life – not a good or productive life but still a life – could be summed up in a couple of sentences whereas her death spawned two paragraphs of newsprint. He skipped through the rest of the piece quickly. Bill had told him the details on Sunday. The body had been found at three in the afternoon by a bargeman moored up in the Surrey Basin at Rotherhithe. Bill had added more graphic details than the newspaper either knew or felt comfortable printing. The actual cause of death was strangulation but she'd suffered before she'd died. And they'd thought Culverton was the Ripper. They were, as Bill had said, back to square one.

He glanced at the rest of the front page, then stiffened.

'Major?' asked Stan. 'You all right?'

Jack didn't hear him at first and Stan repeated the question.

'Yes,' he said absently. 'Yes, fine.' He glanced at the stairs of *On the Town*. The magazine could do without him for a couple of hours. He needed to get to Scotland Yard.

'It's this that's brought me along,' said Jack, putting his finger on a small paragraph at the bottom of the *Chronicle*'s front page.

'*Merchant banker found dead*,' read Rackham. '*The body of Martin Ridgeway, partner in Croft and Ridgeway, High Holborn, was found at his home in Sutherland Park Road, Kew. Mr Ridgeway, fifty-six years old . . . well-known man about town . . . found by his manservant . . . believed to have shot himself . . . married, no children . . . separated from his wife who now resides in France.*' Rackham looked up from the paper. 'No doubt it's all very sad, Jack, but why should I be interested?'

'Because Martin Ridgeway was one of Nigel Lassiter's major investors.'

Rackham's eyes widened. 'Was he, by jingo?'

Jack hitched himself on to the corner of the desk. 'There's something very wrong at Lassiter's, Bill. First of all Culverton, the chief investor, gets killed, Michael Walsh, the secretary, dies and now Martin Ridgeway shoots himself. I suppose he did shoot himself, did he?'

Rackham reached for the telephone. 'Give me a few minutes. That's something I can find out easily enough.'

201

A series of telephone calls followed. Rackham eventually put down the receiver and looked at the impatiently waiting Jack. 'It's suicide, right enough. I've spoken to Superintendent Sykes from Kew and I'd trust his opinion, Jack. Sykes tells me that he was called to the house in Kew yesterday afternoon. Ridgeway returned home from work unexpectedly at midday, looking haggard and ill. Three of the servants saw him. His butler suggested calling the doctor but Ridgeway refused and retreated to his study. Shortly after, there was the sound of a shot. Ridgeway had locked the door but his body was clearly visible from the window. The butler called the police and Sykes had to break the door down. Ridgeway kept a pistol in the study and that's the weapon which was used. There's absolutely nothing to suggest it was anything other than suicide.'

'I met Ridgeway, y'know,' said Jack. 'I thought he was a bit of a creep to be honest. He was at the press presentation at Lassiter's last week and you should have seen him leering at Stella Aldryn. I thought George was going to thump him.'

'He had a name as a womanizer, according to Sykes,' agreed Rackham. 'In fact he seems to have been a bit unsavoury all round. Sykes contacted his firm, Croft and Ridgeway, and got the full story. Apparently Ridgeway had his hand in the till for the last couple of years at least. He was safe enough while old Mr Croft was in charge, but he died two months ago and his son, James Croft, who, according to Sykes, is a very sharp type indeed, took over. He told Sykes he'd suspected something was amiss and spent Sunday going through the accounts. He'd found certain evidence that Ridgeway was embezzling money and informed the man of his findings on Monday morning, adding that he'd arranged for an independent audit to be carried out, starting that afternoon. Ridgeway didn't argue but left the office and went home.' He looked at the newspaper and shrugged. 'The rest we know.' He frowned thoughtfully. 'Jack, you said there was something wrong at Lassiter's. What?'

Jack held his hands wide. 'I don't know, but three deaths, Bill? And the link between them all is Lassiter's.'

Rackham counted them off. 'Culverton was murdered, Walsh died of heart failure and Ridgeway shot himself.'

'There's also the dead girl who George thought he saw,' Jack reminded him.

Rackham gave a snort of disapproval. 'I'm not including imaginary corpses. Jack. I've got enough real ones to deal with, especially when the supposed victim turns up as large as life and, according to you, twice as beautiful. There can't be a link. Apart from anything else, who at Lassiter's benefits from any of the deaths? I mean, we're talking about Nigel and David, aren't we? Nigel wouldn't bump off his two chief investors and although David had a private motive for killing Culverton, I can't see he'd have a grudge against Walsh or Ridgeway, even overlooking the fact one died of natural causes and the other committed suicide.'

'We know there's no love lost between Nigel and David,' said Jack thoughtfully. 'Ridgeway's death following hot on the heels of Culverton's makes things very awkward for Nigel.'

'Murders aren't committed to make life awkward. If David loathes his brother to that extent, it'd make a damn sight more sense for him to bump off Nigel, not merely inconvenience him.'

Jack gave a wry smile. 'True enough. And, granted that Ridgeway invested in Lassiter's, things must be awkward for David, too. Even if they are at daggers drawn, David still needs the Pegasus to be a success if the company's going to recoup the money they've put into it.' He linked his fingers together thoughtfully. 'It was the three deaths so close together that got to me, Bill.'

'If Ridgeway topped himself, it can't be anything more than coincidence.'

Jack clicked his tongue. 'Coincidences happen, I suppose.' He shrugged his shoulders in irritation. 'Never mind. I see you've managed to identify the latest Ripper victim.'

'Yes, much good it's done us. You know, I really thought Culverton was our man.'

'Couldn't he be?' asked Jack. 'I mean, what if this latest killing is an imitation?'

'We've thought of that,' said Rackham. 'After all, everyone knows about the X man and it's easy enough to copy the mark. It could be an imitation, it could be completely unrelated or it could be that Culverton was simply some ghastly creep who harboured obscene photographs and cuttings about the Ripper while the real man is getting away scot-free. It could be any number of things. This chap, Ridgeway, could be the X man, I suppose, although that's too much to hope for. That's as good a theory as any. Don't you see what we're up against, Jack? We can't just guess. Anyone, anyone at all, could be guilty. We simply don't know and I can't see we're ever going to know unless we have that lucky break we talked about.' There was a thin thread of anger in his voice. He pushed his chair back from the desk and, getting up, walked restlessly around the room. 'All the usual sources are a waste of time. Nobody knows anything. Whoever this swine is, he's completely outside the run of everyday crooks and villains.' He perched on the windowsill. 'Forget it. Somehow, somewhere, our man's going to make a slip and when he does, we've got him.'

There was silence for a few moments, then Rackham looked up. 'Sorry, Jack. My temper's a bit the worse for wear. You made a perfectly reasonable suggestion. The answer is, we simply don't know.' He nodded at the newspaper Jack had left on the table, searching for another topic. 'Talking of Lassiter's,' he said, after a short pause, 'there's been a fair old bit of ballyhoo about them in the papers recently. Everyone seems to be getting very wound up about this dinner on the aircraft. You're not invited by any chance, are you?'

Jack shook his head. 'Me? Not an earthly. George tells me that the guests are very important people indeed, people they hope might actually buy the plane.' He got to his feet and picked his hat up from the chair beside him. 'Talking of dinner, are you still joining me for a bite to eat at the club tonight?'

'Curry at the Young Services? Absolutely. I'll call for you about seven o'clock. Is your pal George coming too?'

'He certainly is,' said Jack, doing up the buckle on his Burberry. 'I wouldn't mind a night out with George. I've neglected him a bit recently, what with buzzing out to clubs and . . . Well, after we did our Tarzan act at the factory, it's got better, but I've been feeling a bit iffy about George. Things aren't as they should be.'

'Really? In what way?'

'He bothers me.' Jack frowned. 'It's a bit hard to explain. I keep trying not to let it matter but it does, you know. The thing is, Stella Aldryn called on him the other Saturday morning, the day we went to the Continental. I was out at the time, but I knew she'd been because she left her coffee cup with lipstick on it on the table. When I saw her later, I asked her if she'd been round and she admitted it.'

'And?' asked Rackham.

'Well, she'd asked George not to mention it. Now that's perfectly reasonable, because as she was well aware, people would talk if was known she'd been alone with him in his rooms.'

'They'd have to be pretty stuffy in this day and age. Saturday night, perhaps, but not Saturday morning.'

Jack smiled distractedly. 'Sin only occurs in the hours of darkness, you mean? Anyway, she wanted it kept quiet.' He shrugged. 'Fair enough. It's her business, after all. The point is, George flatly denied she'd been. Even after I'd told him she'd admitted it, he wouldn't have it. He swore blind neither she nor anyone else had called and I don't like it.'

'That's very peculiar,' said Rackham with a frown. 'I can see him not wanting to make a song and dance about it, but why shouldn't he tell you? Especially if you knew already.' He sat down, looking at his friend's worried face.

'It's bothering you, isn't it? Why? Because he won't own up to the truth?'

Jack nodded. 'That's exactly it. The thing is, Bill, he seems so painfully honest.'

'So did Anne Lassiter,' commented Rackham drily.

'Yes, but she had a reason for telling bouncers. There isn't any reason for George to lie. What's more, he isn't embarrassed or evasive about it, as if he was covering up for Miss Aldryn out of misplaced loyalty. It's as if it never happened. It's just . . . well, nuts.'

There was an unconscious emphasis in the last word. Rackham looked up sharply. 'That's it, isn't it? You're wondering if he's quite all there, aren't you?'

Jack wriggled in irritation. 'He doesn't *seem* nuts,' he protested. 'Yet it's either that or he's not the man I thought.'

Rackham let his breath out in a long sigh. 'I can see why it's getting to you. Look, the easiest explanation is that Miss Aldryn told him not to mention it and that's exactly what he's doing. However, you've thought of that. So what's left?' He tapped his fingers on the desk. 'Dishonesty, which you don't think squares with his character, or some form of insanity.' Jack winced. 'I know you don't like that either, Jack, but he does seem prone to this sort of thing. First of all there was his dead girl in the kitchen – admittedly he was ill – but then there was the cat on the roof at the factory. You don't believe there was a cat there, do you?'

'It disappeared pretty quickly if there was,' admitted Jack reluctantly.

'And now this.' Rackham drummed his fingers in another rolling tattoo. 'Look, if it bothers you as much as you say, perhaps he should see someone. Dr Maguire offered to help, I know.'

Jack smiled humourlessly. 'I'm not bringing that up again. He was very short with Anne Lassiter when she suggested it. If he won't take it from Mrs Lassiter he certainly won't take it from me.'

'Well, not Maguire, then, but I think he should see someone.'

'Perhaps,' agreed Jack unenthusiastically. 'Anyway, that's the situation, Bill. I wanted to let you know before the three of us went out together. Incidentally, talking of George, have you had any response from South Africa, by the way? About his legacy, I mean.'

'Now you mention it, I have. I was going to tell you but it slipped my mind.' Jack looked at him expectantly. 'I had a cable yesterday but don't get your hopes up.' Rackham opened a drawer and took out a file. 'Here we are,' he said, finding the cable. 'It's nothing much. All it says is that a George Lassiter stayed at the Faulkner Hotel, Cape Town, from 5th February to 12th March 1922. It's a large hotel and no one remembers anything about the George Lassiter in question.'

'Hang on a mo,' said Jack, picking up a pencil and scribbling the dates on Rackham's blotting-pad. He half closed his eyes and performed a rapid calculation. 'It's sixteen days' sailing time to the Cape.' He tapped the pencil on the blotter. 'That looks to me as if someone signed into the Faulkner just to write the letter to Marchbolt's and be there to await the reply from London.'

'Someone called George Lassiter?' said Rackham softly.

'Someone calling themselves George Lassiter,' corrected Jack with a frown.

Rackham shrugged. 'In light of what you've told me I think it's a possibility, you know.'

'You're right, damn it,' Jack admitted. He looked at the cable again. 'I can't see this gets us very much further. Mind you, we didn't think it would.' He picked up the newspaper. 'I'd better go. I'm meant to be working this morning but when I read that bit in the paper about Ridgeway I thought I had to tell you about his association with Lassiter's.'

'It's useful to know,' said Rackham. He frowned. 'It is odd, Jack, it's very odd, but I honestly think that's all it is. Anything else doesn't make sense.'

* * *

Anne Lassiter put down the magazine she'd been reading as David came into the drawing room. 'Shall I ring for coffee?' she asked.

'In a few minutes,' said David, going to stand beside the mantelpiece. He took his pipe out of his pocket and filled it thoughtfully. They were alone in the room. 'Anne,' he said quietly, 'd'you think my father knows? About Peggy and me, I mean?'

She shook her head. 'I'm sure he doesn't. Not unless Nigel's told him.'

He looked startled. 'How does Nigel know anything about it?'

'Roger might have mentioned it to him.'

'Roger!' He frowned at the bowl of his pipe. 'Anne, I know it's not really any of my business but I'm not sure about Maguire.' He gave her a sidelong, diffident look. 'Are you certain he's the right bloke for you? You know I care.' He glanced down at her. 'Don't bite my head off, will you?'

She smiled. 'No, I won't do that.' Her expression became wistful. 'David, I just don't know about Roger. When I'm with him it's all right but when he's not here ... I don't know.'

'How d'you mean?' asked David curiously.

'He gets his own way,' said Anne. 'He always will.' She sighed in exasperation. 'The truth is I'm attracted to him, but I don't honestly know how much I can trust him. He's older than I am, quite a bit older, and sometimes I wonder if that's a problem. He seems to know so much that I don't. He's clever and sophisticated and can be very good company but I never feel I understand him. He's a very different sort to Thomas.'

David smiled. 'Thomas was the goods, wasn't he? I miss him.' He stopped as he saw the expression on her face. 'Sorry. So do you, I know that.' He concentrated on his pipe again. 'I tell you who reminds me of him,' he said eventually. 'George. They're very different people but there's something about George which makes me think of him.

They were cousins, after all, even if they never knew each other. If Thomas had lived I bet they'd have hit it off tremendously. George is ...' He cast round for the right words. 'He's *reliable*.'

'I know exactly what you mean,' said Anne.

He cocked an eyebrow at her. 'Well?'

She wriggled impatiently. 'It's difficult. When I think of Roger it's so difficult.'

David leaned forward earnestly. 'Don't make a mistake, Anne. That sort of mistake is so very hard to put right. Peggy made a mistake and she spent a long time regretting it.'

'Peggy thinks the world of you, David,' said Anne softly. 'I always knew she did, even though she never said a word.' She paused. 'It's a shame you couldn't keep things to yourself for a bit longer though. She's right about what the police would think. I'm sorry we saw you that day at the factory.'

'So am I,' he agreed ruefully. 'Peggy keeps everything bottled up but she was pretty close to cracking that day. Gilchrist Lloyd had warned her that the firm was in a bad way and she's convinced that Haldean suspects me of doing in Culverton. I think she's wrong, but she's very wary of him.'

Anne bit her lip. 'I think she's wrong about Major Haldean, too. He likes you, David, that's obvious.'

'Well, I like him. I told Peggy as much. I appreciate what he's done for George and there's no doubt about it, he saved George's life at the factory. That was a stunning piece of work.' He grinned. 'Have you read any of his stories? They're clever and sharp, just like him. The only thing which makes me think a bit is that he's hand-in-glove with the police. He's a good man, though. If I was up against it, I'd like to have him on my side.' He gave a humourless laugh. 'Peggy's not convinced. As she says, we're the only people who seem to have had any sort of motive for killing Culverton. She doesn't trust him.'

Anne gave a sigh. 'I wonder if we'll ever find out who did kill him. Have you any ideas?'

David's face was strained. 'No. To be honest, it's getting to me a bit.' He struck a match and lit his pipe. 'I loathed Culverton. He made Peggy's life hell and even now he's dead he's still a problem. He's the reason I don't want the guv'nor to know about how things are with Peggy. In ordinary circumstances he'd be delighted but it's this appalling situation with the police that's the problem.'

The telephone rang in the hall. Anne got up to answer it, then sat down again as the bell stopped. Nigel's voice came through the partly open door as he answered the phone. Anne looked stricken. 'I hope he didn't hear us,' she said quietly.

David shrugged. 'It doesn't matter if he did.' He was about to say more when Nigel let rip with a string of obscenities at the top of his voice. The words were foul. David exchanged a quick, startled glance with Anne and Nigel swore again.

'What the devil's got into him?' demanded David. He strode to the door and swung it open. 'Nigel! What d'you mean talking like that? The whole house can hear you.'

Nigel slammed the earpiece back on its rest and faced his brother. 'Talk? Hellfire, I'd like to do more than talk! That was Mrs Culverton. Do you know what's happened?'

David gazed at him. 'Do you mean to tell me you used language like that to *Mrs Culverton*?'

'Yes, to your precious Mrs Culverton. She wanted to tell us that idiot, Ridgeway, has topped himself. It's in the papers. He's dead, d'you hear me, dead! What the blazes do we do now, I ask you?'

David swallowed. 'You swore at *Mrs Culverton*?'

'Yes, damn it, I swore at Mrs bloody Culverton. So what? Can't you hear what I'm telling you? Ridgeway's dead. My God, David, you'll have to do something now. I need money, d'you hear me? Why don't you speak to her? You can get anything you like out of her. You'll have to lean on her but you can do it, right enough. Roger saw you the other day. You've got her eating out of your hand. If you had any sense you'd get hold of the bloody woman and –'

David's fist shot out, catching Nigel squarely on the mouth. Nigel, flung back by the blow, crashed into the hall table. The table, which held a vase of flowers, went over in a smash of breaking china. The noise seemed to stretch indefinitely, then there was silence broken only by the dripping of water. Nigel, sprawled amongst the wreckage of the vase and spilt flowers, raised himself on his hands and knees, blood swelling from a cut lip. He put the back of his hand to his mouth, gazing at the blood on his hand, thunderstruck. Then, with a murderous glint in his eye, he gathered himself for a spring.

'No!' shrieked Anne. She prepared to fling herself between the two men when the doorbell rang. All three of them turned to look as Corby, who had obviously been close at hand, trod majestically into the hall, stepping through the broken china to the door.

As if absolutely nothing was amiss, he turned from the opened door.

'Dr Maguire, sir,' he announced. 'For you, Mr Nigel.' He coughed. 'Are you at home, sir?'

'Of course I'm bloody well at home,' growled Nigel, pushing past him. 'Come in, Roger. Corby, get that mess cleared up. Roger, go into the drawing room. Have you heard? Ridgeway's dead.'

'That's what I came to tell you,' said Maguire, looking at the shattered vase on the floor. 'What happened?'

'Nothing,' said Nigel quickly, wiping his mouth. 'Nothing much, anyway.' Maguire took off his hat and coat and gave them to the waiting butler. 'Go into the drawing room, Roger. I need to talk to you.'

Maguire looked at Anne. 'I'll see you later. I really think I'd better go and talk to Nigel.'

Nigel walked past David who was standing, a stunned expression on his face, gazing at his fist.

211

Anne touched David on the arm. She wanted to get him away, out of the hall. 'David? Why don't we go into the billiard room?'

'The billiard room?' He drew his hand across his forehead. 'Yes, if you want to.' Although he didn't argue, he didn't move. Anne touched his arm once more to guide him away when the door to the drawing room opened and Nigel came out again.

'Maguire wants to speak to both of us. Not you,' he said curtly as Anne came forward. 'David, I mean.' David looked at him blankly. 'We have to talk. Ridgeway's death has upset the apple-cart good and proper.' David still didn't move. 'For God's sake, man,' snarled Nigel. 'We're still in business and we still have a firm to run.'

David took a deep breath, straightened his shoulders and walked into the drawing room.

As arranged, Bill Rackham called for Jack and George at seven o'clock that evening. 'You've a treat in store,' said Rackham to George as they turned into Trafalgar Square. Lassiter, decided Rackham, looked normal enough and he decided to give him the benefit of the doubt for the time being. 'I think the Young Services does one of the best curries in London. Do you mind walking? I've been stuck behind a desk all day and could do with some exercise.'

'It suits me,' said George. 'Mind you,' he added, huddling into his coat as the wind bit through him, 'I think London has some of the lousiest weather I've ever encountered. If it's not raining or foggy, it's freezing cold.' They walked down Pall Mall and turned right on to St James's Street, their steps ringing in the quiet streets, past the elegant houses with their pillared steps and porticoed doors, white against the soot-blackened brick.

'I see Nigel Lassiter's causing a bit of a stir with his arrangements for Friday night,' said Rackham. 'The River Police have given him permission to land on the Thames between Waterloo and Blackfriars Bridge. There should be quite a crowd to watch him.'

'Yes, the *Messenger* called it a moment of history,' said Jack. 'I'd call it a miracle, granted what's gone on behind the scenes,' he added with a grin.

'Absolutely,' agreed George, laughing. 'I spoke to Stella on the phone earlier and she says that Nigel's working fit to bust and his temper's gone to pot. He'll have a nervous breakdown if he carries on like this. I don't know how she stands the man.'

'Did you ever get to the bottom of what he said to her that day?' asked Jack. George shook his head. 'It was at the factory, at the press presentation,' explained Jack in answer to Rackham's enquiring look.

'What, where you saw the cat on the roof?'

'That's right,' said Jack evenly with a slight warning frown at Rackham. 'After George was safe and we were on terra firma again, Nigel turned on Stella Aldryn and called her a "bloody fool".'

'That's a bit rich,' said Rackham in shocked disapproval. 'He shouldn't use language like that to a woman. It's not on, especially as she works for him.'

'That's exactly what I said,' agreed George. 'It's unfair, isn't it? She can't answer him back properly.'

'What on earth was he talking about?' asked Rackham. 'In what way had she been a fool?'

'That's what we can't work out,' said Jack. 'Neither George nor I could make head or tail of it.' He turned to his friend for confirmation but George had stopped a few paces behind. 'George?'

'Hold on a minute, Jack,' called George. They were on the corner of St James's Street and St James's Place. The house – a very aristocratic house – had steps up to the front door and a balcony on the first floor. The house was surrounded by elaborate wrought-iron railings and flanked by Portland stone pillars topped by lamp standards. To Jack and Rackham's utter astonishment, George ran up the steps and, using the stonework for support, scrambled to the top of the railings.

'What the devil . . .?' Jack and Rackham walked back. 'George, get down,' said Jack.

George smiled at them. 'It's all right. I won't be a tick.' He frowned up at the underside of the balcony, stretched up a hand and grasped on to the underside of the wrought-iron brackets that curled above his head. 'This'll hold my weight, won't it?' he asked, frowning at the bracket. 'I wish my wretched arm was better.'

'George, get down,' repeated Jack. 'You're making a complete idiot of yourself. You can't climb up there.'

'D'you think I'll need a ladder? I'll be all right.'

'George, for God's sake, *get down!*'

'But the cat's stuck.'

Jack and Rackham exchanged worried glances.

'There isn't a cat,' said Rackham, after a glance at the balcony.

George smiled reassuringly. 'Of course there is.' He took a hand off the column to point and wobbled dangerously. 'Look, it's there.'

Jack took the flailing hand and pulled him down. 'There isn't a cat and even if there was you can't shin up the railings. What's come over you?'

'Nothing,' said George. 'I'm fine, Jack, but you can't expect me to leave the poor cat stranded up there, can you?' He shook off Jack's arm. 'Let me go. I won't be a moment.'

Rackham interposed. 'You mustn't climb up there.'

'But what about the cat?'

'There isn't a ruddy cat,' said Jack, losing patience.

George tried to get past him but Rackham barred his way. 'You're not climbing up there. Apart from being dangerous, I bet it's against the law.'

'Leave it, George,' said Jack. 'Come on. Are we going for this curry or not?'

Flanked between Jack and Rackham, George was unwillingly shepherded down the street.

They got to the Young Services, George still vigorously protesting. 'I wish you'd let me help that cat,' he said, as they went into the lobby.

'Drop it, George,' said Jack, handing his coat and hat to the cloakroom attendant.

'It wouldn't have taken me long,' George said stubbornly.

Jack gave a snort of exasperation. He could see how uncomfortable Rackham was feeling and he wasn't alone. 'George, listen to me. I'll grant you saw a cat; I'll believe that the wretched animal was stuck; I'll even concede that, given an absence of anything else to do, you might want to save it; but you cannot, really cannot, start porch-climbing in St James's Place and you are not, really are not, going to dominate the rest of the evening by talking about it. Now, what about this curry?'

They went into the dining room where the subject of cats was thankfully forsaken. They turned their attention to food and, helped by whitebait and hock, followed by curry cooked by the Young Services' Indian chef, the conversation moved on to safer ground.

'By the way, Jack,' said Rackham, looking dubiously at a chilli, 'how did you get on with your search for a club? Did the fancy dress help?'

'Not really,' said Jack, reaching for the bread. 'It's not for want of trying. I seem to have done nothing else but dodge in and out of nightclubs. I was hoping to try and find where Culverton had got to,' he added to George, who was picking at his food in an abstracted way.

'It beats me,' said Rackham, seeing that George wasn't going to respond, 'how few people seem to have had a motive. I've spent days tracing Culverton's associates – he didn't seem to have any friends – and as far as I'm concerned, it's been a complete waste of time. What really annoys me is that we still haven't got a clue where he went after he left the Mulciber. The man seems to have disappeared off the face of the earth and yet we know he went *somewhere*.'

'Well, he didn't go to the Frozen Limit, the 1920, the Gargoyle, the Hesperides, the Crow's Nest, the Good Intentions or the Why Don't You? Oh, and you can rule out the Rainbow's End as well. That's not an exhaustive list, just my haul over the last few nights.'

'It sounds exhaustive to me,' said Rackham. 'You must be stonkered.'

'I am beginning to feel it a bit,' agreed Jack. 'But, although I yearned for vice as ardently as an early Roman emperor, the result is a complete lemon. For all that the papers write about nightclubs being haunts of sin and depravity, full of shameless, flaunting women luring fresh-faced boys to hell to the wail of the saxophone, as the *Chronicle* put it the other day, all those I've been to have been as innocent as Sunday school picnics.'

'So no shameless, flaunting women?' said Rackham with a grin. 'Bad luck.'

'They haven't flaunted themselves at me,' said Jack with feeling. 'Well, a couple – actually more than a couple – have, but their minds were obviously running along the lines of lobster mayonnaise, a pearl necklace or two and a cosy weekend in the country, not enticing me into dens of iniquity.'

'What about the dance hostesses? Haven't they tried to entice or lure you?'

Jack shook his head regretfully. 'They haven't lured, they haven't flaunted, and they haven't enticed, just charged me a quid a time and the price of a bottle of warm champagne for the privilege of a dance and a chat. D'you know it's seventy-five bob a bottle in some places? This is costing me a fortune.'

'Look on it as a little extra something on your tax bill,' said Rackham unfeelingly. 'Mind you, our people haven't turned up anything either. Still, there's a lot of clubs in London.' He turned to George. 'How's your curry? What did you have? Chicken?'

'They called it *Kari de Volaille* on the menu,' put in Jack.

'I feel sorry for the poor creature,' said George, putting down his knife and fork and staring at his plate.

'What, the chicken?' asked Jack.

'No, idiot,' said George. 'The cat. The cat on the balcony, I mean.'

Jack sighed dangerously. 'George, there wasn't any wretched cat. Was there, Bill?'

'I couldn't see one.'

'But it was there!' protested George. 'It was a one-eared ginger tom. You must have seen it.'

Rackham coughed. 'You'll excuse me for mentioning it, Lassiter, but it wouldn't be the first time you've seen things. For instance, there was the cat in the factory.'

'There was a cat in the factory,' said George in surprise. 'Of course there was.'

Rackham tried another tack. 'Well, there was the girl in the kitchen.'

George flushed. 'Come on. You can't count that.'

'You did say how real it all seemed though,' pointed out Jack.

'Well, it did seem real,' countered George. 'It wasn't like a dream, where everything's jumbled up, it seemed real. Even now . . .' He shook his head and picked up the lime chutney. 'It was the detail which was so convincing,' he said, spooning the chutney on to the side of his plate. 'I know I must have imagined it, but I can remember the pattern on her dress and what they said to each other and so on. One said, "We're safe. He's having a bath and she's listening to the wireless," and then, after the girl had collapsed, they didn't react properly. One of the men said, "It's what you wanted. It's what both of you wanted. A perfect death. You've got it." It was so creepy. That bit *was* like a nightmare. It was completely different from seeing that poor cat,' he added, applying himself to his curry once more. 'You must see that, Jack.'

Jack didn't seem to hear him.

'Wasn't it?' prompted George. 'Different, I mean.'

'Yes, it probably was,' agreed Jack absently. He shook himself and smiled. 'Look, never mind about cats. What d'you think of the curry?' He led the conversation on to other topics and the evening – an oddly uncomfortable evening in some respects as far as Rackham was concerned – came to an end.

Rackham was able to say what was on his mind when, having accepted Jack's invitation to join them for a nightcap back in his rooms, he was briefly alone in the lobby with Jack, waiting for George.

'Look, Jack,' said Rackham earnestly, keeping his eye on the cloakroom door for Lassiter's reappearance, 'I think you should be concerned about him. Really concerned, I mean. If there was a cat on that balcony tonight, I'm a Dutchman.' He put his hands wide. 'I said this before but I mean it. I think he needs a doctor.'

Jack sighed reluctantly. 'You might be right, Bill. It's worrying, isn't it? But if he is seeing things, the poor beggar can't help it. Go easy on him, will you?' He gave him a warning look as George joined them. 'Shall we go?'

Once back in Chandos Row, Jack let them into the house with his latchkey and led the way up to his rooms. He put his key in the lock but the door was open. 'That's funny,' he said to George with a puzzled frown. 'I'm sure I locked it.'

They went in. The light in the little hallway was on and, from the sitting room, they could hear a noise, the sort of noise a man makes settling into an armchair.

'There's someone in there,' said Rackham quietly.

Jack opened the door. David Lassiter, who had been sitting in the armchair, stood up as they entered. He looked worried and ill at ease.

'Hello,' said Jack in surprise. 'This is an unexpected pleasure. Er . . . What can I do for you?'

David Lassiter ran his hand through his hair. 'This is difficult, very difficult.' He shifted uneasily from foot to foot. 'I didn't know what to do so in the end I thought I'd tell you. Your landlady said I could wait here. I hope you don't mind.'

'Not in the least,' said Jack easily. 'Why don't you sit down again? We were going to have a nightcap. Will you join us?'

David Lassiter shook his head. 'No, no, I won't do that. It wouldn't be suitable, you know?' He ran his hand through his hair once more. He looked at Rackham and George. 'I hoped you'd be alone. I should have expected George, I know, but I didn't think Inspector Rackham would be with you too. Perhaps it's just as well.'

'What is it?' asked Jack patiently.

David Lassiter took a deep breath. 'I can't pretend any more. I thought I could but I can't. It's been hell, watching you get nearer and nearer.' He swallowed. 'I want to get it over with. It's all for the best.' He looked at Jack with an indefinable expression. 'God knows what Peggy will think but I can't carry on any longer. It'll be better for her this way. You see, Haldean, I want to confess.' He looked at them with tired, defiant eyes, then shrugged hopelessly. 'There's no easy way to put this. I killed Alexander Culverton.'

Chapter Twelve

Rackham made a choking noise in his throat. 'You did what?'

David Lassiter nodded. 'I killed him. I can't stand it any longer. I knew you suspected me.' His voice wavered. 'I could feel you getting closer and closer. I was like an animal in a trap. I knew it was only a matter of time.'

David Lassiter, thought Jack, looked weary to the point of exhaustion. 'Why don't we all sit down?' he said quietly. He looked at Rackham. 'Bill? Is that all right?'

'I'd better hear what Mr Lassiter has to say,' agreed Rackham. He took off his coat and, laying it over the back of the sofa, sat down. 'Mr Lassiter?'

David Lassiter sank into an armchair. 'I don't know where to start.'

George Lassiter, who had hardly moved since they had walked into the room, stepped forward to face his uncle. 'It's not true,' he said, his eyes blazing. 'Why are you doing this? Think what you're doing to us all. There's Anne, there's Grandfather, there's Mrs Culverton. We all trust you. I don't know what you're doing but it *can't* be true.'

David looked at him and the years between them seemed to lengthen visibly. 'It is, George. I'm sorry to let you all down but it's true enough. I'm only human and God knows, I'd reached the end of my tether. Please, will you sit down?' George sank unwillingly on to the sofa. 'That's better.' David Lassiter looked at Jack. 'You're an odd chap. I spoke to Anne about you earlier on. She didn't suspect a thing. I nearly told her, but I couldn't bring

220

myself to do it. Anyway, I said then that you were someone I'd like beside me in a tough place.' His mouth
straightened in a thin line. 'There's nothing you can do but
I hoped you'd understand. You're trustworthy, I think. And
about as dangerous as a rattlesnake. I knew you were on
to me.'

Jack didn't disagree but it wasn't actually the case. He
had wondered about David but only because the man had
a motive, a motive which, he reminded himself, he'd tried
to conceal. Having said that, David possessed the Lassiter
temper in full measure and, yes, he could be violent. His
history showed that. 'Will you tell us why you killed him?'
he asked.

'Peggy,' said David. His expression grew softer. 'It's
because of Peggy. If she'd been happy with Culverton it
would have been different, but she wasn't.' He linked his
hands together. 'He was monstrous. He was a big man,
fleshy and gross, and so bloody fussy about his appearance. God damn it, he used *scent*. His eyes were chilling.
I've never seen such cold eyes in any man. I guessed – it
was obvious enough – that Peggy disliked him but I never
knew she was terrified of him until that evening when
Anne telephoned me and I went round to Peggy's flat in
Kensington.'

'Can you tell us what happened the evening Culverton
was killed?' asked Rackham.

David leaned his forehead on his hand. 'Peggy was
scared. She knew it wouldn't take Culverton long to find
out where she was and she was frightened that he'd force
his way into the flat.' He looked at Jack. 'Did you ever meet
him?' Jack shook his head. 'That's a pity,' said David, more
to himself than to them. 'You'd understand then. Behind
his sophisticated exterior, there was always violence. He
enjoyed watching anything or anyone squirm. I've seen
that for myself. He was a frightening man. I sensed it. I was
always careful not to cross him but then, when Peggy was
so scared ... I knew that the only way she would find

221

peace was if he was dead.' He shrugged, his voice trailing away. 'And so I killed him.'

Rackham coughed. 'How exactly did you do that, sir?'

David Lassiter roused himself. 'How? I . . . I hit him. I saw him leave the Mulciber and I followed him. He went to the Embankment and it was there, by Cleopatra's Needle, I killed him. He fell over and cracked the back of his head on the wall. I meant to kill him. No one saw us. I hit him with a brick. Again and again.' He looked bewildered. 'I don't think I was quite rational. I wanted to make sure he was dead. He deserved to die. I took his clothes off and threw them in the river. I thought it'd be safer that way. I hoped no one would ever know who he was. Even now I'm glad I did it. Peggy's free of him for ever. But I didn't realize what it would be like afterwards. I couldn't stand it.'

'What time was this, sir?'

'Time? When I killed him, you mean? It was before midnight. I heard Big Ben strike afterwards. Does it matter? I've said I did it.' He looked helplessly at the three men in the room. 'What happens now?'

Rackham got to his feet. 'I think I'd better take you to the Yard, Mr Lassiter.'

David Lassiter gave a death's-head grin. 'I might as well get it over with.' He stood up. 'Shall we go now?'

Rackham was about to reply when Jack interrupted. 'There's no need to hurry, Mr Lassiter.' He took out his cigarette case and offered it to Lassiter. Lassiter looked at it as if uncertain what to do, then took a cigarette with an unsteady hand. 'What was the weather like that evening?' asked Jack. 'I know it had been raining earlier but it cleared up later on.' He glanced at Rackham. 'I remember mentioning it to Isabelle as I saw her home from the theatre.' He looked at Lassiter again. 'Had it started to rain when you were out?'

David Lassiter looked puzzled. 'I can't remember. It was fine, I think. Yes, fine.'

Jack pulled on his cigarette, frowning. 'Did Mr Culverton walk directly to the Embankment?'

Lassiter nodded. 'Yes.'

'He didn't get a taxi or go anywhere else from the Mulciber? He didn't call in anywhere?'

David Lassiter shook his head. 'No. He just walked to the Embankment. He knew I was following him after a while. I think I frightened him. I hope I frightened him. I told you, I followed him and I caught up with him by Cleopatra's Needle.' His voice rose. 'Do I have to keep going over it all time and time again? I killed him. What more do you want me to say? You thought I'd done it and now I've told you I've done it. I don't want to say any more.'

Rackham dropped a hand on his shoulder. 'Easy there, sir.' He glanced at Jack. 'We'd better go.'

Jack stubbed out his cigarette and inclined his head to the door. 'Can I have a word with you, Bill?'

Rackham followed him into the corridor. 'What is it?' he asked in a low voice. 'I knew something was biting you. What was all that about the weather? What's that got to do with it?'

Jack put his hands wide. 'Don't you see? According to David Lassiter he attacked and killed Culverton by Cleopatra's Needle before midnight. Where was everyone? How come no one saw him? If it was two in the morning, I grant you the place might be deserted, but before midnight? I've never seen the area completely empty yet. To kill Culverton and dispose of his clothes must have taken ten minutes or so at least, and yet not a single witness reported noticing a thing. The only explanation I could think of was that it was raining – it'd have to be raining cats and dogs, too – and therefore any passer-by had taken shelter.'

Rackham frowned. 'That's odd, I grant you. Actually, Jack, it's damn peculiar. He could have been lucky, I suppose, but I don't like it.' He stood for a few moments in thoughtful silence. 'One part of his story that doesn't ring true was his explanation of how Culverton died. Lassiter says Culverton hit the back of his head but Culverton didn't have any injuries to the back of his head, only the front. I suppose he could simply be mistaken, but it's something I want to clear up.'

'There's another thing,' said Jack. 'We worked out that Culverton must have gone back to the office, didn't we? He'd written *Paris* in his diary but he didn't know he was going to Paris before he left for the Mulciber. But David Lassiter stated he followed Culverton from the Mulciber down to the Embankment. By his account Culverton didn't go anywhere near the office.'

'I thought the word *Paris* was a code, if you remember. He'd written *Paris* in his diary before, when the other Ripper victims were murdered.' Rackham stopped. 'But there's been another murder since then. It seems as if Culverton wasn't the Ripper after all.' He drew his breath in. 'Jack, this doesn't make any sense.' He glanced over his shoulder at the door to the room. 'I know people do confess to crimes they haven't committed but, one and all, they're off their rocker. He's as sane as you or me. Why should he come and confess if he's innocent?'

'Could he be shielding someone?'

'Who?' demanded Rackham in a low voice. 'Peggy Culverton? Maybe that's the answer. She's guilty and he's decided to jump in and save her. He might've thought we knew a great deal more than we did.'

'Perhaps.' Jack didn't sound convinced. 'I don't like it though, Bill.'

Rackham dismissed the problem with an irritated sigh. 'I can't say I'm crazy about it, but I've got to get him to the Yard. Once there I'll go through any inconsistencies with him. However, we did think he was a likely suspect. You've got to remember that, Jack.'

'We thought he had a motive. That's a very different state of affairs. Look, you've got to arrest him. You have no choice about that, I know. I'd just be a bit careful about taking what he says at face value.'

'I will,' promised Rackham.

Jack glanced at his watch. 'It's twenty to eleven. D'you think it's too late to go to Eden Street?'

'Why?'

'Well, someone should tell the Lassiters what's happened and that better be George and myself. I don't think they keep particularly early hours.'

'I can always telephone,' said Rackham.

Jack grimaced. 'This sort of news is bad enough face to face. It'd be rotten for old Mr Lassiter to hear it over the phone. I've got to go round, Bill. Mind you,' he added, 'I can't say I'm looking forward to it.'

The scene at Eden Street was as difficult as Jack had expected. George had telephoned before they left and both Anne and Mr Lassiter were waiting for them in the lamplit sitting room with its warm fire and comfortable chairs. Mr Lassiter sat while Anne stood beside him, their faces alive with apprehension. Anne looked at George, gave a little gasp, and ran to him, her hands outstretched.

'It's bad news,' she said. 'I know it's bad news.'

George, suddenly unable to speak, put his arm round her shoulders and held her close.

Mr Lassiter got to his feet. 'Major Haldean?' he asked, his voice thin with anxiety. 'What is it?'

Jack took a deep breath. 'I'm sorry to have to tell you this, sir, but David's been arrested for the murder of Alexander Culverton.'

Mr Lassiter seemed to age visibly before Jack's eyes. He blindly reached out for the arm of his chair and sank back into it. Anne freed herself from George and, crossing the room, knelt on the floor beside him, holding his hands in hers. It seemed a long time before he spoke. 'David?' he said in a whisper.

Anne looked at George. 'It can't be true,' she said. 'It isn't true.'

Mr Lassiter stirred in the chair. 'Of course it's not true,' he said, his voice a parody of his usual vigorous tone. 'There's been some ghastly mistake. We'll get the solicitor right away and we'll soon have the matter cleared up.'

'David confessed,' said George bluntly.

Jack honestly thought they were going to have another death on their hands. Mr Lassiter doubled up as if someone had hit him a physical blow. George quickly went to the cabinet and, dashing some brandy into a glass, helped his grandfather to drink it. 'We'd better get the doctor,' he said, looking at the old man's colourless face and grey-blue lips.

It was over an hour later. The doctor had been and gone, and Mr Lassiter had been helped upstairs to bed with Anne and George in attendance. Jack, who had been left by himself, looked up as they came back into the room.

'I hope he'll be all right,' said Anne without preamble. 'He's usually so strong that it's easy to forget how old he is. I need to tell Nigel, of course, but he's out.' She fought back a yawn, swaying with exhaustion. 'This has been a dreadful evening. It started off badly but this . . .' She shuddered. 'I can't believe it.'

'What happened?' asked George gently. 'Earlier, I mean?'

Anne put a hand to her forehead. 'It was Nigel and David. They actually came to blows. It's been brewing for some time but it erupted tonight. David hit Nigel.'

'Did he?' asked George, startled.

Jack winced. It was more evidence, as if he needed any, that David Lassiter was not a man to be crossed.

Anne nodded. 'He shouldn't have done, I know, but it was Nigel's fault. He was horrible on the phone to Peggy. He swore at her and David heard him. She'd rung to tell us about Martin Ridgeway. You know about him, don't you? Anyway, Roger arrived in the nick of time to stop a full-scale fight. I can't face Nigel now. I'll tell him tomorrow. I'm not waiting up for him. George, can I have some brandy? I'm so tired and yet I don't feel as if I could sleep.'

George poured her a drink. She took the glass from him and sat on the edge of the chair. 'I wish I hadn't rung David that night,' she said.

Fatigue, thought Jack, was making her talk, the words tumbling from her like a damned-up torrent.

She held on to the glass tightly. 'I knew Peggy needed him. I thought I'd done the right thing.' She shuddered. 'If I'd guessed, if I'd had the slightest idea, how David would react, I'd never have telephoned him and I'd never have covered up for them.' She fumbled for a cigarette from the box on the table, took one and tried to strike a match. Her fingers trembled and the match broke. Jack felt in his pocket for his lighter but George beat him to it.

'Here you are,' he said, pulling a book of matches from his pocket.

She gave a ragged sigh. 'Thanks. D'you know, I'm not sure if that's true. About covering up for them, I mean. I'd like to be honest. I . . . I always thought I was honest.' She looked at Jack with wide eyes. 'Won't they understand? Culverton was a monster. Surely that'll make a difference?'

'It might,' he said. His voice didn't carry conviction. He glanced down, avoiding her eyes, and froze. George had tossed the book of matches on to the table. It was a black, shiny packet with an ornate C embossed on it. He'd seen those matches before. It was exactly the same sort of matchbook that Culverton had left on his dressing table, the matchbook that he and Bill had found when they searched Culverton's office.

He picked up the matches and held them out on the palm of his hand. 'George, where did you get these?'

George looked at him in annoyance. 'The matches? I don't know. What does it matter?'

'It might be very important,' insisted Jack. His voice was urgent.

'I know where you got them,' said Anne Lassiter dully. 'They're from the Continental. They have C on them. C for

Continental.' She buried her face in her hands. 'Oh, what are we going to do about David?' She sat for a few moments, then took a deep breath and drew herself up. 'It's late. You'd better go.'

George reached out and held her hand in his. 'Anne,' he said awkwardly, 'I don't want to leave you like this.'

She tried to smile, an attempt so valiant it twisted Jack's heart. 'That's good of you, George, but you have to go.'

'Can I see you tomorrow?'

'Yes.' She stood up. 'Please come back, George. I'd be grateful.' She put her hand on his arm. 'I'm glad you're here.'

'I wish I could do something,' muttered George.

'There isn't anything. He's confessed. That's the end of it, isn't it? There's nothing to be done.' She leaned on him as they walked to the door. 'Thanks, George. I know you really care. It's not just David, it's Grandfather. I wish I knew he was going to be all right.' Her voice quavered. 'Maybe it's best if he's not.'

George looked at her sharply. 'What?'

She brushed the hair from her eyes. 'Wouldn't it be best? Rather than watch David be dragged through the courts? To say nothing of . . . of afterwards. He cares more about David than anyone in the world.'

'I know that,' said George softly.

'He cares about you, too. Oh, dear God, he was so happy when you turned up. It was like a miracle when you appeared out of the blue. He couldn't get over how you'd come to this house of all houses, that night you were desperate. He kept on saying it was as if it was meant, somehow. It wasn't just you, it was as if his son, Charles, had come back as well.' She was very close to tears. 'He was so happy. I knew it was too good to last. I knew it couldn't last. I wish there could be another miracle or we could put time back but we can't. No one can.'

Jack looked at her, suddenly thoughtful. He pulled the little black book of matches from his pocket, running his thumb abstractedly over the shiny cover. 'Time. No, we can't put time back. We have memories, though. Mrs Lassiter, will you remember for me? You know the night George broke into the kitchen? Can you tell me what you were doing when the policeman rang the doorbell? Please remember.'

Her forehead creased in a puzzled frown. 'I wasn't doing anything. Anything to speak of, I mean. Grandfather was upstairs, I do know that. I remember telling him what had happened when he came down.'

'Was he having a bath by any chance?'

He bewilderment increased. 'As a matter of fact he was. How did you know?'

Jack ignored the question. 'And you? Were you reading or knitting or sorting out household accounts or anything of that sort?'

'No, I don't think so. What was I doing?' Her forehead creased in concentration. 'I was listening to the wireless, I think. Yes, that's right. It was a story, one of A.J. Alan's. I like him. I always make a point of listening to him. I missed the end of the story because the doorbell rang. It was the policeman telling me the area gate was unlocked and then I saw you, George.'

'Don't give up hope,' said Jack. There was the oddest note in his voice, a strong, vibrant note. 'Don't despair. Not yet.'

She looked at him, startled. 'What do you mean?'

'Look,' said Jack, 'you want a miracle. You're wrong, you know. Every so often they do happen.'

She reached out to him, her eyes suddenly bright. 'Major Haldean, is there hope? What can I hope for?' Her hand tightened on his arm. 'Will it help David?'

'To be honest,' said Jack, 'I don't know. But please – don't give up hoping.'

'That was rotten,' said George once they were outside the door. 'Telling poor Anne not to give up hope and so on. I know you meant well, Jack, but David's confessed. You can't get round that. I don't know about miracles and so

229

on but you'd need a magic wand to save him and you haven't got one.'

'No, I haven't,' agreed Jack. He paused, choosing his words with care. 'All I've got is the beginnings of an idea.'

'Will it help David?'

'I don't know.'

'What's the point of that?' asked George in exasperation. 'We're no better off, for all your talk about hope and miracles and so on.'

Jack walked back through the silent Mayfair streets beside his friend. He thought – he couldn't get the image out of his mind – of a street magician who made a dove come from an empty wooden box. That was impossible and yet it had happened. That wasn't a miracle; it was magic.

It was nearly two o'clock when they got back. George was dog-tired and went to bed immediately. More out of a sense of habit than because he was sleepy, Jack got ready for bed. Lying in his darkened room, the luminous hands of the alarm clock on the bedside table counting off the passing minutes of the night, he stared into darkness. He consciously tried to slow his mind down, to stop it from racing.

A black embossed matchbook; a dove in an empty box; *bloody fool*; lipstick on a coffee cup; forty-six thousand pounds; *I think he needs a doctor*; Urbis and Pegasus; the Ripper murders – dear God, the Ripper murders – and cats, lots of cats.

The confused jumble of images gradually stilled. He was standing in the corridor of a house, the Eden Street house, larger and more echoing than he remembered. There were distant voices coming from the other side of a door. It was the wireless. *2LO calling*. All he had to do was push the door open so he could listen properly. The voice on the wireless was important. The voice on the wireless would explain everything.

He woke with a start, knowing that he had been on the verge of understanding. It had been so *clear*. Still half-asleep, he reached out, as if to physically clutch the fleeting thought, but it was gone. The luminous dial of the clock showed the time to be just after five. He groaned in disappointment. Somehow he had nearly got it. He sighed and sat up, rubbed his face in his hands and, getting out of bed, put on his dressing gown.

There was no point trying to go back to sleep. He walked to the bedroom window and looked out over the quiet, dark city. The back yard with its plane tree was a deep well of shadow. David . . . He'd be in a prison cell. He hoped David was asleep. A cat, silhouetted on the wall against the dim reflected glow of street-lights, yowled.

Cats: cats on the board-walk; cats on the balcony; cats on the brain. He shook his head. Bill was right. George hadn't been acting normally, however generous a definition you chose to give to normal. He stiffened and swore, very softly. Cats! But it hadn't begun with cats. It had begun with a man on a night wilder than this, breaking into an empty kitchen and waking into a nightmare.

Was that really where it had all started? Thoughts, pictures and voices kaleidoscoped in his mind then gradually settled in a sequence, glorious in its progression. Of course! All he had to do was start at the beginning and all of it – *all of it* – would fall into place. Paper, he needed paper. He strode out of his bedroom to his desk, reaching for a pencil. He had to get this down while it still made sense. George was the key to it all. If he concentrated on George he'd find the answer. He had thought about illusion, he had thought about mystery, he had thought about a dove coming from an empty box and there it was; he knew the answer and he'd been right; it wasn't a miracle, it was magic.

It was gone six before he threw down the pencil and gathered up his scattered notes. With a craftsman's satisfaction he looked at the plan he had constructed from the odds and ends of facts. It worked. He got up from the desk

231

and lit the spirit lamp for a cup of tea, making more noise than he intended. There were sounds from the spare bedroom and a few minutes later George put his head out.

'Morning, Jack.' He yawned and looked at the clock on the mantelpiece. 'Why ever are you up and about at this hour?'

'It was my idea,' said Jack, reaching down the caddy as the kettle came to the boil. 'The idea I said I had last night. I had a burst of inspiration earlier on.'

George looked interested. 'What's it all about? Will it help David?'

'Perhaps.' Jack hesitated. 'I'd rather demonstrate it than simply tell you, though.' He warmed the pot, spooned in the tea and filled it up. 'D'you want a cup?'

'I don't mind if I do.' George settled down in the armchair, waiting in drowsy, companionable silence while Jack let the tea brew, poured it out and handed him a cup. 'What d'you mean, demonstrate it?' he asked after he had taken a sip.

Jack perched on the arm of the opposite chair. 'I'd like you to come and see someone with me today. It's a chap I know.'

'Okay.' George thought for a moment. 'What sort of chap?'

'He's called Dr Kincraig. He's a nerve specialist.'

Suddenly wide awake, George sat upright, nearly spilling his tea. 'A *nerve specialist*? You mean a loony doctor? I don't need to see him, Jack. There's nothing wrong with me.'

Jack held up his hand pacifically. 'Calm down, old fruit, I'm not saying you're off your trolley or anything like it. It's simply that I'm pretty sure Dr Kincraig will be able to help.'

'He might help you, perhaps,' said George, not noticeably mollified.

'That's exactly it,' agreed Jack. 'I need to see him and I'd like you there too. It's important, George. I wouldn't ask you to come with me if it wasn't. Dr Kincraig's all right. He's a decent bloke.'

'So you say. How on earth d'you know him, Jack? Don't tell me you've ever needed a dingbat doctor, because I don't believe it.' Jack merely smiled. George looked at him with dawning and embarrassed comprehension. 'Oh my God, you did, didn't you?'

'At the time it was tactfully called War Strain. I wasn't sticking straws in my hair, I simply couldn't whack up any interest in things. Anyway, a few sessions with Dr Kincraig put me on the right path and we've run across each other a few times since.' He raised an eyebrow at his friend. 'So, will you come with me, George?'

'Yes, yes, of course,' agreed George, anxious to make amends. 'Absolutely. Anything you say. We'll go now if you like.'

Jack looked at the clock and laughed. 'If we turned up at half past six in the morning he really would think the pair of us had lost our marbles. Let's leave it until after breakfast, shall we?'

Chapter Thirteen

George Lassiter flicked through the pile of magazines on the waiting-room table, decided that the *Windsor Magazine* looked marginally more interesting than the four-month-old *Punch* and took it to the stiffly buttoned shiny leather chair under the window. He was feeling distinctly ill at ease. Dr Kincraig's waiting room was furnished in gloomy good taste, with an oak table, substantial chairs and a solid Victorian sideboard, complete with a Nottingham lace mat and two Chinese vases. A Turkish carpet, its colours faded with age, lay in front of the brilliantly polished brass fender of the cast-iron and tiled fireplace. A reproduction of Landseer's *The Stag at Bay* hung over the mantelpiece. Presumably *The Stag at Bay* was a reference to Dr Kincraig's Scottish origins, but George thought it was a tactless choice.

Dr Alistair Kincraig, a tall, stooping, sandy-haired man with ferocious eyebrows, had greeted Haldean with restrained but genuine pleasure. Both Major Haldean and Mr Lassiter would have to wait, but yes, he could see them that morning. Jack had gone into the consulting room first and had been in there for a good twenty minutes. George, who was not in the mood to be entertained by the *Windsor Magazine* or, indeed, any other publication, felt as if he'd spent most of his life sympathizing with *The Stag at Bay*.

Eventually the door to the consulting room opened and Jack, with Dr Kincraig behind him, came out.

Jack looked very pleased with himself. 'I'm on the right lines, George,' he said. 'Dr Kincraig has been absolutely terrific. He's explained a lot of things to me.'

Dr Kincraig permitted himself a smile. 'I merely confirmed what you already knew, Major.'

'You confirmed what I'd guessed,' corrected Jack. 'Anyway, George,' he added, inclining his head towards the consulting room, 'will you come and join us? I'd like Dr Kincraig's opinion on a few of the things which have been puzzling us.'

George put down his magazine and reluctantly followed them into the room. The consulting room, with two sash windows looking out on to Harley Street and modern, comfortable furniture, was a much brighter place than the waiting room and his spirits unconsciously lifted.

'Take a seat, Mr Lassiter,' said the doctor, indicating an armchair. He sat down at the desk and looked forebodingly at George over the top of his gold-framed spectacles. 'I understand you've got a problem with cats.'

'I haven't any such thing,' said George firmly. He glared at Jack. 'What've you been saying, Jack? Look, I like cats. So what? I like dogs too, and horses. I like all sorts of animals.'

Dr Kincraig cleared his throat. 'D'you have the urge to rescue any other animals apart from cats, Mr Lassiter?'

'I don't have the urge to rescue cats!' George said indignantly. 'Besides, what if I do? You make it sound like something to be ashamed of.'

'Come on, George,' put in Jack. 'What about when we were at the aircraft factory? You were convinced there was a cat on the roof.'

'That's because there was a cat on the roof,' countered George. 'The poor thing was stuck. It was in distress. I know about animals. I care about them. I even know about wild animals, big game and so on, what they will and won't do and how they behave. Sometimes,' he added with a significant look at Jack, 'they're a lot easier to understand than human beings.'

'And the cat in St James's Place?'

George wriggled uncomfortably in his chair. 'What about it? If it wasn't for my arm being crocked I'd have had it down in no time, no matter what you or Bill Rackham had to say about it. I like cats, Jack. I can't abandon the poor creatures, even if you seem to have different ideas.'

He got to his feet and paced round the room. 'Look, doctor, I don't want to seem ungracious, but I don't really know why I'm here. Major Haldean – Jack – assured me you could help but I don't need any help.' He gravitated to the bottom of the tall bookcase which stood between the sash windows, eyeing it up and down. 'If you wanted to help, you could try to help me find out who pinched my money –' George put his hands on the shelves as if to test their weight – 'or tell me what I can say to my grandfather about David –' he stood back from the bookcase and looked around the room – 'or, at the very least, tell me what on earth I can say to Anne.' He walked to the desk, picked up a wooden chair and brought it back to the bookcase. 'Anything else seems to me to be a bit irrelevant.'

He stood on the chair and reached up, his hands clasping the top of the fortunately solid bookcase. 'We have to help David, Jack. If you could tell them about Culverton, then that has to make a difference. Come on,' he added in a coaxing voice, apparently addressing the empty air on top of the bookcase. He made a clucking noise with his tongue. 'We'll soon have you down from there.'

Dr Kincraig and Jack exchanged glances. 'Er . . . George,' said Jack. 'What are you doing?'

'I'm getting the cat down, of course,' said George. 'How on earth it got up there, I don't know.'

Alistair Kincraig rubbed his hands together with deep satisfaction. 'That's absolutely splendid. That's a wonderful demonstration, Major.'

He walked over to George. 'Perhaps if you left the cat alone, Mr Lassiter, it'll find its own way down. I'd be obliged if you'd just be seated for a moment. I'd appreciate a word with you . . .'

Forty minutes later, Jack stood on the pavement outside Dr Kincraig's consulting rooms on Harley Street, looking at

George's departing back. He was off, he said, to Eden Street, to see Anne and his grandfather.

Jack was faced with a decision. He knew enough to go to Bill Rackham but he wanted to know more. He wanted to be sure, completely sure, before he told Bill. He had run through his plans with Kincraig. Kincraig had been dubious but he was a doctor and a professional man who would always err on the side of caution. Kincraig had a full account of what Jack believed to be the truth and instructions to give that account to Rackham should anything go wrong.

He took the black cardboard matchbook out of his pocket, the matchbook George had so casually tossed on to the table at Eden Street last night. It was such an insignificant object and yet it was proof, incontrovertible proof, Culverton had been to the Continental. However, there was nothing to say when he had been. There were plenty of innocent visitors to the Continental. Culverton might very well have been one of them. He might, thought Jack, be barking up the wrong tree. The only way of finding out was to go and look.

Damn it, thought Jack, making his mind up, why not? He grinned to himself. It was about time he had some fun.

It was just on eleven o'clock when Jack walked up the cobbled slope of Tilford Lane towards the Continental. In his pocket was a new rubber-covered torch, complete with batteries.

There were a few passers-by on the pavement but no one paid him any attention. The Continental was getting ready for lunch. The dark blue double doors were open and a white-aproned waiter was sweeping the steps. Jack glanced upwards. The Continental shared a common entrance with the businesses on the upper floors of the building which were, according to the brass plate set into the wall, Wallace and West, Fruit Importers, and the Macedonian Refugee Benevolent Fund. However, unlike the Continental, there were no lights and no sign of life in the upper floors. Business, he thought, must be very thin indeed. In fact, he was prepared to bet there wasn't any at all.

Jack turned the corner, past the end of the terrace which housed the Continental, and on to Saffron Place. A few yards further brought him to a narrow passageway running between the backs of Tilford Lane and Jutland Street. It was called optimistically and, thought Jack, looking at the grime-blackened sign, misleadingly, Dainty Alley. It was an uninviting sort of place, reeking with decay and too narrow for any natural light to ever reach the green-slimed packed earth underfoot. The bricks of the walls, once light yellow London clay, were black with decades of encrusted soot. However, this was the back of the Continental and that made it very attractive indeed. Jack glanced over his shoulder to check he was unobserved and walked down the alley.

Most of the buildings backing on to Dainty Alley had ordinary high wooden gates leading, at a guess, on to minuscule yards. The back gate of the Continental, though, had, as well as a wooden gate, new iron bars set across the entrance. That, thought Jack, was a mistake. It showed there was something to guard. He heard noises from the kitchen and walked on. Sounds drifted up from the shops and houses roundabout. A laugh, a shout and the rattle of dishes told him he had reached the vegetarian restaurant, more than halfway down Tilford Lane and, two doors on, he came across a gate which made him pause. It looked, even by the lax standards of Dainty Alley, so completely neglected. On his walk up Tilford Lane he had noticed a disused draper's shop near the vegetarian restaurant with a faded *To Let* sign in the window. He gave a grin of triumph. This was the place he had been looking for.

The gate was hanging by one rusted hinge and, wincing at the noise it made as it scraped across the stone flags of the yard, Jack pushed it open. Once inside the yard, he paused. The clatter from the vegetarian restaurant continued unchecked and he relaxed.

He didn't know how long it had been since anyone had last entered the yard but, judging from the dark moss between the flags and the sickly ash shoot springing up in the corner, it must be a couple of years at least. The door to the draper's was locked, of course, and he didn't want to break a window because of the noise. He examined the kitchen window and smiled. Drawing out his clasp-knife he slipped it under the beading round the window. It came away easily, exposing the crumbling putty underneath. Within ten minutes he had scraped out the old putty and, digging in behind the glass with his knife, pulled out the entire sheet of glass and climbed in over the filthy sill. His trousers, he thought ruefully, would probably never recover.

The house was deathly quiet and, coming out of the kitchen into the hallway, he saw that the door to the shop stood partly open. He caught a glimpse of the old mahogany counter, dim in the dust-filtered light, but it wasn't the shop he wanted, it was the stairs.

Flicking on the torch, for it was very dark, he climbed up the grimy wooden treads to the third floor. The odd rustle told him that the house had mice – he hoped it was only mice – but no human sound reached him. The door to the attics opened on to a steep staircase. Here, three floors up, there was light from a window high enough to catch the gloom of a November day. The attics had a scattering of junk – old bolts of cloth, some brown paper, parts of a sewing machine – and a little door was set into the eaves.

It was secured by a latch and Jack needed his clasp-knife to open it. Once the door was open he switched on his torch, knelt down and peered inside.

He felt like cheering. As he had hoped, the attic eaves stretched far beyond the confines of the draper's shop, linking all the houses in the terrace. He took off his coat and left it in the attic. Stooping, for it was a small door, he wriggled through on to the sooty rafters.

The wind blew through the narrow gaps in the roof, staled by grime and smoke. The underside of the slates shone with the reflected light. There was, once his eyes had become accustomed to the gloom, enough light to pick his way and he pocketed the torch thankfully, glad to have both hands free. It wasn't high enough to stand upright, but by keeping to the attic wall and crouching down he could step carefully from rafter to rafter. The last thing he wanted to do was break through the plaster.

It took him some time to reach the eaves of the Continental but, granted it was the last house in the row, at least there was no possibility he would come out in the wrong building. He crouched down beside the door to the attics of the Continental and listened. He was at the front of the house and from under the slates came the noise of Tilford Lane – footsteps, voices and the occasional creak of a wheel or growl of a faraway car – but on the other side of the door was complete silence.

A rim of light surrounded the little door, a black bar showing where the latch was. He inserted his knife under the latch and flicked it open. Again he waited, then put his hands on the door and lifted it up and out. The wood grated, sounding unnaturally loud, but no challenge met the sound and Jack, who had unconsciously been holding his breath, gave a sigh of relief.

He gingerly climbed out into the attic. For a moment he stood rigidly, listening for any sound, then relaxed, stretching his cramped muscles and taking stock of his surroundings.

The room was illuminated by a skylight and a partly open door and contained a collection of trunks and boxes. That it was used from time to time was evident from the footmarks on the dusty floor and by a book of matches and a used candle stuck into a champagne bottle placed on a trunk by the door. He picked up the bottle, weighing it thoughtfully in his hand. Now he was actually here he felt the need of a weapon and the heavy bottle would do nicely.

Holding the bottle by the neck, he put the candle stump into his pocket and slipped out through the door.

It led on to a small landing from which a substantial stairwell descended into the house. Through the filthy window at the top of the stairs he could make out a thin slit of sky and solid blocks of the houses overlooking Dainty Alley. These must be the back stairs. He could see the banister rail running down in a succession of decreasing squares to the ground floor below. The back door of the Continental was open, letting daylight into the bottom of the stairwell. A hum of noise came clearly up to the deserted landing.

It was, Jack knew, dangerous, but there was no point in retreating now. He needed some solid facts to back up his theory and those facts lay downstairs. As quietly as he could and once more keeping closely to the wall, he stole downstairs to the next landing.

This was a cleaner replica of the floor above, with a window and a door. He paused for a few moments outside the door, his senses twitching, alert for any sign of life, before he slowly turned the handle.

Everything was quiet. Peering through the hinged side of the door, he could see shelves, a filing cabinet and a desk with a covered typewriter and a letter tray. Offices! He crept into the room, pausing by the desk. The letter tray contained about thirty small brown envelopes, each with a typed name and address, waiting to be posted. It was a bit risky but Jack took one of the envelopes and put it in his pocket. The letter it contained might make useful reading.

He slid open the top drawer of the desk. It contained a desk diary and a bunch of six keys. The keys were labelled *Club, Office, Bar, First Floor, Second Floor, Stairs*. He took the bunch to the door opening on to the stairs and tried the one marked *Stairs* in the lock. It fitted. They, thought Jack, might be useful, but he could hardly walk off with the whole set of keys. With a sudden grin he took the candle stump from his pocket and a sheet of paper from the desk. He lit the candle so that the wax pooled on to the paper, then took impressions of the keys, leaving the wax on the desk to harden.

He looked at the desk diary next. There were various entries, mainly of names. The entry for 31st October made him pause. With a lift of his eyebrows he read *Culverton – the works*. Yes! This was what he had been hoping for. This was real evidence at last. However, it was, frustratingly, all. He wished the diarist had been more specific about what exactly *the works* entailed. He flipped the pages forward. The entry for this coming Friday had a word underlined: *Pegasus*. Underneath it were three names: *G. Stoker*, *A. McCann* and *S. Bierce*. Pegasus? Friday, he knew, was the day on which the Pegasus would take its maiden flight, the day Anne Lassiter had arranged the glamorous and much-talked-about dinner in the air over London. He closed the diary and opened the second drawer. This contained a flat cardboard box. He opened it and drew out a handful of black silk. Masks, he realized, spreading the silk out on his hand. The box contained about three dozen black masks. Of course! If Culverton was concerned enough about his privacy to cut the labels off his clothes, he'd want something to cover his face. He put one of the masks in his pocket, replaced the box in the drawer and looked at the filing cabinet thoughtfully.

He would give an awful lot to go through that filing cabinet but he still had more exploring to do. He picked up the wax impressions of the keys, put them in envelopes from the desk, and, placing them carefully in his pocket, walked quietly across the room to the far door. Once again he paused and listened before he opened it a crack.

It took him a few moments to make sense of what he saw. He was looking into a large, dark, thickly carpeted space. The office had been dingily but adequately lit by natural light from the windows, but the room he was looking into now seemed, at first glance, to have no windows at all. As his eyes gradually adjusted to the gloom, he could make out a sliver of light from above the curtained windows.

Leaving the door open behind him, he went in. This was no use. He needed light. Taking out his torch, he snapped it on, blinking as the beam cut through the darkness. He swept the light round the room. It was set out as a night-club with a bar at the far end. It looked, at first sight, very similar to the Continental. However, whereas in the Continental the tables and chairs were for eating and drinking, the seats in this room were large, luxurious sofas. The space in the middle looked like an ordinary dance floor but it was raised about a foot above the rest of the room. It was, in fact, a circular stage. The torchlight came to rest beside the bar. Here, painted on to the wall and running from floor to ceiling, was a mural of the Eiffel Tower.

Paris! Jack gave a little sigh of satisfaction. He was in Paris, Culverton's Paris. It was here Culverton had planned to come on 31st October. This was the *Paris* he had noted in his diary. Jack realized something else, too. Downstairs, in the Continental, this was the thing which had niggled him. The Continental was decorated with European landmarks but the Eiffel Tower, perhaps the most famous landmark of them all, the one object that sig-nified, to the majority of Britons, France and the Continent, had been missing. He hadn't spotted its absence at the time, but he'd known that something wasn't right.

There were other pictures on the walls, too. These weren't painted on to the plaster but hung like ordinary pictures in frames. That was where the similarity between these and ordinary pictures started and finished. The sub-ject of all of the pictures was, as he had expected, sex. Jack felt a stab of desire, which, as he continued to gaze, was replaced with revulsion. These brutal images weren't about any sort of love, they were about power, the refined and complete subjection of helpless human beings. And he hated it. The paintings weren't coarse or uncultured, they were technically brilliant and only too realistic, but there was nothing here of vigorous high spirits or animal exuber-ance. There was nothing in them to suggest the vitality of men or the sympathy of women. Instead they showed screaming, tortured flesh, perverted for a diseased pleasure and unnatural desire. He put his hand to his mouth, sickened by the room, with its sybaritic furniture and its images of rape and conquest.

He dragged his gaze away and forced himself to walk round the room, taking in the details. There was a door leading, he imagined, on to the main staircase but that was locked. He left the room and went back into the office.

Walking to the back staircase, he listened again for any sound, then relaxed. Going back into the office, he opened the filing cabinet, taking care to support the drawer with his hand so it opened as silently as possible. Inside were a collection of manila folders, each marked with a name. Culverton's name leapt out at him. He had his hand on the file when there came the sound he'd been dreading. In the adjoining room, in that ghastly club, someone was turning the key in the door.

Jack put back the file, delicately closed the cabinet and escaped on to the back stairs. He didn't close the door but pushed it to. Not only did he have to keep quiet, he wanted to know exactly where the newcomer was. As he listened he heard the sound of muffled voices. There were evidently at least two of them. He heard the click as the door to the office from the club opened and the voices got suddenly louder and clearer.

'. . . clear away and see about getting some more champagne up from the cellar.'

Jack put his eye to the crack in the door. There were two men and he could see enough to realize he didn't know either of them.

'Taittinger or the cheap stuff?'

The other man laughed. 'We'd better have enough Taittinger to whet their appetites but you know what this lot are like. Once they get going you could sell 'em anything as long as it looks all right, even if it does taste like petrol. Half of them are off their heads with snow anyway. It helps to keep up appearances, so to speak.'

They both laughed. There was the sound of a drawer opening and closing and Jack saw a hand reach forward and pick up the envelopes from the tray.

'I've got to get these in the post. We'll go out the back.'

Jack couldn't wait. He slipped out of the office, up the stairs and back towards the attic door, sacrificing caution for speed. He groaned inwardly as the wooden stairs creaked beneath his feet and he flattened himself against the wall, not daring to move.

The two men came out of the office door. 'Did you hear something?' asked one.

'I dunno.' The voice was puzzled. 'You don't suppose anyone's creeping about, do you, Steve?'

'I wouldn't have thought so,' came the reassuring reply. Jack breathed a silent sigh of relief then tensed as Steve added, 'We'd better have a look, I suppose.'

Jack sensed rather than saw the moment the men started to climb the stairs. Dropping to his knees, he hefted the champagne bottle and dropped it through the banister. There was an almighty crash as it shattered at the bottom of the stairwell, followed by a startled exclamation from the two men.

'Strewth! What was that?'

Their feet clattered down the stairs and away. Jack momentarily closed his eyes, thanking his lucky stars, then went back into the attic. Taking off his jacket, he used it to hastily brush his footprints away behind him as he made for the safety of the eaves. Once on the other side of the little wooden door he relaxed and, still on edge for the sound of any pursuit, groped his way back along the rafters to the deserted draper's shop.

'Hello, ugly,' said Bill Rackham cheerfully as Jack was shown into his office. He stopped as Jack unbuttoned his coat, revealing his dirt-smeared shirt and filthy suit. 'What the dickens have you been doing? You look as if you've been climbing chimneys.'

245

'Yes, the old whistle and flute copped for it a bit,' said Jack, drawing up a chair and putting his hat on the desk. 'I stopped off at a Gents to wash my hands and face otherwise I think your official watch-dog downstairs would have run me in for vagrancy. I've been visiting a club.'

Rackham's eyebrows shot up. 'Dressed like that?'

'Dressed, as you say, in this self-same pattern of sartorial splendour. Excuse me, I'm feeling a bit above myself. Never mind about my clothes, Bill. I've found the club.'

'The club?'

'*The* club,' repeated Jack. 'The club we've been looking for. The dodgy club. The very shady, very bent and obsessively secretive club. Culverton's club. In a word, I've found Paris.'

'Paris?'

'Paris. It's the name of the club.'

Rackham stared at him. 'Where is it?'

'Not far from Northumberland Avenue. It's in Tilford Lane.'

'Tilford Lane?' repeated Rackham. 'But that's where the Continental is.'

'Absolutely. Paris is part of the Continental. It's hidden away upstairs. That's not all. There's a great many things that puzzled us and I know the answers. I know the why and the where and can make a pretty good guess as to the who. I think,' said Jack, taking out a cigarette from his case and lighting it, 'I'd better tell you the whole story.'

Rackham listened intently. When Jack had finished, he shook his head in disbelief. 'You daft beggar, Jack. What if someone at the Continental had caught you?'

'They didn't,' said Jack easily. 'Relax. Don't you think the risk was worth it, Bill? After all, we know a dickens of a lot more than we did.' He raised an eyebrow at Rackham. 'Enough to act on?'

'Too right,' said Rackham. He looked at the wax impressions of the keys Jack had put on the desk. 'Those should make life a great deal easier. I'm glad you thought to label them.'

'Give me some credit,' said Jack.

'And then there's the letter.' Rackham picked up the brown envelope Jack had taken from the club's office. 'I'd say this alone was worth going for, once you add everything else we know.'

The letter was an invitation, addressed to one Frederick Meredith White, Esq. It looked innocuous enough, requesting the pleasure of Mr White's company at a gala evening on Friday, 30th November at 47 Tilford Lane, from eleven o'clock onwards. The usual entertainment, it added, would be provided.

'Frederick Meredith White, Esquire, eh?' said Rackham, looking at the envelope. 'He's an old friend, in a manner of speaking. I don't suppose you've ever come across Freddie White?' he added. Jack shook his head. 'I recognized the name and address right away. He's originally from a good family, as these things are measured, but he shirked the war and God knows what he lives on. He certainly doesn't work, that's for sure. I once questioned him on a suspicion of being in possession of cocaine.'

'Did you?' said Jack. 'That'd fit. One of the men I overheard said that half the clientele were off their heads with snow.'

'Did he, by jingo?' muttered Rackham. 'So we can add illegal drugs to all the other sins that are accumulating.'

'Do the names I read in the diary mean anything to you?' asked Jack. 'G. Stoker, A. McCann and S. Bierce? I don't know if the S. Bierce is Sholto Bierce, the MP.'

'He could be, I suppose. Jack, you say these names were written under the word *Pegasus*?' Jack nodded. 'I wonder if they're on the guest list for the dinner on board the aeroplane?'

'That's something I can find out.'

'Because if they are, I wouldn't be surprised, granted that we know this gala evening, as they call it, is starting at eleven o'clock, if these three were planning to go on to Paris after the flight. It might very well be their first visit, which would account for their names being written in the diary.'

'Shall we join them?' asked Jack.

Rackham grinned. 'I'd love to spoil the party. It's a matter for the Assistant Commissioner to decide but yes, I can't see why not.' He rose to his feet. 'Talking of the AC, why don't you come and talk to him? After all, as you said, it was your idea.'

Jack glanced down at his grimy clothes. 'Can't I change first?'

Rackham rose to his feet. 'Come on, Jack. Once the AC hears what you have to tell him, he'll be thinking about other things than your trousers.' He smiled. 'In fact, I reckon this is going to be the best news he's had all year.'

Chapter Fourteen

George Lassiter felt Anne's unconscious grip on his arm as the vast flying-boat circled overhead, the Rolls-Royce engines thundering out their stately, rhythmic music. It was Friday night, the night of the maiden flight of the Pegasus, and everything was unexpectedly going to plan.

A line of white lights along the Embankment illuminated the flight path for the seaplane. The lights made dancing white highlights on the choppy water and showed the upturned faces of the crowd, pausing on their journey home to see this latest wonder of the greatest city on earth. On the choked Blackfriars and Waterloo Bridges, hard-pressed policemen tried to keep the traffic moving as London slowed to a crawl. Even the trams on Blackfriars Bridge seemed to be clanking along more slowly as their occupants turned for a final look at what the *Daily Messenger* had called, in a leader which contained more adjectives than information, *A Wonder of the Aviation Age! Another first for Britain!* and, rather more poetically, *A man-made Monarch of the Air.*

It was just as well, thought George, that the crowd had no idea of the frantic efforts, bitter arguments and last-minute compromises that had gone into getting the Monarch of the Air aloft.

After David's arrest, Nigel had stayed at the factory, working flat out. Stella told him how she'd found Nigel asleep, slumped over the drawing board, more than once. He had only eaten when food had actually been put into his hand. Anne had gone to Tilbury to suggest that, in light of what had happened to David, the circumstances were inappropriate for the launch.

Nigel, appalled by the idea, had refused to budge. He didn't, said Anne, seem interested in David or even Culverton. Culverton was dead and nothing could bring him back and, if David had had any consideration, he would have refrained from parading his guilty conscience until after the launch instead of trying to scupper the Pegasus yet again by hogging all the limelight. This line of argument left Anne breathless but, with Mr Lassiter still stricken and incapable from David's arrest, Nigel was in effective control and what he said went.

It had been a desperate race against time and now it had paid off. Nigel's plane was ready – just. George felt a lump in his throat as the magnificent machine soared, banked and turned. Nothing could take away from the enormity of what he was seeing. Although he couldn't warm to Nigel, he had to hand it to the man. The Pegasus was a wonderful achievement. To build an aeroplane that could cross oceans and traverse continents was staggering, and now the Pegasus, with Nigel at the controls, was coming in for what only the most skilful pilot could attempt, a night landing on water.

George returned Anne's grip as Nigel Lassiter, now only twenty feet above the river and slowed to nearly stalling speed, wafted the mighty aircraft down until it kissed the surface of the Thames, turning in a creamy wake to face upstream, hugging the shore. Along the two bridges and sparking down the Embankment, cameras blazed and caught the moment. The thrum of the engines split into a staccato tattoo and spun into silence.

George let his breath out in a whoosh. 'That,' he said, with deep appreciation, 'was perfect.' He looked at Anne, who was grinning in relief. Out on the river, Nigel Lassiter stood up in the open cockpit and waved to the crowd, who responded with a spattering of applause.

'He loves it,' said Anne enthusiastically, temporarily carried away. 'He's worked so hard for this moment. No one ever really believed he'd do it. Even David ...' She broke off, unable to say any more.

George cleared his throat. 'I know,' he said awkwardly. He covered her hand with his, unable to find any words that didn't seem unbearably clumsy. He couldn't, in his heart of hearts, really comprehend that David – *David*, for God's sake – had confessed to murder. Mrs Culverton, he knew, had tried to get David to retract his confession, to change his mind, but he stubbornly stuck to his story. Despite a solemn warning about making a false statement, Mrs Culverton had continued to insist that David had been with her until after two in the morning on the night Culverton was murdered. David, she said, was innocent.

George sighed deeply. He could only guess at the depth of Peggy Culverton's feelings but he knew what effect David's confession had had on Anne and as for his grand-father – well, that was nothing short of a tragedy. He had aged years in the past few days and, for the first time, George realized just how old his grandfather was. Nothing, not the Pegasus or the firm or Anne or George himself, seemed to matter to him any more. The only one who seemed unaffected, thought George, as he watched Nigel climb down on to the wing of the plane, was Nigel.

A group of workers from the Lassiter factory were wait-ing on the shore below the Embankment. They threw a rope to the plane and Nigel secured it, standing as proudly as any captain of old on his quarterdeck as the Pegasus was pulled steadily into the bank.

Anne's face twisted as she heard his shout of encour-agement to the men. 'He hardly seems to have realized what's happened, you know. I wish I was like him,' she added savagely. 'So caught up in my own affairs that I simply didn't know what was going on around me.'

'You don't mean that,' said George.

Anne smiled bitterly. 'Don't I? It would hurt a lot less.' George, unable to find an answer, squeezed her hand once more. Anne blinked very rapidly then, withdrawing her hand, took a handkerchief from her bag and blew her nose in a gesture of finality. 'This is no good,' she said in an attempt at briskness. 'I've got work to do. The caterers are here, I know, but now the Pegasus has landed I have to get everything sorted out.'

'We'll be able to get on board soon,' said George, watching as the Lassiter men tethered the aircraft. They had a temporary jetty ready and Nigel, grinning broadly, climbed out of the aircraft and walked ashore. 'Let's go and see him, shall we?'

They had to wait. Nigel was quickly surrounded by a group of pressmen and more cameras blazed. There were, predictably, questions about David, which Nigel dealt with by ignoring them completely. Gradually the crowd thinned and Nigel caught sight of them. 'Come and join me,' he called with a welcoming wave of his arm.

'She's an absolute beauty,' George said sincerely. 'I've never seen a plane like it. You made a perfect landing.'

Nigel's smile increased. 'Of course, you know something about aeroplanes, don't you? I'd forgotten.'

'George owned a seaplane,' Anne put in.

Nigel ignored her. 'This is the most advanced aircraft in the world. Nothing can match her, nothing. Why don't you come on board?'

'I've got to come on board,' said Anne. 'I'm in charge of the arrangements for the dinner, remember?'

'So you are,' said Nigel. 'You'd better get on with it. We don't have that much time before the guests arrive.' Another reporter hailed him and Nigel looked at her with a touch of impatience. 'Go on, Anne. I'm busy.' He walked past them to where the reporter stood.

Anne turned to George with a rueful smile. 'Did he say thank you or did I miss it?'

'You didn't miss it,' said George curtly. Nigel Lassiter, he thought, was a very difficult person to like. However, he had to admit, as he followed Anne along the jetty and into the passenger compartment in the pontoons, he could build aircraft.

It looked stunning. George followed Anne through the main door. Concealed lights set into the bulkheads shone on polished mahogany and gleaming brass. The entire pontoon was sixty feet in length and it looked more like the stateroom of a luxury liner than an aeroplane. Deep leather seats sat two abreast beside each window and through a door he could see the dining room set with tables.

'Good grief, Anne,' he said in amazement. 'It's more like a hotel than an aeroplane.' He looked round, puzzled. 'Where will everyone sleep?'

'In the dining room.' She led the way through the door. 'All these tables are clamped to the floor by removable bolts. For one thing we can't have them sliding round and for another, we have to use the space for cabins. Once the tables are removed then we can put up stowable night-berths, showers and wash-basins. People – the sort of people we want to attract – simply won't rough it and there's really no reason why they should. We'll have to wait until we actually take off to set the tables, but you can imagine how this will look with linen, china and flowers. We're going to eat in the air, then, before we land, the waiters are going to clear away and, once we're back on the river, Nigel can change and join us for the speeches and drinks.'

'It'll look wonderful,' said George warmly. He ran his fingers lightly round the brass-bound edge of a table. 'Is there a galley? Where will all the food be cooked?'

'The galley's in the crew's quarters, but we're cheating slightly tonight. We're having the food brought aboard already cooked and kept warm.'

'It's a far cry from my old Short 184,' said George. 'Did you have a hand in the design?'

She nodded. 'Nigel didn't have much of an idea what people would actually need on a long-distance flight, so I made some suggestions. One thing I thought about was where everyone would sit after dinner while this room is

253

being prepared for the night. They can either go back in the lounge or outside.'

'Outside?' said George, startled. She nodded. 'Er . . . won't they fall off?'

He was pleased to see Anne's eyes crinkle in a smile. 'We won't let people outside while we're flying. No, this is for the evening, when the Pegasus has landed.' She opened a door in the hull. 'Come and have a look, George. I know it was my idea but I think it's a nice touch.'

He followed her out of the door on to a small landing on the outside of the pontoon. It was surrounded by a guard-rail, and steps, just as on a ship, ran up to the side of the craft. The entire top of the pontoon was laid out as a promenade deck.

'You see the idea?' said Anne. 'I can just imagine sitting up here after the day's flying is over and the Pegasus has come down for the night. We could be anywhere on earth, watching the sunset in the Mediterranean, the Indian Ocean or even the Pacific. Who knows?' She walked to the rails. 'It sounds wonderful, doesn't it?' and she added, more to herself than to him, 'It must be wonderful to be so far away.'

George stood beside Anne at the rails, looking down on to the silent propellers, the black river chopping into strings of crystal where it was caught in the lights from the bridges and the bank. It was a fine, cold night, the distant moon scudding behind dark clouds. The Pegasus rocked quietly in the water, a soothing, gentle motion. 'Would you like to be far away?' he asked hesitantly.

She looked at him with a cynical lift of her eyebrows. 'Is that so surprising? To escape? Yes, I'd like that.'

'I'm glad you're here,' he said. It sounded clumsy and he tried to explain. 'We need you, Anne.' He looked at her unhappy face. He wanted to say *I need you*, but something stopped him. He suspected Anne felt very vulnerable and he didn't want to take advantage of her weakness. She was engaged to Roger Maguire and that was that. He tried to think of Stella, but she seemed very remote. 'The family needs you.'

She shook herself. 'Forget it. Even if I could leave, I wouldn't, not with Grandfather in the state he is. No, I wouldn't go anywhere.' She squared her shoulders and took a deep breath. 'Come on, we've got work to do. This dinner won't arrange itself.' She turned back to the steps. 'Thanks for helping me tonight, George. I appreciate it.'

'Well, I am a member of the family, after all,' said George, following her across the deck. 'Who's coming, anyway? I don't actually know.'

'As many of the great and the good and the seriously rich as Nigel could persuade.' She laughed. 'It didn't take much doing.' She paused by the rail and opened her bag. 'I've got a copy of the guest list here. It's been printed in the papers, of course. It's a shame we've had to limit the numbers so severely. What are you doing afterwards?'

'Nothing very much.'

'Could you stay on board? Nigel wanted me to super-vise the clearing-up but I'd rather take Grandfather home. He's insisted on coming but I think a full evening will be too much for him. I'd be grateful if you'd stay, George. All it really involves is making sure the caterers have done everything and seeing they're safely ashore before Nigel flies back to Tilbury.'

'Leave it to me,' said George.

'I'm not spoiling your evening, am I?' she asked.

'No. I wasn't planning on doing anything after the flight. I'll be glad to know Grandfather's being looked after. I wish I could make things better,' he added impulsively. 'Better for you, I mean. I think it's really sporting of you to do what you're doing.'

He must have looked concerned for she reached out and squeezed his arm. 'Come on. We can't solve any-body's problems by feeling miserable about them and we really do have to start work. There's one thing, at any rate,' she added. 'You're happy. I mean, you've got Stella, haven't you?'

Stella: it seemed almost impossible to bring her vibrant, colourful beauty to mind in this quiet, lamplit place. George tried but his image of Stella seemed garish and artificial. The water slapped against the sides of the pontoons, and on the Embankment the traffic sounded far away. Anne was looking at him quizzically and he smiled. 'Happy? Yes, I suppose I am,' he said.

She shivered. 'Let's go back inside.'

At nine o'clock that evening Jack walked to the police station on Saffron Place. Rackham, wearing a heavy overcoat and muffled up against the cold, was standing by the entrance. He was clearly on edge and greeted Jack with relief.

'I'm glad to see you.' He glanced behind him to the police station. 'This is a massive affair, Jack,' he said quietly. 'There's thirty men involved, including me, and the Assistant Commissioner himself is turning up.'

Jack's eyebrows rose. 'As big as that, eh?'

Rackham nodded. 'Yes, this is it, all right.' Although Saffron Place was deserted, he lowered his voice still further. 'It's a big case in any event but it was the names you read in the diary in the office that did the trick. As soon as we learned that Sholto Bierce really was a guest on the Pegasus, the AC more or less had to be involved. We're dealing with some very important people and we can't afford to get it wrong.' He half-smiled. 'It's a bit like the war, when we went over the top. Everyone standing round, filling in time until the whistles blew, and then into action. It was always the waiting that got to me then, too.' He lit a cigarette. 'I did wonder, granted just how important it all is, if the AC would let me see the case through to the end but he's decided to let me stay with it.' He glanced at the sky. 'Funny to think that the Pegasus is up there, somewhere. It must be strange, flying at night. How on earth can you see anything?'

Jack followed his gaze, looking to where dark, silver-rimmed clouds scudded across the sky. 'I've done some night flying. With any sort of moon the visibility's pretty good. Any reflective surface such as the roof of a house or a sheet of water turns into a sort of opaque mirror.' He grinned. 'Flying's easy. It's landing that's the problem. Nigel Lassiter will get her down all right. He can hardly miss the Thames. I'd liked to have been on board,' he added.

'You're needed here.'

'Fair enough,' Jack acknowledged. 'When are you going to take the men into Dainty Alley?'

'After the Pegasus has landed. I've arranged for them to go in ones and twos, so with any luck they won't draw too much attention to themselves. I'm taking fifteen men in with me and the rest will be stationed on the street. I'll go in first and you bring up the rear. You needn't worry about the men. They're a hand-picked bunch. Most of them were in the infantry during the war and all the men who are coming in with us are experienced trench-raiders. I couldn't ask for a better crowd. We've got a constable posted on the Embankment who's going to telephone when the Pegasus touches down but we'll be able to see it from here, won't we?'

'We'll certainly see her approach the river.' Jack glanced at his watch. 'I'll come and introduce myself to the men, then I'll keep an eye out for the plane.' He stiffened as the wind changed, bringing the far-off, distinctive growl of a series of Rolls-Royce Condor engines. 'There she is now,' he said, pointing.

It took a few minutes for Rackham to pick out what the experienced pilot had noticed right away, then he saw it, a tiny dark moving smudge against the clouds.

'She's got time for a couple of circuits more before she lands,' said Jack knowledgeably. 'Come on. Let's get indoors.'

* * *

The moon was riding higher now, high enough for the occasional gleam of light to penetrate the filthy window of the attic overlooking Dainty Alley. Jack stood beside Rackham, once again listening intently for any noise. Although he had been reassured by Rackham, he could hardly believe how quietly the men had made the passage along the eaves from the deserted draper's shop. Now they all waited patiently, their breathing very quiet. Down below, from the Continental, came the far-off thump of music and from the window came the muted sounds of London.

In the distance the chime of the clock of St Clement Danes, caught and flurried by the wind and traffic, sounded the hour.

'It's time,' whispered Rackham close to Jack's ear. 'Get ready.'

Jack stripped off the hat, gloves and overalls he had worn for his passage through the eaves, emerging, like a butterfly from a chrysalis, in full evening dress with a gleaming shirt-front. He took a black mask from his pocket and adjusted it over his eyes. 'How do I look?'

Despite himself, Rackham couldn't restrain a smile. 'Very sinister. Well done.'

Rackham gave a signal to the men and with a quiet sound, almost like the rustle of leaves, they filed out of the attic and on to the top landing. The music from the Continental was clearer now, sounding up the back stairs. Rackham raised his hand to indicate the men should wait then followed Jack down to the door of the office.

Jack tried the handle. 'It's locked,' he mouthed rather than said.

Rackham nodded and took a bunch of keys from his pocket, the keys which had been made from the wax impressions Jack had brought back. He had a collection of picklocks with him but, if this worked, it was easier. He put the key in the lock, hearing the rewarding click as it turned.

Rackham nodded in approval and gingerly opened the door. The office was in darkness. 'I bet the door into Paris is locked too,' he said very quietly. Together the two men glided across the room to the door of the club. They could hear noises from the other side of the door. There was no music but they could hear the muffled sound of voices.

Jack took the key and unlocked the door, put the keys in his pocket and opened the door a crack, peering into the room. He drew back and shut the door. 'They're all wearing lapel badges,' he said quietly. 'I saw them glint in the light.'

Rackham drew his breath in. 'Damn! What are you going to do?'

'I'll have to risk it.'

'I don't like changing the plan.'

Jack smiled grimly. 'Remember what we used to say in the war. No plan survives an encounter with the enemy. Here goes.' He opened the door again, waited his moment, and slipped into Paris.

It should, George Lassiter thought, have been a perfect evening. The novelty of dining five hundred feet over London had paid off and the guests, hardly any of whom had been on that rare thing, a night flight, had gasped in wonder as the bowl of London stretched out beneath them, rimmed by the moonlit Surrey hills, the Thames like a pewter ribbon, the city a vibrant blaze of light. Then came one of Howgrave and Cheriton's best dinners, with service easily the equal of the Ritz or the Savoy, in a dining room rich with starched linen, fine bone china, gleaming silver and the sparkle of glass.

As the Pegasus finally nosed her graceful way back on to the river the guests had broken into spontaneous applause. When Nigel Lassiter, changed from flying kit to evening dress, had joined the guests in the dining room, he was hailed as a hero. With brandy in hand and the scent of cigars mingling with that of the bouquets of flowers, Nigel had never had a more receptive audience for any of his speeches.

And yet . . . And yet. Whenever Anne relaxed there were tired lines etched on her face, Peggy Culverton hardly spoke, and as for his grandfather . . . George twisted inside as he looked at the old man, a frail caricature of what he had been only days before.

It was over now and the guests had departed. Anne had taken old Mr Lassiter home and Nigel was on shore, discussing the plane's performance with the Lassiter men. The evening had been a triumph. It just didn't feel like it.

Jack stood in the shadows beside the back wall of the club. The room was full but no one had seen him come in. The club was dimly lit, concealed lights shedding a pinkish glow across the sofas and chairs. The only brightly lit area was the bar which stretched across the back wall, gleaming with green bottles and glass. There were, at a guess, thirty or so people in the room, but there was hardly any noise. In front of him was the back of a sofa. He started to walk past it when a sudden burst of laughter made him pause. A girl, naked apart from a few wisps of scarf, leapt up. A man's arms pulled her down and she relapsed back into the seat and out of his line of sight with a brief cry. Jack assumed an expression of unconcern, but no one looked round. Curiosity was evidently not encouraged in Paris.

Here goes, thought Jack, mentally crossing his fingers. He walked with apparent idleness round the side of the room towards the door. A man, his white shirt-front showing pink under the lights, collar open and tie discarded, got up, bottle in hand, reached down and brought a woman to her feet. She, too, was naked, except for a belt of glistening jewels. He put his arm around her with arrogant ownership, then, staggering slightly, led her past Jack and out of the door at the far end. Again, no one showed any interest in their activities. A light flared and shone down, a hard single light, focused on the stage, and a drum started to tap in a subdued rhythm. A woman dressed in translucent gauze, a whip in one hand and holding a thin chain in the other, came on to the stage. She cracked the whip and tugged the chain, dragging another, younger woman in high heels, jewels and chains, with her hands tied behind her back. Jack tore his attention away from the ritualized surrender on stage and worked out his route to the far door.

Rackham wanted the door locked; that was the scheme which they had worked out together with the AC. No one, said the AC resolutely, was going to walk away from this raid. Hands in pockets, he reached the door and lounged against the wall. When he was sure no one was looking, he took the key from his pocket and turned it in the lock. He let his breath out in a silent sigh of relief. Now to get back . . .

He was halfway there when a waiter, who was clearing glasses from a table beside a sofa on which were two partially dressed women and a man in evening dress, stepped back unexpectedly, jarring into him. 'Sorry, sir,' muttered the man, turning round and looking into Jack's face. A startled expression leapt into his eyes.

'Excuse me, sir, but where's your badge?'

'I lost it,' said Jack, attempting to walk away.

The man put his hand out and grasped his arm. 'I'm sorry, sir, you know the rules. You'll have to see the manager. You can't come in here without a badge.' He beckoned to another waiter who hurried over to join them. 'This gentleman's lost his badge. Can you ask the manager to join us?' He turned to Jack. 'You'll have to stay with me, sir, until the matter is attended to.'

Jack had no intention of waiting until reinforcements arrived. Without giving any hint of his intentions he drove his fist into the waiter's ribs, a short, effective punch. The waiter doubled up with a groan and Jack ran for it, back towards the comparative safety of the office. Two more waiters loomed up in front of him, blocking his way, fists at the ready. He tried to duck past them when a third clipped him on the jaw. His head jerked back and his legs

261

were kicked from under him. Sprawling on the floor, he heard the drum stop beating, a woman's scream and the anxious, questioning voices of men. He attempted to get to his feet when a voice stopped him.

'What the hell . . .?' A rough hand grabbed his collar, hauling him to his feet. His arms were pinned to his sides and the mask ripped from his face.

He heard the quick intake of breath from the man looking at him and saw the eyes narrow behind the mask. 'Major Haldean?'

The voice was unmistakable. It was Roger Maguire.

Jack felt a thrill of satisfaction surge through him. He had guessed who was behind the Continental, and he was right.

'Take off the fancy dress, Maguire, old man,' said Jack evenly, looking into the masked face. 'You're finished. I know exactly who you are and what you've done.'

Maguire started back, his mouth working in fury. He turned to address the crowd behind him. 'It's all right,' he called over the noise of the club. 'Nothing to worry about. Please, gentlemen, resume your seats. This is just a little matter I have to clear up.' He turned back to Jack and his captors. 'Take him downstairs,' he said to the waiters. 'We'll use the red room. Major Haldean needs to answer a few questions. A few painful questions,' he added viciously.

That was no good. He had to get his arms free but he was firmly held. 'It's no use, Maguire,' he said. 'I know all about you.' For God's sake, couldn't Bill Rackham see what was happening? Out of the corner of his eye Jack risked a glance towards the office. A waiter was standing outside the door, blocking the entrance. Bloody *hell*!

'Take him away,' spat out Maguire.

Jack laughed. He had to win more time and he wasn't going to be taken out of Paris for anyone. 'Do drop it, Maguire. What do you think you look like, dressed up as Zorro? It's over.'

Maguire snarled and, stepping forward, struck Jack hard across the face with the flat of his hand. 'How did you get in here?'

Jack, temporarily blinded by the blow, didn't answer.

Maguire hit him again. 'How did you get in here?'

Jack, his face throbbing with pain, shrank back defensively. 'I didn't mean any harm!' He was desperate to get his arms free, to make Maguire believe he was really scared. Where the devil was Bill?

Maguire smiled at the terror in his voice. 'Hit him again,' he said to one of the waiters.

Jack struggled, twisting to ward them off. Another blow went home and he sank to his knees. The two waiters holding him dragged him round to face Maguire once more.

Maguire threw his cigarette on the floor and, stepping forward, launched a kick into Jack's ribs. Torn away from the waiters' restraining hands by the impact, Jack rolled away with a grunt. There were dancing lights in his head but with an explosion of triumph he knew his arms were free at last.

He fumbled in his pocket, found the police whistle he was looking for and, with as much strength as he could muster, blew an ear-splitting blast. 'Bad luck, old chap,' he gasped, scrambling to his feet. 'The party's over.'

Chapter Fifteen

Supporting himself against the wall, Jack watched Maguire's face freeze in horror as Rackham's men poured into the room. The blast of the police whistle was like a bomb going off in the dimly lit room. The shrieks of women mixed with the shouts of men and, through it all, Rackham was yelling at the top of his voice.

'Everyone stay where you are! This is a police raid! Stay where you are!' He looked over his shoulder to where Maguire was still standing, surrounded by the waiters, looking on in utter disbelief. 'Make sure you've got him secure,' he called. He raised his voice to a shout once more. 'All the doors are locked and there's no way out!'

Maguire tensed as a policeman approached. Jack, still regaining his breath, watched him intently. He saw his face harden and the gleam of metal as he drew a pistol from his pocket.

'Look out!' shouted Jack and launched himself at Maguire. The crack of the shot bit through the screams, followed by a grunt from the policeman as the bullet tore through his arm. The pistol went skittering across the floor. Maguire hit out blindly, catching Jack on the side of the head before wriggling away, out of his grasp. Blinking, Jack tried to grab him once more and failed. Maguire kicked out, got to his feet and ran for it. Jack rolled away from the flailing feet and, hauling himself up, chased after him.

Maguire dodged round the stage, heading for the back of the room. He leapt on to the bar, sending glasses, trays and bottles flying.

Scrambling after him, Jack saw him fling open a door at the back of the bar. 'There's another door!' he yelled to the policeman thudding after him. 'Lock the damn thing!' Then he was down the staircase, hurtling after Maguire.

The staircase came out in the cloakroom in the lobby across from the doorway to the Continental. Jack saw the white, startled face of the cloakroom attendant as first Maguire, then Jack, pushed their way into the room. Maguire vaulted over the counter, evidently heading for the street, swerving as he saw the police blocking the door.

Jack followed him over the counter in time to see him disappear into the Continental. Women screamed and men shouted as Maguire raced through the dancers on the floor, thrusting them out of his way, heedless of overturned tables and crashing glass. With the part of his mind that never switched off, Jack registered how peculiar it was that the band continued to play as the breathy crescendo of the saxophone was nearly swamped by screams.

Maguire barged his way through a door at the back of the restaurant into the kitchens. A trolley laden with food went over in a smash of lobster claws, cutlery and glass. Maguire ducked round the kitchen table, skidding past bewildered waiters and a white-clad chef holding a pan. Jack saw him reach out in passing and grab a kitchen knife from the table.

He was heading for Dainty Alley. 'Stop!' roared Jack. 'Maguire, you can't escape!' Once Maguire got into Dainty Alley the chase was over, for that entrance was blocked too, but Maguire was armed and Jack feared for the police on the other side of the gate. Jack saw a brief flash of white as Maguire glanced over his shoulder, then the chef loomed up between them, still holding the pan.

Jack thrust the man out of his way in time to see Maguire disappear through the door on to the bottom of the stairwell, the stairs which led up to the attic. There was a creak, a crash as if something had been dropped, followed by an odd, hollow bang, but when Jack reached the stairs Maguire had vanished.

It suddenly seemed very quiet. From behind him the restaurant was pulsating with noise but here on the stairs was silence. Ignoring the chef who had followed him out, Jack cupped his mouth in his hands, shouting up the stairs to the policemen he knew were at the top. 'You up there!'

From the top storey, a policeman looked over the banister rails. He recognized Jack. 'Sir?'

'Come down, quickly. Leave a man on guard. Maguire's escaped.'

The policeman ran down. It only took a moment but Jack was alive with impatience. 'There's no one on the stairs, sir,' said the man when he arrived. 'There's a couple of doors on the way. I suppose he could have gone through one of them.'

Jack shook his head impatiently. 'That doesn't seem right,' he muttered. 'I heard a noise. I can't place it.' He walked into the tiny back yard. The light from the kitchen shining through the stairwell door funnelled on to the flags, making a wedge of sharp-edged shadows. He borrowed the policeman's lantern and shone it round the yard. Nothing. He looked at the high wall and barred gate. There were men in Dainty Alley. 'Hello!' he called. 'This is Major Haldean. Has anyone escaped?'

'Not this way, sir,' came the reply.

Jack swore with impatience and turned back to the stairwell entrance. Then he saw it. There was large square of coconut matting on the floor of the stairwell and it had been moved out of place. He lifted up the mat and there, set into the ground, was a trap door. 'Got him!' he said with deep satisfaction.

He hauled up the trap door, his lips curving in a smile as he recognized the creak. He shone the light down on to a mass of dark water about ten feet below. He put the lantern inside his waistcoat and sat on the edge.

'Leave this open,' he said to the policeman and then, without further ado, swung himself into the water.

He touched bottom briefly, falling against the wall of the tunnel, then the current picked him up and bore him away.

Struggling to the surface and spluttering for breath, he struck out, half swimming, half carried away. It was numbingly cold and utterly dark. This was far more than a sewer, it was a river. The icy water knocked the air from his lungs, and he felt a quiver of fear as he realized he was going to end up in the Thames. Echoing up the tunnel, from far ahead, over the cold rush of waters, he could hear a faint splash. Maguire!

Light, dim reflected light, appeared ahead: he was coming out into the Thames. Then he was out of the tunnel mouth, beached and helpless on the river bank, the water flowing round him as he lay in the mud. The main force of the water thundered over his head as he lay under the lip of the tunnel, but in front of him was the black, light-streaked mass of the Thames.

He didn't know how long he lay there, feeling his chest heave as he took in great gulps of air, but for a few minutes he was unable to move. Then, dragging his way through the mud, he crawled rather than walked to the side of the stream, leaned against the slime-covered stone blocks of the river wall and took in his surroundings.

Thank God the tide was on the ebb. When the river was full the tunnel entrance would be submerged and he would have been carried out into the Thames. With a start of surprise he recognized where he was. He was between Waterloo and Blackfriars Bridge and the Pegasus, close up to the temporary jetty, was riding gently on the river. The jetty was only forty feet or so away, stretching from the shore to the plane.

Then he noticed something else. On the bank of the river, black against the light, a man was sitting, shoulders hunched over in exhaustion. Maguire!

Jack dragged himself to his feet, steadied himself against the wall, then, as quietly as he could, walked to where Maguire was sitting. It was useless, of course. His feet slipped in the mud and shale and Maguire, looking round, caught sight of him.

Unbelievably, he got to his feet and ran. It wasn't a fast run, but it was a run, and Jack, weighed down by his wet clothes with his breath coming in desperate gulps, ran after him. Even in these circumstances, Maguire kept his head. He wasn't running blindly but making for the wall, where an iron ladder led up to the Embankment.

As Jack hauled himself up the ladder, he saw Maguire on the jetty. Maguire ran on to the Pegasus, making for the mooring ropes. He cast off and the seaplane started to drift into mid-stream. As Jack got to the end of the jetty, Maguire scrambled into the cockpit. The door to the pontoon opened and George Lassiter came out on to the little landing stage.

Jack, on the edge of the jetty, put all his strength into a shout. 'George! Help!' He saw George look at him, the surprise clear on his face. Jack took a deep breath and dived into the river.

This time he hardly noticed the cold. He struck out, making for the drifting plane. On the landing stage of the pontoon, George coiled a rope in his hand and threw it. The rope smacked across the water in front of him. Jack grasped it, winding the rope round his hands as George pulled.

As the rope tightened, Jack heard the engines of the seaplane burst into life. He felt the vibrations down the rope as the plane gathered speed, threatening to shake him loose as he battled the current and the backwash, before he thumped against the curving, convex pontoon. George took the strain and Jack heaved himself up, feet scrabbling on the polished wood. He passed the port-holes, glimpsing white tables in the deserted dining room, then he was on the flat-roofed deck, with George's strong hand grasping his coat between his shoulder blades, pulling him on board.

For a few seconds, no more, he lay exhausted. George was asking questions but he couldn't make out what they were. He raised himself to his hands and knees and, with

George's help, staggered to his feet. 'Maguire, George! We've got to stop Maguire.'

The ladder up to the rear of the cockpit was across the deck. They half ran, half slid to it and started to climb, grasping feverishly on to the rungs as the plane tilted. The plane lurched back and hit the water with a shuddering crash. As they reached the cockpit, they saw Nigel Lassiter and Maguire fighting over the controls. Maguire spun round, saw them, and lunged for the joy-stick.

'Take her up! Take her up!'

With a scream from the engines, the vast plane lifted, then smacked down again. Nigel, face working in fury, struck out viciously as Maguire reached forward again. Maguire, flung to one side, shook his head as if to clear it, then sprang. Nigel, one hand on the joy-stick, lifted his arm to keep Maguire away from the controls, and was dragged to one side. His foot slipped on the rudder bar and the plane spun round, out of control.

Jack saw the arches of Waterloo Bridge loom before he dragged George to the floor, flinging an arm over him as the seaplane smashed against the central pier. For a few moments the world was full of rending, crashing metal and splintering wood, followed by an odd interval of near-silence while the engines continued to pulse.

Nigel stood up like a man in a daze. 'The plane's wrecked. *The plane's wrecked.*' He turned to Maguire. 'You wrecked my plane.' He reached out and, taking him by the lapels, shook him like a terrier with a rat. *'You ... wrecked ... my ... plane.'*

Maguire, forced back over the side of the cockpit, raised his fists and started to hit back but he might as well have tried to fight through a brick wall. Heedless of blows, Nigel slammed punches into him.

'Leave them!' cried Jack as George, with a yell, ran to try and pull the two men apart. George ignored him, grabbing hold of Nigel. Nigel paused, looked at George blankly, before saying, his face as calm and his voice as steady as if he were making after-dinner conversation in the drawing room, 'He wrecked my plane.' Then, as casually as if he were swatting a fly, he flung off George and fastened his hands round Maguire's neck.

Maguire's eyes bulged. His knee came up convulsively, catching Nigel in the groin. Nigel grunted, slackened his grip and Maguire struck out. Nigel, caught off balance, fell back, taking Maguire with him.

There was a series of thumps, followed by a single high-pitched, seemingly endless scream. The engine note changed and a slushing, grinding noise filled the air. The engines faltered, coughed, and roared into full life again.

Jack dived for the controls and shut off the engines. They closed down with a roar and the noise of the propellers separated into single notes before they beat to a standstill, leaving only the sound of the river lapping against the sides of the pontoons.

'Jack,' said George, his voice horribly unsteady. 'They fell into the propellers.'

Jack leaned his head back on the seat. 'I know,' he managed to say. 'I heard them. I know.'

How long they were there he couldn't tell. Afterwards he wondered if sheer exhaustion and over-stretched nerves had taken their toll for the next thing he was really aware of was George, standing up in the wreckage of the cockpit, shouting to someone on the bridge. Then George put an arm under his shoulders, helping him to his feet. 'Come on, old man. Rackham's got a boat here for us, but we've got to climb down to it.'

Jack blinked himself fully awake and, thankful for George's support, hauled himself to his feet. Every muscle in his body ached and his ribs, where Maguire had kicked him, yelled a protest. He saw the worried expression on George's face and summoned up a smile. 'I'm fine.'

'Of course you are,' said George with a relieved grin. 'Let's get off this aircraft.'

They picked their way through the smashed cockpit over

the deck and down what remained of the tangled ladder to the boat where Rackham was sitting with two officers from the River Police.

'It's a relief to see you again,' said Rackham as the police steered the boat the short distance to the shore. 'I didn't have a clue where you'd got to until we got a call from the river men.' He paused. 'I gather Maguire bought it.'

Jack stepped on to the bank. 'You could say that. Nigel too.'

'Did he?' Rackham winced. 'That wasn't supposed to happen.' He was silent for a few moments. 'Well, it can't be helped, I suppose. Do you think you can manage the walk back to Saffron Place? We're still clearing everyone out of the club. The AC's directing operations but we can take you home from there – or to hospital,' he added doubtfully, looking at Jack's filthy, torn clothing and mud-covered face. 'My word, you look a sight. I hardly recognized you under all the mud.'

Jack managed another smile. 'You'll eat a peck of dirt before you die,' he said with an attempt at humour and was rewarded by a laugh from Rackham. He felt his ribs gingerly. 'Despite how I feel, I don't think there's anything broken. Where the devil were you, by the way, when that bugger Maguire was giving me the third degree?'

'A waiter came along, saw the office door was ajar, shut it, and stood against the wall. I couldn't open the door without giving the alarm so I decided to wait a few minutes unless you blew the whistle in the meantime.' He looked at Jack. 'So he collared you, did he?'

'Absolutely he did. It was a nasty moment. As I said, a plan never survives the first encounter with the enemy.'

'Jack,' said George soberly as they walked back to Saffron Place, 'how on earth are we going to break the news about Nigel to my grandfather? Coming on top of what's happened to David, this'll kill him.'

'David?' It took Jack an effort to realize that George didn't know the truth. 'David's all right.'

'But he's in prison.'

271

'Not for long. He should be released soon.'

George looked at him in bewilderment. 'But what about Culverton? He confessed to killing Culverton. I heard him, Jack. I was there when he said it.'

'He's all right,' Jack repeated wearily. 'I'll tell you the whole story later but David didn't kill anyone. He'll be fine.'

They walked up Tilford Lane where a single police wagon still stood outside the Continental, rimmed by a party of police. Sir Douglas Lynton, the Assistant Commissioner, broke off from the group. 'Inspector Rackham! This has been a stunning night's work.' He looked dubiously at Jack, then started. 'Good God, Major, I hardly recognized you. I can scarcely congratulate you enough on what you've done.'

'Thanks, sir,' said Jack. He was so tired that it was a real effort to speak and he couldn't get that slushing, grinding noise out of his mind. He didn't want to be congratulated.

'There's one more body to be brought out,' said Sir Douglas to Rackham. 'Three people committed suicide rather than be arrested.' He looked up as two policemen came down the steps carrying a covered stretcher. 'This is the last of them. Who is it?' he asked the leading stretcher-bearer.

The stretcher-bearer shook his head. 'We don't know, sir. It's a woman, that's all I can say. We found her in one of the bedrooms. She'd shot herself.'

Sir Douglas stepped forward and drew back the cover on the stretcher. Jack felt rather than heard the agonized cry that George gave as they looked into the dead, distorted face of Stella Aldryn. It was over.

Chapter Sixteen

Only, of course, it wasn't over. The next day, Rackham, Haldean and Dr Kincraig saw David Lassiter before he was formally released. The records from the club had to be gone through and Rackham, with occasional bursts of inspiration from Jack, started on the task of putting the information he had gathered into a formal report.

It was the following week when the letter arrived. It was from Anne.

. . . I know there's far more to it all than either David or George can tell me. Please, Major Haldean, will you explain what happened? Grandfather and Peggy keep asking me questions and I simply can't answer them.

Jack tossed the letter across the breakfast table to George. 'How come you haven't spoken to Anne? You were at Eden Street yesterday.'

George read the letter, crunching his way through toast and marmalade. He looked, thought Jack, remarkably embarrassed. 'The trouble is,' said George, fiddling with the butter knife, 'it's not so blinking easy. I feel such an idiot, being taken in by Stella, that I'd rather not talk about it, especially to Anne, and, of course, I don't know how she feels about that swine, Maguire. I mean, it's not very savoury, is it? Then again, I know Grandfather is relieved to have David back but Nigel was his son, too, and I don't want to make it any worse for him. Besides that, Mrs Culverton was there yesterday and I can hardly talk about her husband in front of her. To be honest, I've kept my head down.'

'Hmm, yes,' said Jack. 'I can see it's difficult.'

'Why don't you speak to her?' asked George. He glanced at the letter again. 'It's what she wants.'

The grandfather clock in the hall had chimed half past nine when Jack opened the door to Anne Lassiter. Peggy Culverton was with her and, looking very pleased with himself, David Lassiter. 'Come in,' said Jack, taking their coats. 'I asked Bill Rackham and Dr Kincraig to join us, as they can explain parts of the story far better than I can. You've eaten, haven't you?'

'Yes, we've had dinner,' said Anne. 'Grandfather thought of coming, but I managed to persuade him to stay at home.'

'How is he?'

'Better. He's still knocked out about Nigel, but David's news cheered him up.'

Jack looked inquisitively at David Lassiter.

'Peggy and I are going to be married,' said David with a broad grin. 'We announced the news at dinner tonight.'

'Congratulations!' Jack turned to Peggy Culverton. 'I hope you'll be very happy. I'm sure you will be.'

'Thank you.' She looked radiant. All the wariness which he had come to associate with her had gone. She reached out her hand to him. 'We've got you to thank, I know. If you hadn't managed to work things out, it would have all ended very differently. There aren't really words for this sort of thing. You can only guess how grateful I am.'

He smiled warmly at her. 'I didn't do it by myself, you know, but thanks.' He showed them into the sitting room where George Lassiter, Bill Rackham and Dr Kincraig were waiting. 'Make yourselves at home. This calls for something special,' he said, once everyone had sat down. 'Hang on. I won't be a jiffy.'

He was back in a few minutes, holding three dusty green bottles. 'Moët et Chandon,' he explained. 'I've got a case in the cellar.' Anne helped him fetch glasses from the sideboard. 'To the happy couple,' he said, pouring out the champagne. 'You deserve it.'

They drank the toast then Anne looked at him over the top of her glass. 'Will you tell us the story? None of us know what happened.'

'Wait a moment,' said Peggy Culverton. 'Major Haldean, there's something I must know. Was I right about Alexander? Was he the Ripper? I was certain he was but then, when that other murder happened, it seemed as if I'd been wrong.'

Jack took a deep breath. 'You weren't wrong, Mrs Culverton,' he said gently.

She flinched. 'I knew it,' she muttered. 'So he was the X man. In the end I was terrified of him. I seem to have been frightened for so *long.*'

David Lassiter covered her hand with his. 'There's nothing to be frightened of now.' He gave Jack a puzzled look. 'I still can't work it out. I know Nigel was involved but not what he actually did.'

'Nigel, I'm afraid,' said Jack, 'was as guilty as Roger Maguire and Stella Aldryn. The three of them were in it up to their necks.'

David Lassiter and Anne exchanged looks. 'It doesn't surprise me,' said David after a pause. 'He might have been my brother but he was a callous devil. How did it all start?'

'It started,' said Jack, taking a cigar from the box and lighting it, 'when Stella Aldryn met Roger Maguire. That was about three years ago. That they had an affair was obvious, but they had something else in common and that was greed.'

Anne stared at him. 'Roger had an affair with *Stella?*' Jack nodded.

'It came as a shock to me as well,' said George quietly.

'But why?' demanded Anne. 'If he was having an affair with her, why did he bother with me?'

Jack hesitated. 'I think I know the answer but I'll come to it in its proper place. It might make more sense, then. Incidentally, when did Nigel meet Maguire for the first time?'

David Lassiter shrugged. 'Nigel had known Maguire for years. I'd met him occasionally. Naturally I met him a great deal more often after he started seeing Anne.'

'Which makes,' said Jack, staring at the end of his cigar, 'it all easier to understand. You see, what happened was this. Stella was employed as a clerk at Marchbolt's, the solicitors who dealt with George's legacy.' He paused and looked at Rackham. 'We knew that the information about George's legacy more or less had to come from either George himself or the solicitors but what puzzled Bill and me was that the solicitors seemed so honest. Once we knew Stella Aldryn was implicated, it was easy. Bill showed them her photograph and they recognized her at once. She'd changed her name since she worked for them but it was Stella, all right.'

'It explained a lot, didn't it, Jack?' said Rackham. 'For instance, Marchbolt's had apparently written to Mr Lassiter at Eden Street but never got a reply. Stella actually typed that letter – I've seen the carbon – and I imagine she saw it never got near the post-box.'

'It was during the course of her work that she came to hear of the whacking great sum of forty-six thousand chasing a missing legatee,' said Jack, 'and, naturally, she was able to look at the file to discover all sorts of interesting facts about your mother, George. She probably recognized the surname, Lassiter, as belonging to one of Maguire's friends. Anyway, the three of them, Maguire, Nigel and Stella, got together and stole the money.'

'Devils,' muttered George.

'Relax,' said Jack. 'After all, you're getting it back, isn't he, Bill?'

'Certainly, Mr Lassiter,' said Rackham. 'You were clearly defrauded. Both Maguire and Stella Aldryn had a great deal of money salted away abroad. I imagine it was their intention to run for it, should it ever look as if the game was up. I'm happy to say there's more than enough to make good your loss.'

'I told you that, George,' said Jack.

George shifted in his chair. 'I know you did but I'm still hopping mad about it, to say nothing of being taken in by Stella. She must have laughed herself stupid to see what an impression she'd made on me.'

'Grandfather always disliked Stella,' said Anne.

David nodded. 'I never cared for her much, either. She was too wide-eyed and innocent for me. It seemed unnatural sometimes but what really got to me was the amount of time she had off. Nigel didn't seem to notice. I thought it was because he was so absorbed in the Pegasus.'

'There was a much simpler explanation,' said Jack. 'Stella Aldryn was supposedly employed by your firm but the life she lived bore no relation to an ordinary clerk's. She had an eye-wateringly expensive flat in Knightsbridge – where, incidentally, Maguire was a frequent visitor – and lived the life of a wealthy woman of fashion. Naturally enough, she took care that George never saw the flat.'

'So what was she doing in the firm at all?' asked David. 'She must have had some reason.'

'We think she was keeping an eye on Nigel,' said Jack. 'It's a guess but it fits the facts. You see, of the three of them who conspired to pinch George's legacy, Nigel was the one who, from their point of view, was the weak link. He wasn't motivated entirely by greed. He wanted, wanted more than anything in the world, to design and build aeroplanes.'

'He certainly wanted that, all right,' agreed David. 'So what did they do? How did they steal George's money, I mean?'

Jack looked at Rackham. 'Do you want to explain this bit? After all, you're the one who's talked to the solicitors.'

'All right,' said Rackham sitting forward. 'We can assume that Stella Aldryn told Maguire about the legacy. What we think happened then was that Nigel Lassiter took the birth certificate from the desk in Eden Street and gave

277

it to Maguire. It must have been Maguire who travelled to South Africa, as both Nigel and Stella were in England when the legacy was claimed. Maguire gave up general practice about that time and went abroad for a while. In South Africa I believe he booked into the Faulkner Hotel in the name of George Lassiter, made the claim, and came home the richer by forty-six thousand pounds. It's easy enough to open a bank account in a false name, especially armed with a birth certificate, and it wasn't long before the money was divided out between the three of them. We know that,' said Rackham, holding out his glass for Jack to refill it, 'because we've been able to get at their bank accounts.'

David Lassiter's expression was bitter. 'It all rings true. Nigel would have done anything to get his hands on that sort of money. It'd never occur to him to think of Charles's son – you, George – in all this. It was all about the Pegasus, wasn't it, Haldean? He wanted the money to build the Pegasus. Nothing else mattered to him.'

'I think so, yes,' said Jack. 'Anyway, with the money Nigel was able to start work on the Pegasus, Maguire moved from general practice to psychoanalysis and Stella Aldryn left the solicitors, began work as Nigel's clerk and moved into her flat in Knightsbridge. They also opened the Continental, and, in addition, Paris.' He took a long drink and looked into the fire.

'The restaurant, a perfectly good restaurant, probably made money but the real money-spinner was Paris. There are records at the club of who the clients are and who introduced them. Stella, who was very far from the wide-eyed innocent she seemed, found some customers and Maguire channelled his more likely patients towards Paris. Nigel picked a few of his friends. Maguire also supplied dope, which, as a doctor, he could obtain fairly easily. The secrecy surrounding it was absolute. The staff were all hand-picked by Maguire for their broad-mindedness and were ridiculously well-paid to keep quiet. They knew about the dodgy goings-on in Paris, but nothing about murder.'

'The staff might not have known about the murders,' put in Rackham, 'but we think our three had murder in mind from the beginning. The first death happened very soon after the club opened. Jack tells me that this sort of murder club exists in Paris. The name Paris, we thought, was significant.' He looked sympathetically at Peggy Culverton. 'Your husband was one of their first clients. Maguire, who'd been his doctor, introduced him.'

David made a noise at the back of his throat and covered Peggy's hand with his.

Jack looked at her. 'You sensed, didn't you, when he became a killer?' She nodded, unable to speak. David Lassiter squeezed her hand once more. 'You see,' said Jack, apparently intent on blowing a smoke-ring, 'that's what Culverton wanted and he paid – my God, he paid – to do it. The murders threw the police, didn't they, Bill?'

Rackham lit a cigarette. 'They did. For one thing they were so spread out. Culverton was sane, horribly sane, and his urge to kill was controlled by his wallet. Maguire would pick up a likely girl from anywhere in London and take her to the club. One of the bedrooms – the middle floor was given over to bedrooms – was very well insulated. No sound can escape from it.' Peggy Culverton made a little choking noise. Rackham glanced at her then looked away, avoiding her eyes. 'You see, a murderer usually has to dispose of the body but that was all taken care of by Maguire. When the tides were right, the bodies were simply dropped into the tunnel by the kitchens and were washed into the Thames.'

Anne Lassiter's face was white. 'I asked you before but I need to know. Why, with all this going on, did Roger want anything to do with me?'

Jack took a drink. 'I wondered about that. Practically speaking, it gave Maguire another opportunity to keep an eye on Nigel. He was always the most unstable of the three. However, Dr Kincraig has another explanation.'

Dr Kincraig leaned forward in his chair. 'You're probably right about the practicalities, Major, but I think there's a deeper reason why a man of Maguire's type should take up with –' he nodded to Anne – 'a lady such as Mrs Lassiter. You see, he had attracted Stella with little trouble and obviously had no problem in attracting others of her ilk. But to attract a woman such as Mrs Lassiter? Maguire thought the devil of a lot of himself, and to live two lives, one good, one bad, and excel at both . . . man, it's the basis of a deal of psychology and a heap of literature. D'ye never read *Dr Jekyll and Mr Hyde*? It's all there.'

'So I was part of his pretence,' said Anne bitterly. 'I wondered, you know. Even at the time I wondered. And I was flattered, too,' she added. 'I hate to admit it, but I'd never met anyone like him before.'

'Alexander was like him,' said Peggy Culverton. 'Not to look at, I mean, but there were occasions when I caught an expression on his face that reminded me of Alexander.' She shuddered. 'By then I'd started to mistrust my reactions, though. I wondered at one time if I was going mad, seeing the worst in Alexander and seeing Alexander in others.' She looked at Rackham. 'I said, didn't I, that what he had done brought about his death? I was right, too.'

'You were, Mrs Culverton.'

'Who did kill him?' asked David. 'Maguire?'

Jack laughed dismissively. 'What, kill the goose that laid the golden eggs? No. Maguire didn't have a shred of motive. Stella wouldn't harm him and Nigel, as we know, was beside himself. The only people who had any motive were you, Mrs Culverton, and, because of you, David. And, as we know, you're innocent.'

'Despite your best efforts to convince us otherwise,' put in George. David smiled ruefully and said nothing.

'No,' continued Jack, 'Maguire didn't kill Culverton. When he arrived at the club on the night of 31st October he had a problem, though. He had expected to dispose of the body of Bridget Flynn, the girl he had picked up earlier for Culverton's benefit. What he found was that Culverton, who had a history of heart trouble, had not only killed the girl, but died of heart failure in . . .' He paused, choosing his words carefully. 'Well, in the aftermath,' he finished.

Although Anne Lassiter looked blank, Peggy Culverton's reaction told him she knew exactly what he meant. He heaved a mental sigh of relief that he didn't have to spell out the sordid details and hurried on.

'Now it's one thing disposing of the body of a Bridget Flynn, but Alexander Culverton was a well-known man. Maguire couldn't risk the police looking around the Continental and to push him into the river must have seemed the obvious thing to do. Culverton was already naked and to cave his face in and make him practically unidentifiable must have seemed like the best option. It distanced Culverton from the other dead body and, with any luck, he might never be identified. It would certainly take the police some time to work out who he was.'

'Did Nigel know what Maguire had done?' asked David. 'I can't believe he did.'

'No, neither can I,' agreed Jack. 'I think Maguire told Stella Aldryn, all right, but I can't see him confiding in Nigel. If Nigel had known, he would have let it slip one way or another. He nearly let the cat out of the bag more than once. For instance, he threatened Michael Walsh on the day of his murder.'

David Lassiter stared at him. 'Michael Walsh's *murder*? Michael Walsh wasn't murdered. He can't have been. He died of a heart attack.' He paused. 'Hang on. He wasn't a part of this appalling club, was he?'

Jack shook his head vigorously. 'No, he wasn't. Michael Walsh was exactly what he seemed to be, an inquisitive man with too much time on his hands. Nigel knew perfectly well that Walsh was looking into his affairs. He'd caught him out once and didn't want him to try again. Stella Aldryn, too, had reason to be wary of Walsh. Walsh, as I was told, had quite a thing about Stella Aldryn. He followed her about, as George put it. Well, that wouldn't have suited Stella at all. She had far too many secrets, including her flat in Knightsbridge. Walsh was a clever man. Stella Aldryn couldn't risk him finding out that she was more than just a simple clerk.'

'But they didn't have to murder him,' said Anne. 'Surely they could have found another way.'

Dr Kincraig cleared his throat. 'You're assuming, Mrs Lassiter, that murder is a thing to avoid. I've come to understand something of Dr Maguire's psychology and a clever murder is something he would have relished. Major Haldean tells me that Walsh had been badly gassed in the war and that gave Maguire the weapon he needed. It was a very clever murder. I think Maguire must have derived considerable satisfaction from it, because, you see, not only was it clever, it was safe. If it didn't come off they could always try more direct methods.'

'I'm sure there was a very direct method lined up and ready to use,' said Jack. 'I think Walsh should have been murdered the weekend you should all have gone away, but that had to be abandoned. It came off the night Nigel hosted a dinner in the Savoy.'

'But how?' demanded David Lassiter.

Jack held his hand up. 'Wait.' He got up and, walking to the sideboard, stood with his hands in his pockets. 'George, you told us what happened that evening you broke into the kitchen, I know, but it seemed as if you'd experienced a nightmare. You were ill, really ill, and when you told me about it later, you skipped a lot of the details.'

'I was downright embarrassed by it,' said George. 'I thought it must have been a bad dream and I didn't want to talk about it.'

'It wasn't a dream,' said Jack.

Anne gave a sharp intake of breath. 'It really happened?'

Jack nodded. 'Yes, it really happened. The two men and the woman were, of course, Nigel, Maguire and Stella. You know when I cottoned on to the fact that George had been telling the truth?'

Anne looked at him. 'I think I do. It was that night you came to tell us about David being arrested, wasn't it? I said we needed a miracle and you said they sometimes happened. Your voice sounded so odd – triumphant, somehow – that I allowed myself to hope without really knowing why.' She smiled. 'We got our miracle.'

Jack laughed. 'It wasn't really a miracle, you know, it was a sort of magic. Earlier that evening George had told me and Bill a few more details of what had happened that night, such as the fact he could remember the pattern on the girl's dress and, more importantly, what one of the men had said. *He's having a bath and she's listening to the wireless.* D'you see the importance of that? I didn't right away because, George, I must admit that by then I'd started taking what you said and did with a pinch of salt.' He grinned. 'That was the evening you were chasing cats in St James's Street, remember?'

'I remember,' said George. 'There's no need to rub it in.'

'Anyway, Mrs Lassiter, you said exactly the right thing to jolt me into seeing things properly. You said you wanted a miracle and George talked about a magic wand and it made me think about illusions.' He poured himself another drink and held the glass, seeing the bubbles swirl up through the champagne. 'I nearly got it once before, when I saw a street magician in Leicester Square. He made a dove appear from an empty box. I knew I'd seen an illusion, something I knew had to be a trick. But that sort of illusion – that kind of magic – depends on reality. The dove is real and the box is real; it's how they're put together that makes the illusion. Now George saw a murder. A girl died in front of his eyes. He must have imagined it, surely, only he *couldn't* have imagined what was said. *He's having a bath and she's listening to the wireless.* You confirmed that was so, Mrs Lassiter. Your grandfather really was in the bath and you were listening to A.J. Alan. So that meant George must be telling the truth, peculiar though it sounded.'

He lit a cigarette. 'I slept very badly that night. When I awoke my mind was buzzing with what I'd seen and heard. George's nightmare had been real but, just like my dove, it was an illusion. I suddenly realized how that illusion could be brought about and everything fell into place.

283

George and I went to see Dr Kincraig and . . .' He smiled at the doctor. 'Why don't you explain this next bit? You know far more about it than I do.'

Dr Kincraig cleared his throat and sat forward in his chair. 'Very well, Major.' He addressed the room as if he was standing in a lecture theatre. 'What Major Haldean had worked out was that George Lassiter had seen a demonstration of hypnotism.'

'Hypnotism!' said Peggy Culverton, startled. 'You mean look-into-my-eyes and all that sort of thing? They didn't hypnotize George, did they?'

Dr Kincraig was not used to having his lectures interrupted. 'Indeed no, Mrs Culverton. Hypnotism is a very useful tool in dealing with bad cases of nerves and I have often employed it.'

'You've used it on me before now,' said Jack. 'I imagine that's why I twigged it.'

'Just as you say, Major. Now Maguire was a psychoanalyst and was in a position to know about both the theory and practice of hypnotism. There's a lot of nonsense talked about hypnotism because, in this country, it's usually a music-hall turn. However in France, where I studied for a while, it's a recognized medical technique. I usually use it to help a patient relax, as it's fairly easy to induce a trance. There is a popular belief that it is impossible to hypnotize someone against their will. That is not entirely correct. If a subject has a good idea of what the practitioner has in mind, he can fight against it. However, if the subject has no idea of what is to come, it is perfectly possible to put them into a trance without their consent. Such a proceeding is, I need hardly say, completely unethical. Under hypnosis a patient will act in a way which, however peculiar it may seem to an outside observer, makes perfect sense to the person concerned. If, under hypnosis, you give a man a lemon and tell him it is a crisp, juicy apple that he has a great desire to eat, he will crunch through it and be extremely angry if you tell him that he has just eaten a bitter lemon, skin and all. What it can't do is make someone perform an action which they have strong ethical or emotional objections to, such as committing suicide.'

'Well, that's a relief,' muttered George and was instantly quelled by a pair of sandy Scottish eyebrows.

'A great many experiments have been performed,' continued the doctor, 'to determine the limits of hypnotism. Braid and Charcot, the leading authorities in this area, identified three separate states which they could produce at will. There is a state of artificial somnambulism, a state of lethargy or trance, and a state of catalepsy. These states can be engendered, after suitable preparation, by an outside stimulus. It is usually a spoken phrase, although sometimes it can be an action or a piece of music. I refer to this stimulus as the trigger.'

'Catalepsy?' repeated David Lassiter. 'Hang on a minute. That means when you think someone's dead and they're not, doesn't it?'

The doctor nodded. 'Indeed it does, Mr Lassiter. To the unpractised eye – and sometimes, I regret to say, to the practised eye as well – there is no difference between a cataleptic trance and death. Which has led, I fear, to some very unfortunate occurrences. Very unfortunate. Dear me. Yes.'

'But that means . . .' David stopped helplessly. 'What the dickens *does* it mean?'

'It means,' said Jack, 'that what George saw in the kitchen that night was a rehearsal for murder. Walsh's murder.'

He lit a cigarette. 'Michael Walsh, poor devil, with his ropy heart and injured lungs, was still a man and had fallen for Stella Aldryn. That was part one. Part two occurred when Maguire, Nigel and Stella came into the kitchen where they knew they'd be undisturbed and Stella, who had been primed to go off into a cataleptic trance, was held by Nigel who said, "I love you." That was the key word or trigger, if you like. She keeled over and at that point came a knock on the front door. Nigel and Maguire

285

scooted off, leaving Stella who was, to all intents and purposes, dead, and poor George, who had been watching this with his hair standing on end, came out of the kitchen like a bat out of hell, straight into the arms of the policeman who had been knocking at the door. By the time the Law arrived down below, Stella had either woken up or been spirited away, and George was left gargling about dead blondes.'

'But how does that kill Michael Walsh?' demanded David Lassiter.

'I think I understand,' said Anne Lassiter. 'The night George broke into the kitchen was the night before we should have gone away but Grandfather's bad chest prevented us from going. Michael Walsh must have been going to search Nigel's office when we were away and Nigel and Roger surely guessed that's what he'd do. Mr Walsh had to put off his search until Nigel was safely out of the way once more, and that was during the dinner in the Savoy.'

'But –' began David.

Anne turned to him. 'Don't you see? Nigel and the others knew Walsh would try and search his office again so Stella Aldryn must have been waiting for him at the factory. She knew how he felt. He followed her around like a lost sheep. She'd never paid him any attention but if she staged a love scene . . .' She stopped and shuddered.

'If she could get Walsh to say, "I love you," she'd keel over, apparently dead,' said Jack. He looked at George. 'You know how frightening it was, and you were merely an observer. Imagine how Walsh must have felt. He'd be jumpy with nerves and way up high because, at long last, Stella Aldryn had revealed what he must fondly have believed were her true feelings. He had a dodgy heart. Can you imagine the shock when he said he loved her?'

David Lassiter sat back in his chair. 'My God, I can. He always had to be careful. A shock like that would see him off without a doubt.' He looked at Jack in bewilderment.

'You wanted to call the police in the night we found him. Did you guess any of this at the time?'

'No, nothing of the sort,' said Jack regretfully. 'And, I have to say, in the light of his knowledge, the doctor acted perfectly properly in refusing to call the cops. No, what bothered me were the two cigarette ends in the ashtray. It suggested that someone else had been in the office with him and, as we know, they had.'

'What if it didn't work?' asked Peggy Culverton. 'Shock seems so – well, chancy in a way. I've followed all you've said but I think there was a real risk it wouldn't work. What if Mr Walsh hadn't keeled over or what if he'd merely fainted?'

'If Walsh hadn't keeled over, then all that would have happened was that poor Miss Aldryn would apparently have had a fainting fit. That's not a criminal offence. If Walsh had been the one to faint . . .' He broke off and raised his eyebrows expressively. 'Well, I wouldn't like to be helpless and at Stella Aldryn's mercy. Especially when, in the office next door, there were those big yellow and black cushions. It's easy to smother a helpless man. That's the direct method I mentioned.'

'It still seems very elaborate,' said David.

'Does it?' asked Jack. 'Did you think it was murder?' David Lassiter shook his head. 'That's the best sort of murder of all, when no one knows a crime has been committed. Then, just as they were patting themselves on the back for a perfect murder, George fainted at Stella Aldryn's feet. They knew, of course, that George had been welcomed back into the Lassiter fold and I can't imagine they relished having the long-lost grandson and the missing legatee pop up. Stella Aldryn had probably made a point of being in the office to have a look at you, George, the day you went to visit the factory. Do you remember how Maguire and Stella hustled Nigel out of the office, looking for brandy? I'm sure Nigel didn't twig it, but I think Maguire and Stella suspected the worst right away. You were the legatee. I'm certain your days were numbered, but when it turned out you were the unintended witness of the night in the kitchen *and* you'd recognized Stella Aldryn as the dead girl . . . Well, they had to get you out of the way as quickly as possible.'

Anne Lassiter stared at him. 'You mean they tried to kill George?' Jack nodded. She drew her breath in. 'How?'

'I was hypnotized,' said George. 'D'you know, even now I can't get the idea of how Stella appeared to be out of my head.' He broke off with a shudder. 'It's stupid, but I was starting to care about her. Care about her very much.'

'She was a good actress,' said Jack. 'And you must remember that she was very experienced where men were concerned.'

'I know,' said George, 'but it's still hard to believe.'

'Stella Aldryn and Roger Maguire called on George while I was out,' said Jack, stubbing out his cigarette. 'It was the day we went to the Continental for lunch, Mrs Lassiter. I knew Stella Aldryn had called, because she left a coffee cup with a trace of lipstick on the rim. What I didn't know was that Maguire had been there as well. He didn't leave a coffee cup behind because he never drank coffee. I was ridiculously pleased with myself when I remembered that. I asked Stella Aldryn about it that day at the Continental. It must have been a nasty shock for her, but she covered it up very well. And, of course, George denied that she or anyone else had ever been here. I couldn't understand it at the time but once I'd caught on to the idea of hypnotism, it was easy enough to explain. Maguire simply told George to forget they'd ever been and he did.'

'Stella met me in the newsagent's that morning,' said George. 'She asked if you were at home, Jack, and when I said you weren't, told me she had something important to discuss and suggested we come back here. Maguire must have been waiting for the okay from Stella, because he joined us, as if by chance, on the street outside.'

Jack looked across to Dr Kincraig. 'When we came to see you, doctor, I was sure George had been hypnotized and

288

you confirmed that. Even though I was as sure as I could be about what had happened, it was a chilling moment when you put George into a trance and he spelt out what Maguire's instructions were.'

'What were they?' asked Anne.

'I was going to die,' said George. 'He wanted to kill me.'

Anne drew her breath in. 'How?'

Jack, after a glance at George, took up the story once more. 'George was going to have an accident, a spectacular accident. It happened the day the Pegasus was shown to the press.'

'Hold on,' said David. 'Do you mean George's fall from the board-walk?'

Jack nodded. 'That's it.' He walked across the room to the sofa where Boots, the kitchen cat, was sitting curled up beside George, purring gently. He crouched down and scratched the top of the cat's head. The purring increased. 'This old lady had her part to play.' He stood up again. 'Boots has taken a real shine to George. Whenever George comes in, Boots makes a point of coming to greet him. That happened when Maguire and Stella called. I know that, because my landlady told me Boots wanted to get out into the hallway when she heard his voice. I think the presence of Boots suggested the trigger or key word to Maguire.'

'Was it the word *cat*?' asked Anne Lassiter.

'It was the phrase *cat on the roof*. I know you, Maguire and Stella were talking about cats when George and I joined you. When Maguire said *cat on the roof*, George, as he'd been primed to do, climbed up to the board-walk to rescue a totally imaginary cat. Incidentally, George, it was that phrase that led to your trying to shin up a balcony on St James's Street.'

George grinned. 'D'you know, that does have its funny side. But look, Jack, I didn't ask you this before. How come if they wanted to do me in, they didn't try again?'

'They probably were going to try again. After all, Stella only had to say the magic words and you'd climb anything and nose-dive off. It must have seemed such a perfect method, but you'd hurt your arm. You couldn't climb anything and so, for a time, you were safe.'

'You're all right now, aren't you, George?' asked Anne anxiously. She hesitated slightly. 'I mean with cats and so on.'

'I'm not going to start climbing things,' said George with an embarrassed smile. 'Dr Kincraig sorted me out when Jack took me to see him. I couldn't remember a thing about it, though. Apparently he hypnotized me again so I wouldn't give the game away.'

'Major Haldean convinced me it was for the best, Mr Lassiter,' said Dr Kincraig. 'You agreed. As he pointed out, one hint to Stella Aldryn or, indeed anyone else, and the game would have been up.'

'I thought Dr Kincraig said you couldn't prompt someone to commit suicide by hypnotism,' said David. 'How come their plan to make you fall off the board-walk so nearly worked?'

'You misunderstand me,' replied Dr Kincraig. 'A man cannot be asked to commit suicide but he can be asked to think the solid ground is empty air. That's why Mr Lassiter fell.'

'Nigel didn't know about it,' put in Jack. 'He realized what had happened, all right, and was furious with Stella.'

'That's because it interfered with his publicity,' said David, drily.

Jack looked at him. 'Yes. I'm afraid you're right. Anyway, something else happened at the factory that day. Maguire found out that you had a motive to kill Culverton. He didn't act right away but what happened next changed everything, didn't it, Bill?'

'There was another murder,' said Rackham. 'At the time it seemed like another Ripper killing and in a way it was. You, Mrs Culverton, had cut off Nigel's funding for the Pegasus and Nigel, desperate for more funds, leaned on Ridgeway. Ridgeway, a nasty piece of work who had been embezzling money from his firm, agreed to stump up, if he was allowed the ultimate thrill.'

'And the thrill was provided,' said David quietly. 'Dear God.'

Dr Kincraig cleared his throat. 'From what you've told me, Ridgeway was a similar type to Culverton, if something of a poor copy. He borrowed the notoriety of the X man. From his point of view it would have glamorized his crime.'

'He didn't enjoy the glamour for very long,' said Rackham grimly. 'Young Croft, a very sharp sort, had taken over the firm. He knew that Ridgeway had misappropriated funds and arranged a surprise audit. Ridgeway, unable to face the music, went home and shot himself.'

'Nigel was beside himself when he found out,' said David. 'He used some of the foulest language I've ever heard and, what's more, he used it to Peggy. We had a terrific quarrel. I ended up thumping him.'

'He didn't forget that,' said Rackham. 'I think that's what sparked off what happened next.'

'I'm certain of it,' said David. 'Maguire was there. He'd come to discuss the effect Ridgeway's death would have on the Pegasus and the pair of them asked me to come into the drawing room with them. Maguire hypnotized me.' He shuddered and looked at Dr Kincraig. 'I can remember being absolutely convinced I'd killed Culverton. I suppose hearing what Peggy had been through and believing he was the Ripper made that possible. I know I truly did believe it. After you spoke to me, doctor, I remembered what really happened and why. Nigel hated me. There were no two ways about it. I remember their discussion. Maguire put me into a trance and they spoke freely. There were other reasons why I should carry the can for Culverton's death. I had some money from the Urbis that Nigel hadn't been able to get his hands on and my confession would mean the police would stop looking for Culverton's supposed killer. Nigel would eventually have control of the firm and so on, but the reason, the real reason, was that he hated me.'

'Nigel never could care for anyone,' said Anne Lassiter softly. 'He was always alone.'

It was, thought Jack, a very perceptive epitaph.

'It's South Africa for me, Jack,' George declared. 'I want to go home.' He pushed his half-eaten eggs and bacon away and walked moodily to the window. A December drizzle was falling. A taxi splashed its way through the dreary murk that was London. Pedestrians, wrapped in mackintoshes and shielded by umbrellas, trudged along the pavement, each concerned with their own affairs. No one spoke, no one seemed to know they were sharing the world with other human beings. A few more leaves fell off the plane tree outside the window and were trampled underfoot. And yet, no more than sixteen days away, was a land of blinding sun and brilliant blue skies. 'It's South Africa for me,' he repeated.

'You'll have to stay until Nigel's funeral,' said Jack. 'You can't leave your family to face it alone. The inquest was bad enough and the funeral will be really tough for them. And what about the company? I thought you were going to join the firm. I think David might appreciate your help.'

'Come on, Jack,' said George. 'You must see how impossible it is.'

'What? Now you're rich, you mean?'

'Money's got nothing to do with it,' said George in irritation. 'If you must know, it's Anne. I was taken in hook, line and sinker by Stella. How d'you think that makes me feel? If I'd known what was good for me I wouldn't have looked twice at her. That matters to Anne, you know. She didn't say as much but you saw how distant she was at the inquest. I've had my chance and I've blown it.'

Jack gave him a long-suffering look and reached for his pipe. 'Look, old thing, before you eat too much dirt, you might remember she was virtually engaged to Maguire. So far it seems even stevens to me.'

'Rubbish,' said George robustly. 'She was the widow, poor soul, of a really sound bloke. She thought all men were like Thomas. She'd never come across a persuasive devil like Maguire. It's not remotely the same.' He turned to the window again. 'It's South Africa for me.'

Jack sighed and filled his pipe. It was going to be a long time until the funeral.

'I can't,' said Anne Lassiter firmly.

'But why not?' asked Peggy Culverton. 'You do like him, Anne, you know you do.'

'Don't be silly, Peggy. He hardly spoke to me at the inquest. I suppose he's still sore about that woman.' Peggy said nothing, but merely raised an eyebrow. 'I know I still feel pretty chewed up about Roger.'

'You never committed yourself though,' said Peggy thoughtfully. 'Something was holding you back. Why don't you ring George, Anne?'

'I can't possibly do that.'

'Why not?'

'You don't understand. I just can't, that's all.'

'It's hardly the weather for a walk, is it?' grumbled George as they went down the stairs to the hall. 'It's raining cats and dogs and so gloomy you can hardly see your hand in front of your face.'

'Well, stay here then, George,' said Jack in mounting exasperation. 'But I'm damned if I'm watching you march up and down all day like a caged lion. I thought we could go through the park and call at the Criterion for a spot of lunch. It's about time you saw some of the better places London has to offer. It's not all dodgy nightclubs and dingy boarding houses.'

'I know, I know.' George hefted his umbrella and opened the front door to the street. 'Well, if we arc going, let's get it over with.'

The telephone in the hall started to ring. 'Hang on a minute.' Jack stepped back into the house and picked it up, a slow grin spreading across his face as he listened. 'Why don't you ask him yourself? He's standing right beside me.'

He passed the phone over to George and stood back with a smile. 'It's for you.'

Author's Note

In June 1919, Alcock and Brown completed the first non-stop crossing of the Atlantic by air. In November of that year, the two brothers, Ross and Keith Macpherson Smith, flew from England to Australia. These flights, and subsequent record-breaking voyages, demanded huge feats of endurance from both pilots and mechanics. To produce a passenger aircraft – a commercial airliner – that could cross oceans was a truly daunting enterprise.

Short Brothers designed such an aircraft (see *Jane's* for 1919) but this was never built, and it fell to Nigel Lassiter, of the Lassiter Aircraft Company, to try and make the dream a reality. The present volume, as the reader will know, sheds some light on exactly what happened to this ambitious project. Suffice it to say no attempt was made to revive plans to build the twin-hulled, four-engined, forty-seater flying-boat, Pegasus.

The British state-aided airline mentioned in the text is, of course, Imperial Airways Ltd, which was formed in 1924.

The ancient Egyptians first recorded the use of trances over five thousand years ago and the great Chinese healer, Wong Tai, described an induced altered state in c.2600 BC. This knowledge, associated with both religion and medicine, is found in virtually every age and culture, but, as far as Western science is concerned, its father is Franz Mesmer (1734–1815). Two Scots, the physician James Braid and the surgeon James Esdaile, working independently of each other, built on Mesmer's work, Esdaile performing a remarkable series of operations without anaesthetic. In

France, such men as Charcot, Richet and Coué added to both theoretical and practical knowledge of the subject, with which Dr Alistair Kincraig was well acquainted.

As a parting note, it is a sad fact that the damage sustained by Waterloo Bridge proved to be greater than first thought. In December 1923 the centre piers subsided and it was necessary to close the bridge to wheeled traffic for some months afterwards. Jack Haldean always felt a twinge of remorse when walking over 'the finest bridge in Europe' after his part in the story. The reader will be able to judge if he had anything with which to reproach himself.